ARDEN ST. IVES

How to Bang a Billionaire
How to Blow It with a Billionaire
How to Belong with a Billionaire

PROSPERITY

Prosperity
Liberty & Other Stories
There Will Be Phlogiston

Other Titles

A Lady for a Duke
The Affair of the Mysterious Letter
Looking for Group

ALEXIS HALL

Montlake

Published by Montlake, Seattle

www.apub.com

Amazon, the Amazon logo, and Montlake are trademarks of Amazon.com, Inc., or its affiliates.

ISBN-13: 9781542035286 (paperback)
ISBN-13: 9781542035279 (digital)

Cover design and illustration by Philip Pascuzzo
Cover image: © SAHAS2015 / Shutterstock

Printed in the United States of America

Wherever you fit on the gender spectrum, I idolise you, and you're powerful; remember that some of the best artists in the world reject gender norms.
—Bimini Bon Boulash

AUTHOR'S NOTE

Like *Something Fabulous*, this book plays rather fast and loose with history. The language is modern, basically everybody in it is LGBTQ+, and castrati were on the decline in Europe at the time the story is set (although they did still exist; the last castrato survived into the era of voice recording).

I do, however, want to address the way this book handles the intersection between castrati, nonbinary identity, modern readers, and historical context, because I think it's complex and worth unpacking slightly. There are limited surviving accounts of the lives of castrati, and a relatively small proportion of what we do have is in their own words, since castrati tended to be from the kinds of socioeconomic backgrounds that don't let a person get their thoughts recorded for posterity. In particular, the question of how the gender of castrati was perceived by either their society or by the castrati themselves is a thorny one, and, as with most issues of identity, there were essentially as many different interpretations as there were people.

Although many castrati did unequivocally identify as men (and often went to great lengths to prove quite how manly they were, precisely because society said that they weren't), others preferred to occupy a liminal space that was neither "man" nor "woman" and so more closely parallels what we would consider "nonbinary" in modern discourse. That's the direction I chose to go with Orfeo. This does mean that Orfeo is in the difficult position of embracing an identity that was forced upon them by society (and indeed by direct violence), and for some readers that may not be the way they'd want this theme to be handled. I'm mentioning this in advance because I know these issues resonate with people, and I think it's important for us to be able to make informed decisions about the books we read.

Additional content guidance: the nonbinary main character (MC) has thoughts relating to gender dysphoria, and the MC who is a castrato talks (not in graphic detail) about what happened to them. Other content with which readers may prefer not to engage includes (but is not limited to) derogatory/aggressive language aimed at the MC who is a castrato (which is challenged), misgendering, sexual content (on page and graphic), mild acts of violence, kidnapping, a stay in prison, blasphemy, criticism of religious/Catholic practices, talk of getting pregnant, a controlling/abusive relationship, sex shaming (which is also challenged), arophobia, and homophobia.

At its heart, *Something Spectacular* is still primarily the same flavour of whimsy as *Something Fabulous*, and my primary reference point for imagining Orfeo was "rock star," not "trauma survivor" (then again, those things are hardly mutually exclusive, even in the modern day). My aim with this introduction is just to give the book a little context. As ever, I hope you enjoy it.

Alexis Hall
October 2022

Prologue

They said he was the most beautiful man in London.

He being Parsifal Chastaine, the Earl of Southerbrooke. And, even from the perspective of looking down at him from her balcony, Arabella Tarleton was inclined to agree. His softly curling hair was as pale as the moonlight, and his features had a cut-glass clarity to them that perfectly combined masculinity and gentility.

"It is the east," he called up to her. "And Miss Tarleton is the sun."

She sighed a little. "It's night."

"It's Shakespeare."

"For heaven's sake," she retorted. "I am more than aware it's Shakespeare. Books were the only escape I had for the first nineteen years of my life."

"I just meant"—it was hard to tell at this distance, but he seemed flustered—"you look lovely. Like—"

"Like a thirteen-year-old girl?"

"W-what? No. No, like . . . a heroine."

And to think she had once been appalled beyond reckoning because the Duke of Malvern had disrespected Ophelia in her presence. "A heroine who stabs herself? Because a man has overreacted? If that were to be a general pattern for our sex, there would be none of us left."

There was a silence from below. Then, "Miss Tarleton, should I go home? I am beginning to think you might prefer me to go home?"

Something was wrong with her—something deep in her soul—and she no longer knew when the rot had set in. If it had begun with the events of the previous year, when she had fled an unwelcome fiancé, only for her twin brother to welcome said fiancé most enthusiastically in her stead (he was, in fact, still welcoming him nightly, sometimes several times nightly). Or if it was older. If it had spread its corruption beneath her skin the moment she had inescapably concluded that happy ever afters, the ones full of kisses and rose leaves, and promises and poetry, belonged only to fairy tales. But perhaps it didn't matter. Irrespective of the cause, the fact remained: once upon a time she would have thrilled to have a beautiful man offering her the gift of Shakespeare. And now all she felt . . .

All she felt was nothing.

"No," she said, for she owed it to the girl she had once been. "Don't leave. Although please do stop shouting from the garden. You will wake the household."

His Lordship cast around in some confusion. "Where should I shout from?"

"If you came up here, you wouldn't need to shout."

"But Miss Tarleton—"

"Romeo came up," Arabella pointed out.

There was a pause. "I don't think he did. I think he offered an exchange of faithful vows."

"How considerate of him."

"Also," the earl went on, "there wasn't a balcony."

Arabella was beginning to think she would have been better advised to retire alone. Her own fingers were never this annoying. "What do you mean, there wasn't a balcony in the balcony scene of *Romeo and Juliet*?"

"It's a window. 'What light through yonder window breaks?'"

"It could have been a window to a balcony."

"The stage directions say it's a window. Windows, you know, had particular social significance in fourteenth-century Italy."

"And I'm sure the social significance of windows in fourteenth-century Italy was of great concern to the man who believed Verona to be a port."

The earl drew in a breath so emphatically that Arabella heard it upon her balcony. "Miss Tarleton, Shakespeare was a *genius*."

"But clearly not a geographer." She curled her hands lightly over the railing and proceeded—with some effort—in a more conciliatory tone. "My lord, as previously established, we enjoy many advantages over these fictional lovers. I am not a child, nor are we doomed, and I happen to be possessed of a very accessible balcony."

"I . . . ," His Lordship began.

She let the flimsy material of her night rail slip from one of her shoulders. Her skin gleamed silver in the uncertain light. It was a shame, she reflected, that the earl was just an earl. Had he been something better, like a painter, he would surely have wanted to immortalise her.

"Er," he concluded. "Yes."

"Well?" she asked.

Her suitor darted across the garden with gratifying haste, although the haste diminished significantly as he began to ascend the ivy that wound its way to Arabella's balcony. Eventually even the ascent diminished and became a kind of . . . clinging.

"This," panted the earl, "is rather more difficult than it looks."

Arabella frowned at him. "What do you mean? It's not difficult at all. Peggy goes up and down it all the time."

"Why on earth are your lady friends climbing your ivy?"

"No reason."

Having rested on no less than three additional occasions, His Lordship eventually heaved himself over the railing and landed in an ungainly, sweating heap at Arabella's slippered feet. In that moment, it was a little difficult to recall that he was accounted the most beautiful man in London. He was mostly . . . purple. And probably would have been best served by a quiet lie-down.

Arabella Tarleton, however, did not invite people to her bedchambers that they might experience a quiet lie-down. She tossed back her golden tresses. "My lord." It was her best voice. Her sultriest voice. "Kiss me."

"Just . . . just a moment." His Lordship wheezed, pressing a hand to his side. "I've got the devil of a stitch."

There didn't seem much to say to that. Arabella re-covered her shoulder, for it was clearly going unappreciated. "Well, in your own time then."

Moving back to the balcony rail, she let her gaze drift across the darkened garden. It had bloomed riotously to her brother's direction, though there was little to see at the moment, just the shadow of the fountain and the reflection of the moon upon its still waters. "'The beauty of the world,'" she murmured, "'the paragon of animals. And yet to me, what is this quintessence of dust?'"

"Miss Tarleton?" His Lordship came up behind her, his breath warm against the back of her neck. "I don't believe those lines are from *Romeo and Juliet*."

"That is not my story."

And, turning, she kissed him full on his exquisitely shaped mouth. The earl, by contrast, was somewhat hesitant in his responses—at least until Arabella vanquished his qualms by thorough application of her lips and tongue. She was, she knew, excellent at kissing.

When she had partaken of this activity to her satisfaction, she manoeuvred her lover through the socially significant window into her bedroom and shed her nightgown with a serpentine wriggle.

"Miss Tarleton," said His Lordship once again, his eyes owlishly large.

She disported temptingly upon the edge of her bed and spread her legs, easing her fingers into the delicious warmth between her folds. "Come."

"What . . . what do you wish, Miss Tarleton?" The earl moved towards her as if in a daze, which she decided was probably a compliment.

"I wish your mouth or your hand or your cock. Whichever is your preference. Though if the last, I will require you to sheath it."

"I . . ."

He seemed to demonstrate no strong feelings, so Arabella betook herself to the fall of his breeches in order to ascertain if his member was as well formed as the rest of him. Discovering it to be of comfortable length and intriguing heft, and somehow possessed of a smooth, enquiring look, not unlike a curious sheep, she concluded it was fit for purpose.

In response to her salutatory caresses, His Lordship offered several strangled gasps. And then managed, "Miss Tarleton, may we . . . may we kiss a little more?"

Generous lover that she was, Arabella gave her assent, and they fell back upon the bed, their bodies moving together as if in prelude to later symphonies. Altogether, Arabella reflected, it was an entirely acceptable experience. The earl had a sweet, generous mouth that murmured tributes to her beauty and charm as easily as it poured forth the kisses he had requested, and he looked, if anything, even more beautiful in the disorder of his garments. His liberated member was tucked against her, its silken weight a pleasant contrast to the surrounding chaos of tangled linen.

It was then that a particularly intense shudder rolled through His Lordship's body. His eyes screwed themselves shut, and he uttered a deep, heavy groan. And Arabella became unmistakably aware of liquid—warm, viscous liquid—sliding down the interior of her thigh. For a moment she was simply too stunned to react.

"Is that . . . ?" she asked. "Did you?"

The earl rolled off her and stood, attempting to put his clothing to rights with visibly trembling hands. He was not looking at her.

Sitting, she used a corner of the sheet to wipe away her lover's enthusiasm. "What am I supposed to do now?"

"I will . . . I will speak to your guardian on the morrow."

"Believe me," she said, wondering peevishly if His Lordship's pleasure had destroyed hers entirely, "this is not a matter that falls within his expertise."

"I need his consent to wed you."

As it happened, he did not. The only person who could give consent to Arabella's marriage was Arabella. "What has matrimony to do with anything?"

"Miss Tarleton . . ." The earl whirled round so abruptly that a few final drops of ejaculate still clinging to the tip of his penis spattered one of the bed hangings. "I have *ruined* you."

"What? No. At worst you've ruined the bedding."

He stiffened, in a bodily rather than phallic way. "That is . . . that is beside the point. You have entertained me alone in your bedchamber at night."

"Well"—she crossed one leg over the other, her foot tapping petulantly—"you haven't entertained me at all."

The jewellike eyes over which so many ladies, and likely some gentlemen, swooned and sighed grew dark and cold. "Was this why you invited me here? For the purposes of despoilment? Surely you are not in the habit of such . . . such *assignations*?"

The tapping of Arabella's foot increased its rapidity. "My habits are no concern of yours."

"Indeed they are not," agreed the earl, "for I have been sorely mistaken in you."

"The feeling, my lord, is *quite* mutual."

He tucked his cock away with an air of impassioned grievance. "I sought an angel in you, Miss Tarleton. And found only a harlot."

"Nonsense." Her lip curled. "One can be both. Now are you leaving? Or do I need to fling things at your head until you do?"

Since there followed a distinct lack of leaving on His Lordship's part, Arabella seized one of the pillows from her bed and proceeded to beat him with it.

"What are you doing?" demanded the earl.

"I'm thwacking you hence with distaffs."

His hands came up in an effort at self-defence. "What do you mean, you're 'thwacking me hence with distaffs'? You can't 'thwack me hence with distaffs.' You only have a pillow, and I'm a gentleman."

"Considering what you called me just this evening"—Arabella continued to assail him with her pillow—"you are most certainly not a gentleman."

"I spoke only the truth."

"On the contrary. Harlots charge for their services. I sought merely reciprocal gratification. *Reciprocal*"—the pillow burst, spraying the earl generously with white feathers—"being the most significant word in that sentence."

"I—"

Arabella stamped her foot, cutting him off. "No. You have done more than enough for one evening. Or rather, you have done insufficiently, and so I am done with you. Away."

"You," declared the earl, "are . . ."

"Are *what*?"

There was a long silence. "I don't know," he finished despairingly.

There was only one thing for it. Arabella laid claim to another of her pillows and attempted to bestow a further thwacking upon her erstwhile lover. Moreover, by pushing the pillow against his midsection and lowering her head like a very small bull, she found she was able to propel him backwards across the room towards the window and the balcony. "Away. Away with you."

Once again, His Lordship attempted to disengage himself from the beating. "I'm awaying. I'm awaying. For the love of God, Miss Tarleton, I'm *awaying*." To underscore the point, he scrambled over the balcony rail and began swinging down the ivy with far more alacrity than he had initially scaled it.

"Good." Arabella glared down at the most beautiful man in London. "And make sure you stay awayed."

Given the circumstances, it seemed appropriate to add emphasis by way of one final blow, which Arabella duly delivered. Unfortunately, while being whacked with a pillow had damaged little but the gentleman's pride while he was situated upon terra firma, this was not the case when he was precariously hanging from a balcony. He lost his grip, and his attempt to regain it caused a section of ivy to detach itself fully from the brickwork. With a piercing, household-awakening scream, the earl was launched into the air—where he flailed for what felt like the longest second of Arabella's life, before he plunged groundwards very fast indeed.

The splash and the subsequent, rather more bubbly scream that followed indicated he had landed in Bonny's unicorn fountain. Thankfully, in the bowl of it, which was full of water and goldfish. Rather than, say, upon the horn, which was gold-veined marble and would probably have spit him like a suckling pig.

Arabella could hear doors opening. Rapid footsteps. The babble of concerned voices in distant corridors. By the time she had robed herself, her twin brother and his lover were already in the garden, Bonny holding an unnecessarily extravagant candelabra, as Valentine helped the bedraggled earl from the fountain. They were wearing matching purple dressing gowns, trimmed with gold, which was the most obnoxious thing Arabella thought she had ever witnessed.

"Are you morally opposed to discretion?" Valentine turned his gaze up to her. "Or is it some kind of physical aversion, such as some people experience towards peanuts or oysters?"

"I think you'll find," she retorted, "I was perfectly discreet. I was not the one who chose to hurl myself into a fountain."

His Lordship gave a splutter of protest, but it was a weak splutter. "She's a . . . she's a wanton. A . . . a *violent* wanton."

"Yes, yes." Valentine accepted a towel from a delicately hovering servant and draped it over the shoulders of his unexpected guest. "And I'm a sodomite. Now why don't you let Witherspook here take you inside, where you can get dried off and warmed up? Then, when you are in better spirits, we can discuss exactly who is what and whether it means anything of consequence to anyone."

The earl was too wet and shaken for further debate and so allowed himself to be led into the house, leaving Bonny and Valentine in the garden and Arabella still on her balcony.

Bonny apparently saw this as an opportunity to wriggle his way into the crook of Valentine's arm. "You are *the best* sodomite."

"I am quite a good one," the Duke of Malvern conceded, his air of lofty satisfaction evaporating into exasperation as he once again turned his attention to Arabella. "What on earth am I to do with you, Belle?"

The ghost of old bitterness stirred the hairs on Belle's forearms. "You are to do nothing because I am not for you to manage."

"I'm not trying to manage you. I'm trying to . . . to help you."

"I don't need your help," she retorted, more from instinct than by intent.

"So you keep saying, Belladonna." That was Bonny, blinking up at her with eyes as blue as her own, yet infinitely softer. "But you just threw a man in a fountain. That's not the action of an un-help-needing person."

There were pins and needles in Arabella's heart. She didn't *resent* Bonny—she couldn't, he was her twin, his happiness as important to her as her own. In some ways, perhaps, more so. But he had built his life from the stories they used to tell each other, forgiven where she could not forgive, loved where she could not love. And worse, he had made it look easy. As if such joy was the simplest thing in the world to find.

She threw her hands in the air. "Fine. I'm bored. I'm soul-curdlingly, heart-wrenchingly, bowel-twistingly bored. Help me with *that*."

And then she turned and swept magnificently into her bedroom.

Chapter 1

"Letter for you, darling." Glancing up from her book, Peggy's mother gestured with a forkful of bacon, causing it to fly off the fork and land in her husband's teacup. "Oh, bother."

Mr. Delancey de-baconed his tea. "Thank you, pet. I always felt what tea was missing was meat."

"Or meat," suggested Peggy, "could be lacking in tea." She threw herself into her usual chair, Cerberus immediately flopping over her boots in the manner of a dog who hasn't been fed in eight million years. He was some kind of black-and-white pointer mix—long in all directions, especially around the jowls and tail. She smuggled him some ham hock, which made his long, pointy tail even longer and even pointier.

"I think"—another significant gesture from Mrs. Delancey, this one bacon-free—"it's from Arabella Tarleton."

It was definitely from Arabella. The direction had been extravagantly scrawled, and a single teardrop had artfully smeared the dot of one of the *i*'s. Just the sight of it gave Peggy stomach butterflies, but they were practical butterflies. Butterflies who knew what was what, fluttering in spite of themselves. "I'll read it later."

Peggy felt, rather than saw, her parents exchanging glances. It should not have been possible for one's parents to make one feel lonely—but, sometimes, they did. In their eccentric way, they loved her unconditionally; Peggy knew that. But what they had with each other, a lifetime compatibility of incompatibilities, had a way of leaving everyone else on the outside.

"First love," suggested Mrs. Delancey, with the air of someone traversing an icy puddle when they didn't know either how thick or slippy the ice was, "is always tricky."

At that, Peggy laughed. "How would you know? You're each other's first loves."

"Aye, well." Her father shrugged contentedly. "What do you expect? No other bugger'd have us."

"That's not true." Peggy wasn't sure if she spoke from loyalty or challenge. "You're rich as sin—"

"And common as muck," added Mr. Delancey.

"And Mam's . . . well, all right," Peggy conceded. "Mam's peculiar."

"See," cried Mrs. Delancey, who took her vindication where she could get it. "*Tricky.*" She made an emphatic gesture and knocked over the coffeepot, causing her husband and a nearby footman to leap into action before anyone could be scalded.

"Though I don't see," Mr. Delancey went on, once the coffee-based chaos had been contained, "why you'd want to marry anyone who weren't a bit peculiar."

"I'm not peculiar," said Mrs. Delancey, who only yesterday had been trying to induce life into a deceased frog by harnessing the power of a summer storm through a set of copper rods. "I'm *ahead of my time.*"

Peggy's father gazed at his wife. "Tha's the bee's knees, my love."

The gazing continued for quite some while.

"Do you have to be like this," Peggy asked, "at breakfast?" At her feet, Cerberus made sad, starving noises until she fed him a sausage—all too aware that he tried this little performance on everyone, and with such success that he was becoming a lot rounder than he was pointer.

Her parents temporarily ceased their eye-tangling. Mr. Delancey cleared his throat. "You know who I met the other day?"

"Herodotus," suggested his wife.

There was a pause. Mr. Delancey blinked. "You who?"

"Herodotus. Cicero called him the Father of History. I don't know, he was the first person I thought of. Although"—Mrs. Delancey frowned—"now I think further, I suppose the fact he's been dead for over two thousand years renders him an unlikely candidate for a chance encounter."

"Just a bit," agreed Mr. Delancey.

Peggy looked up from the game pie she was enthusiastically carving. "Vlad the Impaler?"

"What?" said her father again.

She shrugged. "First person I thought of. Isn't that what we're doing here?"

"Don't be pert, my child." There was only warmth in Mr. Delancey's voice. "I met the vicar's daughter, Grace. You remember her, don't you, Peggy? She remembers you."

Peggy groaned into the pie. "Oh no. Dad. What is this? Please stop trying to introduce me to eligible young women."

"Which reminds me"—that was Mrs. Delancey—"last Wednesday I had a letter from your cousin Tom—"

"Or men," added Peggy quickly. "Besides, he's my cousin."

Mrs. Delancey nodded. "And very boring and covered in pimples. But I was thinking of that friend of his from Cambridge. He doesn't have any pimples at all, and we had the most wonderful conversation about *The Wealth of Nations*. Perhaps—"

"No." The word came out louder than Peggy had intended, causing Cerberus to sit up with a confused *Aorrw?* She pulled his ears. "Sorry, boy. Nothing for you to worry about." He put his chin back on his forepaws. And Peggy turned back to her parents. "Listen, it's . . . something . . . sweet . . . it's sweet what you're doing, but—"

"We do understand that you love Arabella," put in her mother gently. "That doesn't mean you can't meet other people."

Red faced, Peggy slithered low in her chair until her chin was practically resting on the tabletop. "I *know*. It's just . . . it's not that simple. She'll never love me the way I love her—I don't think she'll ever love anyone the way I want to be loved. But the truth is nobody else makes me feel the way she does."

"Oh, darling." Mrs. Delancey tried to pat Peggy's hand but, finding it out of reach, patted her plate instead. "'This, too, shall pass'—isn't that what they say?"

"I have no idea what they say, but I've been waiting for it to pass all my damn life." Suddenly the game pie had lost its appeal. And Peggy found she was restless in a way that was only partially to do with her body. She stood. "You know I adore you both, I adore you so much, but would you mind awfully if I stormed out moodily?"

"Of course," said her mother. "Go right ahead."

Mr. Delancey nodded. "You do what you need, pet."

"Thank you." Peggy offered them a neat little bow, seized Arabella's letter, and stormed out moodily, Cerberus at her heels.

Of course, she wasn't sure where she was storming moodily *to*, so it soon became more of a brisk walk. Which felt, in that moment, depressingly typical. Belle could keep up a moody storm indefinitely.

Peggy's inadequately dramatic perambulations had taken her from the house and through the gardens, where now she permitted herself to loll against the trunk of a silver birch and *sigh*.

Being in love was a private tyranny.

"Rwror?" asked Cerberus.

"Being in love," Peggy explained, "is a private tyranny."

She had shoved Belle's letter into the pocket of her breeches; it was just a sheet of paper, and probably it contained nothing but nonsense— *Saw the most awful hat today*—but it lay against her like a hand upon skin.

Belle missed her, Peggy knew that. But it wasn't the same kind of missing, just as it wasn't the same kind of love. There'd been a time when *close enough* hadn't mattered. And then it had started mattering. And now it was almost all that mattered. Which wasn't either of their faults. Not exactly. Except there was a hurt, silly part of Peggy that resented Belle for her lack of feelings and some stubborn reciprocal part of Belle that was frustrated at Peggy for having such feelings in the first place.

Semi-reasonably because it had come perilously close to ruining their friendship. Despite a younger, retrospectively more foolish Peggy dutifully reassuring Belle that, of course, it wouldn't ruin their friendship. And, of course, they could still sleep together.

Older, slightly less foolish Peggy indulged in a small groan. Almost worse than bearing the pain of unrequited love was bearing the pain of being so goddamned trite. She was not, she knew, like Belle. She had no wish to be a heroine. Nor did she need to live an extraordinary life. But she thought she could have done better than falling hopelessly for her best friend while deluding herself that this would somehow not lead to emotional disaster.

"The thing is," Peggy told Cerberus, "I could still be with Belle. Except it would be on her terms only. And that would—well. That would make me no better than you."

Cerberus tilted his head, looking faintly offended.

"Cerbs"—Peggy put her hands on her hips—"you're a dog. You're supposed to be loyal and self-sacrificing and straightforward. I'm a person. I have complex needs. I can't live on cunnilingus and devotion. My own devotion, that is." She sighed. "Mind you, I could imagine worse problems than having it the other way round, for all Belle says it's boring. I mean, the devotion is boring. The cunnilingus certainly isn't bor—Christ almighty, is that a dead woman in the stream?"

There did, indeed, to appear to be a dead woman, floating upon the blossom-strewn waterway that wound its way through the little woods that bordered the Delancey estate. She was clad entirely in white, her hair spread like the wine-dark fronds of some fantastical orchid upon the current.

A confused but enthusiastic Cerberus behind her, Peggy charged into the stream and seized the drowned woman in her arms, a process that left everybody involved quite a bit wetter than Peggy had realised it was going to.

The very much alive stranger gave an outraged splutter. "What in the name of Finvarra and Oona do you think you're doing?"

Peggy kept wading towards the bank. "I'm rescuing you."

"Why?"

Peggy paused. "What do you mean, why? Because you were in a stream. People don't like being in streams. Believe me, I know."

"Well"—the woman attempted to toss her head, but all this accomplished was slapping Peggy damply in the face with her tresses—"I *do* like being in streams. I was communing with the naiads."

"Are there," Peggy asked, "many naiads in Sludgy Brook?"

"How am I supposed to know? I was brutally rescued before I encountered any."

"In which case, the next time I'm rescuing someone from drowning, I'll be sure to do it with all tenderness and gallantry."

The stranger gave an angry wriggle. "As well you should, Peggy Delancey. What's the point of rescuing someone at all if you're coarse about it?"

"I would have thought," returned Peggy, with a touch of hauteur, "not dying or being injured would count as some compensation."

She had been slightly startled to hear her name, but then she'd recognised Grace Hickinbottom, the vicar's daughter—who she thought she was fairly justified in *not* recognising because the last time they'd met, Grace had been about fourteen years old. And scrawny. With hair the colour of the village cat, a creature who rejoiced in the name of Pumpkin on account of both his rotundity and his orangeness.

Whereas now she was definitely *not* fourteen. And swathed in a recently drenched piece of diaphanous nothing.

I really need, thought Peggy urgently, *to keep looking at this woman's face.*

Her eyes were dragged inexorably away from Grace's face. Red. Red all the way down.

"For the last time," Grace was saying, her nipples somehow glaring at Peggy through transparent fabric, "I wasn't drowning."

"Is *potentially drowning* really the sort of thing you want me to shrug and leave to chance?"

"I do if your idea of helping a lady involves grabbing at her like the last scone at teatime. Look how you've ruined my flower crown."

Peggy eyed the handful of soggy petals that were being thrust into her face. "You know what you remind me of? That story where Guinevere gets captured by an evil knight and Lancelot tries to save her—except on the way his horse dies, so he has to ride in a cart, and then after he goes through a bunch of trials and duels Guinevere's captor, she tells him to bugger off again because she won't stoop to be rescued by someone who once rode in a cart."

There was a long silence. And Peggy, who had spoken rather more harshly than she'd intended, wished she'd bitten her tongue. Then Grace uttered a melting sigh, her eyes lighting up like stars. "I remind you of Guinevere?"

"Yes?" said Peggy quickly. She cleared her throat. "Yes, you do."

Abruptly Grace unmelted and destarred. "Then why did you tie my hair to a tree that time?"

Had Peggy done that? She couldn't remember doing—oh fuck, she'd done that. Although in her defence she'd been about fifteen and Grace had been following her about like a puppy. "Because you were annoying."

"Arabella Tarleton is annoying. You never tied her hair to a tree."

Peggy gave a little cough. "Indeed I did not."

"Although," Grace went on, with a disconcertingly knowing look, "I suppose you had other means for dealing with Arabella Tarleton when she annoyed you."

It was not an ideal time to be confronted by the far too vivid image of a half-squealing, half-giggling Belle, turned over Peggy's lap, with her skirts bunched about her waist and her stockings slipping down her ivory thighs, her deliciously rounded derriere flushing like the beginnings of a country sunset. It should have been a tantalising memory, and it *was*, but it also brought with it a pathetic little pang: thwarted love, and missing a friend, and probably a non-zero amount of sexual frustration.

Because that was the problem with Belle. She was selfish and infuriating and had no sense of perspective. But she was also undeniably, inescapably *fun*. She made the world shine.

Peggy gave another little cough, no more convincing than the first had been. "A ladygent does not kiss and tell."

"That means yes," said Grace.

"It does not mean yes."

"If the answer was *no*, you'd have said no."

"No, I wouldn't." Peggy subjected Miss Hickinbottom to her sternest look. "I would have said exactly what I said, which is a polite way of saying *It's none of your business.*"

Grace's bottom lip—notably more voluptuous than the cupid's bow of her upper—trembled like ripe strawberries upon a determined breeze. "You haven't even apologised for tying my hair to a tree."

"I apologise," ground out Peggy, "for tying your hair to a tree."

The hair—now fully emancipated from even so much as a ribbon—was promptly tossed over its owner's shoulders, speckling Peggy in little water droplets. "That is a very shabby apology."

"What do you want? Poetry?" The question, Peggy realised a second too late, was asking for trouble.

Grace immediately plonked herself on a nearby tree stump, crossing one leg over the other, a well-shaped ankle flicking restlessly. "Yes," she declared. "Poetry seems appropriate."

"Poetry is never appropriate." With a resigned sigh, Peggy tugged off her coat and dropped it over Grace in a way she hoped might obscure the young lady's distracting breasts without making it look like she was attempting to obscure the young lady's distracting breasts. "You'd better take this. Stop you catching a chill or something."

Grace drew back her shoulders haughtily. "Do I look like I am catching a chill?"

"You look . . ." The breasts were still distracting. "Chill-*y*," concluded Peggy carefully, trying very hard not to stare at the evidence.

"My profound connection to Mother Earth keeps me warm."

"Does it, though?" Peggy wrinkled her nose.

Grace chose to ignore this. Really, she had more in common with Arabella Tarleton than she knew. "You owe me some poetry, Peggy Delancey."

Chapter 2

The truth was, Peggy was beginning to feel the tiniest bit guilty. It was not, after all, good form to go around tying people's hair to trees, even if they deserved it. Probably especially if they deserved it. And the fact Grace had grown up very lovely indeed—and was currently very underdressed indeed—was certainly no influence upon Peggy's thinking. Propping her booted foot upon the tree stump next to Grace and leaning forward, with her elbow upon a knee, she attempted a tone of conciliation. "I'll concede that I owed you an apology, and I should have delivered it more graciously. I'm truly sorry. Tying your hair to a tree was beastly of me. But what the devil makes you think I know anything about poetry?"

Grace tilted her head slightly, her lambent gaze turned upon Peggy. "You have a poet's eyes."

"I absolutely do not," said Peggy firmly, "have a poet's eyes."

"Yes, you do. They're so deep and dark and full of sorrow."

Peggy rubbed the eyes in question. "I think that's actually a bit of water from the brook? You were throwing it about a bit, Grace."

"You remind me," went on Grace, undeterred, "of Lord Byron."

That did not sound good. "Self-conscious about my weight and dressed like a prick in clothes that don't belong to me?"

Grace frowned.

"Not," Peggy added hastily, "that he has anything to be self-conscious *about*. As Bonny says, sometimes one just happens to be a roly-poly gentleman with a lot of love to give. The Albanian dress, though? That's just downright peculiar. You know who should dress as Albanians?"

"No?"

"Albanians. Seems only fair."

"I feel"—Grace was still frowning—"you're rather missing the point."

"So's Byron."

"Peggy," snapped Grace.

"What?"

"Stop talking about Byron."

"You brought him up."

Grace's foot was still flicking as restlessly as a tiger's tail. "I was talking about you. I was being nice about you. And you clearly don't care. Just like you didn't care when you tied my hair to a tree or interrupted my communion with nature."

"It was very nice," Peggy tried, "of you to be nice about me, Grace." Even if being compared to Byron wasn't exactly going in Peggy's Big Book of Compliments.

"It *was* nice of me." Grace gave a decisive nod. "So now it's your turn to be nice back."

That sounded . . . quite a bit more promising. Peggy gently lifted what Belle used to call her *carnal eyebrow*. "What did you have in mind?"

"I told you before: a poem."

So not promising at all, then. "And I told you, I don't have a poetic impulse in my body."

"Have you ever tried?"

"What if I just licked your quim?" asked Peggy, somewhat desperately. "I'm exceptional at that."

There was a little pause. Then Grace uncrossed her legs with an air of significance, the fabric of her gown bunching between her thighs in a way that managed to be simultaneously concealing and tantalising. "Is that so?"

"Well," suggested Peggy. "Why don't I try, and you can let me know?"

"I do . . . I do like the sound of that."

And, just like that, they were back to promising. The grass by the stump was soft and mossy—likely a little muddy, but that was one of the many advantages of breeches. That, and pockets. Since Cerberus had long since got bored of observing two people talking by a stream and had ambled off on some canine adventure of his own, Peggy dropped to the ground, her hands coming to rest lightly upon Grace's knees.

The knees did not yield in the slightest.

"After," said Grace, "I get my poem."

"Oh, for—" Peggy closed her lips firmly, for it would have been ill mannered to finish the exclamation. She pressed her head against the side of Grace's leg, a gesture which, even she had to admit, spoke more of abjection than sensuality.

One of Grace's feet rose again, her toes brushing Peggy's shoulder before settling against it. The scent of . . . honestly Sludgy Brook rose up around them, but beneath it was something far sweeter, the unmistakable intimate tang of skin and desire. "Don't you want to lick my quim, Peggy?"

Peggy had made the initial suggestion on the grounds that it was preferable to poetry. But now she was en route to quimsville—or had believed herself en route to quimsville—she was discovering she did, indeed, very much want to be there. "Yes, but—"

"I'm very wet," remarked Grace, with the air of someone offering idle commentary on the weather or the state of the roads.

"Thanks for the update."

Heaving a sigh, Grace twitched her gown a little higher, revealing a sweep of a thigh and the merest flash of pink flesh crowned in gleaming, autumnal hues.

Peggy groaned, all too aware of the excited heat gathering within her drawers. "Fine. You win. I'll . . . I'll compose you a poem. But on your head, be it."

"Not my head." Grace gave a triumphant little giggle, which—or maybe Peggy was quimstruck—was almost endearing.

Sitting back on her heels, Peggy tried to think of anything that wasn't Grace's bare legs and re-distracting nipples. "There once," she suggested.

Grace nodded approvingly.

"Was a lady called Grace?"

"Go on?"

"Who had. Um. A very nice face?"

It was clearly not what Grace had been hoping for. Her encouraging expression was beginning to look increasingly unnatural, like a tablecloth draped over a rotting corpse.

"Her eyes," tried Peggy.

"Good. Yes. My eyes."

"There were two?"

"Oh."

"And"—hope bloomed in Peggy's heart, the words flowing more naturally as she espied an end point—"the rest of her'd do . . . for a hasty carnal embrace."

"I," said Grace in a small voice, "I was hoping for a sonnet."

"Then get Lord Byron to lick your quim."

"I don't *want* Lord Byron to lick my quim."

"Then how about"—Peggy cast Grace a look she had developed over her extensive acquaintance with Arabella Tarleton—"we leave the sonnet writing to him, and the quim licking to me?"

"I suppose."

Grace was still a little pouty, but she leaned back upon the stump, looking—Peggy had to admit—very much like the sort of wild forest nymph she might have enjoyed knowing she looked like. It almost made Peggy wish she'd been a poet after all. She dropped a kiss to the inside of Grace's knee and was rewarded by a sigh and shiver.

"I feel like I've waited forever for this," Grace murmured, arching her back in welcome.

Peggy ran her kisses a little higher. "To have your quim licked?"

It was a complicated business, keeping your end of the conversation going when your mouth was occupied, but Belle (oh, Belle) had loved words almost as much as she'd loved to be touched. And Peggy, of course, had loved to please her. Although, were she to be completely honest, that had been as much vanity as selflessness. Committing your-self to the business of being an attentive lover gave you a sort of armour somehow. As if with every toe-curling, heart-stopping, scream-inducing climax you were saying: *You may not love me, but you will remember this.*

"Goodness no." Grace was laughing. "Are you not beholding me? I get my quim licked whenever I wish."

"I'm beholding you," Peggy confirmed, shoving Grace's garment impatiently out of the way.

One of Grace's hands alighted upon Peggy's head, her fingers mov-ing through Peggy's waywardly inclined curls. "No. I meant you, Peggy. I meant you."

An anxious, faintly curdled sensation settled in the depths of Peggy's stomach. "Because of my reputation?"

"Because of how long it's taken you to see anything and anyone that wasn't Arabella Tarleton."

Oh no. Oh no no no no no. Sitting back on her heels, Peggy was obliged to cease her beholding. "Grace, I . . . I don't mean to sound, you know, above myself here. But you don't . . . you wouldn't be . . ." She cleared her throat, pushing the hair Grace had disarranged away from her brow. "Look, you're not in love with me, are you?"

Grace rocked forward slightly on her tree stump and gazed down at Peggy with an expression of utter incredulity. "Of course I'm in love with you. I've been in love with you for years."

"But I tied your hair to a tree. You can't be in love with someone who tied your hair to a tree."

"You've apologised."

"Yes, but I still did it," Peggy protested. "I'm clearly a very bad person."

"And you rushed to my rescue when you thought I was drowning in a stream."

"Very cruelly. Destroying your flower crown and upsetting the naiads."

"There weren't any naiads," Grace pointed out.

"There could have been, though. How can you be in love with someone so potentially disrespectful to naiads?"

"Peggy." Grace's eyes had gone shiny again. And, leaning down, she cupped Peggy's cheek gently. "The way you feel you're unworthy of love is so very"—she heaved a deep and tender sigh—"romantic."

Peggy shied back a little at that. "What? I don't feel I'm—I'm very worthy of love, I'll have you know. I'm great. All I mean is, I don't think *you* should be in love with me. I think it's a bad idea."

"Were you in love with Arabella Tarleton because you thought it was a good idea?"

"No. I just . . . was."

"You see?" None of the shine had faded from Grace's eyes. "The heart is a wild bird, Peggy. It can neither be governed nor caged. It simply flies as it will upon the winds of emotion."

Peggy had seen a dissection once: as far as she was concerned, the heart was squashed red meat. It certainly wasn't flying anywhere. "Being in love with someone who doesn't love you is . . . well, I'll be honest with you, it's one of the worst things in the world that isn't, I don't know, war or poverty or slavery or syphilis."

"Oh, Peggy." Another earnest sigh from Grace. "You're so beautifully wounded."

"I'm not wounded," yelled Peggy. "I just don't want to hurt you."

"Then," suggested Grace, "don't?"

Pushing herself to her feet, Peggy indulged in a windmilly gesture of frustration. Maybe she *should* try falling for Grace Hickinbottom: normally only Belle could make her windmill. "It doesn't work like that—believe me, I know. And while I'd like nothing better than to continue with"—this gesture was a lot less windmilly and a lot more specific—"what we were doing, I shouldn't—I can't—if you're expecting something from me I'm unable to give."

"You mean," said Grace slowly, "you aren't in love with me."

This felt *horrible*. But it also felt like an occasion in which honesty was required. "No."

"And you don't want to lick my quim a little bit in case you fall in love after?"

Part of Peggy—a particular part—hesitated. Then she shook her head. "I'm not going to fall in love after."

"How do you know?"

"Because . . ." Peggy hung her head in defeat. "Because I'm still in love with Arabella."

Grace gave her the hardest stare Peggy had ever received in her life. "*Why?*"

"What do you mean why? It's just the way my heartbirdmeat is right now."

There was a long silence. Then Grace rose to her feet with far more hauteur than a slightly damp woman in a transparent dress should have possessed. "Well," she said. "I always thought it would be terribly interesting to be in love with someone beautiful and damaged, with a disdainful lover in her tragic past. But now I see it's just inconvenient."

That was, unfortunately, completely accurate. Peggy drooped even further. "I'm sorry."

Grace just stuck her nose in the air like an angry hunting dog. "Excuse me, please."

They were in a forest clearing by the edge of a brook, so there was no necessity for anyone to excuse anyone. But Peggy obligingly took a step backwards anyway.

"Hmph," declared Grace, sweeping past.

Peggy offered an apologetic bow.

Grace kept on sweeping. Then she paused, glancing over her shoulder. "Oh, and one more thing, Peggy Delancey."

"Yes?"

"If you should ever come upon me drowning in a brook again, do me the honour of leaving me to die."

There was no good answer to that, so Peggy just bowed again.

Bowed and felt terrible and thought of Belle's letter, which was still in the pocket of her breeches.

Chapter 3

Somewhat inevitably, Peggy was on her way to London. Belle's letter, as much as she had been able to make it out, given its unsolicited brook dunk, had read, *I desperately need your help. Please come.* Which was, as missives went, particularly Belle-like in that it inspired a lot of emotion and gave absolutely no information.

London, too, had a tendency to be emotion-inspiring. Unfortunately, that emotion was mostly dread. Peggy's family was rich enough, and probably eccentric enough, that she could have done as she pleased. But there would still have been the whispers, the questions, the laughter, and the incomprehension. They—that nebulous *they* of the beau monde—would have made a scandal out of something that felt, to her, as ordinary as breathing, and she was not sure she could have borne it. The worst of it was that she didn't even dislike dresses. She enjoyed them. But in London they felt like a prison. Like a lie she was telling about herself.

Or maybe she was a coward. If Valentine, the Duke of Malvern, one of the proudest men she had ever met, could live openly—brush off the ridicule as if it was nothing more than dust upon his sleeves—why couldn't she? Maybe, and here she allowed herself a private smirk, you had to be a duke. Or maybe he had learned how to inhabit a world where the only thing that mattered to him was love.

Love again. She sighed. If she was very lucky, she might grow as weary of it as Belle claimed to be. Not for the first time, she wondered if she should have stayed in Devonshire with Grace, but it was hard to imagine what kind of future they could have—what with Peggy still in love with Belle and Grace in love with a version of Peggy who didn't actually exist. Of course, not every affair had to *have* a future. Except none of them did, that was the problem, and Peggy had no idea what "the future" even entailed for someone like her. Whoever she fell in love with, whatever choices she made around them, it felt as though she would be saying something about herself she didn't want to be saying. And the one thing she did, perhaps, want to say—*I can't imagine anything better than having someone to drop their bacon in my tea at breakfast*—seemed banal beyond belief. Bonny's duke had gone on a cross-country chase, crawled through a cellar window, and taken a bullet for love. And all Peggy could manage was—

She honestly had no fucking idea.

The view from the carriage window had been gradually giving way from narrow streets to wide ones, from grey stone to gold, and the hustle-bustle of thousands of lives to the ordered serenity of less than a hundred. The Delanceys had their own fashionable Mayfair townhouse, not that it saw much use from either of her parents, but Peggy could not have taken up residence there alone, and the thought of (figuratively) digging up a great-aunt or hiring a chaperone made her feel faintly nauseous. Young ladies required chaperones. She was not a young lady. Although, frankly, the thought that *anyone* required a chaperone was faintly insulting. If the only thing preventing every social occasion from descending inexorably into an orgy was the watchful eye of a trained orgy-preventer, then that reflected poorly on the disposition of everyone involved.

In any case, Peggy was staying with Belle. And that there could be deemed nothing improper about that just demonstrated a fatal lack of imagination on the part of society. Belle, in turn, was staying with her twin and her twin's in-everything-but-name husband, in *their* fashionable Mayfair townhouse. And Peggy—emerging stiff-limbed from the carriage, with her skirts twisting around her ankles—was greeted with warmth and hastily concealed surprise by the butler. Because of course

Belle had written her a frantic plea for aid and then not actually told anyone Peggy was coming.

"Good heavens." Valentine emerged into the sun-washed splendour of the entrance hall. "Peggy."

"Yes," confirmed Peggy, dropping her reticule, then a glove, then her other glove, then her shawl, and finally her bonnet, as she attempted to strip off her pelisse. "That's me. I'm here."

Valentine's bootheels clicked across the marble floor as he hurried towards her. "It's wonderful that you're here."

"Belle didn't . . . think to mention it, I suppose? That she'd invited me?"

"Arabella wouldn't think to mention it to me if my hair was on fire."

In spite of everything, Peggy smiled. "She wouldn't, would she?"

"You know you're always welcome in our home."

And then Valentine made a strange, puppetlike movement that Peggy briefly thought heralded some kind of nervous collapse, before she identified it as a shy man's attempt to offer a hug that he had subsequently decided might not have been welcome.

"Oh, come on," she said.

She held out her arms, and Valentine promptly enfolded her. He was an unexpectedly capable hugger, which was to say he hugged like he meant it—neither rushing nor lingering but pressing her warmly to him in something that felt almost like gratitude. That was the Duke of Malvern's secret truth, for all the others he laid bare before the scorn of his peers: he did not have many friends, but those he cultivated he truly treasured. Peggy couldn't have said when she'd grown so fond of his pompous arse. But here they were.

"Are you staying long?" he asked once they had parted.

Peggy shrugged. "Depends on Belle."

"Well, if you're not too tired, perhaps after dinner we could gather in the library and"—a touch of pink crept across the top of his oh-so-aristocratic cheekbones—"indulge ourselves in a round or two of the dictionary game."

"You know I'll just say everything's an ornamental pot."

He smiled then, and Peggy reeled a little internally from the way it changed his whole face from abstractly handsome into something rather glorious. "But Peggy, ornamental pots are not the same without you."

"Oh my God." Belle's voice broke upon them as abruptly as if she'd dropped a piano on their heads from the floor above. "Must it always be the same story with you, Malvern? First you steal my brother, and now you're trying to steal my friend."

Valentine gave a kind of strangled yelp and leapt away from Peggy so hastily it was almost comical. "What? N-no. Miss Tarleton, I assure you I—"

"I'm joking," said Belle, "you utter knobhead."

She sailed gracefully down the stairs towards them—looking beautiful and ethereal and, frankly, *studied*. Practicing her attitudes in the mirror was one of those character traits that could be endearing in certain contexts, and frustrating in others.

Right now, it was fifty-fifty. Tilting forty-sixty in favour of frustrating when Belle claimed Peggy's arm with stagy possessiveness. Peggy loved her too well, as a friend above all else, to protest and embarrass her, but Arabella Tarleton had no right whatsoever to be possessive. And yet, in her own strange way, she was.

"In any case"—Belle was already trying to draw her away—"you can't have Peggy tonight. *We* already have plans."

Valentine's eyes narrowed with, to Peggy's mind, understandable wariness. "What plans?"

"We're going to visit our dear old friend Lady None of Your Business," retorted Belle. "You're not my keeper, Valentine."

He gave a soft cough. "Well, I'm your guardian, so technically I am."

"Then you may guard"—Belle made a show of patting herself down before presenting him with the digitus impudicus—"this."

To Belle's visible irritation, Valentine merely shrugged. "In which case I'll be at your disposal the next time you need a young man extracted from a fountain or a young lady's father dissuaded from taking a horsewhip to your hide."

"As you will." Belle dismissed him with a roll of her eyes and a sweep of her hand before dragging Peggy upstairs and into her room. Once again, Peggy could have protested. And, once again, she didn't. Less than five minutes under the same roof as Belle and it already felt as though no time had passed. That nothing had changed. Peggy least of all.

"Do we really have plans tonight?" she asked. Because, after days in a carriage, she didn't feel capable of much beyond soaking in a hot bath.

As ever, Belle's room was in a state of extravagant chaos, books and papers and garments strewn everywhere. Pushing a pile of lacy petticoats to the floor, Belle threw herself down upon the unmade bed. "Yes, we're going out. To a musical soiree."

"Did I miss something in your letter?" Peggy looked around for somewhere to sit before giving up and perching next to Belle. "When you said *I desperately need your help*, did you in fact mean *I desperately need your help . . . to party?*"

The look Belle turned on her was one of genuine hurt. "I *do* desperately need your help."

"At a musical soiree? What use could I possibly be? Unless you're looking for someone to fall asleep in the back row?"

"You won't fall asleep," Belle told her, with ill-deserved confidence.

"I will. There hasn't been a pretentious art form invented that can keep me conscious."

Belle gave a little moue of exasperation. "Can we forget the soiree, please?"

"Believe me," Peggy muttered, "I'd like nothing better than to forget the soiree."

"Peggy!"

"What?"

Pushing herself to her knees, Belle was silent for a long moment, regarding Peggy with eyes narrowed to icy-blue chips. Then, "I don't understand why you're being so disagreeable all of a sudden."

"Maybe"—Peggy regarded back—"because you've yoinked me all the way to London for no bloody reason? Unless it's just for whatever satisfaction you get from knowing you can snap your pretty fingers and have me come to heel like a damn dog."

It was too much. And Peggy realised this the moment the words left her lips. She could have blamed Grace for stirring things up. The journey for giving her too much time to think. But no. It was all her, and her own resentful heart.

She braced herself for a retort from Belle. Maybe even some flying soft furnishings. But, to her horror, Belle simply covered her face with her hands and started crying. And not in the way Belle usually cried, which was for the sake of theatrics, and because she could look usefully beautiful doing it. This was something else entirely: full of private pain.

"Oh God. I'm sorry. I'm so sorry." Peggy gathered Belle to her—which, after a second or two of resistance, Belle allowed. "I'm such a beast. I didn't mean it."

"No-no." Belle made the sort of undignified sound she would never normally have allowed. "It's not you, Peggy. It's . . . it's me. I'm just so . . . so *miserable*."

Peggy kissed the top of her head a little helplessly. "Darling, darling."

"And I'm tired," Belle sobbed, "and I'm bored and I don't . . . I don't fit anywhere."

"You're Valentine's ward now. You can fit wherever you want."

"But don't you see?" Lifting her head, Belle presented Peggy with her swollen eyes and very red nose. "That makes it even worse because I *still* don't fit."

"Fit how?" asked Peggy, somewhat overwhelmed by this sudden flood of emotion. While she was well aware that Arabella Tarleton was not always who she pretended to be, Peggy had somehow let herself forget that she wasn't wholly invulnerable. That was the problem with loving someone who didn't love you the way you wanted: it was too easy to lose who they were in your own feelings.

Belle drew in a deep, shaky breath. "I have to fall in love, Peggy. I *have* to. It's what women are for."

"People who aren't women fall in love too." Peggy was relieved to note she sounded only *slightly* defensive.

"It's not the same, though. You've read the same books I've read. Beheld the same world I have. Love is supposed to be our consolation."

"Your what now?"

"Our consolation. For the fact we have *fuck all else.*"

It was not a perspective on love that Peggy had previously considered, but then her own situation was rather unique in the freedoms it offered, both financially and personally. "I think," she said carefully, "that may be true for a lot of women, but it doesn't have to be the case for you. You're independently wealthy. In a few years you could even have your own household. Or travel—you've always wanted to travel."

"By myself?" Belle's voice rose. "Alone? Forever? Until I am eaten to death by scarabs on the banks of the Nile?"

When talking to Belle, it was important to focus on what mattered and not allow yourself to be distracted by hypothetical scarabs. "You're not alone. You have Bonny—"

"Bonny left me for Valentine." Belle heaved a sigh. "As was only right. Valentine is everything he's ever wanted."

"And me? Do I not count?"

"Of course you count. But, Peggy"—fresh tears gathered in Belle's eyes—"you're going to leave me too."

Peggy scowled. "Right. Because pelting down to London at a moment's notice is exactly the sort of thing people do as a farewell gesture."

"Not now. Perhaps not even soon. But inevitably: when you fall in love yourself."

"Chance would be a fine thing."

"It's what you *want*," Belle said heavily. "It's what everyone wants. Everyone except me. In the great dance of life, I will be the eternal wallflower. With no-one to hold my hand when the last notes fade and the musicians leave us to the dark."

Something sharp and acrid was rising to the back of Peggy's throat. "And being with me isn't even worth thinking about?"

"Of course I've thought about it."

"I'm honoured." Rising, Peggy tried to walk off her feelings. But navigating the room was hazardous and just made her feel even more restless. A strange combination of trapped and untethered. "For God's sake, Belle, I love you. I've loved you for years. I'd do anything for you. I'd never leave your side. And I definitely wouldn't let you get eaten to death by scarabs on the banks of the Nile."

The colour fled Belle's face, leaving it chalky and tear mottled. "Please don't. I *hate it* when you talk this way. You know that."

"I know." Peggy pulled at her hair, feeling sick and foolish and deeply, unbearably hurt. As she always did. "But I wish I could understand what's so intolerably repulsive to you about me being in love with you."

"It feels *wrong*," cried Belle. Not, Peggy noticed, bothering to dispute the whole *repulsive* angle. "I can't explain why."

"Does it matter? I'll never mention it again. We can still be together." Except that would be a mistake and Peggy knew it would be a mistake. But it seemed, just for an instant, better than whatever was happening now. This tear-your-skin-off breaking up of two people who had never really been together. "I'll be your lover and your companion, and never ask for more."

Belle crumpled back down onto the bed, looking for a moment very small and very broken amidst the sheets and discarded dresses. "You'd find me lacking. You already do. And, in the end, you'd despise me."

"And you really think the answer here"—Peggy returned to Belle's side, placing what she hoped was a soothing hand between her shoulders—"is to find some stranger and make yourself fall in love with them? I'm not sure it works like that."

"Why can't it work like that?"

"Well," tried Peggy, "because . . ."

"Not every experience comes naturally to all people. Perhaps I am simply under-practised in matters of love. I mean"—and here Belle brightened visibly—"remember when I thought I might not enjoy anal pleasures? But having made the attempt, I discovered I enjoyed them very much indeed? And now I partake of them often, and gladly?"

As it happened, Peggy *did* remember. She remembered very vividly. And it was an odd thing to feel slightly wistful about. "I just don't think love and, um, anal are the same?"

"How would you know?" Belle pouted a little. "You responded to both from the outset. Perhaps we are simply fashioned differently, you and I?"

Peggy opened her mouth, then closed it again. This was so typical of Belle. She could make you question almost anything.

"Besides," Belle went on, with the burgeoning confidence of someone who felt they were winning an argument, "do you know what Bonny told me about Valentine?"

"Do I *want* to know?" Given the context, this did not sound like it was going anywhere Peggy wanted to be taken.

"Yes." Belle nodded. "It's rather lovely, but if you ever try to claim I said so, I'll kill you with my garter."

"I can think of worse ways to go."

That earned a giggle from Belle. "Don't you dare raise that eyebrow. You know what it does to me."

It was almost, though not quite, an invitation. And perhaps in the past Peggy would have taken it anyway, because sex was a lot easier than talking. They were good at sex and had only got better at it. Talking they'd been good at once, but the reverse had occurred. Looking back, Peggy wondered if sex had ever helped *really*. It certainly didn't seem as though it would help now. Even though it would have been a relief to lose herself in pleasure and closeness and something she could half pretend was love.

Except such pretending wasn't fair to Belle. Wasn't fair to either of them.

Chapter 4

"Tell me about Valentine?" she asked instead.

"Oh." Belle's eyes gleamed with the joy of other people's secrets. "Bonny said that he—Valentine, I mean—only feels sexual desire for Bonny."

That did not seem like much of a revelation. "Bonny *would* say that. He's wildly vain."

"No, but until Bonny, he had never felt anything like it for anyone."

"If there was ever a man to strike me as a late bloomer, it's Valentine."

"It's *more* than that, Peggy. It's . . . who he is." One of Belle's hands caught up Peggy's, squeezing it slightly frantically. "Don't you see?"

"I suppose," Peggy conceded. "Though what I mainly see is something that isn't our business."

"What if"—Belle's grip intensified to the point of pain—"what if I'm like Valentine?"

Peggy cast her mind over Belle's varied selection of lovers. "I don't think you're like Valentine."

"Maybe I'm like Valentine *for love*."

It made sense. Or did it make sense? It was often hard to tell with Belle. So Peggy tried a neutral "Oh?"

"Why not? If Valentine only became interested in sex after meeting Bonny, maybe I just need to sleep with the right person, and then I'll fall in love?"

Peggy's heart had abandoned its usual *ba-dum ba-dum*, adopting instead a wavery, sad-cat wail of *I'm not the right person, I'm not the right person.* "And, um"—she tried to keep the wavery sad-cat wail out of her voice—"how's that working out?"

"Terribly," declared Belle. "I've ravished half of London, to no avail."

"Poor you."

"There's no need to be mean, Peggy. It has had its compensations, I will admit, but it's been hard work, and I'm getting quite bored."

"It's a wonder you're not getting quite poxed."

Belle released Peggy's hand abruptly. "I won't be shamed, Peggy, even by you." Her tone was—Peggy had to admit, deservedly—cold. "Especially by you."

"I know," said Peggy quickly. "I'm sorry." Because she was. The comment had come from somewhere mean and bitter, and Belle did not deserve it.

"You know"—Belle was gazing at her in genuine sorrow—"I wish it was you as much as you wish it was you. Do you not think my life would be a thousand times better if I knew how to love you? Do you think I don't *want* to love you?"

"Belle . . ." It came out as somewhere halfway between her name and a groan. "Don't take this amiss, but it's very hard to keep track of what you want one moment to the next."

It was the sort of remark almost guaranteed to rouse Belle to fury and theatrics. But instead, she just said very quietly, "The same as everyone else, I expect. Freedom, happiness. Not to feel powerless and alone." There was a pause. The sort of pause that gave Peggy ample time in which to feel like an absolute arse, and, while she was grappling with that, Belle went on: "I am trying. I have been trying. I would have married Valentine, as I was meant to, and I would even have tried to be a good wife. But then he abandoned us—and I realised I'd never been real to him for a moment. I was just a . . . a toy he could pick up and play with and break and forget about and pick up again at his whim."

"He certainly didn't cover himself in glory," Peggy admitted. "But—and I'm not defending him, mind you—it's clear he had his own . . . matters to attend to."

"And his matters will always take precedence over the feelings of others, simply because of who he is, and what he has."

Peggy, far too conscious of all the ways her own wealth and the protection of her family gave her own *matters* more precedence than they might have otherwise, offered an awkward little shrug. "You mean the whole . . . duke thing?"

"He's a duke?" Belle lifted her brows impishly. "Are you sure? He's never mentioned it."

And Peggy laughed through her freshly breaking heart. Because it hurt, it hurt so much, to feel such joy with someone you could never have. "And you really think," she asked, flicking what she hoped Belle would interpret as a tear of mirth from the corner of her eye, "falling in love is the answer here?"

Like dying stars, the light faded from Belle's eyes. "What other answer is there? Remember, I spent years living a thousand imaginary lives with Bonny, and I never found the shape of mine the way he did his. And then I thought if I could just . . . *be* a heroine, as the books describe, then maybe love would find me, and everything would finally make sense. But none of it has worked, and I'm still here and I'm still me—and all I see for myself is a future as some half-ghostly adjunct to my own twin's happy ever after."

In that moment, Peggy's own unhappiness seemed small and straightforward and more than a little selfish. It was all very well to cast yourself as the thwarted lover in your own story. But it still made you the inconstant friend in someone else's. She slid off the bed, dropped to one knee, and took Belle's hand in hers. "I'm sorry," she said.

"There's no need." Belle looked down at her, with that deep affection that was not love in the way Peggy had always wanted it to be. "Really, you've always made a far better romantic hero than I."

At this Peggy gave a snort and pressed her brow to the back of Belle's hand. "Oh, don't you start."

"She was," Belle murmured, "a 'verray, parfit, gentil knyght.'" And then, "Please say no if it's too much, but I . . . I don't know what else to do. Will you help me?"

"Help you fall in love?" Peggy glanced up. "I'm not sure I can. I mean, I'm not sure anyone could."

Belle gave an exasperated little squeak. "Not that part. You see, I think I've . . . I think I've found someone I might want to . . . to try with?"

Jealousy stretched dragonishly, or perhaps like a mild-to-severe case of indigestion, somewhere in the depths of Peggy's gut. "I thought you said you'd been trying."

"Yes, but this time feels different."

From Peggy's perspective, it seemed very much the same, but she also did not quite trust her perspective when it came to Belle. Love had compromised her. "How so?"

"I . . ." Belle hesitated. "I don't quite know. But they're one of the most remarkable people I think I've ever seen. And . . . if I can't fall in love with someone like that, maybe I'm simply beyond hope?"

The indigestion-jealousy-dragon thrashed its tail. "Aren't you expecting a bit too much from love?"

Standing abruptly, Belle pushed past Peggy and took an energetic turn about the room. For all Belle may have personally considered her stint as a heroine a failure, she certainly had the mannerisms down. She looked, Peggy thought, almost unbearably beautiful when animated. At rest she was perilously close to a fashion plate, composed and picture perfect with her golden curls and drown-in-me eyes. In motion, she was something altogether wilder and more complicated: every season in one, from the summer tempests of her passions to the unyielding winter of her loyalty, and the soft autumnal quiet of her care.

"What do you mean," she cried, "expecting too much from love? It is the uniting bloody force of humanity, is it not? Playwrights and poets and philosophers have been banging on about it for centuries."

"Well," Peggy tried, "maybe they're wrong?"

"Wrong? Are you telling me that Shakespeare is wrong? That Sappho was wrong? That Shelley is wrong? All these people are wrong, and I—only I, in all the world—am right?"

So that had been less comforting than Peggy had intended. "Must it be about right or wrong? Could it not be that Shakespeare, Sappho, and Shelley are Shakespeare, Sappho, and Shelley and you're . . . you're you?"

"I . . ." Belle put a hand to her brow, but for once it did not seem like theatre. She looked, for a brief moment, truly and utterly exhausted. "I don't know anymore. But I do know I'm sick of feeling like this. And this could be my opportunity to have . . . something. Something of my own."

Peggy was conscious of a somewhat vertiginous sensation: that nagging certainty of having missed something or failed to say what you'd meant to. Or, worse, needed to. But the moment was slipping away, and Belle didn't *seem* angry with her. So Peggy just offered what she hoped was an encouraging grin. "You know I'd do anything for you, Belle, but I'm hard-pressed to see what any of this has to do with me. I can't . . . make you fall in love. Or make someone else fall in love with you."

"That's exactly my problem, though." Belle's eyes were wide and unexpectedly vulnerable. "I don't know how to make someone fall in love with me. I've never tried."

"I think," said Peggy gently, "the fact that many people have fallen in love with you regardless suggests trying isn't necessary. You just have to . . . um. Be yourself?"

"Be myself." Belle's tone was flat. "I hope that doesn't become widespread advice on the subject of love because it is neither helpful nor encouraging."

"I'm not sure what else I've got."

"Well"—Belle gave the floor an irate little stamp—"it's not good enough. You don't understand: this isn't some ordinary boring duke whose attention I wish to claim. This is someone . . . someone special. Someone *spectacular*."

Frankly, Peggy couldn't imagine many people more spectacular than Belle herself. "Even someone spectacular will adore you, given opportunity."

"That's the problem, though," cried Belle. "I've given them ample opportunity to adore me. And they have thus far failed to do so. What's wrong with them?"

"Perhaps they don't favour women?"

"If rumour is to be believed, they favour everyone. Sometimes they even favour several people at the same time."

"And," Peggy asked carefully, "this . . . this is the sort of person you feel is the sort of person you want to fall in love with?"

Belle tossed the spun-gold waterfall of her hair. "You'll understand when you see them."

"You sound half in love with them already." Peggy did her best not to sound grumpy. Unfortunately, she sounded grumpy.

But Belle just shook her head regretfully. "No. I'm mostly annoyed they don't seem to have noticed me at all." She frowned. "Why haven't they noticed me? I put a lot of effort into being this beautiful."

"You are beautiful," Peggy agreed. "And you would be, even without the effort."

The look Belle turned on her was at once exasperated and fond. "Sometimes, Peggy dearest, you're so very not a girl."

"I'm aware. As you should surely be aware that love is about more than how you look."

"I know that—I've read a million books—but one must start somewhere. Except I'm getting nowhere. Which is where you come in."

While Peggy had not read a million books, she had read some, and she had moreover a long-standing familiarity with Belle's schemes. "I absolutely point-blank refuse. Nothing you say or do will change my mind, to pretend to be in love with you—when I am actually in love with you—to make some stranger jealous."

"How dare you." Belle struck a pose of affront—*pose* being the word. "I wasn't going to suggest that. I wasn't going to suggest that *at all*."

"It's a terrible idea. It won't work. It never works, not even in fiction." To say nothing of the fact that it would make utter mincemeat of Peggy's heart.

"What I was thinking," Belle went on, as if she really had been thinking it, "was that you could play Cesario to my Orsino."

"I already am bloody Cesario to your Orsino, only without the prospect of a happy ending."

"Which surely makes you perfectly placed to carry my suit for me." Peggy ruffled her own curls fretfully. "When was the last time you saw that play? Because it ended very confusingly for everyone."

"I'm talking about the principle, not the outcome." Belle's eyes grew wide and earnest. "Please, Peggy? *Please*. It's probably my last and only chance of happiness."

This also bore all the hallmarks of a terrible idea. But it was better than the last terrible idea. And Belle seemed genuinely happy. Besides, what else was Peggy going to do with her life? Turn down sex with vicars' daughters and talk to her dog?

"If I must," she said, as she had said so many times before. "But I'm not building any willow cabins."

Chapter 5

People who held private concerts were the worst. Not content with letting opera stay at the opera, where it belonged, they insisted on creating additional opera spaces in the world at large and forcing them on their acquaintances. Worse, they actually cared about music, so whereas at the theatre you were free to people-watch (or in extreme cases leave early) and the proprietors didn't give two figs as long as they got paid, at a private event you had no choice but to act like you were paying attention.

Lady Farrow—the host of this evening's entertainment—was a particularly extreme case. She cared about music passionately, and blithely assumed that the whole world shared her passion. Her husband was a similarly artistic soul, though he was poetical rather than musical, and the ton had breathed a sigh of relief when they ultimately chose to wed each other. While they were both in many ways eligible—he was titled, she was handsome—their marriage kept their excessive creativity contained to a single household.

Right now, Lady Farrow was exclaiming rapturously in the direction of Belle—something something had one in London something something 1790s—and Peggy was wishing there was food. That was another problem with private, or indeed public, concerts: you were supposed to sustain yourself on culture, and thus the best you could hope for was watery wine and biscuits. Surely Belle wasn't attempting to fall for a music lover? It didn't seem the sort of thing she would countenance.

She was a bit like the god of the Old Testament in that regard: thou shalt have no other loves before me. Although she was also considerably more generous because thou couldst fuck whoever thou wanted.

Her eyes roved the lethargic crowd, trying to imagine who— amongst the visibly reluctant attendees—could possibly have caught Belle's interest. That laughing gentleman? This adorably bespectacled lady, who was halfway to catching Peggy's?

"Lord Southerbrooke," exclaimed Lady Farrow.

Which was when Peggy turned to behold the loveliest man art or imagination could have fashioned. Dark-eyed and moonlit-haired, he was as pristine, as perfectly symmetrical, as a sculpture. Peggy braced herself for the gut-stab jealousy, yet nothing came. Perhaps she was simply too awestruck. If this was who Arabella Tarleton had chosen to fall in love with, it was hard to fault her.

"I'm so glad you came." Lady Farrow was mid-pleasantry with the vision of unbearable magnificence.

The vision gave a surprisingly awkward bow for a vision. "Of course, Lady Farrow. I am—I am quite excited."

"One hears that about you," murmured Belle from behind her fan.

"I don't think you've met Miss Delancey? This is the Earl of Southerbrooke, Miss Delancey. My lord, Miss Delancey."

Peggy offered a social grimace. She did not entirely enjoy being addressed as Miss—it was unavoidable, but she still felt it like a pin through her heart, trapping her in a taxonomy of someone else's making.

"Of the Devonshire Delanceys?" enquired the earl, politely.

His eyes were a brown so deep the light seemed to lacquer them. "Stunning," said Peggy. "I mean stunned. I mean hello."

"And of course," went on Lady Farrow smoothly, "you recall Miss Tarleton?"

As one, Belle and His Lordship turned from each other without a word, the former gliding away with her head held imperiously high, and the latter stalking off in the opposite direction. Peggy stared after them, bewildered, and abruptly devoid of her companion.

"Good lord," came a mischief-filled voice at her elbow. "The double cut direct, beautifully executed. I haven't seen one of those since . . . oh . . . 1813."

"What happened in 1813?" asked Peggy, turning to greet Sir Horley Comewithers, who had naturally gravitated to the single site of drama in the room.

He smiled his impish smile. "Lord Hardywicke and Lord Clusterpick both wore the same hat."

"At the same time? Didn't that make it difficult for them to snub each other?"

"Very droll." Sir Horley, Valentine's self-appointed best friend and a renowned troublemaker, leaned in to kiss her cheek. "No, they were wearing identical hats independently. And they haven't spoken since. How are you, my dear Peggy? What brings you to London?"

Peggy jerked her thumb towards Belle, who was still mid-glide— albeit liable to be interrupted by a wall if she continued—and tried to ignore the sympathetic flicker in Sir Horley's eyes. It felt too close to pity. "What brings you to a . . . a whatever this is?"

"Sugar plum, I wouldn't miss it for the world. Haven't you heard? Lady F has secured one of those"—he gave an indiscreet discreet cough—"Italian singers."

Wonderful. Not only would Peggy be forced to spend several hours listening to people singing, but she wouldn't even be able to understand what they were singing *about.* "Why are there so few English operas?"

Sir Horley flicked open a fan of his own—a very beautiful one, in lavender silk—and struck a contemplative pose. "I suppose it might have something to do with the fact we semi-recently cut the head off our king and closed down all the theatres. Well, I say *we.* I mean some dullards with unflattering haircuts."

"I'm beginning to see where they were coming from."

"And anyway," Sir Horley pressed on cheerfully, "we have Purcell. Arne. Lampe. *Handel,* although I suppose he was technically German and wrote mostly in Itali—why is your face doing that?"

"I don't know. I can't see it. What's it doing?"

"It's glazing over."

"Can you blame it?"

Before Sir Horley could assign his preferred measure of culpability to Peggy's face, Lady Farrow moved to stand by the dais at the front of what, in happier times, was probably the ballroom. She gave a little cough that nobody paid attention to and then a vigorous clap of her hands, which they did.

"Thank you all for coming," she said, smiling upon her guests as Peggy imagined Lucifer might smile upon new arrivals in hell. "I've prepared an absolutely *marvellous* programme for you tonight."

Peggy couldn't quite repress a groan.

"Music," Lady Farrow went on, casting her eyes to the ceiling, "is, of course, my greatest passion."

Sir Horley put his lips close to Peggy's ear, concealing them both behind his fan. "Makes one rather pity her husband, does it not?"

"As the bard himself said: 'The man that hath no music in himself, Nor is not moved with concord of sweet sounds, Is fit for treasons, stratagems, and spoils; The motions of his spirit are dull as night, And his affections dark as Erebus.'"

"Treasons, stratagems, and spoils it is then," muttered Peggy.

Sir Horley lifted his brows. "Those dark affections, though. They sound rather exciting."

Lady Farrow made a gesture of general beneficence. "Starting us off tonight will be Miss Drearingpole and Miss Stodingplonk, who will be performing for us Charles Burney's Sonata no. 1 Book 1 in F for Piano Four Hands: II: Allegro."

"Oh no." Peggy elbowed Sir Horley urgently. "I haven't heard Sonata no. 1 Book 1 in F for Piano Four Hands: I. How will I understand the plot?"

"As for the rest of the delights in store, well"—Lady Farrow fluttered coyly—"you must simply wait and see."

Something stirred the room then. A name passed from mouth to mouth like a kiss.

"Now," concluded Lady Farrow, leaving Peggy at once relieved she was concluding, and heart-sinky because that meant the musical part of the evening had become inescapable, "can I please ask you all to take a seat?"

It was at this moment that Belle popped up like a shark beneath a shipwreck, seizing both Peggy and Sir Horley. "Come. We need to be at the front."

"Need we?" asked Peggy.

But Belle was already dragging them through the crowds, and since resisting would likely have left all three of them in a pile on the floor, Peggy allowed herself to be dragged. She was, at the very least, successful in her attempt to convince Belle to secure them a place by the aisle.

"So I don't knock against anyone's knees," Peggy explained, "when I get so bored I absolutely have to run out screaming."

"I don't think you'll run out screaming." Sir Horley shamelessly claimed the seat Peggy would have chosen. "But you may fall asleep, so probably best for everyone concerned if you go in the middle."

Grumbling, Peggy flopped down between Belle and Sir Horley. "Where have I heard that before?"

"It doesn't reflect particularly well on you if you've heard it anywhere."

Belle gave a traitorous peal of laughter.

"Hey now"—Peggy turned to her—"you're supposed to be on my side. Don't encourage him."

"But I love encouraging Sir Horley," declared Belle.

It was at this moment that Miss Drearingpole and Miss Stodingplonk emerged onto the dais to a scattering of applause and took their seats by the large pianoforte that currently occupied the centre of the stage. They were a pair of equally serious-faced women who moved in almost eerie accord and proceeded to gallop their fingers over the piano keys, filling the room with a barrage of notes that only increased in speed and intensity as the piece continued. A single lock of Miss Drearingpole's hair detached itself from her brutal chignon and began to bounce violently at her temple. Upon Miss Stodingplonk's upper lip trembled a drop of perspiration, bright as a broken diamond. As one, Belle and Sir Horley leaned in, almost squashing Peggy in their eagerness to conference.

"They are at it," Sir Horley whispered.

"Like *wild cats*," Belle agreed.

Peggy gave a little cough. "In the absence of our dear Valentine, I feel compelled to observe that they do seem like very good friends."

At which point the young lady who was sitting behind Peggy tapped her on the shoulder until she turned round. "Excuse me"—the irate young lady's eyes barely strayed from Miss Drearingpole and Miss Stodingplonk—"but you're supposed to be appreciating the art, not enjoying yourself."

Not for the first time in her life, Peggy wished for a hat to tip. "My apologies."

After Miss Drearingpole and Miss Stodingplonk had completed both Sonata no. 1 Book 1 in F for Piano Four Hands: II: Allegro and Sonata no. 2 Book 1 in D for Piano Four Hands: II: Allegro, they took their bows and left the stage, only to be replaced by a long-nosed gentleman who subjected them to the full thirty minutes of Mozart's Flute Concerto no. 1 in G Major. He was followed by a statuesque lady in a pearl-bedecked turban who swept the cover from a harp and played a succession of Rosetti sonatas whose rippling rise and fall sounded so . . . liquid-like that they left Peggy squirming with an abrupt need to wee.

And, God in heaven, as a peek at Sir Horley's pocket watch confirmed, they were little more than an hour in. They were then permitted the briefest of aural respite as a small orchestra of about twelve musicians assembled itself on the dais. This turned out to be in service of gratifying the company with some sections from *Artaxerxes*, despite at least some elements of the company (i.e., Peggy) remaining staunchly ungratified by *Artaxerxes*.

A soprano who, under less trying circumstances, she might have found extremely pretty moved to the centre of the stage and—as people were unaccountably wont to do in opera—burst into song for no reason. As her clear, crystalline voice filled the room, Peggy wondered if anyone else was sensible of the irony of a two-to-three-hour piece of musical theatre opening with the line "Still silence reigns around." It was all she could do to prevent herself from muttering "We should be so lucky" under her breath.

As the selection from *Artaxerxes* meandered onwards, Peggy did her level best to fall asleep, as Sir Horley had predicted. But the problem with music in general, and opera in particular, was that it tended to be . . . loud. And loud was not conducive to rest. There were periods when Peggy would almost manage to slip into blessed insensibility, but then something emotional would happen, the music would crescendo, and she would be viciously recalled to her surroundings, and the equally vicious crick in her neck.

Further opera followed, mostly the sort of arias that lent themselves to the sort of vocal showing off that made the experience of listening less pleasant for your audience; then a string quintet—which was basically a string quartet that didn't know when to give up—performing that Boccherini minuet that pursued one from ballroom to ballroom like every bad decision you'd ever made. By the time a solemn young man had spread himself abaft a cello, Peggy was oddly comforted: the C. P. E. Bach concerto he played sounded like someone sobbing under their bedclothes in the dark, but it spoke to her present mood.

Next came a rousing rendition of Beethoven's "Come fill, fill, my good fellow," the name of which reduced Sir Horley to a fit of giggles that had to be stifled in Belle's handkerchief. Only for them to overcome him again immediately when a barrel-chested, florid-faced man began to encourage the aforementioned filling in a rich bass-baritone.

"There's a comma," Belle told him, struggling with mirth herself, "between *fill* and *my good fellow.*"

Sir Horley nodded, hopelessly flushed, with tears caught on his lashes. "I know. But. But you can't *hear* a comma."

"This is a worrying insight into your sex life," observed Peggy.

"No, it isn't," retorted Sir Horley. "My sex life is merry and mellow, and I've filled many a good fellow."

The lady behind Peggy tapped furiously on her shoulder. "You're enjoying yourself again. It's very distracting and inappropriate."

"Sorry." Peggy resumed her disconsolate chair slump. "Sorry."

Chapter 6

"Peggy." Belle's hand curled over Peggy's forearm so tightly her nails dug into the underside of her wrist. "Peggy. It's . . . it's them."

Abruptly, Peggy realised she was almost horizontal in her chair, and it was probably only Belle's grip that was stopping her from sliding onto the floor. She righted herself and shook her head. "Mrrfgh?"

"It's *them*," said Belle again, as if a greater emphasis on *them* passed for explanation.

"Mrgfh nnfff mrggh?" Peggy wiped the smallest—smaller than small, miniscule, barely visible—touch of drool from the corner of her lips.

Belle was making a peculiar jolting motion with her head—as if she was trying to point using only her eyes. Standing on the dais was the next, and Peggy sincerely hoped final, performer. They were tall, taller perhaps even than Valentine, but as slender as a reed, their limbs long and graceful, giving them something of the aspect of an Old Testament angel. An earthbound seraph, fiercely and perfectly androgynous. Clad in plainest black, with their dark hair drawn sharply back, they offered their face—with all its beauties and its paradoxes—to the world with a kind of defiance. The soft curve of their cheek and jaw. Their long, aquiline nose with its uneven bridge. A mouth from a Renaissance portrait. Feathered brows above deep-set eyes. And, oh God, those eyes: as black as the lashes that framed them, with a sheen like polished jet, and a single sweep of silver across the lids.

It was a shame they were here to make a noise, and thus contribute to the general ruination of Peggy's evening, otherwise—

Otherwise what?

This was Belle's person. Well, Belle's potential person. And there were rules about that kind of thing. Rules that Peggy would have cut herself open rather than break. Certainly not for as little as a night or two of passion with a beautiful opera singer. When Belle's love—even if it came in its own shape—was worth more to her than almost anything in the world.

Peggy cast her a sideways glance, abruptly and unaccountably melancholic, memories of Belle unfolding like paper dolls. It was hard to believe she'd once almost been frightened of her own shadow, a silent, wary-eyed child who had grown into a restless, angry adolescent. And now? Now she just seemed lost. Maybe she'd been lost for a long time, and nobody had noticed. Never seen the curtain come down on the play.

Fuck, what was wrong with her? Where was all this coming from? Oh—probably the small string and harpsichord arrangement on the stage, which had been layering soft, sad harmonies over the silence while Peggy's mind had been adrift.

"This singer, then," she wondered aloud. "Are they going to . . . you know. Sing?"

Sir Horley and Belle put a hand on each of her knees in an almost simultaneous gesture of "Hush now."

So Peggy hushed now.

And then, from between the singer's parting lips, slipped a note of such unutterable purity that it damn near stopped Peggy's heart. The aria—whatever it was—couldn't have been much longer than three minutes, and she didn't have a clue what was being sung about, only that it felt as though someone was delicately stripping the skin from her bones with a silver blade. There were no vocal tricks, no embellishments or flourishes: just the performer's voice merciless in its power and perfection like nothing Peggy had ever heard before.

It was beautiful, but it was beautiful in the way that the night was beautiful in winter, when it was at its blackest and coldest, and you felt as infinitesimal as the distant stars. It was beautiful as only the bloodiest sunsets and the most jagged mountains were beautiful. Terrible beauty, beauty that wanted to drive you to your knees and drink the tears from your eyes, the sort of beauty to rend skies and topple cathedrals, as impossible as the flame of Prometheus.

Peggy had not come out tonight seeking a glimpse of the numinous, but the numinous was staring right at her regardless.

It took her a moment to realise that the aria was over. That the room was still, hollow in its fresh silence.

Then, an explosion of applause.

"So . . ." Peggy lurched to her feet. "I'm not very—I'm feeling a bit . . ." She could taste blood at the back of her throat. Her breath was knives. Her pulse a stampede of wild horses. "I think I might . . ."

Then the walls closed in, the ceiling rolled over like a dog wanting its tummy scratched, and the ground vomited itself into her face.

❦

"What just happened?" she asked.

"I think"—that was Belle's voice, coming from someway above her—"I think you fainted?"

"What? No. No, I didn't."

"Then you . . . cast yourself involuntarily on the floor. Or, at least *towards* the floor. Sir Horley caught you before you hit it. And then carried you out into the garden so you could get some air. It was rather dashing of him."

Peggy digested this. And disinclined though she was to give such a fanciful tale much credence, it did seem to explain some things. Like, for example, why she was in the garden when, last she'd checked, she'd been inside the house. "I'm sure I didn't faint," she said stubbornly.

"You know"—Belle soothed her brow with a cool hand—"if you wanted to leave, you could have just said."

A pause as Peggy continued digesting. "Did I really faint?"

"Just a little bit. Round the edges."

"Oh God."

"Darling, it's fine. These things happen."

"They don't happen to me." Peggy made a valiant attempt to lever her head out of Belle's lap, only to plonk it immediately back because moving made her temples pound and her vision swim. "I don't even know why I did."

"Perhaps you had a powerful reaction to the music?"

"Belle, you've met me. Do I seem like a person who has powerful reactions to music?"

Belle gave a little shrug. "Farinelli's voice was rumoured to make people spontaneously orgasm."

"In that case," said Peggy firmly, "I definitely fainted. There were no orgasms, spontaneous or otherwise."

"What if it was emotional orgasm?"

"It was not an orgasm of any kind."

There was another silence, broken by Belle sighing into a nearby cloud of wisteria. "They are . . . they are a good choice, aren't they?"

"A good choice?"

"To try and fall in love with. When I first heard them sing, I . . . I thought that feeling might be what being in love is like?"

It probably said something about Belle that she assumed love would be so . . . overwhelming. "I couldn't tell you, Belle. I'm not even sure I *liked* . . ." Peggy briefly ran out of words. "Whatever that was."

"You know it was glorious," returned Belle simply. "Besides, you don't act as if you *like* being in love with me either."

"Only because you don't love me back."

"And if I did"—Belle's hands stilled in her hair—"it would become a tame thing?"

Peggy wasn't sure how to answer that. Was what her parents had a *tame* love? Perhaps to some people, it might look that way. It certainly wasn't anything she could imagine sharing with Belle. Then again, all her romantic fantasies of Belle had been *about* Belle—what she needed, what would make her happy—and it had never really occurred to Peggy to wonder about her own needs. Her own happiness. Typical, really. Only she could find a way to write herself out of her own forever. "I suppose not," she said finally. She pushed herself gingerly to her elbows. "Look, I know you want my help with the whole—with *them*. But I think I need to go home and pull every blanket I can find over my head. I'll be available to visitors again circa 1850."

Belle made a concerned noise. "Are you unwell, still? Should I have a doctor brought?"

"No, I'm not unwell. Just a bit at-home-every-blanket-I-own-over-my-head-not-seen-until-1850-ish."

"You know you can't do that. If you do, everyone will think you're embarrassed."

"Yes," said Peggy, "because I *am* embarrassed."

"Well, you shouldn't be. We can say you ate a bad grape or something."

"Is fainting what happens if you eat a bad grape?"

"I don't know." Belle made a faintly impatient gesture, as if the medical consequences of inferior-grape consumption were entirely beneath her. "I've never eaten one. In any case," she went on briskly, "even if you want to go home, you'll still have to go through the house."

Peggy surveyed the garden. "What if I climbed over that wall?"

"It's quite a tall wall, and you're wearing quite a flimsy dress."

"What if I took my dress off?"

"I think you'd probably find running around London in your underwear even more embarrassing than fainting at a party."

That was . . . probably accurate. Peggy sighed. "Fine. We can go back in. But I'm leaving as soon as I can."

With a nod, Belle rose from the bench where they'd been resting. "Thank you for coming with me tonight."

"And," Peggy reminded her, "for coming to London in the first place."

"That too."

"And for all the other harebrained shit you've dragged me through."

Belle's eyes flashed blue and shocked in the spill of light from the house. "Excuse me. What harebrained shit?"

"Um, how about the time you decided we were going to run away to America because you didn't want to marry Valentine?"

"What else was I supposed to do? Marry Valentine?"

"You told me he was a monster. When he was clearly just as confused as the rest of us."

"He seemed monstrous to me." The night was not cold, but Belle wrapped her arms around herself against an involuntary shiver. "You don't know what it's like, Peggy, to be helpless and penniless. For God's sake, you don't even have to be a woman all the time."

Except to those who would insist she could not be anything else. Peggy stood, and was relieved that the ground, the sky, and the bits in between stayed where they were supposed to. "Let's not do that."

Belle offered a conciliatory hand. "You're right. I'm sorry."

"It's not . . . you know it's not . . . that I'm not—" Peggy broke off, with no idea what she was trying to say. Not uncomplicated? Not invulnerable either? The problem was, it wasn't anything she'd tried to talk about before, not even to Belle. And she wasn't sure she knew how to explain the parts of herself that didn't always fit together when she wanted them to. That went unseen even, she feared, by herself.

Unfortunately, by the time she was even 30 percent of the way towards articulating any of it, Belle had already moved on. "We should get back to the ballroom," she said, stiffening her spine like a soldier going into battle. "Falling in love with Orfeo isn't going to happen by itself."

Peggy wasn't wholly convinced it was going to happen at all. But maybe she just didn't want it to. Which wasn't to say she didn't want Belle to be happy. It was just that it would be sort of typical if she was embarking upon a spectacular romance with Peggy's assistance while Peggy herself was . . .

What? Standing around and pining?

"Come on, Peggy." Belle gave her a little tug that could have been either encouragement or exasperation and was probably a bit of both. "I'm sure hardly anyone even noticed you fainted . . . I mean, briefly assumed a non-voluntary horizontal position."

"What about Sir Horley catching me and carrying me out?"

"He did it very discreetly."

Sir Horley didn't have a discreet bone in his body. Not even the tiny ones in his toes. But Belle could be catastrophically convincing sometimes, and Peggy was going to have to deal with the fashionable world at some point (running away in her underwear notwithstanding). So she put on her best "I did not faint and, on the off chance I did, I'm fine with it" face and let Belle draw her back through the French doors.

The moment they stepped across the threshold, though, the room fell silent. Heads turned. It was the sort of reaction that Belle adored and Peggy hated. She was just re-evaluating the run-through-the-streets-of-London-in-her-undergarments strategy when the crowds parted, and there was the singer—the singer in whose vicinity she had possibly maybe fainted a little—gazing at her with unmistakable curiosity.

Fuck.

And now they were coming over.

Double fuck.

They'd changed since their performance, shedding all their previous austerity in favour of a dark-teal frock coat into whose skirts was woven a pattern of peacock feathers in emerald, sapphire, and indigo. Even that sly streak of silver across their lids had gone, replaced by lavish tinctures in shades that matched their coat, sweeping from their inner eye almost to their temple, their lashes artificially lengthened by the application of turquoise feathers. Unbound, their hair was almost perfectly straight and fell to their waist, not quite black, Peggy realised, but a deep brown—lighter than their eyes, darker than their skin—in whose strands the candlelight found shades of honey, mahogany, and autumn hickory.

Triple quadruple *quintuple* fuck. Because apparently they did not need to be singing to be glorious. Peggy's heart gave a doomed and traitorous flutter.

"So there you are, mio principe." Their spoken voice, it was a relief to note, did not rend any skies, topple any cathedrals, or make Peggy faint. It was perfectly ordinary, if slightly accented.

The words, though. They were so unexpected that Peggy actually glanced over her shoulder. "Who? Me?"

They smiled, one corner of their mouth slightly more curved than the other, drawing Peggy's attention to the trio of tiny beauty marks upon their cheek: the smallest a direct course north-easterly from their lips, the second a little larger, positioned diagonal to the first, and the third as decisive as a full stop, just below their cheekbone, with a paler freckle waiting like a lover at its side. "Yes, you," they were saying. "I thought you had fled me. And left not even a jumping slipper behind."

Peggy was as lost as Pythagoras in the triangle between those beauty marks. Lost enough to forget she hadn't introduced Belle. To almost forget she was there at all. "Sorry, a . . . a what kind of slipper?"

"A jumping slipper." They tilted their head. A simple gesture but rendered fantastical by the accompanying flicker of their feathered lashes. "You do not have this story of the little ashes girl?"

"Oh." Peggy was a clodhopper. She was hopping all the clod. Because of fainting and beauty marks and a mouth whose smile she wanted to lick and—*God damn it.* "Er. Yes. Yes, we do. But it's a glass slipper. Not a jumping slipper." She made a valiant attempt to de-clod her hops. "Not that slippers of any kind are usually the hallmarks of princes."

"Is it not," they returned, "the nature of princes to dress as they please?"

Peggy shrugged. "Depends on the courage of the prince."

"Or the circumstance. And, in any case"—another of those disarmingly crooked smiles—"I am glad for the opportunity to meet you."

"Not because of the . . . the . . ." Peggy mimed an ungainly swoon. "I hope it didn't disrupt anything."

Their eyes glinted wickedly. "Had it been in the middle of my performance, we might now be having a very different conversation. But no. You have paid me the highest of compliments, I think."

This was excruciating. Although—on the bright side—being mortified was distracting Peggy from the very real possibility she might like the person Belle liked. The person whose attention she was currently monopolising. "It probably wasn't—I mean, I probably just ate a bad grape. I mean, those grapes. When they go bad, they go really . . . um, bad." She elbowed the unusually silent Belle. "Don't they?"

To her surprise, the singer seemed genuinely saddened, watching her from beneath the dazzle of their tinctures. "Ah, be generous with me, mio principe. Let me have this. There is no shame, you know, in feeling art in the body as well as in the soul."

"Fine," Peggy grumbled, undone—as ever—by the faintest hint of vulnerability. "You were so good I fainted. Happy now?"

They pressed both hands to their heart, their nails buffed to a soft shine. "Rapturously. They say that when Farinelli performed, he—"

"Made people come, I know."

"Moved his audience to tears?" they finished, after a crescent-moon sliver of a pause.

Peggy opened her mouth and closed it again. Then tried a neutral, "Sorry. Yes. That does seem more likely."

"I suspect"—the singer adopted a contemplative aspect—"that when he wanted to make people come, he used other means."

Peggy was going to kill Belle. She was going to kill her with a shoe. "You're right. Yes. He probably did."

"As," they went on, "do I."

"Good to know," said Peggy, not thinking about it. Not thinking about it *at all*.

Another pause, rather more gibbous than the last. "It occurs to me, I have not yet learned your name, mio principe."

Peggy was still thinking about it. "I'm your prince." What, no. Wrong. "Peggy. Sorry. I'm your Peggy. Sorry, not your Peggy. The Peggy. Well, a Peggy. Margaret, that is. Margaret Peggy of the Devonshires. I mean the Delanceys. I mean Delancey. Of Devonshire."

"You seem to have a lot of names, PeggyMargaretPeggyDevonshireDelanceyDevonshire."

"I go by Peggy," explained Peggy.

"I begin to understand why. I am Orfeo."

The singer offered their hand, and Peggy—forgetting where she was and who people thought she was—took it and kissed it. And was oddly gratified to see those painted eyes gently close, even if only for a second, and feel upon her lips the faintest of tremors. "Just Orfeo?" she asked. "You seem to be as under-supplied on the nominative front as I am the reverse."

"There is no *just* about Orfeo," they retorted. But then they gave a shrug. "What alternatives do I have? Take the name of my teacher, my patron? Become yet another Senesino?"

"Are there a lot of them?"

"Oh yes. They must have mutilated more than the average number of children in Sienna."

"Er," said Peggy. "Do they?"

"Not me, of course." Orfeo fluttered their lashes, but the smile upon their lips was bitter. "I took this wound in a war. I was kicked by a horse or gored by a boar. I have always been this way."

Impulsively, unthinkingly, Peggy took their hand again. Felt, once more, that surprising, revealing shiver. She wanted to tell them how very beautiful they were but didn't quite dare with so many people watching and listening, and with her best friend at her elbow.

"There's no need to look so stricken," murmured Orfeo. "I find I would rather be honest than speculated about."

"I wasn't speculating."

"Of course not. But everyone else in this room is wondering what I am or what I am not, if I am this, or if I am that, and, most particularly, what it means for them. If they desire me or if they fear me. Or if I am simply too disruptive to all those things the world insists must be *so* or *so*."

"I think"—Peggy offered a wry smile—"you're well aware that most people have already made up their mind on the desire front."

Orfeo laughed but did not dispute it. And Peggy tried not to be as helplessly entranced by their arrogance as she had been by their vulnerability. "Have you?" they asked.

"Have I . . ."

"Decided you desire me?"

Peggy wondered if she could faint again. Sadly, her body did not oblige. So she cleared her throat unconvincingly and tried, equally unconvincingly, to pretend any of this conversation had been for Belle. "You, err, you've met my friend, Miss Tarleton, haven't you?"

Orfeo turned their glittering, searching gaze on Belle, and—for a split second—Peggy was wildly, irrationally jealous. "Of course," they murmured. "How are you tonight, Miss Tarleton?"

At which point, impetuous, sharp-tongued Belle muttered something that sounded very much like, "Nrflghe."

Oh God, maybe she really *was* in love with Orfeo. Or maybe she'd decided that being in love meant acting like an idiot: books would certainly have been little help there.

Which meant, as usual, it was Peggy's job to bring the sensible.

Chapter 7

"We *both* loved your performance," she said into the nrflghing silence. Orfeo inclined their head. "I am honoured. We are falling out of fashion, I think, so cannot always be assured of so warm a reception."

It was almost imperceptible—perhaps so imperceptible that Peggy was probably imagining it—but something about Orfeo had changed. They offered the same warmth, the same curious gaze, the same tantalising play of humility and theatricality. But it was as though they had gilded themselves, somehow. Until they were nothing but the gleam of reflected light.

Belle's lips moved. "Nergh—errr?"

"She finds it difficult to believe that you wouldn't be welcome anywhere," Peggy explained, although, for all she knew, Belle might have been saying she thought hedgehogs were delicious with olives.

Orfeo's eyes flicked back to Peggy's. "Sometimes too much beauty is too much pain. Not everyone likes to be reminded that the one"—they lifted their hand palm up, then gracefully turned it—"can be the other."

"Nrgfgh." Belle nodded eagerly. "Nrghgrghfn."

It seemed appropriate, at that juncture, for Peggy to kick her in the ankle. "It, um—it definitely sounded sad. The song—aria—thing. You sung." Still no help from Belle, and Peggy was drowning. What was music *about* anyway? "Was it a love song or . . . or. Not a love song? Or . . . oh God. It wasn't one of those ten-minutes-before-you-jump-off-a-tower-or-stab-yourself-with-a-sword songs?"

The corners of Orfeo's mouth twitched, first the one, then the other, and then they were smiling. "Oh, mio principe. What a pleasure you are. You truly know nothing of opera, do you?"

"Not a damn bean," Peggy admitted.

"And yet I still reached you"—stepping forward, Orfeo put their hand over Peggy's heart, which immediately started somersaulting in her chest—"right here."

Peggy tried to defend herself with a bad grape, but the words had dried on her lips.

"That is what music is, you know." Orfeo had not moved their hand. "The only force in the universe at whose feet language will lay her crown."

"No, but . . ." From Peggy's perspective, it was less a case of language laying down her crown than turning up drunk and disorderly, and falling headfirst into the soup tureen. "But what *were* you singing about?"

To her surprise, Orfeo broke her gaze, lashes sweeping across their eyes like a stage curtain. They were even, she thought, blushing a little, the blood gathering beneath their skin. "It will . . . it will ruin it for you."

"Well, now I think I have to know."

"Trmfffgh," said Belle.

"What was that?" asked Peggy. "I don't speak mouse."

"Trees," Belle managed. "They were singing about trees."

"Trees?" repeated Peggy. "As in . . . big and leafy?"

Orfeo nodded. "It is the opening aria from *Serse*, by your Handel. An utter failure, by the way."

"I mean, if it's about trees . . . I can kind of see why?"

At this Orfeo laughed—a rough, oddly unmusical sound that they quickly swallowed. "It is not solely about trees. Just the opening aria."

"And the rest?"

"Oh, the usual things opera is about: mistaken identities, romance gone awry, the King of Persia learning that, for all his power, love is not his to command."

"What about trees?" asked Peggy. "Are they his to command?"

And, once again, Orfeo turned their face away, their laugh vanishing into their shoulder. It hurt Peggy, in some tender private place, to think that this would be the part of themself they chose to hide. "He does not wish to command trees, *Peggy*, he merely admires this one particular tree. And wishes it to grow in peace and harmony."

Peggy shook her head. "I can't believe you sang a love song. To a *tree*. And it made me . . . And I fainted."

"I told you"—Orfeo glanced towards them again, the deep shine of their eyes like a private island amidst the shimmer of their tinctures—"it is not the words that matter at such moments."

There was a long silence. Before Peggy's thoughts manifested themselves as "You must really like trees, huh?"

Orfeo's hand, she realised, was still against her heart. Had been resting there as if it was the most natural place in the world for it to be. It took only a step to bring them flush to each other, Orfeo's head as graceful as a flower as they lowered it to Peggy's neck—where they hid, for the briefest of moments, their laughing. Transformed it to nothing but breath and the movement of their mouth against Peggy's skin, a silent butterfly of secret mirth.

"Ah, mio principe." They lifted their head again, their gaze almost sorrowful. "You distract me from my duty to Lady Farrow. She must have the opportunity to exhibit her singer, must she not?"

"Must she?" Peggy wondered.

"But"—and here Orfeo hesitated for the first time that evening—"perhaps you would care to visit me tomorrow? I will be . . ." Another pause. "How is it said? At my toilette from, shall we say, eleven?"

"From eleven? How long are you intending to be dressing?"

"As long as it takes for you to visit me."

This could not have been what Belle had in mind when she'd asked for Peggy's assistance. Peggy glanced towards her, hoping for some kind of steer. Unfortunately, before she could receive one, they were interrupted by the approach of a tall, striking man. He was dressed with elegance rather than extravagance, and was radiating such ill-suppressed fury that Peggy took a protective step in front of Belle.

The stranger, however, had eyes only for Orfeo, who turned to face him with a lack of surprise that was its own indictment. "Lord Asham."

"You," began Lord Asham. "You . . . you . . . by God, if you were anything of a man, I would call you out for . . . for . . . whatever it was you did with my wife."

Orfeo's brows lifted provokingly. "If you are uncertain what I did with your wife, my lord, it is no wonder she sought it with me."

There was a long silence. Lord Asham's complexion had fluctuated from dark red to practically grey so quickly it would have had Peggy concerned for the vascular health of a less vigorous-looking fellow. "You admit, then, that you dishonoured her?"

"I admit no dishonour in pleasure."

"Pleasure?" The word exploded incredulously from Lord Asham. "What pleasure could some unmanned half creature offer anyone?"

Peggy sucked in a shocked breath. The sort of breath you take when you've had the wind knocked out of you and you aren't sure if you'll ever breathe again.

But Orfeo barely reacted, a slight tilt of their head, and the slant of their gaze, somehow emphasising the height difference between them and Lord Asham. "You know, I have never understood the great value your type of man is so determined to put upon manhood. It seems a"—Orfeo paused—"a great fuss"—their eyes slid unmistakably downwards—"for a small matter."

"You"—apparently oblivious to Orfeo's implication, Lord Asham leaned in—"have defiled my wife."

"Are you sure?" Refusing to fall back, Orfeo extended a hand contemplatively, their attention upon the sheen of their nails. "A few seconds ago, you claimed I was incapable of it."

"There is no telling what unnatural thing an unnatural thing may be capable of."

This was too much for Peggy. The words may not have been for her. But they could have been. They could have been for anyone who had ever felt as she did. "Listen," she tried. "Maybe we should—"

Except then Orfeo cut her off with a flicker of their fingers and a smile like the edge of a knife. "I begin to think, Lord Asham, that you have come here tonight because you wish to find out exactly what I am capable of and what others may be capable of when they are with me."

The last dregs of colour drained from Lord Asham's face. Peggy was prepared for another explosion, but when he spoke it was in little more than a poisonous whisper. "You gelded whore."

What happened next could only have taken seconds. But they were the slowest seconds of Peggy's life. She saw Lord Asham draw back his arm. The sudden tension in Orfeo's shoulders as they braced for a blow. There were only moments to act, and Lord Asham was bigger than Peggy. Stronger too. She could have interposed herself, of course, but that would have probably got her whacked in the face. And she could have tried to grab his hand, but that would have . . . probably got her whacked in the face. A scene that Belle would have found satisfyingly heroic. But, deep down, for all she might secretly want to be sometimes, Peggy knew she was not really a hero.

She was just a person.

A person who didn't want to stand by. But who also didn't want to get whacked in the face if she could help it.

Moving swiftly behind Lord Asham, she reached up and covered his eyes with her hands. Pressing her two fingers against his lids, she took a neat step backwards. The gentleman gave a yelp and an undignified flail, staggering after her. Because that was the thing about height and strength: it didn't count for much when you were being dragged about by your eyes.

She dropped to one knee, leaving the temporarily blinded and helplessly struggling Lord Asham no choice but to follow her down. He was heavy and startled, and, truth be told, Peggy was not the *most* inclined to steady his descent, which meant he landed arse first and sprawling upon the ballroom floor.

"What the fuck," exclaimed Lord Asham into the abrupt silence, "was that, sir?"

Peggy shrugged. "I could ask you the same question."

He twisted his head round. "I mean . . . miss. I apologise for my—but how did you—why did you. This is highly inappropriate."

"I can see you're not having the best evening," said Peggy, finding, almost in spite of herself, a whisper of sympathy, for his confusion if nothing else. "But you really shouldn't go around trying to slap people."

"Nor should you assault them and force them to the ground."

"That was an action-and-consequence-type situation." Disentangling herself from Lord Asham, Peggy scrambled to her feet, only to catch her hem beneath her heel and tear it soundly. "Fuck it."

A hand reached down to her—Orfeo's hand—and she took it, letting them draw her fully upright. "Did he hurt you? That was . . . that was a wholly unnecessary thing for you to do for me."

"It was very necessary," retorted Peggy. "He was going to hit you."

Orfeo's expression was difficult to read. Distant in a way it hadn't been before. Or perhaps it was just the faint smearing of the paint around their eyes that made her feel that way. Like she was seeing them suddenly from far away or through a misted glass. "And you think I cannot take a blow?"

"I think you shouldn't have to."

It was at this moment Lady Farrow burst from amongst her guests, dragging with her a servant who looked like he had been chosen based on an incidentally intimidating demeanour, rather than any particular eagerness to break up a fight at a soiree.

"Orfeo," she cried. "Orfeo. I'm so sorry. I had no idea. Whatever were you thinking, Charles?" This last to Lord Asham, who had regained his footing, if not his composure. "This is a temple to Terpsichore. Not some tavern for you to brawl in. I've half a mind to have you thrown out for insulting the guest of honour."

"*That*—" Lord Asham flung an arm in Orfeo's direction but got no further.

Lady Farrow nodded to her servant. "Teaspout? Please remove Lord Asham until such time as he is able to honour the sanctity of music."

"But I just clean the knives and boots," protested Teaspout. "How am I supposed to remove a gentleman? I haven't been trained in gentleman removal yet."

"I categorically refuse to be removed." Lord Asham widened his stance like a boxer preparing to take all comers.

A muscle in Lady Farrow's cheek twitched. "Charles, you're embarrassing me in front of the—"

"The what?" sneered Lord Asham. He once again gestured towards Orfeo. "*That*? Do you have any notion what it did to my wife?"

Perhaps it was precisely because the words made her flinch that some prideful, self-protecting imp made Peggy speak up. "I think at this point you're the only person here who needs clarification about what your wife has been doing. But maybe you could, you know, ask her about that?"

Lord Asham spun back to Peggy, watching her with the sort of inevitable wariness that followed grappling someone by their eyes. "Do you presume to lecture me about my own marital relations?"

"Well, something's clearly not right with them," Peggy pointed out.

"Charles." Tentatively, Lady Farrow took him by the sleeve. "I really do need you to leave. You're making a spectacle of yourself."

"*I'm* making a spectacle of myself? When . . ." Here Lord Asham turned to Orfeo. Except suddenly he seemed to lose the will to fight. His shoulders sagged. And his next words seemed as much for himself as anyone. "I just don't understand. Why would she—what's wrong with me? What can someone like you possibly give her that I can't?"

Orfeo regarded him for a long moment before offering another chill blade of a smile. "More than you have a hope of imagining, caro mio." They glanced towards Peggy. "I will see you tomorrow, I hope?"

"Um." Unprepared, yet again, Peggy nodded. "Yes."

Then they sketched a bare skeleton of a bow. "Forgive me, Lady Farrow." And with that they were gone, vanished into the waiting, whispering crowd.

"You"—Lady Farrow began physically dragging Lord Asham across the ballroom, no mean feat, but he was obviously too dazed to resist—"are leaving. That *creature*, as you called them, is Montcorbier's protégé, and they're the toast of Europe. You have no idea what a coup it was for me to get them. And do you think anyone is going to remember that now? Do you think people are going to be talking about how the wonderful music I provided stirred their hearts and enriched their souls?" She paused, somewhat out of breath, and gave a little growl. "No. They will talk of how Lord Asham lost a fight with a girl before revealing to the world he has no idea how to fuck. You have ruined my party, Charles. Ruined it."

Peggy watched them leave, *I'm not a girl* withering to silence on her lips.

"My sugar plums." Sir Horley, who had somehow secured a glass of champagne—this being one of his strange and special talents—stepped from the alcove where he'd been watching the various exchanges with ill-concealed delight. "It's such a pleasure to have you both in town. You make everything so much more interesting."

"I do not," protested Peggy. "I go out of my way to make things as uninteresting as possible."

"Maybe you're just the sort of person upon whom interest naturally accrues?"

"You mean I'm a human tailor's bill? I'm not sure that's the shining compliment you think it is." Peggy sighed. "I can't believe I've been here less than a day and I've caused a scandal."

Sir Horley finished his mysterious champagne and opened his fan. "Oh, you'll be fine. The fact you threw one of our most prominent Corinthians to the ground like Achilles slaying Hector is a mere detail in the far more titillating story of Lord Asham unmanned by a eunuch."

"They're not a eunuch," said Belle, as she gazed somewhat distractedly after Orfeo, despite their being long gone. "They're a castrato. Those are different."

Peggy shot her a peeved look. "Don't you mean *nrghfle nrrggh nrrghnurgle?*"

To her surprise, Belle actually blushed. "I'm sorry . . . I . . . I was caught off guard."

"'Caught off guard'?" repeated Peggy. "No. Caught off guard is when you trip over your shoelace or you forget someone's name. It was like you'd become a ghost. Or a mouse. Or the ghost of a mouse."

"As I say"—Belle's eyes flashed with a touch of her usual spirit—"I was caught off guard. They're . . . very beautiful. And famous. I've never spoken to someone famous before."

"And you still haven't," Peggy told her.

"Besides," Sir Horley added, "you already know a famous person. You know Emily Fairfax, don't you?"

Somehow, Belle managed to pout impatiently. "Yes, but I wasn't aware she was my favourite novelist when I first met her. Also, as you may recall, I was quite busy being forced into matrimony at the time."

"I have a wonderful idea." Sir Horley insinuated himself between Belle and Peggy, taking each of them by the arm. "My keenly honed sense of such things tells me that nothing of further interest is likely to happen here. Why don't we go back to Valentine's, drink his best brandy, and complain about all our acquaintances?"

Belle gave an eager little squeak. "Oh yes, let's. Valentine will be so annoyed, and our acquaintances are so very worth complaining about."

"And we"—Sir Horley flashed his slightly vulpine grin—"are so very good at complaining about them."

Given Peggy's day had been spent on a coach and her evening at a private concert where she'd fainted, started a fight, and . . . and experienced some feelings it had been very unhelpful for her to experience, it was hard to see how things could get any worse. Even if they involved Belle and Horley. "Let's go," she said.

Her intent had been to depart with swiftness and certainty. Except on the threshold of the ballroom, she could not help but pause. There were lessons, she knew, to be learned about turning back. And yet—like the hero of every story ever told—she turned back anyway.

If Orfeo's height had not made them easy to find, their mode of dress would have. They were the bright centre of the room, as if every other colour had gazed upon their beauty and, finding itself wanting, drawn back in dismay. Surrounded by admirers, they had no reason to notice Peggy, and Peggy was sure she didn't do anything to attract their attention. But notice her they did, their eyes finding her as surely, as effortlessly, as a compass pointed north. It lasted less than a second. She told herself it was nothing. That it meant nothing. But she felt it, somehow. A look that was just for her and all for her. As undeniable as the hand Orfeo had pressed to her heart or the laugh that had unfurled its secrets against her skin.

And oh fuck. She was fucked.

Chapter 8

The plan to steal Valentine's best brandy was somewhat impeded by the discovery that the library was already occupied. Valentine was positioned by the fireplace with a handkerchief and an air of studied nonchalance, his hair hopelessly tangled, while a flush-faced, wide-eyed Bonny waited on the other side of the room, clutching the back of the sofa he was standing behind.

Perhaps unsurprisingly, Sir Horley was the first to speak. "Are we interrupting?"

"Sir Horley"—Valentine's jaw tightened like he was trying not to grind his teeth—"you should know by now you are always interrupting."

"I do have a wonderful sense of timing," agreed Sir Horley, sailing triumphantly into the room. "Now, how about you pour us all a drink, I draw this sofa closer to the fire, and we all have the cosiest of . . . whatever a tête-à-tête is when there's more than two people."

"Tête-à-tête-à-tête?" suggested Peggy.

"How about"—Bonny's hands had tightened on the sofa back—"you leave this where it is, and I stay where I am too?"

Belle's eyes narrowed as she glanced from Valentine to Bonny and back again. "Bonbon, are you not wearing unmentionables?"

"Well." Bonny's flush deepened. "Now that you mention it, not . . . not entirely."

"Does *not entirely* mean *no?*" asked Peggy.

Bonny lifted a shoulder in a rueful shrug. "A little bit."

"Oh my God," Belle cried. "Were you? With him? In here?"

"I mean," said Bonny. "Obviously?" This earned an *urgh* from Belle, and he went on. "Do you really believe there's a single room in this house where we haven't? Oh, except the servants' quarters. Valentine said that would be an abuse of power."

"But just to be absolutely sure"—Peggy eyed the surrounding furniture—"you haven't abused any of these chairs?"

"No." Bonny had a, frankly, magnificent pout. "We were in the window seat."

"The window seat?" Belle didn't quite shriek. But it wasn't *not* a shriek either. "That's my reading nook. I can't believe you despoiled my reading nook. How am I supposed to enjoy a pleasant afternoon with *The Even Truer and Even More Shocking Confessions of Sir Willoughby Harkness* knowing you've probably ejaculated up the wall next to me?"

"I didn't ejaculate up the wall," protested Bonny. "I ejaculated into Valentine's face."

There was a long silence, broken only by Sir Horley trying to stifle his giggles behind his fan.

Valentine cleared his throat. "Thank you, my heart, for sharing that with our friends."

"I'm so sorry." Bonny had both his hands over his mouth. "It just . . . I didn't mean . . . I'm flustered and I'm not wearing any trousers. Would you all please turn away for a moment?"

A few minutes later, Valentine had taken his preferred seat by the fire, and Bonny—fully mentionable—was curled up on his lap. Sir Horley, having re-positioned the sofa, had taken full possession of it with Belle, which left a chair for Peggy on the other side of the fireplace. It wasn't far from the rest of the little circle, but it was a reminder, as if she needed one, that, while she'd been kicking her heels in Devonshire, trying to get over Belle, the others had been here. Together. Forming their own set of habits, their own particular dynamics.

It was good. Change was good. More than that, change was necessary. But once it had just been the three of them—Belle, and Bonny, and

Peggy—and now Bonny had Valentine, Sir Horley and Belle were clearly thick as thieves, and Peggy was meant to be helping Belle pursue romantic and sexual fulfilment with someone else. Someone Peggy wouldn't have been wholly averse to seeking romantic and sexual fulfilment with herself. Gah.

"Valentine," Sir Horley was saying, "tell me you still have that rather fine cognac? An 1811, wasn't it?"

Keen to be, if nothing else, useful, Peggy crossed to the sideboard to retrieve a decanter. "I'll see to drinks."

"Thank you." Bonny, who had a peculiar talent for rolling himself up small, nestled further into Valentine's shoulder. "I'm too cosy to move."

Peggy snorted. "As if you were going to."

"No," Bonny agreed, "but Valentine would have. And then I'd have been forced to move anyway, which would have been a tragedy."

"Yes"—Sir Horley accepted the glass of brandy Peggy had poured for him—"your life is full of hardships, you poor boy."

"It is," Bonny exclaimed, nearly bouncing off Valentine's lap. "I'm probably the first person in the world to experience a panicgasm, and now I'm exhausted. Someone should write a medical pamphlet about me."

Peggy set two glasses of brandy down on the table next to Bonny and Valentine. "Yes, but the scientific method would require you to re-produce the results."

"God"—an expressive shudder from Bonny—"no thank you. I like to linger in my pleasures. Savour them to the last drop."

Sir Horley leaned forward, eyes and teeth wickedly aglint. "Do tell me more about your pleasures, Bonaventure."

"Bonny," growled Valentine. "Stop telling him about your pleasures."

At which point both Bonny and Sir Horley collapsed into helpless laughter. Belle just shook her head. "Every time," she said. "Why do you react every single time? I mean, I don't care what you give yourself conniptions over, but you surely must be aware that they do this deliberately?"

"Being exasperated is Valentine's way of showing he cares," Sir Horley explained. "So I give him plenty of opportunities to be exasperated with me."

"And"—that was Bonny—"being jealous turns him into this delicious, possessive manticore of a man. Which makes me feel very loved."

This earned another, even more emphatic *urgh* from Belle.

"There there, princess." Sir Horley uncrossed his legs and patted one of his knees. "Put your feet here, and I'll rub them for you. Because that will make you feel very loved."

As ever, Belle needed little encouragement to accept being petted. "Why do the prettiest shoes always pinch the most?" she asked plaintively.

Gently, Sir Horley drew off the shoes in question, which were of the high-heeled, heavily embroidered variety that Belle favoured, and dug his thumbs expertly into her arches. "Because we erroneously insist that beauty is pain."

And, just like that, Peggy was thinking of Orfeo. The way their voice had soared so tenderly and so impossibly. It had been a bare handful of hours ago, and yet already the memory was slipping away from her. The words, the music, even the way they had looked when they sang. She might as well have tried to cling to the taste of a lover's mouth or the scent of someone else's skin. Because it was not, in aftermath, the details that mattered. Just the feeling.

Except that particular feeling was a vast ship. A ship of . . . *things*. And in its wake came a host of other feelings, capering like incorrigible dolphins. Old longings and newer ones, carefully disregarded sorrows, and the particular loneliness that struck only when you were surrounded by people who cared for you.

She took a swallow of Valentine's excellent brandy. *Buck up, Margaret Delancey.*

"How was your evening?" Valentine was asking. "And I hope to God you weren't waving that fan about in public."

"What would be the point"—Sir Horley glanced up from his ministrations—"of having a fan that one didn't wave?"

Valentine shifted as best he could beneath Bonny's determined snuggling. "You'll be talked about."

"Sweet Valentine, I am already talked about. It's just everyone lacks the words to do it properly." An odd smile, half-mocking, half-melancholy, curled about Sir Horley's lips. "Besides, I am not the one living openly in marital bliss with another gentleman."

Valentine's arm tightened around Bonny. "Yes, and the ton can mock or condemn us as they please. It need mean nothing to either of us because—"

"You're a duke," everyone chorused.

And Valentine hid his laughter and his blushes in Bonny's golden curls.

"For myself," Sir Horley mused, once the general mirth had faded, "I am sorry it is no longer usual for gentlemen to carry fans. Perhaps I can inspire a resurgence."

"And if you did?" Valentine slanted a brow at him. "Would we then return to bows and buckles, and shoes with diamonds in the heel?"

Sir Horley uttered a sound of unabashed longing. "Oh, that we could. Bloody Brummell has a lot to answer for. Something tells me he's condemned us to a century or more of boring fashion."

"I'd rather dress like Brummell," Valentine said, "than dress like my grandfather. At least, if his portrait is anything to go by."

Bonny gave a little squeak. "Is he the one in head-to-toe apricot satin? I would *love* to see you in head-to-toe apricot satin."

"Well, you shall not." It was Valentine's stern voice. The voice that absolutely nobody paid heed to anymore. He turned his attention back to Sir Horley. "Now, I believe you were supposed to be telling us about your evening?"

For all Sir Horley's faults, perhaps the most significant was his soft heart. So, on this occasion at least, he chose to spare Valentine the spectre of apricot satin. "Indeed, I was. And it was an utter delight. Peggy fainted, then started a fight. Best night out I've had in ages."

"Flower"—Bonny was gazing at Valentine with the half-dismayed, half-accusing look of someone who has had all their worst fears about missing out confirmed—"you've been taking me to the wrong kind of operas."

"As far as I'm aware," murmured Valentine, "it's not usually a contact sport."

To no-one's surprise, Bonny was not discouraged. "Maybe it should be. Maybe then people would pay attention to the stage instead of to each other."

Peggy had thought Belle entirely lost to the satisfaction of having her feet rubbed, but now she declared, "They would if Orfeo was singing. Oh, Peggy"—she sat up suddenly, knocking Sir Horley's hands away—"you liked them, didn't you?"

"No," said Peggy, too quickly. "I mean, maybe. I mean, I don't know them. I mean, why does it matter?"

"Yes." Bonny, too, had acquired an unusual air of alertness. "Why does it matter what Peggy thinks of some singer?"

Belle lifted her chin proudly. "I trust Peggy's judgement."

It was all Peggy could do to restrain an unflatteringly sceptical laugh. "No, you don't."

"Yes, I do," Belle protested. "I trust it. I just don't heed it."

"Belladonna . . ." It was Bonny's "You are my twin, and I know you too well" voice. "Who is this Orfeo to you?"

Belle squirmed a little. "If you must know, Bonbon, I'm thinking I might fall in love with them."

There was a long silence.

"Why?" asked Bonny, finally.

"Why?" Belle simultaneously lost control of her emotions and her volume, leaping off the sofa as if neither could be contained. "You have only spent half our lives talking about love and dreaming about love and inventing stories about love, and now you are living a life of love, and you—of all people—ask me why I might seek love for myself?"

"I just meant"—Bonny shrank a little further into the crook of Valentine's arm—"why Orfeo?"

"Why not Orfeo?" retorted Belle. "At the very least I am unlikely to be bored."

Languorously, Sir Horley drew her back down beside him. "My sweet child, I think you can ask a little more of love than that."

"Can I?" The animation seemed to leave Belle's limbs, and she drooped against him. "Love does not seem amenable to me in general. Or I not amenable to love."

"If it's any consolation," Sir Horley told her, "we might all do well to be a little more like you."

Peggy's eyebrow twitched. "You mean, *you* would do well. Who is it this time?"

"The same." Sir Horley heaved a sigh. "With me, it's always the same."

"Still?" asked Peggy. "Will no-one rid you of your turbulent priest?"

A rare blush crept across Sir Horley's cheeks. "I have no wish to be rid of him. That's the problem."

"He brings you nothing but strife. I don't understand what you see in him."

"His cock?" Sir Horley suggested. "Something about the girth, I think?"

"As if," Belle put in tartly, "you do not have your pick of phalli. You know it's more than that."

Sir Horley cringed. "It must be my vanity, then. After all, most of us lose our lovers to time, indifference, or a rival's charms. Mine is taken from me by God himself."

"You mean"—Belle's voice had lost none of its tartness—"fawning parishioners and a comfortable living."

"Dear one, I adore you, but your idea of advice is a slap in the face."

Belle shrugged. "Then I hope it will bring you to your senses. You are worth more than a man who refuses to choose you."

"You forget"—Sir Horley's hand closed around hers, his voice softer and more serious than it was wont to be—"we were not all raised to expect love as our birthright."

Now Peggy thought about it, she realised how little Sir Horley actually spoke about himself—which was to say, he spoke a lot, about everything, but she had only the vaguest impression of his background. A rich aunt, perhaps? And no other family.

"But," Sir Horley continued briskly, "that is more than enough of that. Do you know if Orfeo returns your interest? You didn't find being literally unable to converse with them an impediment to romance?"

Belle cast him an impatient glance. "I'm working on it. And Peggy is helping."

"About that," said Peggy. "I'm still not sure . . . how exactly?"

Or—in all honesty—that she wanted to.

"The fainting was genius," Belle declared.

"The fainting was an *accident.*"

"Nevertheless . . ." Belle heaved a sigh. "It was more attention than they've ever given me. Why aren't they giving me attention? I always get attention."

Somehow Peggy managed not to roll her eyes. "Maybe, and this is just a wild guess, it's because their presence renders you incapable of human interaction?"

"Well"—as ever Belle seemed blissfully unconcerned with any of the practicalities of her ideas—"you can speak for me, can't you?"

"How?" asked Peggy again.

Belle waved a nonchalant hand. "You can figure that out when you see them tomorrow."

"I'm going then?"

A confused blink from Belle. "Why wouldn't you?"

"Oh, I don't know. Maybe because this is a flat-out terrible plan?" Even as she spoke, Peggy found herself wondering if she was protesting too much. If it was obvious to the others that she was protesting too much. Because, of course, she wanted to see Orfeo again. She wanted to see them again for all the wrong reasons.

"You always say my plans are terrible," Belle went on, unperturbed, "which is why I pay no attention when you do. You're basically the boy who cried wolf for terrible plans."

Peggy gave a wronged splutter. "Not true. If that story was about me, I'd be spending my whole life pointing at wolves going, 'Look, everybody, a wolf,' only for the rest of the village to insist it's not a wolf at all, just a doggy-looking sheep, and then getting their faces eaten off."

Springing from the sofa, Belle went prettily to her knees beside Peggy's chair. Deployed her biggest eyes and softest lips and—dammit. "Please, Peggy," she said. "Just this once? For me?"

Peggy's initial reply was a groan. The groan of someone who knew they'd been defeated before they'd even taken to the field. "Just this once. And if it's a no, it's a no, and that's the end of it. And if it's a yes"—oh God, why did the possibility of a *yes* fill Peggy's throat with frogs and bile—"you're on your own. I can't spend the rest of my life as your love translator."

There was a stir of movement from the far side of the fire as Valentine untangled himself from Bonny and rose. Such was his stature that his shadow unfurled across the library walls like a fairy-tale monster. "You shouldn't be spending any of your life as her love translator." He turned to Belle. "What is this in aid of, Arabella?"

"'In aid of'?" repeated Belle, with an atonality that served as its own warning.

Not that Valentine had ever been good at recognising warnings, especially when they came from Belle. "Yes. What is this . . . this new *concern* of yours about? Are you trying to annoy me?"

Now Belle was on her feet again too. "A-annoy you?"

Peggy's eyes met Bonny's eyes met Sir Horley's eyes as they all tried desperately to catch Valentine's. Unfortunately, he was glaring at Belle and didn't even notice that Sir Horley was none-too-subtly passing his hand across his throat in the universal gesture for "You need to stop what you're doing right now or you'll suffer a dire misfortune."

"I thought"—Valentine pressed his fingertips to his temples—"we had moved beyond communication that involved your repeating my own words back to me in increasingly theatrical accents."

"I thought," returned Belle, practically quivering with fury, "we had moved beyond your belief that my life has anything to do with you whatsoever."

Valentine, too, seemed to be fighting slightly with his temper. "Our lives are connected. We have commonalities of—"

"Oh no," said Bonny quickly. "You leave me out of this. Both of you leave me out of this."

"We care about the same people," Valentine tried again. "Surely that means more to you than whatever game you're playing with me."

"What makes you think"—Belle's voice wavered, then steadied—"I'm playing a game?"

"Aren't you?" Valentine demanded. "With your parade of unsuitable suitors? And now this opera singer? Who you know you cannot marry."

Belle tossed her hair, but Peggy saw the gesture for what it was and for what it had always been: empty theatricality cast across a long-wounded heart. "I will marry as I damn well please. As you promised me I could."

"No, I . . ." For the first since he'd parted company with his chair, Valentine faltered. "I mean, you cannot marry them in the legal sense."

"You cannot"—Belle made little quotations with her fingers—"*legally* marry Bonny, and yet—"

"Yes but," Valentine began.

Lying back against the sofa, Sir Horley opened his fan and dropped it over his entire face.

"But we're," Valentine was continuing, "Bonny and I are . . . whereas you are . . ." He gestured towards Bonny. "We . . . and you . . ."

"Still requesting to be officially stricken from the records of"—visibly lost for words, Bonny circled his hands in the air—"whatever this is."

"He means"—Belle drew herself coldly—"that you are men—and I am not—and therefore—he considers me bound by the very rules you have already deemed irrelevant to your happiness."

"I neither said that," insisted Valentine—who, due to what Peggy presumed was ducal inexperience of manual labour, had still to learn that the best thing to do in a hole was stop digging—"nor did I mean it. Besides, what will you do if you do not marry?"

Belle stamped her foot. "I don't know. Be eaten to death by scarabs on the banks of the Nile, if I so desire."

"Why would you want to be eaten to death by—"

"Because it would be my *choice*," Belle cried. "And for the last fucking time, not everything about me is about you."

With that, she turned on her heel and swept from the room—an exit whose drama was slightly marred for Peggy because she'd caught the sheen of tears in Belle's eyes.

The library door slammed.

The fire, unable to read the room, crackled merrily.

"Flower," said Bonny, finally. "I love you with all my heart, exactly as you are. I would never want you to be otherwise, but, sometimes, just sometimes, I wish you could be a little bit . . . not."

And with that, he hurried after his sister.

The library door slammed again.

"Well," remarked Sir Horley, from beneath his fan, "someone's sleeping on a divan tonight."

Valentine cast him a haughty look. "Of course I will not be sleeping on a divan. My house contains many bedrooms."

"Emotionally," Sir Horley told him, "you will be sleeping on a divan."

"Emotionally"—Valentine heaved a sigh—"I will be sleeping on the floor."

"Or in the stables," Peggy offered.

"Under a bridge," agreed Sir Horley.

"Are you quite finished?" asked Valentine.

Partially lifting his fan, Sir Horley peeped at Peggy. "I don't know. Are we?"

"Yes"—Valentine's expression grew severe—"you are."

"You've nothing to worry about." Sir Horley righted himself. "That boy is about as resentful as a syllabub. You'll be forgiven by morn."

Eager to be done with the conversation—to be alone with her thoughts—Peggy got to her feet. Her head spun a little, on the evening, on the brandy, on the memory of Orfeo's breath like fingertips against her skin. "I'd better turn in," she said. "I can't face Lady Farrow on anything other than a full night's sleep."

"Why would you have to?" asked Sir Horley.

Peggy gave him a look. "Bit rude, otherwise? Show up at someone's house. Refuse to talk to them."

"You do know that Lady Farrow isn't Orfeo's patron?"

Somehow, Peggy managed not to roll her eyes. "How would I know that? I don't art."

"They're one of Montcorbier's . . . projects."

"Montcorbier's projects?" Peggy's tone sharpened.

"Oh—well." Sir Horley looked slightly uncomfortable. "He's kind of a . . . a . . . collector."

Of the Marquess de Montcorbier, Peggy had heard little and cared to know less. "A collector of what?"

"Art? Rarities? Beautiful things."

Lifting her brandy glass from the table, Peggy drained the last few drops. "Well, he sounds like a great person. Can't wait to meet him."

"It's more that"—again a display of uncharacteristic uncertainty from Sir Horley—"you probably shouldn't cross him."

"I've no intention of it," muttered Peggy.

And, in that moment, she sincerely believed she spoke truly. That she would visit Orfeo tomorrow and petition them on behalf of Belle, and that would be the end of the matter. Then again, she'd believed that when Belle had told her she wanted to run away to America, they would get as far as the nearest inn before Belle got bored, got distracted, or otherwise changed her mind.

And look how that had gone.

Chapter 9

Peggy was having a bad morning. She couldn't find a single dress she wanted to wear in all the clothes she'd brought. Her hair was annoying her. And nothing would make her décolletage sit right. It was one of those days when, had the choice been hers, she would have bound her chest.

Most of the time, Peggy liked her body. It was not, she knew, what fashion would have preferred it to be—for that, she would have needed to look like Belle, whose diminutive frame and tiny waist made the rest of her positively voluptuous—but, in many ways, she liked that too. Hers was not a body shaped to please the eyes of others. It was a body she had fashioned for herself through fighting and horse-riding and running about after Belle (Belle, and other ladies, and the occasional willing gentleman).

Unfortunately, sometimes she was required to clothe it in ways she was not in the mood to clothe it. And that left her feeling lumpen and uncomfortable and *wrong*. Like a dog with a new collar it wanted nothing more than to scratch off.

Her reflection, with the ringlets that wouldn't curl, and the bosom that seemed to Peggy as if it had been attached to her with birdlime, was scowling. It rubbed its nose. Shifted from one foot to the other. Then sighed, shoulders slumping.

Both it and Peggy were going to be late.

And, in abstract, she knew she looked fashionable, even dashing, in her fawn poplin walking dress with its bold blue satin embroidery. But for whatever reason—vanity or something more complicated—she was reluctant to meet with Orfeo when she was feeling out of sorts. When she wasn't feeling like herself.

Better, though, to get it over with. To fulfil her promise to Belle and then . . . well. Who knew what happened then. Maybe Peggy went home was what happened. Tried to decide what to do with her life without the Tarletons turning it into one unnecessary escapade after another. There had to be a non-delusional clergyman's daughter (or son) who would be willing to—

And there she stopped again. Whatever followed "willing to" was simply too vast for her brain to fold itself around. Willing to love her back? Willing to commit their future to her? Willing to—

No. She couldn't. Because the thought led to scary places. Scary not for their own sake. But because some part of her truly feared they could not be hers.

Better to spend her days pointlessly in love with Arabella Tarleton.

In any case, the carriage ride to the Marquess de Montcorbier's Grosvenor Square mansion was too short to allow Peggy to fret herself into too deep a chasm. Mainly, she passed the time trying not to pick at her sleeves or prod at her bosom. Upon arrival, she encountered Lord and Lady Farrow, who were in the process of departing, still clad in the same garments they'd been wearing yesterday, and who contrived to greet her in a manner both abashed and smug. By way of answer, she went to tip her hat, then remembered she wasn't wearing a hat, and ended up tugging one of the plumes set into the crown of her bonnet instead.

The marquess's butler—a chilly, stately gentleman—observed the to-and-fro of Orfeo's visitors with impassivity. And then, after a footman had helped divest Peggy of her outerwear, he led her upstairs to Orfeo's chambers. It was probably just her fractious mood that made her read disapproval into the set of his back.

Orfeo's room, even compared to Belle's, was a tumult of extravagance and disorder. The latter, rumpled sheets upon the bed, clothes cast across every surface, was surely Orfeo's doing, but she could not tell if the decoration—rococo splendour in cream and gold—was to their taste or the absent marquess's. As for Orfeo themself, they were seated at an ornate dressing table, attired in a negligee of pale-pink silk, their hair in tangles down their back.

"Um," said Peggy. "Hello." She wasn't entirely sure where to look. The robe wasn't much of a garment. It was more of a . . . haze, really, and through that haze she could catch glimpses of gentle curves and smooth brown skin, and stockings embroidered with roses. When it came to people clad in little more than nothing, Peggy's recent luck had either been very good or very bad.

Orfeo glanced at her through the mirror. They were wearing the remains of their tinctures from last night, though these were mostly smears this morning. "I was not certain you would come, though I had hoped to be more together if you did. Lord Farrow was reluctant to leave. That is," they added, with a touch of haste, "as a hibernating bear is reluctant to leave a warm cave. Not as an importuning gentleman is reluctant to accept a dismissal. In case you are inclined, once more, to defend my honour."

"You know," Peggy suggested, "you could just say thank you. Or never mention it again. I'm good with either."

"I *should* say thank you." Orfeo lowered their lashes, still feather-touched from the night before. "But that would involve admitting how much I have learned to take violence for granted."

Folding her arms, Peggy leaned a trifle louchely against the door-frame. "You often get into fights at parties?"

"Is it really a party without a fight?" Orfeo smiled, white teeth and weary eyes. Then they reached for a ewer and began to pour water into a basin. "But you were, and are, very gallant, mio principe."

Peggy did not, right now, feel very gallant. To distract herself, she surveyed the chaos of paints and powders and who knew what spread over Orfeo's dressing table. "Is there anything I can do to help?"

They shook their head. "Not at all. Just . . . sit, keep me company a little? I have a thousand questions to ask you."

"Sit," Peggy repeated, glancing around her.

"Oh"—an idle wave of Orfeo's fingertips—"put anything on anything."

"The thing is, I think you've already put everything on everything."

Orfeo only laughed and made another "Well, it's your problem now" gesture, so Peggy gathered up a bundle of clothes from a nearby chair—a gilded thing, on cabriole legs, hand-carved with a crest of foliated flowers and upholstered in gold—drew it forward, and perched on the edge of it, her lap full of silks and satins and velvets, from which drifted the scent of Orfeo's skin, as honey-sweet and rich as acacia blossom. She tried to think of something to say, something about Belle, that would feel natural. And—helplessly lost in the unexpected intimacy of holding fabric that had held Orfeo—came up absolutely blank. Wetting a cloth in the basin, Orfeo had begun to clean their eyes with brisk, efficient motions.

"Do you really sleep"—Peggy made a gesture meant to encompass the gown and the paint—"like this?"

"My guests sleep." They peeled the feathers from their lashes. "I do not."

"Is that," Peggy asked. "I mean. Aren't you tired?"

They gave a little shrug. "What is the alternative? My lovers wish to go to bed with Orfeo. They do not wish to wake up with Giovanni Rossi."

"That probably depends on the lover."

"Well, perhaps *I* do not wish them to wake up with Giovanni Rossi."

Now Peggy was the one to shrug. "Then that's your choice."

"You know"—Orfeo's tone was playful, but there was something brittle beneath it—"I thought I said I wanted to ask you a thousand questions. And yet here you are, asking questions of me."

"I suppose," Peggy offered, after a moment's thought, "I feel everyone benefits from a fair distribution of questions."

"In my experience, people are only too happy to talk about themselves."

Peggy was starting to worry she wasn't being a good guest. And she still hadn't managed to mention Belle. "I'm not . . . *not* happy to talk about myself. But I'm definitely not the most interesting person in the room."

Again, the reflection of Orfeo's eyes sought hers. Without the kohl and the paint, there was something unexpectedly naked in their gaze. The starkness of their dark eyes. Their very ordinary lashes. "I would not be so certain of that, Peggy of Devonshire." From amongst the pots and vials upon the dressing table, they picked up a silver-backed hairbrush, embossed with a relief of an apple and a snake amongst curling vines and scrollwork, and began to drag it rather viciously through their hair.

It made Peggy wince. "Let me," she said, once again trying to find somewhere to place Orfeo's discarded clothes as she abandoned the chair not so very long after claiming it.

"Let you . . ." It was the closest to off balance Peggy thought she'd ever seen them. Even when being threatened at a musical soiree. "You want to brush my hair?"

"Why not? You're clearly doing a bad job of it."

"Whose hair is this? Mine or yours?" But they did not resist as Peggy slid the brush from their fingers.

"You should be kinder with it," Peggy murmured. Orfeo's hair was a silken weight in her hands as she began dividing it into sections, draping them first over one shoulder, then the other.

"What are you doing?" Orfeo demanded, the dance of goose pimples across their neck and shoulders belying the sharpness of their tone.

Taking up a section of hair, Peggy closed her palm around the strands, holding them together as she eased the brush gently through the ends and teased out the knots. "It's better this way."

"Longer, you mean."

"I didn't realise you were in a rush. I thought there were a thousand questions I was to answer for you."

Orfeo's eyes had already grown heavy-lidded in the mirror. "Why do I get the feeling you don't like that?"

"I don't mind it." Now that the brush was moving effortlessly through the bottom few inches of hair, Peggy unclasped her hand and re-settled it further up. There she repeated the process, using the bristles of the brush to part the tangles in stages, instead of trying to force her way through all at once. "But there's no need to be so bossy about it."

At this, Orfeo startled. "What an outrage. I am not bossy."

"No?"

"Perhaps," they conceded, "I can be a little imperious."

"Perhaps," Peggy agreed. There was something almost hypnotic in the motion of the brush, the soft scratching sound it made, as rhythmic as a purring cat, especially now it was moving unhindered through the strands. She ought to have been used to it, having brushed Belle's hair often enough, but she had to admit as much as she'd enjoyed that—taking care of the lover who did not quite love her—she had never found it quite this . . . *sensuous*. Perhaps it was the sheer abundance of Orfeo's hair, or its straightness in contrast to Belle's clusters of fashionable curls, the way the light lost itself amongst the dark strands.

Orfeo's lashes fluttered in some disarming combination of arrogance and self-mockery. "You do recall that I am very famous and important? People expect me to be a little imperious."

"What else do they expect?"

"Dio caro, is there ever an end to what people might expect? And"—Peggy suspected they were trying to sound stern, but they, too, seemed lulled and softened by the steady cadences of her brushing—"you are doing it again."

Orfeo had another beauty mark, tucked just beneath the lobe of their left ear. Peggy wondered if they knew it was even there. If anyone had noticed it before. Put their lips to it, in secret worship. "Doing what again?"

"Asking all the questions."

"Fine." The section of hair Peggy was working on was now completely smooth, slipping through her fingers in a long silken caress. She let the task of selecting another section and starting, once again, at the bottom distract her. There was, she had to admit, something a little unsettling in Orfeo's curiosity. It wasn't that she minded. It was just she wasn't used to being the sort of person to arouse curiosity—at least not in a good way. Mostly, she was used to being the sort of person who was simply there. The one who stood at others' sides. "What did you want to know?"

"Everything," breathed Orfeo, with no hesitation.

And it was such a Tarleton answer that Peggy laughed. "Can you be a tiny bit more specific?"

"Where are you from? What—"

"Devonshire."

"Yes, but what are your parents like. Are you in love? What are your passions? What is your favourite colour? What is the thing you most regret? When is the last time you wept? How does the first scent of spring after a long winter make you feel? Do you like cake? When you touch yourself at night, what do you think of? Have you ever had your heart broken? What do you think happens after we die?"

The brush had stilled in Peggy's hand. "Uh," she said. "Blue."

"Dark or light?"

"Dark."

Orfeo tilted their head slightly. And gave a soft "hmm" as if Peggy had said something significant.

"Why?" she asked.

"Why not? It is something to know about someone, is it not? And it is the something you chose to tell me."

"No . . . I mean . . . why any of this?"

"You seem," Orfeo murmured, "to have stopped brushing my hair."

"What? Oh."

Turning their head, Orfeo nudged kittenishly at Peggy's hand. "Please continue. I was enjoying it. Nobody has ever brushed my hair for me before."

It was hair brushing. Just hair brushing. It shouldn't have meant anything. It was barely even flirtation. But Orfeo admitting their pleasure in it made Peggy's fingertips tingle. While she very carefully did not imagine all the other ways they could share pleasure. Although—oh hell, she was imagining it—her brain took her to some surprisingly non-lurid places. Some lurid ones, too, of course. But mainly how they might taste upon her lips. How it would feel to hold them.

And that reminded her of Belle. Or not of Belle personally. Rather, the story of Tam Lin, which used to be—probably still was—one of her favourites. How Tam Lin's love had to seize him from his horse before the fairy court could claim him back. She wondered if Orfeo would be like that, a lion and an eagle and a fiercely burning flame before they were finally just themself, safe and spoiled in Peggy's arms.

Right. So now wondering was banned, alongside imagining.

"Nobody?" she asked, in a senseless effort to erase every thought she had. "You don't have a maid or a . . . a valet?"

Orfeo lifted a shoulder in an idle shrug. "I do not need one."

The room—and the tendency of Orfeo's hair to tangle—strongly suggested otherwise. And Peggy, somehow, didn't like the thought of them, alone amongst someone else's splendour. "You're living in the house of a marquess. You should have your own attendant."

That only made Orfeo laugh. Once again it was startlingly rough and a little too loud, and, once again, they smothered it with their hand. It was, perhaps, the only hint that the person before her could ever have been Giovanni Rossi. "Mio principe, there are two kinds of people in the world: those who pay and those who are paid. I am one of those who is paid."

"I thought you said"—Peggy smirked into the mirror—"that very few things are either *this* or *that*."

Orfeo's mouth firmed into a stubborn line. "Well, this is such a thing. Moreover, it ensures I remain somewhat in control of when and how I am gossiped of."

"Not all servants are gossips."

"It is not a matter of morality," Orfeo said, a little coldly. "It is a matter of . . . economy. Poverty strips one of choices. Do you think my father gladly gave me to the priests? Or do you think he felt it was the only thing he could do, for me, and for his family?"

"You don't"—Peggy swallowed, uncertain whether this was a fair thing to ask—"blame him, then?"

"What use is blame? You cannot eat it or sell it or warm yourself with it at night."

"That's very . . . very . . . something of you. I'm not sure, in your position, I'd be so something."

"What is my alternative? Lamentation? For what I might have been, if not Orfeo?"

With so much of Orfeo's hair untangled, the brush could sweep the whole length of it uninterrupted—and each long stroke made them arch, catlike, to her touch. "Maybe not lamentation . . ."

"I love my art, Peggy. There has not been a voice like mine since Farinelli." They spoke, for once, without arrogance. Just a cool, clear certainty. "Who knows, perhaps I will surpass him?"

"Is that what you want?"

"Is it not what everyone wants? To be remembered is to be immortal." Orfeo broke off suddenly and laughed, as if they had intended a joke. "And you have still only answered one of my questions."

It was a blunt way to turn the subject, but Peggy could not blame them. For all her hands were full of their hair, Orfeo was still a stranger to her. She had no right to be pressing and prying as she was. The problem was, they did not feel quite like a stranger. And talking to them was a slightly dizzying thing. It left her alert, breathless, eager to test them, and the limits of herself. Like fencing with a well-matched partner—thrust, parry, riposte, and back again—though how they were to declare a victor she did not know. She was not even sure if victory was the intent. They might each of them have been equally willing to bare their throat to the other's blade.

If only they knew how. Or dared to.

Chapter 10

"There were a lot of questions," Peggy said. "I'm not sure I can remember them."

"Well," Orfeo admitted, "I'm not sure I can either. But I remain wild to know you, Peggy of Devonshire."

There was a faint pause, Peggy contemplating the reality that there was not even a pretence left that she was de-tangling Orfeo's hair. She was simply brushing it, the way she sometimes brushed Belle's: idly, contentedly, simply to make it shine. "Is this how you normally get to know people?"

"I . . ." One of Orfeo's rare hesitations. "In all honesty, I have not formed the habit, so I have no notion how such matters are normally accomplished."

"How can you not have formed the habit?"

"Well, I was raised at a conservatorio that I was forbidden to leave, and then I sang in church choirs until I met the marquess. I have since travelled the courts and theatres of Europe, and, after my season in London, I will surely do so again. But"—their eyes flashed impudence at Peggy in the mirror—"since you are such an expert, enlighten me. How do the English *get to know one another?*"

"Nothing simpler," returned Peggy. "We exist in each other's vicinity for about a year, then spend the next five years enquiring about each other's health and remarking on the weather, at which point one or other of the involved parties may assay a mild expression of regard.

And then you are friends. A decade or so after that, it may be possible to hug, or admit to a personal feeling."

Orfeo turned on the cushioned bench, leaving Peggy hovering over them with a hairbrush and nothing to apply it to. "Since I neither have two decades to spare, nor talent for either banality or repression, may we try my way?"

"Why?" she asked, suddenly flustered, and not just by the purposeless hairbrush. Without the mirror between them, there were no more reflected selves. Just each other. And Orfeo, in their wisp of nothing, with the smooth river of their hair flowing across one shoulder, and their face stripped of all its cosmetic distractions. She wanted to rest her fingertips upon the bow of their lips. Her mouth upon the bump that marred the line of their nose. She wanted to place a kiss upon each beauty mark like a pilgrim at prayer.

It was only when Orfeo spoke that Peggy realised she had been staring. "You keep asking why."

"And you keep not telling me."

Orfeo lowered their lashes. "It is not such an easy thing to explain, mio principe."

"Neither is 'when I last had my heart broken' or 'how spring smells' or whatever it was."

For the first time, a silence came between them that was not quite comfortable, and Orfeo seemed no more certain how to break it than Peggy was. It probably didn't help that their relative positions meant she was essentially standing over them. So she sank to a knee upon the rug, only catching her heel upon her hem a very little bit.

"Look," she said finally. At the same time, Orfeo offered, "Please try to understand."

And then they both fell silent again.

"Please try to understand," Orfeo tried a second time, "life at the conservatorio was very restricted. It was music and singing, and praying and confession, and very little else—though what any of us were supposed to have to confess, I have no notion. But I was surrounded by people who . . . who had been made as I was, who had the same dreams I did, but were still not like me. And now I am—"

They broke off, their eyes briefly distant, and when they continued, Peggy could not tell if it was a new direction or what they had been trying to say all along. "And, afterwards, with the marquess, I met . . . I met men who loved men, and women who loved women, and those who loved both and neither. I met women who dressed as men, and men who dressed as women, and men who were not thought such when they were born, and women likewise, but for all my searching there has been no-one quite like you."

"Great," drawled Peggy. Rare specimen: London Zoo. *Peggius bizarricus.* "Thanks."

Most people took Peggy pretty much at face value. But Orfeo's eyes widened. "You mistake my meaning."

"You just said you turned the world over like a kid looking for wood lice under a log and found only me."

They gave an impatient jerk of a shoulder. "You recall, I presume, that I am *quite busy.* Opera does not sing itself. Besides, the world is vast and people infinite in their variety. Magnificent as you are, surely"— their tone softened—"you cannot believe yourself a lone star in the firmament?"

"I sometimes feel like a lone star in the firmament. I mean . . . not a star. Just, you know. The other thing."

Leaning forward, Orfeo pressed their lips lightly to Peggy's brow. "Do not we all, tesoro mio."

"Just out of curiosity," Peggy asked (never mind she could still feel the exact shape of Orfeo's mouth against her skin), "what exactly do you think I am that you've been trying to find?"

At this Orfeo smiled that wide, slightly lopsided smile of theirs. "Why, someone like me. Someone neither *this*"—they turned one palm up, then the other—"nor *that.*"

Abruptly breathless, Peggy sat on her heels. It was a strange, disorienting experience to have something she was used to explaining to others offered back to her as if it was simple. "Is that what . . . what you see? In me?"

"Is it not correct?"

"N-no"—Peggy tugged at the neckline of her dress, half convinced her heart was going to burst out of her chest and bound about the room like a puppy. "It is. I am. I . . . I really am. It's just, you know."

Another of Orfeo's inquisitive little head tilts. "I don't think I do know. Can you explain for me?"

"When you . . . tell people. They either say you're not, that you can't be. Or they nod and smile, trying to be nice, and that just feels like they don't believe you in a different kind of way. So then you're left wondering if you're making it all up."

There was a silence. Then Orfeo flowed from their seat in a cloud of transparent, blossom-scented silk and knelt before Peggy. "Oh, mio principe," they murmured.

"Shush. It's not—it's just . . ."

Except Peggy wasn't quite sure what it *wasn't*. Or what it *just*. Only that she was suddenly tired. And maybe she'd been tired for a while.

Like this, Orfeo was taller again. Bowing their head, they laid it against Peggy's shoulder, swaying into her as gracefully, as naturally, as a flower upon the breeze. "Sometimes"—the words were little more than breath against Peggy's neck—"I wonder if I am because I was made to be. Because it is easier to confront the world with what it fears than fear myself."

Peggy didn't know what to say. So she held them instead, tightly enough that it was—for a little while—hard to find the edges of where she ended and Orfeo began: they were just bodies together, as certain as the spiral upon a seashell.

"Perhaps had things been otherwise," Orfeo went on, "I would have been a farmer like my father. Married some sweet peasant girl. Had children of my own. Never dreamed in music and lived for the gleam of a thousand candles."

"Would you have been happy?"

"With some of it, perhaps. A family of my own. Or I am simply being contrary, regretting only what I cannot have. But as for the rest, it is absurd, is it not? That we think to be a man—whatever a man is made of—so great and precious. A small price, if you ask me, for a great gift. Hardly a sacrifice worthy of a god."

"What does God have to do with anything?"

"Remember, I was raised by priests. God is everything."

"Surely you can't . . . you can't think God was responsible for what was done to you?"

Orfeo's laughter stirred the hairs at the nape of Peggy's neck. "The God I knew as a child demanded penance for the wayward thoughts of a dormitory full of sopranos who did nothing but serve His glory. I have long thought ill of Him, but I do not dare to disbelieve."

"Maybe you should turn Protestant?" suggested Peggy. "I don't think our version of God cares about anything very much."

Orfeo actually gasped. "Goodness, I could not. Have you seen your ghastly churches? So square and grey. And your crosses, absent of their subject, with no suffering to glorify."

"Big suffering enthusiast, are you?"

"I am Catholic, mio principe. What do you think?"

"I think," said Peggy firmly, "your God is a dick and doesn't deserve a damn thing from you. And I also think whether you are born or made, you are who you are, and who you are is . . . you know . . ."

Sitting back a little, Orfeo regarded her with slightly parted lips. Brightly seeking eyes. "This sounds like it will be flattery. Please do finish."

"I'm embarrassed now," Peggy muttered.

"No. You must." Orfeo's expression was so solemn it could only have been mockery. "You have heard, I hope, that we sopranos are hatched from the eggs of a particular sort of Tuscan cock? These cocks brood for many days, and, when laid, the eggs are celebrated with flattery, caresses, and money. And so you see it is only right that I am celebrated with those things still."

"I brushed your hair," Peggy pointed out. "I've celebrated you plenty today."

"But"—and now there was no hint of playfulness in Orfeo's manner—"I wish to hear what you were going to say."

Peggy growled. "Fine. I was going to say you're . . ." It was Belle's word. Not Peggy's. But it was still the right one. "Spectacular. There. Are you happy now?"

"Are you aware," Orfeo said, "how often you ask me if I'm happy? The answer is yes, again. I am very happy when I am near you."

"You've only met me twice."

"And both times you have made me happy. That is more than most people accomplish."

"Cynical, aren't you?"

But Orfeo shook their head. "Impossible, knowing you exist. And that nothing made you, but you."

Lost for words, and quite undone, Peggy's mouth said: "Fuck."

"Pardon me?"

"Oh, just. I'm not used to . . . any of this, actually."

"I did not wish to tell you," Orfeo admitted. "I was afraid it would be too much. I do not need you—I do not need anyone—to grant me permission to exist in the world. And I do not believe I shall ever truly know if I am who I was always meant to be, or if I became who I am because all other choices were taken from me, but . . ." And here they broke off, half laughing, a coppery flush upon their cheeks. "Ah, it is simply good that you are here, Margaret Delancey. I cannot say it better than that."

And, in that moment, Peggy found she was perilously close to laughter too. Laughter that felt at once like relief and release. As if she'd been holding her breath for her whole life. "It's good you're here too, Orfeo."

"You'll stay with me, won't you?" they asked. And there was that look again: raw and eager, with no mischief or theatricality to soften it. "While I am in London? I do not have a decade, but I have a season; is that time enough?"

"Um." It was starting to dawn on Peggy that this had gone off track. Gone off track in a major way. Gone so far off track the track was no longer visible even on the horizon. It was, in other words, a complete disaster. And, also, a little bit the best thing that had ever happened to her. "Time enough for what?"

"To accommodate your English mores. To enjoy each other."

Fuck fuck fuckitty fuck. "This . . . enjoying? What kind of enjoying would it be?"

"In whatever fashion feels right. I am not trying to seduce you. Well . . ." Orfeo's unadorned lashes fluttered artfully. "I am. But seduction is of more than the body, is it not?"

"I see." Peggy offered them a sardonic look. "As you seduced Lord and Lady Farrow?"

"No, Peggy, I fucked them. As a matter of professional pride. But I like that you are jealous. That bodes well for me, I think."

"I'm not jealous."

More fluttering. "Let's say you are."

"I'm *not*." Peggy thought about it for a moment. "No, seriously, I'm not."

Taking Peggy's hand, with all its calluses and the scrapes she just naturally seemed to accumulate, Orfeo ran the pad of their thumb over her knuckles, then kissed the same spot. "As you say."

"People don't belong to people," Peggy insisted. "I'm just trying to work out—I know you think I'm—that we're . . . and maybe we—" She discovered she had no idea what she was trying to say. Unfortunately, having made that discovery halfway through saying it, she had no choice but to continue.

Continue as she should have started.

Instead of letting herself get distracted by hair brushing and flirting and talking and telling Orfeo the sort of things she'd never told anybody.

"So"—her voice wavered and went pitchy—"my friend, Arabella Tarleton?"

To give Orfeo credit, they gave a soft hum, as if this was not a massive non sequitur—a phrase young Peggy had always confused with secateurs and now imagined as a huge pair of scissors slicing the conversation asunder. "The tiny, peculiar blonde?"

"She's not peculiar." Peggy paused. "Actually, yes, she's quite peculiar. But she's also my dearest friend, and—"

"Oh." Orfeo let out a soft breath, nearly a sigh. "You are in love with her?"

"No. Yes. I mean, it's complicated."

"I have no personal experience, but if we are to believe several centuries of art, then I am not sure there is such a thing as simple love."

"She's not in love with me," Peggy explained carefully. "And I'm in the habit of being in love with her. Which, for the record, still feels exactly the same as being in love."

"And you think"—Orfeo's expression offered her nothing—"spending time with me will trespass on your love? Are you sure that will not be a good thing for you?"

"Right." The thought dragged itself out of Peggy's throat like ribbons on a kite string. "Because I want to spend my life falling in love with one unavailable person after another."

Orfeo shifted slightly away from her, a sudden wariness in their posture that made Peggy feel like she'd sprouted bubonic pustules. "I am not inviting you to fall in love with me, mio principe. I am already in love with music. I gave up my balls for her, after all; she is not a mistress to play false."

This was already beginning to feel familiar. All too familiar. And that was not Orfeo's fault—in some ways it had nothing to do with them—but grief was a dragon when it roared, engulfing everything in its indiscriminate fire. "Good for you. But the thing is"—Peggy clambered to her feet, her skirts now hopelessly creased, and the rest of her little better—"I'm just an ordinary person. I want and feel ordinary things. I don't have a higher calling or some kind of magic immunity to occasionally falling for people I care about."

"Peggy . . ."

"I mean, I'm not saying I *would*. But I'm straightforward. Knowing someone means liking them means caring for them means love sometimes."

Orfeo had remained on their knees and was now gazing up at Peggy, a position that, by accident or design, gave the whole scene an air of incipient tragedy. "I do not disdain ordinary things. They are simply not an option for me." Something like sorrow deepened their dark eyes. "I am offering you everything I can."

So very much the story of Peggy's life. "I can't tell you," she told them, "how sick I am of hearing that." Orfeo flinched and she relented. "I know it's not you. But I can't get myself embroiled in another complicated compromise—"

"Not everything you do not envision is a compromise. It can just be . . . something different."

Peggy huffed out a sigh. "You should know I only came here because of Belle."

A tiny pause. Then, "Only?"

"Mainly," Peggy said, hoping it wasn't a lie. "She likes you. Or might like you. Or wants to like you."

"Well"—Orfeo seemed unsurprised by the news—"I am afraid I am not interested in her. I am interested in you."

"And you think I'm just going to go with that?"

At last, Orfeo rose, moving to the bed with the sort of careless grace Peggy could not have replicated in a gazillion years of trying. There they disposed themself upon the disordered sheets, looking like something from a particularly racy portrait. All they needed was a handful of hovering cherubs and someone to feed them grapes. "I will sleep with your Belle if that's what your friendship requires."

"What?" The word clanged out of Peggy's mouth with all the élan of a dropped dress sword. "No. That's not . . . that's not how friendship works. What the fuck is wrong with you?"

"Ask any satirist in Europe, and you may receive whatever answer pleases you." They put a hand rather theatrically to their brow, though Peggy thought she discerned real distress beneath the posturing. Or maybe she just wanted to. "This is beginning to frustrate me, mio principe. How many times, in how many ways, must I lay bare to you the fact I have no experience in this? It would be no hardship to fuck your beloved: she is beautiful and seems to know what she wants. I enjoy such lovers."

"Useful information," said Peggy.

"And do not think"—Orfeo's voice slipped as effortlessly into irritation as they shifted registers in song—"I do not see you when you do this. When you . . . take refuge in small words, as if the less you say, the less you have to care."

"Or," suggested Peggy, not at all defensively, "this is how I talk."

Lowering their hand, Orfeo used it instead to make another gesture—even more sweepingly dramatic than the last. "I don't understand. I wish for us to be close. I'm trying to please you."

"By offering to fuck people for me?"

"But"—Orfeo's lips curled wickedly—"I am so very good at it."

Belle, too, professed herself good at fucking. Perhaps she should get together with Orfeo, after all, and they could good fuck each other merrily. "Not everything is a . . . a . . . performance, Orfeo."

"Not for you," they said softly. No pretence at teasing this time.

"I think"—snakes, live snakes, she was sure of it, were twisting in Peggy's stomach—"I think I'm going to have to go."

"Because of me?" asked Orfeo. "Or because of your friend."

"She's a bit fragile just now. I don't want her to think I betrayed her." Because it would be a betrayal, wouldn't it? To seek intimacy with Orfeo—emotional or sexual—after everything Belle had confided in her? And even if betrayal was too strong a term, it certainly wasn't the act of a friend.

For a moment Orfeo was silent, their delicately feathered brows pulled into a slashing frown. "Or is it because of you?"

Peggy's thoughts screeched to a halt, though the snakes continued to writhe "Um. Me?"

"Yes. Rejecting what I can offer because of what I cannot. Denying us both anything we might share together because we will never have some hypothetical future that was taken from me when I was nine years old."

"Maybe"—Peggy's voice rose—"that's the future I want, though."

"And you think knowing me will stop you having it?"

"I think . . ." Somehow Peggy couldn't stop the words spilling out. "I think you're just someone else who'll break my heart."

"And so you pre-emptively break mine?"

"Oh, come on." Having grown up with the Tarletons, Peggy was not someone given to wild gesticulations, but she gesticulated now. And few could have called it tame. "We're little more than strangers. Nobody is breaking anyone's heart."

The corners of Orfeo's mouth twitched as if, had the situation been otherwise, they might have smiled. "*Sorely disappoint me* did not carry the same rhetorical weight."

"Again, we're not on the fucking stage."

Peggy was braced for a sharp retort. Certainly Orfeo was more than capable of them. But they just sighed. "Is this to be how we part, then? Does it make it easier?"

"Not remotely," said Peggy.

Then—not really knowing what else to say or do—she turned and left.

Chapter 11

Returning to Valentine's, Peggy was consumed by the urge to fling herself into Bonny's unicorn fountain and float there, in the cool clear water, amongst the sun dapples and rainbow fish.

It was not, however, an option.

Or rather, it was an option because if there was ever a household where a whim to fling oneself into a unicorn fountain would be respected, it was Bonny and Valentine's. But Peggy didn't think she was the sort of person to express herself by acts of unicorn-fountain flinging. She was the sort of person who expressed herself in a long walk. Or a melancholic silence. Or going to tell her friend that her plan to fall in love with an opera singer wasn't going to fly.

According to the butler, Miss Tarleton was in the lavender drawing room, a room that had suffered somewhat from Bonny's ongoing experiments in what he called *style*. When literally everyone had confirmed the results of this particular experiment were hideous, an eyesore, ghastly to behold, he had finally permitted Valentine to soften the extremity of the lavender with creams and pearly greys, even some flashes of powder blue amongst the soft furnishings, and thus the room had become useable again. Even, on a good day, pleasant.

Peggy had been hoping to talk to Belle alone, but the whole household was already assembled: Bonny sprawled across a chaise, deep in a book, while Belle, Valentine, and Sir Horley were gathered around a chessboard.

"Hmmmm," Belle was saying, as she stroked an imaginary beard. "The Plotwoddikins defence. A bold choice indeed."

They were playing Devonshire chess, a game which did not exist, but which Belle and Sir Horley used to torment Valentine. Peggy couldn't quite remember how it had started—only that Valentine was too good at actual chess, and usually won, and was bad at winning. He did not crow like Bonny and Belle did, but he got smug while pretending to be modest, which was somehow worse. Hence Devonshire chess, a local variant that, according to Sir Horley and Belle, required its masters first to discern the rules by observing the play of others. Needless to say, Valentine had been attempting to discern the rules for quite some time.

"How was your visit?" asked Bonny, looking up from his book, albeit slightly reluctantly.

Peggy flopped into a chair. "Non-ideal."

"Hah," Sir Horley exclaimed, in great triumph. "You think yourself so cunning, but you have left me an opening."

Belle put on a show of examining the arrangement of the pieces. "How dare you. I have not—oh. Oh no. I see it now."

"Where?" asked Valentine, in equal parts bewilderment and fascination.

"There." A sweeping gesture from Belle towards, as far as Peggy could tell, a random spot on the board. "This is unfortunate for me."

"Very unfortunate," agreed Sir Horley. "And, ungentlemanly as it may be, I'm afraid I shall press my advantage by boffling your knight."

Belle uttered a piteous cry. "You monster." Then she bit her lip. "There must be some way I can prevent this catastrophe." Leaning her chin upon her hand, she once again surveyed the board. "Alas," she concluded, after a small spell of time. "I do not think there is. Very well, sir." She moved one of her bishops to an arbitrary space. "My knight is boffled."

"That," observed Valentine, "is a bishop."

"Of course it is." Sir Horley rolled his eyes. "Normally, of course, she would have boffled the knight with the rook, but I have obliged her to use the bishop because I have placed my king contra mundum."

"Which," Belle added sharply, "you would have noticed had you been paying attention, Valentine."

Valentine inclined his head. "How foolish of me. I do apologise."

Of course, if Belle and Sir Horley had been paying attention, *they* would have noticed the struggle of that stern mouth to hide its smile. Peggy had long since suspected—and Bonny had confirmed—that Valentine knew exactly what game was being played and delighted in it.

"Do you by any chance," Peggy asked, somewhat more harshly than she had intended, "want to hear the outcome of this damn mission you sent me on?"

Belle gave a squeak. "You know I do."

"Do I know that?" It wasn't fair, Peggy knew, to be angry at Belle. She could hardly have expected her to wait like a puppy with her nose pressed forlornly to the window for Peggy's return. But wasn't there a middle ground between that and cheerfully messing about with her friends while Peggy was getting her heart kicked into the sun?

Abandoning the chessboard, with its boffled knight, Belle flew to Peggy's side, perching prettily on the arm of her chair. "Tell me everything."

"There's not much to tell." It wasn't really a lie. Because there *wasn't* much to tell about the conversation as it related to Belle. On account of Peggy being literally the worst love emissary ever invented. Great. Now she was hurt, angry, *and guilty.* "They said they're in love with music and don't have space for anyone else."

Belle was silent for a moment, her face locked into a kind of stillness while all the light faded from her eyes. "Oh," she said at last. And then, in a small shaky voice, "I . . . I suppose that makes sense."

"I mean," said Peggy, somehow feeling worse about everything, "does it?"

"You've heard them perform. If I had such a talent, it would probably be the most important thing in my life too." Belle heaved the world's bravest sigh. "What . . . what were they like?"

"Orfeo?" asked Peggy, instinctively stalling for time.

"No"—Belle contrived some semblance of her usual manner—"some other soprano."

Oh God. Fascinating? Beautiful. Tender. Bitter. Melancholy. Driven. Secretive. Conflicted. Perfect. Peggy's snakes were back—not writhing this time but coiled heavily inside her. "Complicated."

"You"—Belle was still trying very hard to sound undaunted—"are the worst gossip, Margaret Delancey."

"You didn't send me to gossip. You sent me to declare your interest." Which Peggy had done inadequately at best. Actively halfheartedly at worst. "And I . . . I did a bad job of it. I'm sorry."

"Oh, Peggy." Sliding into her lap, Belle cast both arms around her neck. "I'm sure you were wonderful. You're not responsible for Orfeo's choices."

Not for their choices. But there was no getting away from the fact that Peggy had barely mentioned Belle at all. "I could have made your case better."

"I'm sure you did your best," said Belle, consolingly.

But I didn't, Peggy wanted to protest, feeling unworthy of consolation. *I did the bare minimum.*

"Besides," Belle went on, encouragingly, "as rejections go, I suppose I can take succour from the fact it . . . it was not really about me?"

This might have made Peggy feel better. Apart from the fact that, while it wasn't *really* about Belle, and it might genuinely have had something to do with music, it was also more than a little bit about Peggy.

"I still don't understand"—this was Bonny, somewhat plaintively—"why you were so determined to be in love with this . . . this singer person in the first place."

"Oh?" Belle's brows went up, her tone turning sugar-sweet and deadly. "Haven't you heard? It's to annoy Valentine. My whole life revolves around him, you see."

Comfortably accustomed to navigating his lover and his sister, Bonny ignored this. "And the actual answer?"

"I don't know," Belle admitted. "I suppose I thought . . . they might be the sort of person it was easy to fall in love with."

"Falling in love just happens." Bonny flung his arms in the air to emphasise his point.

"Except that's the thing, Bonbon, it doesn't just happen to me."

"That's not true," protested Bonny immediately. "It can't be. Love is for everyone."

Seated as they were, Peggy felt Belle's shoulders slump. "You have no idea how very much the opposite of reassuring you're being right now."

"Belladonna . . ." Bonny's tone gentled. "You will find someone, I know you will."

"I . . . I am not so certain." Rising from Peggy's lap, Belle moved about the room, her steps distracted and uncertain. "I am beginning to think I am doomed."

"I can go back," Peggy yelped. "I can try again. Or maybe if you spoke to them yourself, they'd be able to see what a wonderful person you are—"

"Oh, Peggy"—Belle cut her off—"you're sweet. Don't be silly. It's over. I couldn't love you, and Orfeo doesn't want to even try being loved by me, and now I don't know what I am to do." She paused grimly. "Other than die alone."

Leaping to his feet, Bonny uttered a cry of dismay. "Don't say that. You're just . . . wary or . . . or . . . hurt . . . or . . . or . . ."

"On the contrary"—Belle's voice was unusually soft—"I begin to think I might always have been like this."

Bonny gazed at her, his eyes wide and already beginning to shimmer with tears. "Oh, Belle. Oh no. How are you to live to happily ever after now?"

"I . . ." said Belle. "I don't know."

And then, in perfect unison, they both burst into tears before hurling themselves onto the nearest items of furniture. Surprisingly, it was Sir Horley who rose and went to pat Bonny's heaving shoulders—his face being buried in a cushion—and Valentine who arranged himself decorously next to Belle. Peggy, meanwhile, was sure she was getting a headache. The sort that stormed in your temples and had probably been there for longer than you realised.

She felt bad—a new, subtly different shade of bad to swirl with all the other accumulated bads she was feeling—because she was having a hard time not wishing she was still with Orfeo.

Despite the way their conversation had ended. If it needed to have ended at all . . . except no. It definitely needed to have ended. She owed it to Belle. And to her own sense of fair play.

But still.

The memory of them sparkled on her tongue, like lemon juice on a summer day, tart and sweet and sharp. Exactly what you needed.

Her sigh was lost amidst the tumult of two Tarletons weeping.

If she closed her eyes, she could drift upon the scent of Orfeo's skin, the softness of their voice, and the precisely chosen words it enwrapped, the paradox of their eyes that could reflect such warmth, such mirth, and—when needed—such utter disdain.

It was infatuation. What else could it be? After all, she knew nothing of Orfeo beyond what she'd been told, or able to glean, from two conversations, a fight, and some gossip. Whereas the Tarletons . . .

The beautiful, impossible, infuriating, endlessly self-absorbed Tarletons, with their loud stories and their big dreams and their inability to compromise on even the slightest thing: they had been the first people outside her own family who hadn't laughed when she had solemnly explained to them that she didn't think she was a little girl *or* a little boy, thank you so very much. Bonny was her first friend. Belle her first friend *and* her first love. You didn't imperil something as precious as that for a season with a stranger.

You just didn't.

Chapter 12

Peggy was trying not to be wretched. Which was especially hard because she had no possible reason to be wretched. She was young, rich, moderately attractive—fortunate by any metric—and she had good friends, none of whom were presently trying to enlist Peggy in their romantic misadventures. Although, to be fair, that might have been because they were too busy arguing with each other. And, when they were not arguing with each other, communicating solely through Peggy. If she had to ask Bonny to pass the salt for Belle, or vice versa, one more time, she was going to throw them both out the window. And the salt after them.

It did make her wonder, though, just how long Belle had been quite so scared and quite so unhappy. And wasn't that some guilt to go with her guilt? Because what kind of friend didn't notice their friend's unhappiness? The sort of friend who was so determined to prove herself the perfect lover she lost track of everything else. It was embarrassing.

Of course, being in love with someone didn't just go away. And maybe it never would. Maybe loving Belle would, in some small way, always be part of her, like the scar on her thumb from when Bonny—in a rush to get somewhere—had accidentally shut a door on it. But in the same way that little scar had once been a hideously swollen and concerningly misaligned digit, radiant in hues of meat red, sunset purple, and apple green, so had something changed, quietly and naturally, in the love that had once felt so painfully all-consuming. Which Peggy should probably not have been comparing to a squashed thumb.

Having a squashed thumb was a generally unpleasant and awkward experience. Loving Belle . . . loving Belle had always been easy.

Although no longer having it be the centre of everything left Peggy oddly hollowed out and directionless. Or, perhaps, she had been directionless the whole time and hadn't noticed because she'd been distracted by her dogged pursuit of a woman who, it turned out, had known what she wanted—or rather what she didn't want—all along. Much as Bonny, aged nine and three quarters, had looked up from the story he was writing and declared he would marry a duke for real someday.

Her mind kept drifting back to Orfeo and to their conversation. All the things she had said to them that she barely dared to even *think* and, in that moment, had turned into weapons to hurt them both. Her insistence that what she was looking for was an ordinary life—was that even true? Did people who were looking for ordinary lives fall in love with people like Arabella Tarleton? Did they agree to run away to America? Act as a second in the most incompetent duel Peggy thought had ever taken place on English soil? Proposition—propositionish . . . propos-ish-on—famous sopranos on behalf of their friends? Or was that just what you were left with if you didn't fit anywhere else? If you were neither mother nor father, nor husband nor wife. It was not a reality that Peggy normally let herself contemplate. It hurt too much.

And, in any case, the point was the very definition of moot. Trying to figure out what she could or could not have, who she could or could not be with, was very much dependent on actually finding someone to figure it out *with*. Someone who wasn't her romance-oppositional best friend, an opera singer committed exclusively to their career, or a clergyman's daughter with a fatal case of poetry.

Honestly, Cerbs, said Peggy, in her head, to the dog who wasn't there, *I do know how to pick 'em.*

Then again, she wasn't sure it was fair to include Orfeo with the others. For she had neither been the pursuing nor the pursued. And when she'd been with them, it had felt . . . well, it was hard to describe how it felt. Not like it felt with Belle, who she had known for a good chunk of her lifetime, with the clutter of memories—joy and sorrow and old hurts, and above all abiding familiarity—that brought with it. There was nothing familiar about Orfeo. It was all new, new and fascinating, and . . . *galvanising*. A brisk walk on a spring morning, when half the world was mist, and the rest potential, and the sky was all the colours that would fade in daylight.

In any case, there was no use dwelling. Or daydreaming. Or sidling up to Belle, now she believed she was condemned to a life of loneliness and despair, and asking if she would mind terribly if Peggy took up with the very person she had herself enlisted Peggy's aid to pursue. Besides, she had no notion what taking up with Orfeo would actually entail. If she was being foolish, as they had suggested, to reject one thing on the basis that it was not another thing. Or if, alternatively, she had finally learned to protect her stupid heart.

Except, would it have really been so bad to . . . to try? Maybe they could have been friends? Never mind the way Orfeo looked at her, with such hope and hunger in their eyes. And never mind that Peggy probably looked at them the exact same way. It was, honestly, odd, a little disorientating, to feel so much about someone you knew so little. But it was the *wanting* to know that scratched at her constantly like an animal at the door.

Wait. This was dwelling. She was not supposed to be dwelling. But there were, unfortunately, very few antidotes to dwelling. The best she could manage was keeping busy. And, perhaps, her busyness seemed less natural than it could have because Valentine had somehow agreed to be her fencing partner in the mornings. Not that, given his dislike of both mornings and fencing, he was a particularly good partner, but Peggy appreciated the offer for what it was: an act of kindness.

Like most gentlemen of his class, Valentine had learned to fight as a young man and, like most gentlemen of his class, subsequently allowed the skill to atrophy completely. This was, in Peggy's estimation, no bad thing in general, as dukes had enough advantages without also being able to stab people. But it did mean she spent an hour or so a day standing in the garden trying to goad Valentine into doing anything other than extending his sword at face height and retreating.

If nothing else, it was probably reasonable exercise because circumventing a long, pointy object held by a much larger person required considerable dexterity, even if the much larger person in question was doing very little with their long, pointy object.

"You know"—Peggy backed off, panting—"you *can* attack."

Valentine stifled a yawn in his sleeve. For some reason, morning Valentine was one of the most ducal versions of Valentine, maybe because the rest of him hadn't woken up yet. "That seems like a lot of effort for little reward."

Peggy lunged. "The reward is not getting hit with a sword."

Parrying clumsily but still, given his superior reach, effectively, Valentine disengaged and stepped back. "I'm not getting hit with a sword now."

"But what if this was a duel or something?"

"Excuse me"—Valentine turned her blade again—"I have been in a duel, and I acquitted myself very creditably."

"Neither weapon discharged."

"And thus no-one was hurt and honour satisfied." He paused. "Bonny was still rather upset with me, though. So even had I not found being in mortal peril rather wearisome, my duelling days are well and truly over."

Rather wearisome, indeed. Peggy remembered his grey face, and how his hand and his voice had shook, especially when he understood how close he was to losing Bonny. It had been the first time she had seen the man behind the monster he was playing. "Yes, but it'll be more fun if you did . . . something . . . anything else?"

"Fun for whom?" asked Valentine. "You know I don't enjoy perspiring. It is bad for one's shirts."

"That's not what Bonny says."

This, Peggy knew, was a little mean of her. But if she had hoped to spur Valentine into action, she was to be disappointed. Instead, he gave a little yelp and dropped his sword. "One does not wear a shirt on those kinds of occasions."

"Unless you're in the library?"

"Margaret Delancey." Valentine put his hands on his hips. "You are an imp."

Hooking her foot under Valentine's blade, Peggy flicked it into the air and caught it with her spare hand before offering it back to Valentine. "Say it with your sword."

He gave a heavy sigh and then made a halfhearted thrust which Peggy put aside easily, riposting directly to his chest.

"Ow," said Valentine.

"Sorry," said Peggy.

It was at this moment that they were interrupted by a footman, hurrying towards them across the still dew-touched grass. "A visitor for . . ." And here he paused, first for a moment and then a longer moment. "Your Grace's guest," he finished, with an air of having completed a difficult job to his own satisfaction.

Peggy grinned at him encouragingly, pleased to not have been *miss*-ed.

"Well, I should hope so," returned Valentine, one hand still to his chest, where he had received exactly no injury. "Anyone who called on me at such a time would be instantly cut from my acquaintance."

"I have shown . . ." Once again the footman seemed to be wrestling with something. "Your Grace's guest's guest to the garden room."

"Did my guest give a name?" asked Peggy, a trifle warily. While she retained a certain amount of popularity amongst fortune hunters, she did not cultivate a wide circle in London, and therefore wasn't often called upon. Most likely, it was only one of her parents—they didn't like to leave the country, or each other, but she was an indifferent correspondent, so they sometimes popped in to make sure she wasn't dead. Or Grace, she supposed. Knowing her luck, it could have been Grace Hickinbottom, come to demand more love and poetry.

The footman was too professional to weave from foot to foot, but he gave every impression of wanting to. "Orfeo?"

"Orfeo," Peggy cried. "Oh God. *Orfeo?*"

"That was the name I was given."

"Hell's bells." She glanced wildly at her shabby breeches and sweaty shirt. "I'm not dressed. I can't see them like this."

"I am not dressed either," Valentine protested. "I have no coat."

Orfeo? Orfeo here? To see Peggy? After everything she'd said? What could they possibly—

She discovered she was running in a little circle. "I have to . . . I can't . . . What can I do?"

"I thought it best," put in the footman, "to put your guest in the garden room because Mr. Tarleton—"

"Bonny's there?"

The footman just nodded.

"Fuuuuck." Peggy shoved her sword into Valentine's hands. "Hold this." And then she took off at full speed towards the house.

The garden room was a new addition, built for Bonny by Valentine. Or rather paid for by Valentine. Built very much by other people. It was an excruciatingly romantic room, all arched windows and exquisitely painted murals of waterfalls and wildflowers. The doors opened directly onto the terrace, making it hard to tell where the inside ended and the outside began, and the lavish collection of plants—humble though they were—seemed to have been chosen specifically for the bloom of their bright colours and the attraction they offered to bees and butterflies alike. It was Bonny's favourite place to spend what he and Valentine erroneously believed to be the morning. Which was to say, it was where they took breakfast, usually at about noon.

Sure enough, Bonny was there now, teacup in one hand, book in the other, while all around him swirled the softness of butterfly wings and the contented drone of pollen-drunk bees. And there, too, was Orfeo. They were in breeches and boots, both dark, over which they had cast a full-skirted frock coat in a soft, lustrous shade of gold. Its buttons, likewise, were gold, as was the velvet collar and the small capes at the shoulders. A wholly absurd garment that Peggy immediately and desperately coveted.

"So," Bonny was saying, his voice high with nerves, "you're a castrato?"

Orfeo made the slightest motion of their head. "The preferred term is *soprano*."

"Yes but. I mean. Did they. I assume you've. You know. How is that for you?"

"And how," murmured Orfeo, in their sweetest, most deadly tones, "are your testicles, mio caro?"

"Hello," yelled Peggy, barging into the centre of the room.

Turning to her, Orfeo extended their hands in greeting and then leaned in to kiss her, first on one cheek, then the other—a manoeuvre that Peggy entirely failed to handle with grace, first freezing, then bashing her nose into Orfeo's, and finally planting an abortive kiss of her own into the empty air. "Buongiorno, mio principe," they remarked. "We are discussing our genitals. Do yours have anything they wish to contribute?"

Peggy opened her mouth. Then closed it again. Then managed, "Err no. No, they don't. Sorry."

"How strange." Orfeo's lashes—today their tips were golden, to match the coat, and a subtle line of the same shade drawn across their eyelids—fluttered. "I assumed it was an English custom."

"No." Bonny hung his head, curls flopping winsomely. "It's not an English custom. I was being quite phenomenally rude. And I'm sorry."

Orfeo simply lifted a shoulder in dismissal if not outright forgiveness.

"I shouldn't have . . . it's just that it seems like a lot to . . . for—the thing is," Bonny admitted torturously, "I don't really like opera at the best of times."

"That," Orfeo told him, "is because you have no soul."

Bonny's eyes widened. Shock, with a touch of amusement. "You do know my husband's a duke?"

Another of Orfeo's half shrugs. "And I have sung at the courts of kings."

"And I suppose"—Bonny changed tack—"I am to leave you scandalously alone with my friend here?"

"Given that she is not a woman," Orfeo returned placidly, "and I am generally accounted to be not a man, I am not certain what strictures we would be breaking?"

It was oddly sweet to see Bonny—silly, dreamy Bonny—trying to play protector. But it was also the very opposite of necessary. "Bonaventure," said Peggy, "shove off."

This inspired a certain amount of pouting, but—not being Valentine—Peggy was immune. "I will if you want. But, Peggy"—he cast a jumpy, suspicious look at Orfeo—"do you actually know anything about . . . about . . . this person?"

"I know you've not done a very good job at welcoming them into your house."

But then Orfeo made a languid gesture. "I will not be staying long, Signor Tarleton."

Oh. Peggy had no cause to be disappointed. She hadn't expected to see Orfeo at all, so fretting over the length of their visit was foolish. Except there it was, so very baldly stated: this was fleeting, a courtesy. It meant nothing.

Bonny, meanwhile, was in the process of leaving, his book cradled protectively to his chest.

"I'm sorry about that," Peggy said, when he was finally gone.

"Not at all." Orfeo offered the faintest smile. They were wearing a tall hat, in silk rather than beaver, with a veil that dipped coquettishly across one eye and served only to accentuate the gold-touched intensity of the other. "I am many things that people find frightening."

All the same, Peggy was going to be Having Words with Bonny later. "Do you want to sit down?"

They shook their head, a hand drifting up, almost protectively, to adjust the position of the veil. "There is no need. I know I should not have come."

"Maybe not," Peggy agreed. "But I'm glad you're here."

There was a small, difficult pause. "I wondered," said Orfeo at last. "Would you care to see me at the King's Theatre? Tomorrow is opening night, and the marquess has not yet returned from his travels, so I have the use of his box."

This was the last thing Peggy might have expected. And left her scuffing in confused awkwardness at the floor. "I'm sure I could use Valentine's."

"Or you could accept what it is in my gift to offer."

"You know I probably won't faint again."

"That is not mandatory." Orfeo smiled, somewhat uncertainly. "But I would like it if you were there."

"I mightn't," Peggy pointed out, mostly joking, but definitely only mostly.

It won a soft laugh from Orfeo. "It is up to you, of course."

"You really want me to come?"

They inclined their head slightly. "Not if you would truly hate it. But I have no particular friends in London, and my welcome, irrespective of my ability, is less assured here than it is in Europe."

"I won't hate it," said Peggy quickly. "How could I? It's what you do, after all."

"It's what I am."

It was not, in all honesty, a splendid moment to be reminded that Orfeo had chosen music over Peggy, and Peggy had chosen nothing over something. So she focused on the logistics of opera instead. "I mean, I probably won't have a clue what's going on."

"Oh"—Orfeo made a stagy, airy gesture—"it's very simple, mio principe."

"Is it, though?"

"Of course. I play the son of the prefect of the Royal Guard of Persia, who has recently assassinated the King of Persia."

"Wait. Sorry." Peggy was already lost—although, from the glitter of Orfeo's eyes, she was intended to be. "Which of you did the assassination?"

"My treacherous father—pay attention. I would not assassinate the King of Persia, for I am close friends with his son, and am also in love with his daughter."

"You're in love with the daughter of the son of the assassinated King of Persia?"

"No, with the daughter of the King of Persia. And," Orfeo went on, their hands moving in time with their rapid speech, "the son of the King of Persia happens to be in love with my sister too. Except unfortunately a general in the Persian army is also in love with my sister and has supported my father in his treacheries in order to claim her hand in marriage."

Peggy's brain was reeling. "And that all fits in three to four hours?"

"Darling, that all takes place before the action begins."

"Great," said Peggy. "Can't wait."

Orfeo laughed again, their eyes—or at least the one eye not partially obscured by the veil—impossibly warm.

And Peggy became instantly worried she might do, or say, something very silly indeed. "Sorry, uh. Are you sure you won't sit down? Or tea. I can . . . we can . . . tea."

"I should not. Also, I do not enjoy tea. I cannot for the life of me understand why your nation is so obsessed by it."

Peggy shrugged. "I don't know. Maybe we're all too polite to say we don't like it? The tea is optional, though. For you, anyway. I think if a British person tried to opt out, we'd get thrown into the sea or something."

"Is not, traditionally, the tea thrown into the sea?"

"Only by Americans."

"I . . ." One of Orfeo's rare and fleeting hesitations. "I still should not. I would ask for more than a visit to the opera, and you have already told me no, and there are few things I find less pleasant than someone who cannot accept a no, so I have no intention of becoming such myself."

They weren't asking. They'd just made it very clear they weren't asking. And yet Peggy irrelevantly choked out an answer anyway, "You know . . . Belle . . . me . . . I can't . . ."

"I do know," Orfeo cut in sharply. "You do not need to explain again."

Peggy hung her head wretchedly. "Sorry."

"Come to the opera if you wish. Or not, if you do not wish."

"I'll come," Peggy promised, desperately wishing she could offer more, but not quite daring to.

"Thank you." Stepping forward, Orfeo put a hand lightly on her shoulder, leaning in to whisper. "And don't forget to bring me flowers."

Peggy's whole body reacted to their proximity. The heat of their breath. The scent she remembered from having sat under a pile of their clothing. "Um . . . what kind?"

There was a pause that seemed at once too long and too short, Orfeo's mouth close enough to Peggy's ear that she could almost feel the shapes it made as they laughed and whispered, "Blue roses." Then they stepped away again sharply, regarding Peggy with an expression she could not read.

"Are you all right?" she asked. Like an absolute fool. Because clearly neither of them were.

They tilted their head slightly, something sorrowful in their eyes, though their mouth was curled into its uneven smile. "I think I did not express myself properly when last we met."

"Didn't you?"

"No." Their gaze slipped away again. "When I spoke of my searching, I did not make it clear enough that the miracle was not that I found someone like you. It is that the person I found was you."

"Orfeo . . ."

But they cut her off again, this time with a laugh. "Don't forget my flowers, Peggy."

And with that, they offered a neat bow, re-adjusted their hat and the position of the veil, and departed, the shimmer of their gold coat fading. The click of their bootheels swallowed by silence.

Chapter 13

It was Bonny, in the end, who had told Peggy that blue roses—or blue flowers of any kind, really—did not exist. Or rather, that they were extraordinarily rare because something something natural pigments something something delphiniums something something bluebells.

"Why," Peggy had asked, in frustration, "would they ask me for an impossible flower?" And then she paused. "Oh."

Bonny, to whom pausing was alien, rushed on regardless. "I have no idea. I always ask for flowers I can definitely receive. What's the point otherwise?"

The point, Peggy thought, suddenly understanding, is that you *expect* to receive them. And someday she was going to like somebody who didn't see their life as a story they were telling instead of something they were living. Or, then again, maybe she wasn't. Maybe dramatic beyond all reason was her type.

Oh fuck. It was her type, wasn't it?

Which was not to say Peggy couldn't be a little bit dramatic too. Especially when confronted with so-called impossibilities. Which was why she spent her afternoon shopping for white roses and blue inks, and her evening cutting stems and stuffing flowers into jugs containing different measures of water and ink, in the hope they would absorb some of the colouring. By mid-afternoon the next day, she had a collection of . . . well. Mostly still-white roses, if she was honest. But a few of them had a distinctly bluish tinge to them. And one, while it was not blue exactly, had a soft turquoise glow to its petals. She wrapped it up carefully, hoping it had enough water to sustain it through what was inevitably going to be a long, long opera.

Her companions for the evening turned out to be Sir Horley, which was not surprising, because the fellow was secretly quite cultured, and Bonny, who was clearly feeling guilty for his earlier behaviour. Perhaps predictably, Belle had lost interest in opera and opera singers since Orfeo had rejected her by proxy. And Valentine was in the bath, an occasion of great ceremony and several hours' duration, and it was testament to the depth of Bonny's remorse that he was missing it.

Peggy had dressed rather daringly in an evening gown of crimson merino trimmed in gold braid and swansdown. Her bosom, tucked behind a pearl-buttoned bodice, was behaving entirely as it ought, and she felt . . . not beautiful, exactly, because it wasn't the sort of word she'd ever wanted for herself, but bold and strong and *right*. Of course, Orfeo had an opera to perform in, and music to give their heart to, so was unlikely to notice Peggy, in red or otherwise. She liked it, though, knowing she would see Orfeo doing what they loved while showing the world who she was. Or part of who she was. A part that was true.

They made, Peggy thought, a rather impressive party. Sir Horley was always polished, especially in evening wear—with his bright hair, dark clothes gave him the air of a fox from a fable. And, beneath the auspices of Valentine's tailor, Bonny looked as pampered as a housecat, the rainbow of paste rings he used to wear replaced by real jewels, the cost of which Peggy didn't think it was her place to contemplate.

Out of respect for Orfeo, and at Peggy's insistence, they arrived at the King's Theatre not long before the first act was due to start and found it surprisingly busy. The Haymarket was lined with carriages and the theatre vestibule, with its lavishly painted apse, thronged so vigorously with people that Peggy had to cradle her rose protectively. Whether it was discomfort, curiosity, or genuine enthusiasm that they inspired, Orfeo had been right about the power of their reputation.

Normally the beau monde wouldn't grace a performance with their presence until well after dinnertime.

As they took their seats in the absent marquess's box, which was on the second tier, and thus ornamented with a somewhat incongruous selection of nymphs and dolphins, Bonny was still interrogating Sir Horley about the plot.

"And he gives his son, who he did the murder to help, the blood-soaked murder weapon because?"

"Because," Sir Horley explained for the ninth time, "it's an opera."

"And then condemns his own son to death, even though he knows he did the murder, and he did the murder explicitly for his son, because?"

"Because . . . ," Sir Horley began.

Bonny waved an exasperated hand, colours flashing on his fingers in the brightly lit auditorium. "Yes, yes, it's an opera. But surely that doesn't exempt it from making any narrative sense."

"Actually, it rather does." Taking out his mother-of-pearl monocular, Sir Horley fit it to his eye. "Just try to enjoy the sound and the spectacle, dear one. When somebody comes to the front of the stage alone and makes everything about them, that's called an aria. You'll relate."

Now Bonny was pouting. "I know what an aria is. I have been to the opera before. But what if I don't relate. What if I get bored?"

"Then you can watch Lord Galvan frigging Mrs. Bedyle—his hand is completely under her skirts."

"Where?" Bonny bounced in his seat. "I can't see. Can I borrow your—"

Wordlessly, Sir Horley passed over his monocular.

"Oooh." There was a long pause. "He can't be very good at it," observed Bonny, finally. "He's taking forever."

Peggy, meanwhile, was feeling . . . feeling something? Because while the ton had—as usual—come to look at each other, they had also undeniably come for Orfeo. All these people, drawn in wonder, to hear a voice that still sometimes flicked at the edges of Peggy's dreams like a mermaid tail upon the horizon. And Orfeo, for whatever reason, had wanted Peggy. Been the one to look in wonder. And she'd said no. Out of loyalty to Belle. And being scared.

And because she was an idiot. Clearly, she was an idiot.

Then came a flurry of sound from the orchestra: a fast movement followed by a slow and another fast, during which Lord Galvan enjoyed no further success with his lady. Or, more to the point, she enjoyed no further success with him.

"What," remarked Sir Horley, having reclaimed his monocular from Bonny, "is Miss Langley wearing? That colour makes her look like she has jaundice."

Needless to say, Sir Horley did not long after retain possession of his monocular. "You know"—the device swung back and forth like the trunk of a very small, distressed elephant as Bonny surveyed the boxes on the opposite side of the auditorium—"I think Mr. Welbekin is padding his garments again."

Sir Horley squinted. "His shoulders normally look like that, don't they?"

"Oh." Bonny giggled. "Not his *shoulders*."

It was at this moment that a man and a woman swept onto the stage, and for a disorientating handful of seconds Peggy almost didn't recognise Orfeo in the noble soldier risking all for a stolen evening with his beloved in the palace gardens. For whatever reason—something something pope something something—Peggy had acquired the notion that castrati often took the roles of women upon the stage, and while she hadn't precisely been expecting to see Orfeo cast as one, she also hadn't quite imagined them portraying this sort of very conventional romantic hero.

Of course, she'd seen them play a part before, one deliberately designed to challenge or confirm someone else's assumptions about them. But with her, she was beginning to realise, they had only ever been Orfeo.

And that was oddly humbling.

Especially now she knew they were also capable of this. Of inhabiting another person's story so completely that she could barely see the joins anymore.

The voice, though—for all it was Arbace who sang his sorrow and his love—the voice, with its heart-piercing beauty, could not have belonged to anyone but Orfeo. It spread its wings across the audience, startling them into silence, and filling the vastness of the auditorium with its strength and splendour. Peggy's breath tangled hotly in her throat, and a succession of shivers ran up the exposed skin between the puffed sleeves of her gown and her opera gloves—though, thankfully, she didn't faint this time.

To her right, Sir Horley had leaned forward to rest his elbows on the velvet-covered balustrade, monocular trained upon the actors rather than the audience. To her left, Bonny was wriggling in the grip of some kind of emotion, but since he hadn't run screaming out of the box, she assumed it was positive. Below, the young guardsman with Orfeo's voice—having bid farewell to his lover—had ill-advisedly agreed to look after the bloody sword with which his father had just murdered the King of Persia. No way that would be coming back to haunt him.

Needless to say, it came back to haunt him. While his best friend, the king's son, was out murdering his brother, having been manipulated into believing he was responsible, Orfeo's character was arrested in the palace gardens and denounced by all his loved ones in a series of brutal arias.

And that was when Peggy realised she was . . . watching an opera without resentment and only a small amount of bewilderment. She was probably missing most of the nuance of the story, but maybe there wasn't that much nuance to catch? Lovers, friends, dead emperor, scheming father with poor judgement. Honestly, she was quite drawn in. Some of it, especially the parts where it was just people sing-talking at each other, went on a bit. But she supposed the plot had to be moved somehow. And not everything could be a magnificent aria about . . . whatever arias were about.

It wasn't necessarily how she might have chosen to spend her evening. But she could have watched Orfeo forever, just to marvel at them, and marvel at the idea that a person of such extraordinary talents had found something marvellous in her. Because if Peggy had to step to the front of the stage and deliver an aria from the depths of her heart, it would probably go something like:

> I am mildly conflicted about my life sometimes
> And it is hard to know how to be yourself
> When everything in the world is full of other people's ideas
> About what things are and mean.
> But mostly I am very lucky with the people who love me
> And fine. Mostly I am fine.

Arbace, meanwhile, had been left alone, forlorn, impossibly conflicted, unable to defend himself on the whole murder issue without denouncing his own father. Which certainly put Peggy's problems, such as they were, in perspective.

Suddenly, he stood, the music swelled, and a fresh hush fell across the audience. Anticipation leapt from nerve to nerve, breath to breath, like a living thing. And then Orfeo, whose character had been silent and distraught through the last run of arias, broke once more into song. Peggy wasn't sure exactly what he was singing about—probably his misfortunes—only that Orfeo's voice rose and fell like the waves in a storm, gathering power and breaking afresh, as Arbace paced about the stage, trying to escape his fate, only to be confronted by it again at every turn.

Peggy had never heard anything like it. Not even at Lady Farrow's musical whatever-it-was, when she had first heard Orfeo sing. That had been, she understood now, an exercise in pristine restraint. This was Orfeo unleashed, their voice sweeping with unimaginable ease from its powerful tenor to its shining soprano, through a dizzying array of liquid runs, leaps, trills, and roulades, as Arbace reeled from despair to determination and back again.

It was frankly magnificent, the vocal complexity of the piece only increasing with every foiled escape, until the very beauty of it was exhausting.

Sir Horley had tucked his face into the crook of his elbow and seemed to be crying very softly.

Startled—for while Sir Horley liked opera, and art in general, more than the rest of them, he was not particularly emotional—Peggy put a hand on his shoulder. "Are you all right?"

He snuffled softly. "I'm drifting down a cruel sea."

"I mean," said Peggy, "aren't we all?"

Orfeo's final flourish was a succession of rippling notes Peggy could only describe as "very high," capped by another that was even higher. And yet there was no shrillness to the sound at all: just something rich and vigorous that felt as triumphant as a soldier upon the battlefield.

Bonny's fingers were gripping his own curls. Peggy had a hand clutched to her heart. Because the soiree had been little more than a glimpse of this: the kind of beauty that did things to you. Hurt you and healed you and humbled you.

Left you not quite the same.

The act was over. The stage bathed in silence. And then the applause was rapturous.

"I'm not sure"—Bonny's face was white—"if I now completely believe in God. Or still don't."

Peggy raised a brow. "What's God got to do with anything?" Though he did seem to be coming up a lot lately.

"Oh, you know." Bonny shrugged. "Don't you ever see something so wonderful that it feels impossible it could have just *happened*?"

Emerging, red-eyed, from behind a handkerchief, Sir Horley made a visible attempt to project his usual insouciance. "You feel the hand of the watchmaker."

"But then," Bonny went on, "Orfeo didn't just happen, did they? They were made."

"We were all made," Peggy pointed out.

"Not with . . . not how . . ." A succession of expressive gestures from Bonny. "That's not the hand of a watchmaker. That's the hand of a surgeon."

"I'm sure," Sir Horley drawled, "the pope would say God guided the hand of the surgeon."

"Yes, well"—Bonny pouted—"the pope also believes I'm wrong, so I don't care what he would say."

Sir Horley's look, as it often was when it alighted upon Bonny, was indulgent. "Well, what do *you* say then?"

"I don't really know," Bonny admitted. "I feel . . . I suppose . . . sort of privileged to have experienced"—he flailed his hands—"*that*. But I also feel guilty for admiring something I feel shouldn't exist. And yet if it stopped existing, wouldn't we just be taking something beautiful out of the world? These are big questions for a small Bonny."

Unlike nearly every man-inclining man of her acquaintance, Peggy was not particularly susceptible to Bonny being winsome. "Maybe they're not yours to ask? Orfeo's who they are. This is what they want to do, however it came about that they're doing it."

"And they are," murmured Sir Horley, "quite remarkable. So much so I . . . I'm sorry, I can't stay."

"Err . . ." Peggy, who had resumed her typical theatre-attending slouch, sat up again. "What? Why?"

He made a uselessly inarticulate gesture.

"Because you're drifting down a cruel sea?" Peggy asked. "I thought you were just . . . moved by the music?"

Visibly discomforted, Sir Horley rose. "I find I'm just not in the mood for emotions in general."

"Are you ever?"

"Well. No. But the negative ones I particularly deplore." Sir Horley rolled his eyes—apparently at himself. "They're so wearisome to everyone."

"You don't have to go, though," Peggy protested. "Even if you end up crying during—"

"Now now."

"Even if," Peggy corrected herself, "you end up experiencing a negative emotion during an aria, I thought you were supposed to *arrive* after the first act of an opera, not *leave*."

"What can I say?" Sir Horley struck a pose by the curtain that divided the box from the corridor beyond. "I'm an *innovator*." He paused. "And, by the way, I probably ought to mention, I'm getting married."

Bonny, who had been swinging his chair on its back legs, crashed to the carpeted floor and lay there in an expressive heap. "How can you be getting married?"

"The usual way, I imagine. Church and vicar. Family and friends. Unfortunate woman."

"But," Bonny spluttered, "but you said you'd never get married. Because you, because you're. You know."

"Well, my aunt has other ideas."

Rolling himself to his feet, Bonny righted his chair. "Is it up to her?"

"She's my only family." There was an unexpectedly serious note in Sir Horley's voice.

Bonny's lip quivered—as it was often wont to do when he was confronted by a worldview that did not match his own in all specifications. "Aren't *we* your family?"

Sir Horley heaved a heavy sigh. "It's not the same, darling, and you know it."

"I *don't* know it," protested Bonny.

Entirely futilely, as it happened, because Sir Horley simply turned and departed, abandoning Bonny and Peggy in the box of an absent marquess.

"Should . . ." Bonny wrinkled his nose nervously. "Should we go after him?"

Peggy shook her head. "I know you Tarletons like to leave in the hope of being followed. But, as a general rule, people don't weep at an aria and then run away because they want company."

"Fine." With a heavy sigh of his own, Bonny cast himself violently back in his chair. "This is the worst opera ever."

Peggy, who was sitting on her chair like a normal person, gave him a look. "I don't think Sir Horley getting married is really the fault of *Artaserse*."

"No, but now I'll forever associate it with dreadful news, and I wasn't a devotee to begin with."

"Well, think how Sir Horley must be suffering," Peggy returned. "He actually likes the opera."

"Clearly"—Bonny was gazing at her with big, faintly accusing eyes—"Sir Horley has bigger problems right now. What is happening, Peggy? Everything was perfect, and suddenly our lives are falling apart."

"What do you mean?" asked Peggy warily.

"Well, Belle has given up all hope of love. And Sir Horley is being forced into matrimony. And you—"

"What about me?"

"Aren't you going to be tragically in love with Belle forever? Like"—and here something almost approving crept into Bonny's voice—"a preux chevalier?"

Peggy flinched. "Firstly, no, I hadn't planned on it. And, secondly, preux chevaliers weren't a thing. There's nothing romantic about knights. They were just rich, armoured bastards who killed people."

This observation drew a sound from Bonny like she'd actually stabbed him. Meanwhile Peggy was merely feeling stabbed.

"And I'm sure," she went on with more confidence than she felt, "Belle will find someone other than Orfeo to be in love with. Someone she's actually spoken to, for example?"

"But what if she doesn't?" demanded Bonny. "What if Orfeo was her last and only chance? What if she's *broken*?"

This was the last thing Peggy needed. She was perfectly capable of feeling guilty by herself, without Bonny inadvertently contributing. "I don't think we should say she's broken just because—"

"Just because she can't love?" interrupted Bonny, more than a little hysterically. "How is that not broken? How can she possibly be happy if she can't love?"

Bonny and Belle were so very alike, in so many ways—although as they'd grown up and, to some extent, grown apart, it tended to mean they just got stubborn about different things. With Bonny ever more committed to a world that looked like a storybook and Belle ever more convinced that she wanted something else entirely. Never mind what any of this might mean for Peggy, about whom there were no stories, to either cleave to or turn from.

"Maybe," she said finally, "she'll be happy in a different way. Not everyone has to be happy the exact same way you're happy."

There was a long silence—or as silent as it was possible to get in an interval at the theatre, which was to say quite noisy indeed. Finally, Bonny said, "But . . . but I'm *so* happy."

"Good for you."

"No, but," Bonny tried again, "I'm *so* happy. And . . . and I feel guilty about it because nobody I care about is as happy as me. I mean, except Valentine. Obviously *he's* happy because I'm completely fabulous."

"You're completely something," Peggy muttered.

"Why are you always mean to me?" Bonny asked. "You're never mean to Belle. You always take her side and—"

"I think you'll find I take the side of whoever isn't being an idiot."

"And me wanting the people I love to be happy is me being an idiot?"

"Only because you've found a way to make it all about *you* and *your* happiness."

"I can't believe," Bonny said, in his whiniest voice, "you're making me out to be some kind of . . . some kind of . . . *villain* over this."

Peggy laid her forehead against the cool metal of the balustrade surrounding the box. "I'm not saying you're a villain, Bonny. I'm just saying . . ." What was she saying? She tried again. "Look, I know you think being with a duke is the only happy ending that could possibly exist for anyone. But maybe it . . . it *isn't?*"

A pause while Bonny re-assessed literally everything he believed in. Then, "Are you sure? Because dukes are *the best.* They've got heaps of money, and everybody has to do whatever they say."

In spite of herself, Peggy laughed. "You're such a little . . ."

"Constant source of joy?" Bonny suggested helpfully. "Pocket-sized bundle of bliss?"

"Just, please . . ." Peggy was enormously tired, and even the balustrade had stopped helping. "Try to remember that not everyone is you."

Bonny drooped beside her like a trodden-on flower. "I'm sorry, Peggy. I really am. I just want to help. On the subject of which"—he de-drooped abruptly and shuffled his chair closer to hers—"what about you?"

This was the problem with Bonny. He was 90 percent predictable and 10 percent menace. "What about me?"

"Well, Sir Horley wants a priest, and Belle wants a soprano, and you . . . what do you want?" Bonny wriggled in his seat with the air of a bird fluffing its feathers. "*See. I'm listening.*"

Images raced across Peggy's mind like birds against clear sky: the sound of familiar footsteps upon a path, a strand of someone's hair curled across a pillow, the way the world smelled at dawn, the resolute click of a front door that was yours, a child's hand in hers. And Orfeo, in all their pride and tenderness, sleeping sated in her arms.

"There's nothing to listen to," Peggy told him roughly. "Because," she lied, "I don't know what I want."

Chapter 14

When the performance was over—it had culminated, in a flurry of recitative and, despite its ominous beginning, with nobody murdered except the people who had previously been murdered, and love broadly triumphant over . . . more murder—Peggy asked Bonny to excuse her for a moment.

"You're *abandoning* me?" he cried, with predictable drama.

"Yes, in the untamed wilds of this theatre."

Although, to be fair, the theatre was *quite* wild—wild with applause for the whole cast, though especially for Orfeo, who was taking a bow amidst such a tumult of flowers that Peggy's slightly blue rose was beginning to feel like no tribute at all. She'd thought to try and sneak backstage while everyone else was still seated (or rather standing and clapping) because she wasn't sure she'd be able to in the crush and clamour, but—given how very . . . celebrated Orfeo already was—perhaps she wouldn't be permitted to attend on them at all. The thought made her feel oddly queasy, even though she also knew she had no special rights. She had no great name to recommend her, wealth but not *great* wealth, and even in a red dress she was only moderately attractive. In short, she was nobody. And all she'd done for Orfeo was reject them. Reject them and bring them a squashed, badly dyed flower as a sort of . . . *Oops, sorry, I wish I / you / the world was different.*

Despite her concerns, she was allowed backstage, where the noise of the audience was, somehow, even more overwhelming than it had been in the auditorium. It was not necessarily *louder*, but there was a weight and expectation to it that pressed against Peggy's heart like too many bodies in a crowded room. She was hustled and bullied through narrow corridors, her footsteps drowning amongst the clatter of other footsteps moving even more quickly than she was, then pushed through a door and . . . left.

In some ways, it was a relief to be away from both the theatre goers and the theatre, um, doers, and yet Peggy couldn't quite shake the sense that she was trespassing. The room was sparsely decorated, the furniture—such as it was—chosen for practicality rather than beauty, but some quintessence of Orfeo lingered. Some scent upon the air. A suggestion of their fingertips against the mirror glass. It was certainly a lot tidier than their bedroom at the marquess's house had been, though that wasn't on its own so very surprising. Peggy already knew that Orfeo played many roles, both on and off the stage.

It wasn't long before the door opened again, and, this time, it was Orfeo—in the process of pulling a wig from their head. Apparently they had not been expecting her, for their reaction was a visible start and a muttered "Cazzo," the wig slipping from their fingers to the floor as they put a hand to their chest.

"Er," said Peggy. "Sorry."

Orfeo's eyes were wide beneath the paint. "W-what are you doing here? I am not fit to be seen."

Hadn't she been invited? Oh God, how seriously had she misread the situation. "They let me in. I thought you . . . didn't you tell me to . . . come?"

"To see me sing, yes. Not to see me covered in grease and sweat."

It was true that what had been a captivating illusion of grandeur from a distance had transformed up close—like Cinderella at midnight—into rumpled fabric, paste jewels, and smudged makeup. And yet beneath it all, Orfeo was radiant, their eyes as bright as diamonds, as if the trappings of a costume could no longer contain their beauty. "I can't believe," Peggy told them, "that you discerned my terror of grease and sweat by the power of mesmerism. Honestly, it was a fear buried so deep inside me I hadn't even realised I had it."

Having picked up their wig again, Orfeo pushed past her to the dressing table, where they set it upon a stand. There, they plucked at it idly, picking out some of the tangles, refusing to look at Peggy—though the mirror reflected their exhaustion in the hunch of their shoulders. "I prefer to be alone after a performance."

Oh, this was going fantastically. Peggy gave herself a small internal cheer in her most sarcastic voice. "I'm sorry. I didn't know. I'll leave. I just came to bring you this." She made a "Here, have it" gesture with her rose, which was withering rapidly in its paper wrappings.

Still Orfeo didn't look at her. "Put it . . . somewhere, if you please."

"Yes. Right. I will do that." Peggy slid it onto the edge of the dressing table, nudging it over to Orfeo like it was a naked blade. "And now I'm going."

"Grazie."

"Just . . ." She paused. She was not, in all honesty, feeling much like a miracle. More like someone who had gone where they weren't wanted. "Just," she tried again, "you could be covered in alligator guts and you'd be beautiful. I'd still find you beautiful. There's nothing in the world could change that."

Orfeo said nothing by way of reply. But as Peggy had her hand on the door handle, she heard the faintest rustle of paper from behind her. And then, "Peggy, what is this?"

"What you asked for."

"But"—Orfeo's tone was a wall, offering no emotion, concealing all thoughts—"blue roses do not exist."

"They still don't," Peggy admitted. "That's ink."

She turned to find Orfeo, in their stage finery, their brow and neck streaked with perspiration, and their hair still caught beneath a wig cap, holding Peggy's rose between their fingers. They looked . . . she could hardly tell. Perplexed? Almost angry. "It was a joke. Blue roses are impossible. Do you think we live in some kind of fairy tale?"

"No," she said slowly. "I don't think we live in a fairy tale. But . . ." She took a deep breath that, no matter how long she kept breathing, didn't seem to quite fill her lungs. So she stopped, air exploding out of her mouth again in a wheezy huff, and attempted to keep talking. "But maybe I'm less scared of impossible things than I thought I was?"

What happened next was something of a blur. Peggy wasn't even sure she'd done it. Except she must have. Because Orfeo's shoulders were against a free-standing mirror, and one of their legs was flung across Peggy's hip, and her hands were tangled half in their hair and half in the wig cap, and . . . and . . . oh God. They were kissing. They were kissing *so much* that she heard the glass creak behind them.

"That," Orfeo murmured against Peggy's mouth, "will be seven years' bad luck if you are not careful."

"Fuck it," Peggy growled in answer.

And kissed them again. Again. Again. The sort of kisses that stripped you bare. Lips and tongues tumbled together like everything you'd ever decided not to say. While she wasn't one to boast, Peggy was an assured lover. Considerate, competent . . . some other things probably. In any case, it wasn't relevant. Because she was none of them now. She was a ravenous desperate mess, and Orfeo was melting against her like being mouth-attacked by a ravenous desperate mess was all they'd ever wanted in the world.

Their hair—released at last—was pure silk, falling over Peggy's wrists. And they, too, were a thing of silk, lithe and strong, and rough and smooth, coiled around Peggy like they would never let her go. They were everywhere, warm, and yielding, drawing her closer, deeper. And beneath the sweat and the grease and the makeup was something that was so undeniably, irrefutably Orfeo that it felt to Peggy as recognisable as harbour lights, guiding her exactly where she was supposed to be.

"You know," said Bonny, "I've been standing here, clearing my throat discreetly, for quite a long time."

Horrified, Peggy leapt away from Orfeo. "Oh fuck."

"Not quite." Bonny was blinking in a fashion Peggy chose to read as condemnatory. "But if you'd kept going."

She could feel a smear of stage makeup congealing on her cheek. "I w-wasn't going to keep going. I mean, we were just . . . It's not what it looks like."

"It looked a lot like kissing," said Bonny ruthlessly.

"It felt a lot like kissing," Orfeo agreed. They were still pressed against the mirror, their hair in tangles, their eyes heavy-lidded with pleasure, and their mouth slick and swollen from Peggy's. Their voice, though. Their voice was ice. "But I'm interested to know what you thought it was."

This was not going well. Peggy flailed slightly. "I'm not saying it wasn't kissing. I'm saying there's . . . there's context."

Orfeo still hadn't moved except to fold their arms tightly across their chest. "If there is context, Margaret Delancey, you should have explained it to me before you kissed me."

"I know . . . it's . . . it's just it's complicated. And I . . ."

"Yes," said Bonny, "you should have."

She turned on him. "Will you *please*—"

"Perhaps"—now Orfeo's voice was a blade—"you could both leave my dressing room? I have said, have I not, I prefer to be alone after a performance."

Peggy hung her head. "You did . . . say that. I'm sorry, Orfeo, I—"

"I have not asked for apologies. I have asked you to go away."

"Yes but—"

They stooped suddenly and swept Peggy's rose from the floor. It looked very sorry for itself indeed, its petals faded and curled, barely blue at all in the oily candlelight. "You should take this."

"But," she protested wretchedly, "I brought it for you."

Orfeo shook their head. "I told you to bring blue roses. You said yourself, this is ink."

There was nothing for it except to take the damn rose—even though Peggy hadn't wanted anything less in her life. And, after that, there was nothing for it but to leave. She walked as quickly as her gown and slippers permitted, which was still fast enough that Bonny had to break into a run to keep up. It shouldn't have been in any way satisfying to her that he had to, but she was clearly just a vindictive person tonight.

Pushing their way through the crowds, they found Valentine's carriage stuck in a line of other carriages. Casting her rose into the gutter, Peggy climbed inside and threw herself into the far corner, where she huddled. Bonny settled opposite, uncharacteristically silent. And there they waited for the coachman to extricate them from the rest of the traffic.

"How," muttered Peggy finally, "how did you even get backstage?"

Bonny gave a long, slow blink. "That's what you're asking me? Well, all right. I told them I was a duke, and they let me through. It works in most situations."

There was another long silence. From the street outside came the sounds of coachmen shouting at other coachmen to "get out the bleeding way!"

"I'm starting to see," said Bonny finally, "why Orfeo wasn't interested in my sister."

Horrified, Peggy looked up. "It's not . . . I wasn't . . . you're not going to tell her, are you?"

"Of course not." Bonny's reply came gratifyingly swiftly. And then, "You're going to tell her."

Peggy's heart fell through her stomach, and then the bottom dropped out of the universe. "Oh my God, I can't. She . . . she'll never forgive me. It was bad enough after she thought I'd sided against her with Valentine."

"It's not the same."

"How?" asked Peggy, her voice rising sharply.

"Because that was about her, and this is about you." Bonny blinked again. "At least, I'm assuming it's about you. It would be very odd behaviour if it wasn't."

"She'll still feel betrayed."

Bonny just shrugged. "Maybe. But you still have to talk to her."

"Do I, though?"

"Well . . ." Bonny pulled a face. "Only if you care about, for example, not being a *dreadful* human being."

He was right. Or maybe he wasn't right. It was hard to tell because Peggy couldn't think properly through the fog of self-disgust. She'd tried . . . she'd tried to be loyal to Belle and honest with Orfeo. And all she'd done was fuck everything up for everybody, including herself.

Because how hard was it actually? Not to kiss someone your best friend wanted? Not very hard. The world was full of people Belle either didn't want or had already had. Peggy could have kissed any of them with impunity—with the possible exception of Grace Hickinbottom, who had too many feelings of her own. And yet she had kissed Orfeo. Who, in that single catastrophic moment, it had felt impossible *not* to kiss.

And she could taste them still. Feel them still. All their supple strength and softness. They had welcomed her clumsy passion until, in breath and heat and mouth-upon-mouth, body-to-body, they learned tenderness together.

Oh God. Oh fuck. She'd done an awful thing to two people, and . . . and . . . yet how was she supposed to regret it? To not want it? No matter what it meant—or didn't mean—for Belle.

Peggy let her head thunk against the window as the carriage finally began, at a snail's pace, to move.

Chapter 15

She had to talk to Belle. Peggy knew she had to talk to Belle. She lay awake all night, thinking how she had to talk to Belle. Except in the morning she felt so wretched she didn't want to get out of bed. And then that somehow led into another night and another morning, and the days were slipping away while she claimed to be "not well."

An excuse that was as implausible as it was embarrassing, because Peggy had a reputation for being irritatingly vigorous. If a cold went round, she either didn't get it full stop or was over it in a day, at which point her still-afflicted loved ones would be inclined to view her general health and well-being as a personal insult. And yet in spite of all this, sometimes it was perilously easy to stay in bed. It didn't happen often—not *often* often—but every now and again a great . . . she wasn't sure *tiredness* fully described it. A sort of soul-deep stagnation, when nothing about her, or about anything else, felt like it made sense.

Of course, what didn't feel right at the moment was that Peggy had done something terrible. So maybe she wasn't really stagnating. Maybe she was just hiding. As much from herself as Belle.

It was just . . . she wasn't supposed to be like this. She was the quiet one, the devoted friend, the careful lover. She didn't lie or sneak around. She didn't get half-obsessed with strangers, especially when someone she cared about had—reasonably or otherwise—pinned their entire future on the stranger. She definitely didn't throw people against mirrors and kiss them like she wanted to climb inside them and build a willow cabin next to their heart.

She was *supposed* to be a bit boring.

The way Peggy saw it, everyone sort of got one . . . one *thing* that they were allowed to make trouble over. Something that other people had to deal with or accommodate or politely ignore. The problem was, with her, *she* . . . who she was . . . that was already the thing. Which meant now, she was not only *her*—someone she already secretly worried she might have made up in her head, and yet was the only version of herself that fit—but *also* someone who messed up, made bad kissing decisions, and couldn't make other decisions. Someone, in other words, who hurt in horrible ways the very people she most cherished.

It was, frankly, no wonder she couldn't get out of bed. She didn't deserve to get out of bed. She deserved to spend the rest of her life shunned by all, and being slowly nibbled to death by moths. The big furry ones that seemed inexplicably threatening, despite being little more than wings on a stick.

Eventually, though, Belle barged in. In fairness to her, she had tried knocking first and Peggy had pretended to be asleep, and then Belle had called out, "I know you're pretending to be asleep," and Peggy had pretended to be asleep even harder, and finally Belle had come in. She looked pretty and bright, in a sprigged muslin morning gown, and was carrying a tray of toast and tea—upon which only some of the toast had been eaten—and Peggy had betrayed her.

Pushing her head under several pillows, Peggy gave up pretending to be asleep and began pretending to be legitimately dead.

"Peggy," sighed Belle, managing to sigh a name with no aspirations in it, which was, somehow, typical of Belle's immense capacity for bending the world to her will. "Peggy, what's wrong?"

Peggy made muffled noises.

"I brought you some toast. I would have brought you more toast, but Bonny passed me in the corridor and completely stole a piece."

Peggy made more muffled noises.

"At least try to drink some tea, darling?" There was a clack as Belle put her tray on a nearby table, then a soft flump as she sat down on the edge of the bed. "You aren't really ill, are you? You never get ill. It's annoying."

"I'm ill," Peggy lied. "I've got . . . tuberculosis."

"Wouldn't it be easier," Belle suggested, "if you just told me what the matter is? Because I think having tuberculosis will get quite complicated for you quite quickly. I shall get Valentine to call for a doctor, and you'll probably have to go to a sanatorium in Switzerland or something."

"I don't have that kind of tuberculosis. I have the lying-in-bed-being-left-alone kind of tuberculosis."

Belle's fingertips stroked gently through Peggy's tangled hair. "That's a very specific kind of tuberculosis."

"Please stop being nice to me."

"I'm not being nice to you," Belle said. "I'm selfishly trying to make you get up because I'm bored of being stuck with Bonny and Valentine. Also Bonny says Sir Horley is getting married, but Sir Horley won't talk about it, and I don't know what to do."

Drawn, very much in spite of herself, Peggy lifted her pillow just enough to be able to peep out from under it. "Isn't Sir Horley's marriage Sir Horley's business?"

"No." It was Belle's "You are a fool who has said a foolish thing" voice. "It's our business. Because we care about him."

"He seems to feel his aunt cares for him," Peggy pointed out.

"Do you believe that?" Belle tossed her ringlets emphatically. "Do you?"

"Well, not really. But it's hard to tell. He doesn't mention her much."

"Exactly," declared Belle, as if this was incontrovertible proof. "And hasn't he always said he wouldn't get married? Yet now he is? Doesn't that strike you as suspicious?"

"It strikes me as someone changing their mind."

"Oh." Belle blinked. "You think he's suddenly decided that marrying someone he neither loves nor desires is a *good* idea?"

"Most people do, Belle. It's kind of how it's supposed to work."

"Would you, though?"

"No, but then I won't be getting married at all. On account of the way I'd probably have to wear a silly pink dress, and the vicar would be 'Do you take this woman?' and I'd be 'What woman?' and then remember they were talking about me."

Belle looked briefly abashed. "I'm sorry. I wasn't thinking."

And had Peggy possessed any more than zero legs to stand on, on the whole being-a-bad-friend front, she would have said, *You never do.*

"I still need you, though," Belle went on, irrepressibly. "We have to help Sir Horley."

"It hasn't even been established he wants help. And"—Peggy pulled herself abruptly into a sitting position—"I am done helping you, Belle. You do not need my help. With anything. Ever again."

There was a bewildered silence. "But why?"

"Just . . ." Peggy still couldn't bring herself to say it. "Just because."

"Because of Orfeo?"

Urgh. Urgh. A thousand miles of urgh. "Yes."

"It wasn't your fault I asked you to woo them for me and they said no."

"It's not," Peggy tried. "The thing is . . ."

"Peggy, dearest Peggy." Belle, unhelpfully, gave her cheeks a little squeeze. "You are the best and kindest person. You should not, however, blame yourself for—"

"I kissed Orfeo," yelled Peggy. "I kissed them. I kissed them a lot. And I only stopped kissing them because Bonny caught us kissing."

A silence rolled ominously through the room. "Why?" asked Belle finally.

And Peggy, having told one truth, had no choice but to go on telling others. "Because I like them. I really really like them."

Belle made a noise. It was a clipped little "hmph." Then she got to her feet and began to pace.

"I'm sorry," Peggy said pleadingly. "I'm so so sorry."

Belle paced.

"Are you . . . are you really angry with me?"

"Yes, Margaret." At last Belle paused, turning back to Peggy, her cheeks flushed and her eyes bright with tears. "I'm angry with you."

"I didn't mean to . . . I swear to God, I didn't mean to. It just happened. Which isn't to say"—Peggy was burbling, and she knew she was burbling—"it isn't my responsibility, because it is. But it wasn't my intent. I'd never do anything to hurt you, Belle. Never never never. You have to believe me. Please believe me."

Belle looked no more reassured. "I'm not angry because you kissed Orfeo. I'm angry because you didn't think to tell me *any* of this before. How selfish do you think I am?"

It was probably for the best, Peggy decided, to assume that was a rhetorical question.

"Well," Belle conceded. "All right. I'm *somewhat* selfish. But not so selfish I would ever think of my happiness over yours or expect you to sacrifice your happiness for mine."

Put like that, Peggy was beginning to wonder if she had, in fact, acted rather foolishly. "Um," she said. "Sorry? You can slap my face if you like?"

"I'm not going to slap your face. That would be violent, abusive, and inappropriate."

"You shoot people with guns."

"One person. Once. By accident. Because I was frightened." Belle paused, thoughtfully. "I might pull your hair, though."

"You can pull my hair."

Sitting back next to Peggy, who humbly bowed her head, Belle very gently tugged at one of her curls. "You are the biggest baconwit sometimes, Peggy Delancey."

"I'm not that big a baconwit," Peggy protested, albeit meekly. "And I really am sorry."

Belle huffed a sigh. "You don't have to be sorry. You haven't done anything wrong. Or whatever wrong you have done seems to have been mostly enacted on yourself."

"And Orfeo," muttered Peggy.

"They didn't like you kissing them?"

"No, they did," said Peggy quickly. "They definitely did. But I . . . I still behaved badly."

"Because of me?"

"A little bit because of you. But mainly because of me." Peggy drew her blanket-covered knees up to her chin and hunched over them. "You know I love you, don't you, Belle?"

"How would I know something like that?" Belle widened her eyes comically. "You never talk about it."

"Ha ha. No, but I mean. I love you and I'll always love you. But I think maybe I clung so hard to being in love with you because it was . . . because. Um. It felt safe."

"Thank you." Belle's tone was wry. "That's very flattering."

"I just mean, I didn't have to think about anything."

"You are full of compliments today."

"About me," Peggy clarified hastily. "I didn't have to think about me. About what a relationship means for me."

"Why does it have to mean anything?"

"Because I'm worried what it will mean to other people."

Leaning over, Belle kissed Peggy's anxiously wrinkled forehead. "Maybe, for now, you could just worry about what it means to Orfeo."

"It doesn't mean anything to Orfeo. I wasn't lying when I said that their life belongs to music."

"That doesn't seem particularly healthy or fulfilling."

Peggy tried to draw her knees up even more but was prevented by the limits of her own body and the physical laws of the universe. "It's what they want."

"Is it?" asked Belle. "Or is it all they've been told they can have?" That should not have felt like hope. "Do you think?"

It was at this juncture that Belle appeared to run out of supportive energy. "How would I know? You're the one who's been kissing them."

"Once," Peggy said firmly. "I've kissed them once."

"For long enough to get interrupted doing it. That must have been quite some kiss, Peggy Delancey."

It seemed like a good moment for Peggy to hide her glowing-red face. "It was."

"Then what are you waiting for? Go and do it again."

"You . . ." Peggy briefly looked up again. "You really don't mind?"

"Oh, Peggy. You *arse basket*. Did you really think I would stand in your way?"

"But what about you? And the scarabs? You made me feel Orfeo was your last chance at . . . I don't even know? Love or happiness or whatever?"

"Well . . ." Belle's mouth tightened. "That may be true. Or it may not."

"You want to try and fall in love with someone else?" asked Peggy hopefully.

At this suggestion, though, Belle just shook her head grimly. "I don't think so."

"Ah."

"I suppose," Belle went on quietly, "I rather liked the idea of being in love with Orfeo. They seemed so . . . I'm not sure how to explain it. Detached, I suppose, from everything I feel trapped by. Except lately I've begun to wonder . . . I've begun to wonder . . ." She broke off, biting her lip. "Peggy, what if there's nothing wrong with me?"

Peggy blinked. "Believe me, darling, there's a lot of things wrong with you: you're dramatic and demanding, and sharp-tongued and high-handed, and more than a little bit self-absor—"

"Yes, yes, ha ha." That had earned a full Tarleton pout-scowl. "I am speaking specifically of love. Perhaps it need not matter that I do not fall in love? That, despite my best efforts in that direction, I . . . I find it tiring and tedious and a little bit incomprehensible. It . . ." The pout-scowl vanished, replaced by something a lot more uncertain. "It does not make you think less of me, does it?"

"Of course not," exclaimed Peggy. "I mean, it was bloody inconvenient when I wanted you to be in love with me. But it . . . it seems to be who you are, maybe?"

Belle gave a sharp little nod. "And just because I am not romantically inclined does not mean I do not experience love at all. You might not have realised this about me, but I am a very loving person."

"You are. In your way."

"Indeed I am. Why"—Belle struck a lofty pose—"only today I discovered my dearest friend had, perhaps, not worked as tirelessly on my behalf as she could have done."

"Belle . . ."

"And," Belle continued triumphantly, "I forgave her instantly, without qualm or second thought, because I do, truly, want her to be happy."

In spite of herself, Peggy was conscious of a certain squishiness in the heart region. "Thank you. But you wouldn't have to forgive me if you hadn't tried to *Twelfth Night* me in the first place."

Belle's eyes narrowed. "Your tuberculosis is improving then?"

"I . . . I might not have tuberculosis," Peggy admitted.

"You don't say. Now"—another of Belle's favourite poses, chin uplifted, hands plonked firmly upon her hips—"don't you have an opera singer to be kissing?"

"I do." Peggy flung off her blanket. "I just need to do something first."

Belle's delicately retroussé nose twitched. "Is it wash?"

"Two things," declared Peggy. "I just have to do two things first."

Chapter 16

One very hot and thorough bath later, Peggy was banging on Valentine and Bonny's door. "Are you decent?"

"Never," came Bonny's answer.

"Are you decent enough," she tried again, "that I can come in?"

"That depends on your definition of *decency*."

"Is any part of you inside Valentine or vice versa?"

A longer pause than Peggy would have thought necessary to figure it out. "No."

Nervously, she pushed open the door and went in. Bonny and Valentine's bedroom was a small palace, albeit a surprisingly restrained palace in terms of its decorations: tall windows set into cream-painted panelling, lots of light and space, a vast four-poster whose soft blue hangings matched the curtains and, Peggy thought, Bonny's eyes. Both Valentine and Bonny were in the bed or, in Bonny's case, on it. He was stark naked, on his front, with his legs swinging idly behind him, a copy of *Clermont* propped up in front of him and a half-eaten piece of strawberry cake in his hand.

"Hello," said Bonny, unperturbed.

"Hello," said Peggy, also unperturbed. She had seen Bonny unclad almost as often as she'd seen Belle. In very different contexts, obviously. But they had swum together often enough, and Bonny, in general, saw little benefit in hiding the bounty nature had bestowed upon him—by which he meant his arse. And, indeed, it was currently pale, plump, and delectable upon the rumpled sheets.

"I don't suppose"—Valentine was sitting at the head of the bed, reading the morning paper, and decorously swathed in a pearl silk robe—"it has occurred to you that Peggy might have preferred you attired?"

Bonny turned a page. "I see little benefit in hiding the bounty nature has bestowed upon me."

"Have you considered," asked Valentine mildly, "that perhaps not everyone wants to see your bounty?"

"Don't worry"—Peggy waved a cheerful hand—"I've seen it plenty. And his front bounty too."

Valentine got that abashed, faintly jealous look he often got at the thought of Bonny in the context of anyone else. "I presume, though, that isn't your reason for this visit?"

"It could be," protested Bonny.

"It's not," put in Peggy firmly. "I was wondering if I could borrow Periwinkle?"

If Valentine was possessive of his husband, he was almost as possessive of his valet. Actual alarm settled over his features. "Why? What for? For how long? This is very irregular, Peggy. A man's valet is his castle."

"A man's valet"—Bonny knocked his foot reassuringly against Valentine's arm—"is a person."

"Yes, but he's *my* person. We've been together for a very long time."

"The thing is," explained Peggy, "I've decided to take back Calais for the British crown, and I think Periwinkle would be exactly the right person to ride at my side."

"No." Still visibly alarmed, Valentine cast aside his paper. "Absolutely not. He could be harmed, or killed, or unavailable to me when I need him. I'm sorry but—"

"She's joking, flower," said Bonny in a singsong voice. "Because you're being unreasonable about your valet."

"Periwinkle"—Valentine's lip quivered slightly—"is very special to me."

Peggy was getting the distinct impression she'd started something she wasn't prepared for. "Um," she tried.

"If he's that special to you"—Bonny's tone was now sliding towards petulant—"maybe you should put your tongue up *his* arse for a change."

"I do not want," Valentine retorted, "to put my tongue up Periwinkle's arse, Bonny, on account of his being my valet. I want to put my tongue up your arse, on account of your being the man I love."

Peggy cleared her throat. "You know I'm still here? I can come back if you want to keep arguing about anilingus. But I wanted to see if maybe Periwinkle would"—she ran her fingers through the fall of her curls—"cut my hair?"

"I'm not sure he has any experience with—" began Valentine before Bonny's previously affectionate foot kicked him in the shoulder. "I apologise," he said instead. "I did not think that through. But"—his eyes sought Peggy's, his expression both caring and inescapably confused—"have you thought this through?"

She shrugged. "How much thought does it require? Hair grows back."

"What if you don't like it?"

Trying not to gnaw the inside of her cheek, Peggy told herself that Valentine was just a cautious person. "I don't like it now."

"Why not?" Valentine had that faintly wounded expression other people sometimes got when you spoke of changing your appearance, however trivially. "Your hair is beautiful."

"And it'll still look beautiful"—surprisingly, this was Bonny—"if it's shorter. But even if it didn't, even if it looked appalling, it wouldn't matter, because it's Peggy's hair and she can do what she likes with it."

She gazed at him, startled but pleased. "You really listened to me the other night, huh?"

"Maaaaaybe." Bonny flicked over a page. "And I'm assuming you returned the favour."

"Maybe," Peggy conceded.

"And let me guess: Belle doesn't hate you?"

"Why would Belle hate Peggy?" asked Valentine, who had risen with the typical reluctance he displayed whenever he was obliged to leave his bed before he was completely ready—which, being a duke, he seldom was—and had gone to ring for Periwinkle.

"Something about an opera singer," offered Bonny.

And, mercifully, Valentine didn't press the matter, perhaps because he was too worried about his valet being so taken by the process of cutting Peggy's hair that he quit Valentine's service instantly. Periwinkle did not, as it happened, quit Valentine's service instantly, but he was otherwise perfectly amenable to the task. Indeed, if he thought there was anything unusual about the request at all, he kept his silence, and a couple of hours later, Peggy had a fashionably windswept look that—even she had to admit—wasn't likely to discourage romantically inclined young ladies from asking her for poetry.

It was the oddest feeling, looking in the mirror afterwards. Like she was lighter all over somehow, the stir of air against the back of her neck such a tiny thing, and yet so profoundly . . . *freeing*. At first she wasn't sure if she recognised herself. And then she realised it was the opposite: that she was only just beginning to.

She had packed mostly for London, which meant sixty-seven thousand subtly different styles and types of dresses, but she had at least one pair of pantaloons right down at the bottom of her travelling trunk. She pulled them on and bound her breasts before digging out a loose lawn shirt and a brown velvet tailcoat. Unlike Valentine, she was not willing to labour for several hours over the perfect cravat, so she tied an easy barrel knot and left it at that.

Once again, the image in the glass disorientated her, simply by looking how she wanted—in this moment—to look. Probably there would come a time when she wanted long hair again. Tomorrow she might go back to gowns. She didn't know, she couldn't tell. But that in itself carried a kind of rightness with it. Not having to decide.

With a bounce in her step—her new shorter hair bouncing right along with her—Peggy set out for the marquess's house. She didn't bother calling for a carriage because having to call a carriage to take you to the other side of the same damn square was the sort of nonsense society inflicted on ladies. And she wasn't—had never been—a lady, and she was through with letting people force her to pretend to be one.

"I've come to see Orfeo," Peggy told the impassive butler who had admitted her last time.

If he recognised her, he gave no sign of it, beyond the faintest curl of his lip. "Orfeo isn't here."

Peggy cringed slightly. That sounded like a brush-off. The sort of thing a servant would tell you if you'd pissed off their master, or a guest of their master, past the point of redemption. "When will they be back? Can I wait?"

"I mean"—somehow the butler contrived to curl his lip even more, without changing his expression in the slightest—"they are no longer resident. At least for the moment."

"Where are they resident, then? Did they say?"

"I did not enquire."

Whatever Peggy had been planning for—and honestly she hadn't got much beyond *Hello, sorry I kissed you*, or rather *Not sorry I kissed you, can we do it again*—she hadn't considered the possibility of Orfeo just . . . not being there. "But I thought . . . that is . . . wouldn't the marquess want to know? Where they were?"

"I'm sure His Lordship could locate his guest should he so wish."

God, was this her fault? Surely not. She'd behaved pretty awfully, she'd be the first to admit that, but "I have suddenly left my home" didn't, in any world, connect to "We had a bad kiss." Or rather, "We had a good kiss that ended badly."

"I don't suppose," she tried, "you know *why* they left?"

The butler was radiating that "I want you to go away" energy so endemic to butlerkind. "Again, I did not enquire."

"And they didn't leave, I don't know, a note? A forwarding address? A message of any kind?"

"I don't believe they would have had time to."

He was fucking with her. Peggy was increasingly convinced he was fucking with her. This was going beyond butler and into obstructive. "Why," she asked with frankly outrageous patience, "would they not have had time to leave a message?"

"The men who took them away seemed possessed of quite a sense of urgency."

Peggy's mouth fell open. "Wait, what? They were taken away? Men took them away?" She surged forward so forcefully that the butler actually took a step back. "You'd better tell me exactly what happened here, or . . . or I'll use every tool at my disposal as someone who isn't a butler to make your life somewhere between mildly and vastly unpleasant."

"I believe," said the butler hurriedly, "the men were bailiffs, intent upon recouping a debt."

"Oh my God. And you just let them drag Orfeo off to prison or worse?"

The man's mouth compressed in a sour line. "What was I supposed to do? As you have been at pains to remind me, I am a mere butler."

"I don't know. Sold a candlestick?"

"As a general rule, my master prefers I watch over his possessions, rather than dispose of them."

"But Orfeo is your master's guest. His . . ." Suddenly Peggy realised she had no idea about the relationship between Orfeo and the marquess and didn't want to even approach suggesting there could be anything possession-like about it. "Patronee?"

"That may well be"—there was a sneer in the butler's voice—"but that is nothing to do with me. And now I bid you good day."

The door closed in Peggy's face with the finality of a "fuck you." She was beginning to see why Orfeo mistrusted servants. And whatever was she to do? She'd been braced for an uncomfortable conversation, not to find Orfeo gone, dragged off like a criminal with no-one to help or speak for them. When had it even happened? While she'd been moping uselessly in bed? Would the theatre know more? Surely it was at the very least *relevant* to them if their lead soprano had just . . . vanished?

She sprinted back to Valentine's house and took a carriage to the King's Theatre, where, after some insisting—insisting went so much better in trousers—the manager told her that *no*, he hadn't heard from Orfeo, and *no*, it wasn't unusual because singers (especially Italian singers) were unreliable shits, and *this*, by the way, was why they had understudies, and fuck this whole ruddy business. So that was that, and Peggy was no closer than she had been to discovering Orfeo's circumstances or whereabouts.

It crossed her mind that their patron might be able to help, but she had no idea who or where he was, beyond his name and what Sir Horley had told her about him. She could have gone back and yelled at the butler—something that had been only passingly effective the first time round—but even supposing she found out how to contact the marquess, it was likely to take weeks for a letter to arrive and just as long for him to come back, assuming he cared enough about his protégé to set off immediately.

Cared about or at least felt protective enough of?

In any case, that would still be an untold amount of time Orfeo was . . . in prison? Even the thought was outlandish. And more than a little terrifying.

That left Peggy with only one course of action. She told Valentine's coachman to take her to Newgate—might as well start with the worst-possible option—and climbed aboard. Thankfully, following a liberal series of bribes, it did not seem Orfeo was in Newgate. Next she tried the King's Bench out of a sense of what, under the circumstances, passed for optimism, as it was supposed to be . . . better? If you had money and connections, which, while it was strange to think of a debtor having money, Orfeo surely had access to money and connections aplenty.

They were not at the King's Bench.

"Uh," said Peggy to the coachman who had found himself on a whistle-stop tour of London's penitentiaries, "Marshalsea, I guess? And then the Fleet?"

It was a short journey across Southwark to what was now the second site of Marshalsea, although she disembarked at Saint George's Church, as the prison itself clearly hadn't been constructed with the expectation of carriages. It was long and narrow, a rectangular huddle of pressed-together houses, surrounded first by a slender yard, all paved over, and then by high stone walls, topped with spikes. There was something about the sight, even after visiting two other gaols today, that made Peggy's throat tighten. Some combination of the cramped quarters and the lack of light, the way the spire of Saint George's fell across those squalid little buildings like the shadow of a blade.

At the gate, she engaged the turnkey—a shuffling, stooping fellow by the name of Tampin—in what was becoming a familiar ritual of questioning, blandishing, bullying, and bribing. To her surprise, and burgeoning horror, this time it bore fruit: Orfeo, or the *Eye-talian*, according to Tampin, was here. After plying him with an additional handful of coin, Peggy was admitted, the heavy iron gates opening just enough to allow her through, then slamming shut behind her in a fashion she would have found unnecessarily dramatic had it also not been ominous on some fundamental, soul-clenching level.

Chapter 17

Inside, the walls swallowed what was left of the light, and the stench from the nearby wells mingled almost unbearably with the fetid reek of too many bodies in too close proximity. Peggy wrestled her handkerchief over her face, but it didn't help. Likely the only thing that might would be amputating her own nose, which could lead to other problems down the line. Keeping close to Tampin, from necessity rather than comradeship, she followed him through the gatehouse and the keeper's lodge and finally out again into the prison yard—if such a mean strip of stone could so be called. Everywhere she looked was a sense of stagnation and decay: even the greyish weeds, what few of them grew, were as brittle as skeletons.

And this was where Orfeo had been taken? Of course, Peggy knew in abstract of such places—of debtors and criminals and punishment—but nothing could have prepared her for the reality of it. The sheer inhumanity of people corralled with less consideration than cattle for infractions that, ultimately, in no way justified the consequences.

Of the barrack-like block of houses that comprised the main prison, some of the rooms had been given over to shops or, Tampin explained, lay within the gift of the turnkeys themselves for the more genteel—by which he meant more solvent—type of prisoner. Apparently Orfeo was not this type of prisoner, so it was to Staircase 3 that they made their way and up Staircase 3 they climbed. The smell here was even worse, and worse, too, was the noise. It rose and fell with ceaseless inharmony, a constant impingement upon the senses. Another reminder of too many people living too closely upon each other.

At the stop of the staircase, the wood of which was dark with rot, Tampin made a great show of knocking upon a rickety door. From within, Peggy could hear voices, but she could not pick out Orfeo's amongst them. At the knock, however, silence fell—or the nearest thing to it that was possible within the walls of Marshalsea.

After a borderline-unreasonable wait, the door creaked open a crack, to reveal a diminutive, wiry gentleman in a shabby black coat that would once have been extremely well cut indeed.

"Good afternoon," he said, in a broad South London accent, and an air of great hauteur. "To what do we owe the pleasure of this unanticipated visitation?"

Before either Peggy or Tampin could answer, another voice called out, "Who's calling, my love?"

"Whom," said the man in the doorway, "shall I say is calling?"

"Tampin," said Tampin. "With a guest for the new one."

The man's soft grey eyes flickered over Peggy. "A guest, you say? And no calling card. Most irregular."

"What's that?" came the second voice.

"A caller," relayed the first man, despite the fact his companion could blatantly hear everything that was happening, "without a calling card."

"No calling card?" repeated the other. "What is the world coming to?"

"No manners," agreed the first man. "No fucking manners at all."

Peggy flailed upon the threshold. "This is a prison. I didn't bring my calling cards. Can I just come in, please?"

"A prison." The man in the doorway sucked in an outraged breath. "How very dare you. Why, you stand before the residence of no less a person than the Duke of Marshalsea himself."

"And," added the man from inside, "his lovely duchess."

The lovely duchess fluttered his eyelashes.

"Right." Peggy repressed a sigh. "Margaret Delancey, of the Devonshire Delanceys, to see Orfeo, if you please. Sorry not to have left a calling card. No snub was intended."

The Duchess of Marshalsea looked intrigued. "Of the Devonshire Delanceys, you say?"

Peggy nodded.

"The Devonshire Delanceys?" asked the Duke of Marshalsea, still within. "Not the Hampshire Delanceys? Or the Somerset Delanceys? Or the Up-Your-Arse Delanceys?"

"Definitely not the Up-Your-Arse Delanceys," Peggy said. "They're a cadet branch, and we don't acknowledge them. Look, can I just see Orfeo? Please?"

Keeping his body in the doorway, the Duchess of Marshalsea turned to the room behind him. There was a brief pause. Whispered conversation. And then he turned back. "Orfeo is not at home to visitors."

"Oh, for God's sake." Peggy reached, as she had been reaching on a fairly regular basis, for her coin purse. "How much to see Orfeo?"

The duchess recoiled. "Is it treason"—he glanced over his shoulder—"to attempt to suborn through means of material gain a member of the British aristocracy?"

"No, my love," came the answer. "That's just how society works."

"Fair dues." The duchess returned his attention to Peggy. "Five bob, please."

Peggy paid up.

"You still can't see Orfeo, though."

"What? Why?"

The duchess curled his lip. "Because, Margaret Delancey, of the Up-Your-Arse Delanceys, they don't want to see you."

Peggy was having a non-ideal day. Probably not quite as non-ideal as having been arrested for one's debts would have been. But it was still not good. She'd seen more gaols, and been more worried, than in the rest of her life combined. "Well," she called out, "I'm happy you've made friends *in prison*, Orfeo. Is it really the time, though, to be holding a grudge?"

"Nothing but time in prison, ducky," said the duchess. "It's kind of the whole point."

"Oh, come on." Peggy paced in the sweltering corridor. "I'm sorry. I'm so sorry. I was trying to see you to say sorry before I learned you'd been dragged off by bailiffs. And I'm still sorry. Not for kissing you, obviously, but for being an arse about it. And . . ." Her eye fell on Tampin, who was still standing there, watching the proceedings like a sheep at the theatre. "Do you not have somewhere to be?"

"Not really," said Tampin.

"Right," said Peggy. "No problem. Glad you're having fun." It crossed her mind that maybe he'd lied to her and Orfeo wasn't here at all, and now she was just paying to embarrass herself in front of strangers, but she wasn't sure he'd have the wherewithal. Tampin's capacity for criminality gave every impression of topping out at corruption—which, given his job, probably seemed for the best. "Orfeo?" She raised her voice again. "Please? I really am sorry, and I really do want to see you. If you ever felt inclined to kiss me again, I wouldn't be an arse about it. And, also, if you don't want to kiss me again, I would understand that too. But, whatever your stance on the whole kissing thing, it's probably not good that you're in prison right now? And maybe we should do something about that?"

A murmur from beyond the door. "They wish me to tell you," the duchess explained, "that there is no *we* here."

"This is a long way to go for pride."

"Apparently you have absolutely no notion how far an Italian will go for pride."

"Orfeo"—Peggy tried to sound less irate and more conciliatory—"I'm literally begging you."

"It doesn't seem very literal to me," remarked the duchess, who was evidently a helpful sort.

"Well, let me come in, and I'll be as literal as you like."

"Can I come in too?" asked Tampin.

Peggy eyed him. "Who knows. Did you bring a calling card?"

The duchess stepped out of the doorway with a flourish. "Tampin is always welcome at our court."

Their court was a square room, not more than ten feet across, with a sloping ceiling and a single window. It would have made an acceptable cupboard. For three people to sleep in and live, and receive two visitors, it was unendurable. A matched pair—well, matched in terms of sagginess, scruffiness, and the general air of broken-downyness—of single beds were shoved against two of the walls, their heads closing away part of a corner, and into the third wall was set a fireplace, currently unnecessary because of the smothering closeness of the air. This left very little space for anything else, and yet space had been found, for ramshackle heaps of personal items—mostly books and fabric and sundry objects—that gave the room the mien of a particularly haphazard pawnbroker's, and a rough wooden table with a set of clearly scavenged chairs.

At this table, Peggy found Orfeo, clad only in boots, breeches, and a linen shirt, all rather the worse for wear, their lank hair partially caught up in a queue. And, with them, one of the biggest men she had ever seen, heavy-set and broad-shouldered, though slightly run to seed. She could also have described him as one of the ugliest men she'd ever seen—his face and hands were a map of fading scars, his eyes an unprepossessing pond-water green, and his nose had been broken so many times it was little more than a shapeless bulge—but that felt unnecessarily judgemental. He was lounging quite at his ease, in a magnificent coat that had been painstakingly constructed from scraps of cloth.

"Um," said Peggy politely. "Hello? Your Grace?" And then, to Orfeo, "Are you all right?"

They made a dismissive gesture. "As you see, quite well."

"What happened?"

"Apparently"—their shrug was equally dismissive—"some people thought I owed them money. I did not have any money. So here I am. That does not, however, explain what has brought you to—what do they call it again? The Palace of Marshalsea."

"I was looking for you. I came to apologise."

One of their brows twitched sceptically. "This is quite a trip, for an apology."

"Well," Peggy said ruefully, "I owed you quite an apology."

"And this is the apology?" Orfeo's tone was not encouraging.

The duke and duchess offered little gasps, as if they had put their thumbs to a hot stove.

"Well, I was mostly shouting the apology through the door. But yes." Peggy dropped to one knee before Orfeo, trying not to think too hard about the state of the floor. "I fucked up, and I've come to beg your forgiveness."

"I am not sure I'm very inclined towards someone who doesn't know what they want."

The truth had never felt less like a clean blade. It cut jaggedly and deep, but Peggy suspected she had earned its wounds. Orfeo, who had little reason to trust anyone, had trusted her. And she had failed them. Rejected them. Let her uncertainties rule her, when she should have trusted back. She bowed her head, ashamed.

"Not all of us have our lives irretrievably bent towards being famous opera singers," she pointed out—though Marshalsea was a strange place to speak of the complexities of freedom. She risked an upwards glance, but Orfeo's expression offered nothing. "It's . . . it's not that I don't know what I want," she went on. "It's more that I don't know how to have it or what it might mean if I do. But none of that changes the fact that I want you."

Finally, a flicker in Orfeo's eyes. The faintest suggestion of light.

"I want you," Peggy repeated, a little startled by how easily the words came. How overdue they felt. "Whatever that looks like. Whatever it means. However long it lasts. The rest I'll . . ." She flapped a hand. "I don't know. I'll work out someday. It doesn't matter."

"And your so-dear friend?" asked Orfeo, more than a little bitterly.

Peggy blushed. "Well, we talked and—"

"And she gave you permission? I am not sure that is the compliment you think it is."

More hot-stove noises from the duke and duchess.

"We talked," Peggy said, trying again, "and it was right that we did. I should have told Belle I couldn't do what she asked the moment I met you. But I didn't, and I'm sorry for that too. The truth is . . ." She paused, biting her lip. "The truth is, I'm a bit of a coward, Orfeo. There."

It was not the sort of speech she would ever have imagined making in front of an audience. Or, indeed, at all.

"You came here," offered the duchess unexpectedly. "That don't seem like the act of a coward."

Peggy peered over her shoulder. Given the limited available chairs, Tampin had claimed one, and the duchess was comfortably enthroned upon the duke's lap—an arrangement, Peggy suspected, that might have been undertaken even had the seating possibilities been otherwise. "I'm not a coward about doing things. I'm a coward about . . . myself."

Something seemed to soften in Orfeo. "You're not a coward, mio principe. Sometimes living, simply as we are, is the greatest act of courage there is."

"I'm not always very good at living," Peggy admitted, taking this hint of understanding from Orfeo as permission to rise. "It's easier to be . . . um. Part of someone else's story—does that make sense?"

"And yet"—Orfeo was regarding her steadily—"you keep trying to be the hero of mine."

"Some hero, to kiss you and run away after."

Their mouth quirked up very slightly, their beauty marks dancing. "A hero with a little bit of anti-hero is the best kind of hero."

"Is it, though?" wondered Peggy. "Also, can we do something about this prison situation you're in at the moment?"

It was strange how . . . ordinary Orfeo appeared in this particular setting. A slightly too-tall figure with dull hair and tired eyes. And Peggy didn't care in the slightest. "I have no idea," they said. "But if you mean to initiate a gaolbreak, you should probably wait until you are not right next to the turnkey."

Tampin gave a little start. "What?"

"They're teasing, darling," said the duchess, reaching out to pat his arm.

"I was thinking more"—Peggy tried to pace but found nowhere to pace to—"what about the marquess; surely he wouldn't want . . ." She waved a hand. "*This.*"

Orfeo glanced away. "I am beginning to suspect my patron may not be best pleased with me. I think he might believe I am growing, hmm, distracted?"

"Yes, but there's *not pleased* and then there's *actual prison.*"

"What do you think prison is, Up-Your-Arse Delancey?" The Duke of Marshalsea spoke up suddenly, his voice a low rumble.

"It's where . . . we." Suddenly Peggy found herself on uncertain ground. "Put criminals?"

The duke turned the dull sheen of his eyes upon her. "It's an exercise of power. How do you think any of us got here?"

"You . . . couldn't pay your debts?"

"Because?"

"You . . . didn't have enough money?"

"Because?"

"Financial mismanagement?" Peggy squeaked.

Sliding an arm about the duchess, the duke drew him closer. "Why don't you tell this young person of your financial mismanagement, my love?"

"Once upon a time," said the duchess, in a weary, singsong voice, "there was a tailor with a small but successful shop. Wanting to expand his business, he fell into debt for 40s. On attempting to repay the debt, in the full amount, he was told the debt was now 60s. Foolishly, he refused and was the very next day served with a Marshalsea writ. The tailor, still afflicted with foolishness, took the case to an attorney, who advised him to defend it, the first step of which required him to pay the attorney 25s." The duchess paused, settled his head against the duke's shoulder, and then continued. "The next day he was served again, with a notice of declaration. On return to the man of the law, 2 guineas were demanded to plead the case, which the tailor—believing in the justice of his cause—paid again. Another week, and this time the tailor received a notice of trial. For this, the lawyer now charged 5s, citing briefs, fees to counsel, subpoenas, and so on. Being, by this point, unable to lay hands on any further funds, and having parted with . . . what had I parted with?"

"£3 7s," returned the duke.

"Indeed. So," the duchess went on, "having parted with £3 7s in order to save 20s, the tailor could no longer retain the lawyer and therefore was obliged to suffer judgement to go by default. A judgement which consigned him to prison, and here you find me still, my landlord, on learning of my incarceration, having seized all my other possessions."

Peggy cringed. "I . . . I'm sorry. That's . . . that . . ." A cut from Peggy's quarterly allowance would have covered it.

"It's a common story," said the duke.

"Is yours?" she asked.

To that, he simply shrugged. "Most likely. But don't worry"—the duke offered her a cracked half moon of a smile—"we're all coming into money tomorrow."

Getting the sense she'd blundered over some invisible line, Peggy turned back to Orfeo. "Look, can I ask, how much do you owe?"

"I have no idea," Orfeo told her loftily.

"If you don't know how much you owe, how do you expect to get out?"

"Well"—their glance was infuriatingly proud—"I am coming into money tomorrow."

"You're coming into money," said Peggy fiercely, "right the hell now."

This seemed to cut through their self-conscious languor. "Peggy, no. I refuse."

"What's the alternative? You stay here?"

"Are we insulted?" asked the duchess. "Tampin, my duck, are you insulted? When you labour night and day to squeeze every last drop of liquidity from your beloved charges?"

Tampin looked more than a little alarmed. "Here now, I'm not like you gents. I ain't one for squeezing anything."

"I *have* been staying here," Orfeo pointed out, ignoring the interruption.

"And the plan is just to wait for . . . wait for what exactly?"

"My patron will . . ." They broke off, flushing slightly. "My patron will forgive me. He always does. I am too valuable for him to do otherwise."

"You'll be less valuable if you get, I don't know, smallpox. Or dysentery."

"And the damp," added the duchess, "can't be good for your voice."

There was a long silence. Then Orfeo's shoulders slumped, their hand drifting nervously to their throat. "There's a writ somewhere."

"I have it." The duke drew a piece of paper from an interior pocket and carefully unfolded it, spreading it over the table. "There . . ." Orfeo barely glanced his way. "50s to a Mr. Ridmark, a milliner."

Peggy cast a frustrated look at Orfeo. "Or I can leave you here to get dysentery and die."

"What you need to do"—the duke drew her attention back towards the writ—"is find two respectable property owners to guarantee the debtor will appear at trial or otherwise pay their dues. Or you can get an affidavit from the original creditor that the debt has been paid off."

"And then Orfeo will be free to go?"

The duke made a "not quite" motion. "After the discharge fee of 10s 10d."

"Hang on," said Peggy. "What? You have to pay money to leave the prison you were put into for not having any money?"

"We don't make the rules." The duchess settled himself more comfortably upon the duke's lap. "And your coat don't fit proper across the shoulders."

Peggy rolled her eyes. "Yes, I was going to stop by Weston's, but, oh, I couldn't on account of not being explicitly a man."

"Perhaps I'll do it for you," murmured the duchess, "next time you come by. Assuming you do, of course."

"Why would I not?"

"Because nobody *actually* pays off someone else's debts. And, besides"—he smiled, looking younger, unexpectedly boyish in such a grim place—"I might have died of dysentery before then."

Peggy stood, pulling her coat—which truly did not fit well across the shoulders—more tightly around her. "Don't joke about it. Dysentery isn't a joke. I think there's actual blood . . . coming out of . . . bad places."

It wasn't the best goodbye she'd ever given. But, in her defence, it was her first time in prison.

Chapter 18

Peggy passed a restless, useless night, worried about Orfeo and feeling nebulously guilty for being rich and comfortable. Physically comfortable anyway. Emotionally speaking, she was quite the opposite.

She'd gone straight to Ridmark the milliner's after leaving Marshalsea. The shop had been closed, but she had been loud and annoying enough that Mr. Ridmark had, in the end, admitted her. Peggy was no more satisfied to be mistaken for a gentleman than she was to be mistaken for a lady, but—if one had to be mistaken at all—being mistaken for a gentleman came with certain advantages. Specifically, greater tolerance extended for being loud and annoying.

In any case, once Peggy had disrupted a not particularly innocent milliner's evening, he proved amenable to settling the debt and offering the required affidavit, especially when Peggy offered a more than reasonable rate of interest and compensation for the disturbance. She would have preferred to return to Orfeo immediately, but even in His Majesty's judicial system there was a limit to what bribery could accomplish, and she did not think she would be admitted to Marshalsea after dark.

She did, however, turn up a little after dawn in order to reprise her strategy of wearing breeches, and being loud and annoying and rich. It worked, and she was greeted by a sleepy-eyed Tampin, who contrived to do everything even more lackadaisically than the day before. This included letting her settle Orfeo's accounts, which in turn included both admittance and discharge fees, rent, and other sundries which she was sure were either made up or illegal or, in some cases, made up and illegal.

The room Orfeo was sharing with the Duke and Duchess of Marshalsea was somehow even more cramped than she remembered, chill without a fire, and grey-washed by what little early-morning light its single window admitted. The duke and duchess were still abed, pressed together like two pieces of punctuation beneath the blanket they shared, but Orfeo was awake, seated at the table, much as they had been yesterday, in their shirtsleeves, with their hair drawn loosely back from their face. There was an odd stillness to them, so very different from their usual animation, or the magnetism that infused their performances.

"Um," said Peggy. "Hello."

They glanced her way. "So here you are again to rescue me, mio principe?"

"I wouldn't call it a rescue. I haven't fought a single dragon or solved a single riddle."

One of their eyebrows flicked up sharply. "That you know of."

"Do you want me to get back in my cart, Guinevere?"

"I . . . I beg your pardon?"

Peggy sighed. "Never mind. Just, you're free to go."

"And of course"—Orfeo offered a thin smile—"you want nothing in return."

"What I want is for you not to be in prison. As far as I'm concerned, that's win-win."

The Duchess of Marshalsea stuck his head out of the blanket. "She came back for you, didn't she? Can't you argue with her somewhere else? We're trying to sleep."

"Yes," said Peggy. "Can you argue with me somewhere else? Like my carriage, for example. Well, Valentine's carriage. But still. In the carriage I have waiting."

Rising, Orfeo swept into a curtsy. "As you will."

"And leave your coat," added the duchess. "It hurts my soul, it does."

Not wanting to add a secondary layer of argument to the argument Orfeo clearly still wanted to be having with her, Peggy stripped off her coat and put it on the table, along with some coins to cover alterations. She didn't have much hope of ever seeing the garment again—and she wouldn't have voluntarily come back to Marshalsea if someone, for a change, had paid her—but she didn't want to be rude. And the duchess was right: the coat really *didn't* fit across the shoulders.

Orfeo had no possessions to gather, so they were ready to leave the moment Peggy was. Or would have been if not for—

"Why is Tampin standing in the doorway with his hand out?" she asked.

"Tip," said the duke.

"Tip?" repeated Peggy. "He's a turnkey, not a waiter."

"I've got to eat," Tampin pointed out, his hand unwavering.

"You can buy food with the rest of the money you've extorted from me. You can buy enough food to treat the entire prison to pie and mash."

Tampin's mouth turned down sadly. "You don't think I'm good at my job?"

"You're lazy"—Peggy started counting on her fingers—"corrupt, apathetic, careless, immoral, and by all accounts a bit dim."

The duke gave a muffled chuckle. "An excellent turnkey then."

"Fine." Sighing, Peggy pressed a shilling into Tampin's palm. "There. Thank you for your service."

And, with that, they really were at liberty to leave. It was a relatively short journey down the rickety staircase, across the yard, and out through the gates. They walked in silence, which made Peggy too aware of every noise: the tap of her bootheels, the clang of metal behind them, the way the trapped and ceaseless sounds of Marshalsea gave way to the everyday noise of London. Which did not feel so everyday once you'd been locked away from it, even if only for a little while. The sky had not yet found any blueness, so it was a cloud-streaked pewter. Nevertheless, Orfeo turned their face up to it like a flower, and Peggy was relieved to see them do it. She didn't need their gratitude, exactly, but some sign of . . . something? That was good.

They made, she realised, a rather outlandish pair just then: Orfeo dishevelled, both of them coatless, and, in their own particular fashion, ambiguous. It should probably have made her feel self-conscious. But instead, it just made her defiantly happy.

"Where should I take you?" Peggy asked once they'd reached the carriage. "My place? Your place? The Fleet?"

Orfeo's eyes flicked to hers. "You don't have to take me anywhere."

"So, I'll just leave you on the street then?"

"I am not . . ." They broke off and then continued anyway. "I am not your *problem*, Peggy."

"I don't see you as a problem." She didn't quite kick one of the carriage wheels in frustration, but her foot hovered. "Are you still annoyed with me because of the kiss? Or are you annoyed because I got you out of actual prison? Because that seems a really unfair thing for you to be annoyed with me over."

"I am not annoyed," they told her, in a voice that sounded just the opposite. "I do not like feeling—and you may deride me for the irony of this—indebted."

"But you'd be fine," Peggy snapped, "if I was the marquess?"

"I do not *like* the marquess," Orfeo snapped back. They put a hand to their brow, trying to gather themself. "That is . . . it would be my money they were paying with."

"Then you can pay me back with your money. Now where to?"

Some of the rigidity left Orfeo's shoulders. "Your home, I suppose?"

"Let's go." Having duly instructed the coachman, Peggy pulled open the carriage door and ushered Orfeo inside.

"You should probably sit downwind of me," they remarked as they took a seat. "The accommodations in Marshalsea were far from salubrious."

"I'll live."

Silence enveloped them afresh as they travelled.

"Orfeo," Peggy tried finally. "I feel . . . it's . . . I don't like that you seem to be treating the fact you like me as something bad? This"— she flapped a hand to indicate a general sense of everything—"hasn't changed how I see you or how I think of you. And it definitely doesn't mean you owe me now."

"In this world, everything is a transaction of some kind."

It was like running at a wall. "What did you mean"—she changed tack—"when you said you didn't like the marquess?"

Orfeo flinched very slightly. "I should not have said that. It is rather gauche, is it not, to speak ill of one's patron."

"Well, if he had you thrown into debtor's prison . . ."

"He did not," said Orfeo quickly. "It was more that he did not prevent me being thrown into debtor's prison."

"Has that happened before?"

One of Orfeo's shoulders lifted in the barest of shrugs. "Once. In Italy. Financial management does not interest me. I am"—they cast her a wry look—"after all a star."

"You can be a star who is solvent."

"I *am* solvent." Orfeo sounded perilously close to offended. "I believe I am quite well paid."

"You believe?" Peggy had not meant to be so interrogative. This was not her business. But it also made absolutely no fucking sense.

At this, Orfeo rubbed a hand wearily across their brow. "The marquess manages such matters for me."

"The same marquess you don't like? Who can't even give you a servant to help you get dressed? Who got you sent to debtor's prison? *Twice.*"

"I should not have said I do not like him. He is a good patron. Without him, I would still be singing for cardinals."

"Why don't you like him?"

At last Orfeo turned from the window, through which they had been watching London sweep by in an anonymous blur of houses, shop fronts, and passing carriages. "I'm not sure. I just . . . don't. Truthfully, I do not like many people."

Peggy raised a sceptical brow.

And Orfeo half smiled in response. "Oh, I like to dazzle them. I like them to remember me with awe and longing. I am even happy to enjoy them for a night or so, singly or in groups of two to six."

"That's a very specific number."

"Any more and it gets unpleasantly confusing."

"Good to know."

"Glad to be of service."

Another silence, though it was slightly more comfortable than the last. "My patron thinks I am vain and undisciplined," Orfeo offered abruptly. "And he is correct. Though I have every right to be vain."

"And every right," Peggy suggested, "to be undisciplined."

"Ah, but that is wasting what God has given me, or diminishing the sacrifice I made, or some such thing. Life at the conservatorio, though, was only discipline, and I find I am often resentful of whatever should occasion gratitude." They slanted another look at her, their eyes full of shadows. "What it comes down to, I think, is that I am simply not very nice."

"For what it's worth," Peggy said, undaunted, "I have a really poor history of being attracted to niceness."

One of their hands alighted fleetingly upon her knee. "I grow increasingly concerned you might be a good person. You deserve some-one nice."

At this she rolled her eyes. "Fuck nice. I deserve someone spectacular."

"What about that ordinary life you hold so dear?"

"Ehh . . ." Peggy swished her hand through the air, clinging to the courage she had found in Marshalsea. "Fuck that too."

Chapter 19

Once they arrived at Valentine's, there was a new awkward discussion to be had over whether Orfeo wanted their own room or to share with Peggy. Mainly what they wanted, however, was an understandably expedient bath, so Peggy had arranged one—slightly more conscious than she had been prior to her Marshalsea visit that arranging a bath basically meant making other people provide one. But such was the efficiency and, she hoped, well-paidness of Valentine's domestic staff that they heated the water and carried it upstairs in abundance, and all before breakfast.

Under normal circumstances, watching a . . . well, she wasn't yet sure what Orfeo was to her . . . in any case she might have enjoyed watching them bathe, except for the fact that had she herself just spent the best part of a week in debtor's prison, she would have valued privacy. So she left them to it, kicked off her boots, and lay down on her bed. Just for a moment. Resting her eyes.

And was awoken what felt like many disorientating hours later by the whisper of her name.

"Mrghf?" she said attractively.

"You may be glad to learn"—Orfeo's voice was full of silken promises—"that I am feeling a lot more grateful now."

Opening her eyes, Peggy found the room honey gold with sunlight and Orfeo sitting on the other side of the bed, partially draped in a sheet. Their hair was a perfumed curtain, curling slightly at the ends from dampness. "Oh God."

"No"—and here Orfeo's lips turned into a wicked smile—"I am quite other."

"I told you in the carriage, you don't need to be grateful."

Leaning over her, Orfeo stroked a fingertip across Peggy's throat, where her hastily pulled-off cravat had left it bare. "Perhaps I wish to?"

"This . . ." An involuntary shiver got in the way of whatever sensible thing Peggy had been about to say. "This," she managed, "can't be transactional to me."

"You struck a man down on my behalf. Brought me impossible roses. Removed me from debtor's prison. I should at some point say thank you, no?"

Peggy flailed her feet out of the blankets. "You just have."

The sound Orfeo uttered had a lot less sensual promise in it and a lot more exasperation. "I must give something back."

"You must not."

"I would *like* to."

"Orfeo . . ." Pushing herself upright, Peggy rubbed the sleep from her eyes. "I'm confused. One minute you're annoyed with me; now you're trying to coitus me."

Their lashes fluttered. "I'm a prima uomo. You should expect me to be unpredictable and tempestuous."

"Then why don't you surprise me by being thoughtful and communicative?"

A frown pulled their brows together. "Are you *rejecting* me?"

This was all moving too quickly for a half-exhausted, half-aroused Peggy. "What? No?"

Orfeo rolled away and lay on their back, a hand behind their head, one knee slightly raised to expose the supple length of their thigh. "You gave every impression of wanting me when your friend was posing an obstacle. Is liberty less appealing than you thought it would be?"

"No, getting fucked because you think it'll even some score you're keeping in your head is less appealing than—well, it's not appealing at all."

"Oh, Peggy." Orfeo had a Belle-like ability to sigh whatever Peggy-related utterance they felt needed sighing. "We have had this talk: I am good for music and for fucking, and you may have your choice of either."

"Well," Peggy told them, "I want more than that."

Their expression turned distinctly sardonic. "And to think you insisted this was not to be a transaction."

"I'm only asking for what you offered when I first came to visit: a chance to know you, whatever that looks like."

"I offered that?" murmured Orfeo. "You must have swept me quite off my feet."

"You swept me back." Impulsively, Peggy turned and covered them, sliding her body into the cradle of their thighs like it belonged there. "With your music and your beauty and your audacity."

"Audacity," they repeated. "You are good at finding words I like."

Peggy wrapped a hand around one of Orfeo's wrists and pressed it languidly to the pillow. "I'm sure I can find more."

"You do understand"—their voice had dipped into its softest, most slumbrous register, their breath slipping as slow as honey from between their parting lips—"that nothing has changed. There is no happy after ever I can offer you."

"Then let's be happy now."

"And this"—Orfeo curled their fingers towards their palm, brushing the backs of Peggy's—"makes you happy?"

"I'm in bed with a *star*, aren't I? What's not to like?"

Orfeo laughed at her attempt at theatricality. "No, I meant . . . this specifically." They shifted beneath her and pushed a little against her grip. *"This."*

"Oh. Well." Peggy felt herself blushing a little. "*This* is definitely fun."

There was something unexpectedly uncertain in Orfeo's eyes. "It is your preference?"

"It's *a* preference. But I have a lot of preferences. Frankly, I have so many preferences, I'm not sure you can really call them preferences. What about you?"

"I prefer—as with any other performance—to be in control of what happens to my body."

She released them immediately, lurching sideways to land in a graceless flop on the bed. "Oops. Sorry."

"That is the thing, though, Peggy . . ." Shedding the already inadequate sheet, they followed her over, skin again, and the rough silk of their hair, their paradox of strength and softness. "It is too tempting to lose myself with you. I wish I had known how it would be when I invited you to visit me."

"What were you expecting?"

"To do what I always do. Beguile and intrigue—potentially fuck senseless—and leave after, I suppose. Instead, I ended up asking you for all sorts of things, and then feeling utterly crushed when you would not, or could not, give them to me."

Peggy ran a hand gently down the curve of their flank, feeling against her palm the soft quiver of responsiveness that rippled through them. "Well, I'm still beguiled and intrigued, and you can still fuck me senseless. As long as you're doing it because you want to, not because I got you out of debtor's prison, where you shouldn't have been in the first place."

"Ah, don't." Ducking their head, Orfeo tucked themself against Peggy's shoulder. "You have no idea how much simpler it is to be nothing but Orfeo. Touch me again?"

It was such an odd mixture of command and entreaty—but Peggy would not have resisted regardless. "How do you mean?" she asked as she traced the long groove of their spine with the pads of her fingers. The occasional scratch of her nails.

They shivered sweetly and pressed closer. "Orfeo belongs to music and to the marquess. That makes it easy to be shameless. To feel neither anger nor bitterness nor pain."

"I'm pretty sure feeling anger, bitterness, and pain are an inevitable part of being alive."

Their teeth nipped at Peggy's jaw. "And how often do you feel angry, bitter, and in pain?"

"I mostly get as far as mildly annoyed," Peggy admitted. "And occasionally lovelorn."

"There was a time when singing was the only freedom I had." Sitting up, straddling Peggy—who was more than happy to be straddled—Orfeo tossed their hair back, their naked shoulders gleaming golden-brown through the dark strands. "Perhaps it still is?"

"It doesn't have to be." Peggy sat up, too, gathering Orfeo into her lap. It was odd to be clothed when they were naked, but Orfeo seemed to have no self-consciousness about it at all. They seemed as effortlessly comfortable in their skin as they were in peacock feathers and gold.

"How?" asked Orfeo, a hint of fresh frustration in their voice. "And remember, before you promise me it is simple, that I was fashioned for a life of worship and restriction."

"I suppose . . ." Peggy thought for a moment. "I suppose I'd start by managing my own finances."

"But I have no head for business."

"That's why you hire someone who does—and before you say you don't or can't trust anyone, that's why you hire the right person for you."

Orfeo's expression had grown shuttered and haughty. "How is this different from what the marquess does?"

"Well—what does he do for you exactly? What happens when you need money?"

"Oh . . ." Orfeo gave an apathetic shrug. "I just buy whatever I please, and the marquess settles the bills."

"Except when he doesn't," Peggy pointed out, "and you end up in debtor's prison?"

"It may well have been an accident."

"Do you even know how much you earn?"

After a moment, Orfeo shook their head. "The marquess did not think I needed to be concerned with trivialities. I have never wanted something I was unable to purchase. But then . . . I mostly purchase clothes."

"And millinery."

"Ah yes." Orfeo's laugh danced across Peggy's lips. "My fatally expensive tastes in millinery."

Peggy recalled the bill. "It must have been quite a hat, Orfeo."

"I hope at least it was several hats?"

"It was one hat."

"Does it make it worse or better," they asked, "if I cannot even remember which of my hats it was?"

"It makes it even more important for you to know what the fuck is going on with your money. Has Lady Farrow paid you for appearing at her godawful soiree yet? I mean, I assume you were getting paid?"

Orfeo's eyes went wide with outrage. "What do you take me for, mio principe, an amateur?"

"Right." Peggy disentangled herself from Orfeo and leapt off the bed. "We start there."

Orfeo pushed themself onto an elbow—impossibly inviting, with their long limbs, and all the exquisite ambiguities of their flesh laid bare, elements of masculinity and femininity both, proving the lie of either. "Starting where? And what? You may not have realised, but I am quite exceptionally naked."

"I've . . ." Peggy swallowed. "I've noticed."

"And I had presumed," Orfeo went on, with a lazy cat smile, "we were going to fuck."

"Oh, we are going to fuck, all right."

"I had hoped our fucking might surpass *all right*."

"No, I mean"—Peggy scratched her ear self-consciously—"we are *definitely* going to fuck. Just not if there's any possibility you believe you're beholden to me."

Orfeo offered her a wryly exasperated look. "First your friend whom you love, then some fears for a very particular future, now some arbitrary moral qualm. I will begin to think you all talk."

Returning to the bed, Peggy slipped her hand between Orfeo's thighs, her touch assured, possessive, even a little taunting. "How is this for talk?"

"B-bold words indeed," said Orfeo, their quickened breath catching beautifully.

"See"—putting a knee upon the bed, Peggy leaned over them— "I've read your Machiavelli . . ."

"I wouldn't call him *my* Machiavelli. He was a very strange man."

"In any case, I've read what he has to say about princes. Does this please you, by the way, to be touched like this?"

"Certainly it does . . ." Orfeo arched into Peggy's caresses, pleasure-greedy as ever. "You will not bring me to fulfilment in such a fashion, but I enjoy it. Truthfully, I enjoy your touch in many ways. It has lingered upon me, each time."

"Then it can linger another."

"You are cruel." The words were offered without rancour. Almost as incitement.

"No, I'm not." Peggy shook her head. "I'm *selfish*. In this at least. As a prince should be."

"Did Machiavelli say that? Forgive me, my capacity for sociopolitical discourse has been compromised by your hand upon my cock."

"He didn't exactly say that, and you have a very pretty cock, by the way."

"Of course I do. And it may be appreciated without fear of complication, unlike so many others."

"Actually"—Peggy moved lower, to softer places, where the skin was smooth and hot and intimate—"my cock can *also* be appreciated without fear of complication. Or cocks, I should say, because I have several."

"Well endowed, aren't you?"

"I really am," admitted Peggy, laughing. "And I'll happily introduce you. But we were talking of Machiavelli, remember?"

"Put your fingers inside me, and I won't remember my own name."

She had nothing to ease her entry, so she settled for a slow circling instead. Against the pads of her fingers, Orfeo was at once supple and tender, the muscle yielding slightly like their mouth to her kiss. "Machiavelli . . . ," Peggy went on.

"Why do I feel I am in an unplanned threesome?"

"Machiavelli claimed that what was virtue in others could be the opposite for princes, and vice versa. And therefore . . ." With one last, lingering caress, Peggy drew back.

Orfeo uttered a sound of discontent, a rough thing, like a tiger deprived of prey. "This behaviour seems like it would be vice in anyone."

"What behaviour?"

"Provoking me. Stirring me. Leaving me unsatisfied." Lounging back upon Peggy's pillows, they let their fingers drift the length of their body, lingering in the spots that presumably delighted them the most—nipples, the taut skin of their flanks, the satiny interior of their thighs. "If you wish to view the matter selfishly, then I can assure you that there is . . . as the saying goes . . . much *in it* for you."

Peggy arched a brow. "Is there now?"

Orfeo's first answer was nothing more than a quiet gasp, wrung from their throat by their own ministrations. It was an odd thing to be jealous of and yet, in some small way, Peggy was, wanting to keep the power over their reactions to herself. At least for a little while. "Yes, I am very beautiful, especially when I come. And afterwards you shall find me delightfully pliant."

That did sound far too tempting. "I think," said Peggy, breathing carefully and not leaping on Orfeo in a wild frenzy, "you're misunderstanding my commitment to selfishness."

"Oh?" Orfeo's tone matched the lazy enticement of their hands.

"Mm-hmm. You see, it's not that I don't want you or that I want you to be frustrated or unfulfilled . . ."

"Glad to hear it."

"It's just"—Peggy wrapped a hand about their wrist to still them, something Orfeo readily allowed for all their teasing—"whatever I am to you, or whatever I become, I need it to be for myself alone. And not for even the shadow of a sense of obligation."

Orfeo's eyes were intent upon hers, dark and seeking and unexpectedly soft. "Ah, Peggy. I am too proud and have been too graceless."

"I like that about you," blurted out Peggy, lost in their gaze. "I mean, the first one. I don't think you've been the second."

"You know I have. I will pay you back as soon as the marquess returns. And, in the meantime, there is no-one I would rather owe a moderate amount of money to."

"You're just saying that because you want to be fucked."

"Maybe." Orfeo glinted a grin at her. "But I think I do trust you. It's a little odd of me. I am not sure I have ever trusted anyone before."

"Well, you'll find I'm trustworthy to a fault. It's probably why people keep dragging me into their nonsense."

"And yet now you are the one trying to drag me into nonsense."

"I'm not," Peggy protested. "You know how you said you don't like people very much? Have you ever slept with somebody you liked?"

"I sleep with people for all kinds of reasons . . . curiosity, boredom, appetite."

"That wasn't the question."

Orfeo scowled. "Then, I suppose . . . no, I have not. It has never seemed particularly relevant."

"Well, it's different," Peggy told them. "It's special. In its own kind of way."

Orfeo was still scowling, but there was something sweetly resigned in it too. "You are not going to make a romantic out of me, Peggy. I only play one on stage."

"I'll settle for you remembering it . . . us . . . what we do together."

"You think I am in danger of forgetting? You need to have more confidence in yourself."

That made Peggy laugh. "I don't think you'll forget. But I'm not going to let you cling to any excuses when you look back."

"What excuses do you believe me liable to entertain?"

"Who knows. But I do know that I can't have your music or your future, and I wouldn't take them anyway. So I'll have you now, and I'll have you completely."

"In case you haven't noticed"—Orfeo's expression was somewhere between irritated and amused—"you aren't having me at all."

Peggy patted their knee encouragingly. "Let's go get you well paid. Then I'll see you well fucked."

"Lady Farrow has probably already sent the money to my patron."

"I very much doubt it, Orfeo. I mean, she's rich and he's rich. So she won't have bothered to pay, and he won't have bothered to ask her. Neither of them care."

"And *I* should care?"

"I thought you were supposed to be celebrated in flattery, caresses, and wealth?"

Orfeo was silent for a moment. "Indeed I am. And perhaps you are correct that I owe it to myself to be more concerned with the last."

"I've never known anyone to go to prison for lack of adulation."

"Ah, but"—Orfeo, still visibly aroused, indulged in a languid stretch—"I wither without it."

"Come on. You're stalling."

"I'm not dressed. And all my belongings are elsewhere." Flipping onto their front, Orfeo rested their chin on a platform of their folded elbows and swung their legs up coyly. "It's almost as if the world is telling us to stay in bed."

Chapter 20

Peggy did not think the world was telling them to stay in bed, and she had proven expertise when it came to prolonged bed-themed vacations. But the feeling she remembered from the first time she had visited Orfeo at the marquess's townhouse was back, filling her with a sense of . . . she hardly knew how to describe it. A sense of boundlessness for both herself and the world in general. Like she could just *do* things. Not simply watch them happen.

Although, in this particular instance, what she'd made happen was to borrow some of Valentine's clothes as well as his carriage. He'd seemed fairly relaxed about this, having no present need for either (he and Bonny were picnicking on the drawing room floor), and Orfeo, too, raised no objections—perhaps because of Valentine's exquisite tailoring or because most garments were costumes to them. To anybody, now Peggy thought about it. Seeing Orfeo in relatively sober attire— buff-coloured pantaloons, russet coat—reminded her of Lady Farrow's Musical Whatever. The way they had stepped onto the stage in nothing but black, as if they wanted no distractions from their voice. Like this, even in borrowed clothes, there were no distractions from the endless fascinations of their beauty. The darkness of their eyes and the curve of their mouth, at once so sensual and so cynical.

"What are you staring at?" asked Orfeo, from across Valentine's carriage.

"You," Peggy admitted.

"That much I had gathered for myself."

She winced a little. "You're just so absurdly lovely to look at."

"Oh." Orfeo pushed back a lock of their hair, which they had left loose, a heavy fall of inky black, and smirked. "Yes I am, thank you."

"That's, er, quite a way to take a compliment."

"What is the alternative? Call you a liar?"

"Well no, but—"

"How do you take them?"

"Compliments?" Peggy thought about it a moment. "The usual way? You know, flailing, scuffing, assuming the person was mistaken, deluded, or exaggerating."

"Badly, then?"

"Is it, though?" asked Peggy.

"Yes," said Orfeo. "All you are doing, with your inability to accept sincerely offered praise, is making everyone around you uncomfortable."

"Well, they should have thought of that," retorted Peggy, "before sincerely offering me praise, shouldn't they?"

"Peggy"—leaning across the space between them, Orfeo put their hand upon her hand—"you are endlessly strange and endlessly delightful."

She gave a frantic squirm. "What. No. What? Wait. Strange? Am I strange?"

"Yes, I do not know how someone so bold can also be so self-effacing."

"I'm complex," muttered Peggy aggressively. "It's part of my unique charm."

"It is. And the best thing about it"—Orfeo's smirk, if anything, grew smirkier—"is that I know how to make you flustered."

"Why would you want that?"

"Because it is endearing. And, as we have discussed at some length previously, I am not a very nice person. Besides, you recently left me in a state of"—they paused for a moment, almost visibly trying out words—"excessive concupiscence, for which I am now exacting my revenge."

"I was pretty concupiscenced myself, you know."

"Indeed. And"—Orfeo tweaked one of Peggy's curls—"it suited you."

"Oh my God," she protest-whined. "Stop it."

"Why does it trouble you so much?" asked Orfeo, making no attempt to hide the fact they were laughing at her.

"I don't know. Not everyone likes being the centre of attention."

"You have been the centre of my attention since—I would say since you fainted at my performance, but while that was amusing, I think it was only after you had additionally grappled a man and later brushed my hair that I understood how truly disruptive to my peace of mind you were going to be."

It was a glimpse of Peggy as she was not used to seeing of herself or thinking of herself. "Those are odd things to be attracted to."

"I think it was not the individuality of them, but the sum of them."

"I see," said Peggy, who didn't.

They gave a little shrug, their gaze sliding fleetingly from hers. "You make me feel safe."

It wasn't the first time someone had said something like this to her. "Thanks. I'm sure that's very attractive."

"It is. After all, I used to think the marquess did."

"And now he doesn't?"

"I suppose it is more that the world opened less to me than I thought it would when I left the world of church choirs with him."

"How come?"

Orfeo's fingers drummed an absent tattoo on the side of their leg. "I have travelled Europe, performed at the courts of kings and emperors, and upon some of the greatest stages of our times. I followed my curiosity and seduced as my fancy took me. But it has never occurred to me to think about money. Or that thinking about it could feel like freedom."

"It's odd, isn't it," Peggy asked, "what can feel like freedom?"

Turning to her, Orfeo gently wound one of her curls around a finger. "I like this."

"Me too."

"But Peggy?" Their eyes were intent on hers. "Can it be enough for you?"

"I said it was. Is."

"What changed then?" Their tone was light enough, but they did not break her gaze. "When we first spoke, you were adamant I was not worth it."

Peggy swallowed a yelp. "Oh my God. I didn't mean that. I was just tired of falling in love with people who didn't want the same things I did, and scared of getting my heart broken all over again."

"I have never broken anyone's heart before." Their smile was one of their distant ones. "I will not break yours."

"I can't lie, Orfeo," she said. "I'm not exactly going to be delighted when you leave."

Their eyes slid away from hers. "Even if I stayed, I would take more from you than I gave."

"What do you mean?"

"I can offer you neither name nor legacy."

"I already have a name," Peggy pointed out. "And as for children . . ."

"Yes?"

She wanted to tell them she didn't care. That it didn't matter. That she'd never—

"Do not mistake me for a fool," Orfeo murmured. "I would prefer you didn't lie to me."

"Look," she said, finally. "I don't know. I just don't know."

"And if you had to answer to no-one but yourself?"

A glance out the window confirmed that their destination was still too far away to furnish her with a convenient excuse to end the conversation. "Then. Yes. I mean, probably? Except"—it was hard to think about such things, let alone speak of them—"it could cost me . . . cost me *myself*."

Orfeo tilted their head curiously. "In what way?"

"Well, because if I had a child, then everyone would look at me like I was—they'd say I was—" Bile filled her throat, and she fell helplessly silent.

"Peggy." They tapped her lightly on the knee. "You cannot let who people think you are keep you from being who you are. Few know that so well as I."

"Either way"—Peggy pulled a bright smile out of somewhere—"it's not a today problem. Or even a tomorrow problem."

Orfeo's gaze was warm, though their eyes were sad. "It need not be a problem for you at all."

"Just," said Peggy, with awkward vehemence, "don't think any of that means I want this, with you, any less."

"And what exactly do you think *this* is?"

She would have done anything just then to try and banish their pain. "An adventure of my own for once."

It worked, or partly worked—winning the flash of a smile from Orfeo. And the words themselves felt true enough. There would be time later to think about her future. And, if she had to choose, she would rather have a present with Orfeo—home, family, even heartbreak be damned.

⟨§✿⟩

Their arrival at Lord and Lady Farrow's house was first checked by the butler and then by Lady Farrow herself after they had convinced the butler to admit them.

"I'm sorry"—she blinked at them from amongst her correspondence—"but you want what?"

Orfeo slid a step behind Peggy, as though they were attempting to hide behind her.

"Money," said Peggy crisply. "Orfeo wants to be paid."

"Paid?" repeated Lady Farrow.

Peggy offered a cool stare. "I assume you weren't under the impression that an internationally renowned opera star was performing at your home solely from the goodness of their heart?"

"Well . . ." Lady Farrow looked as though she might, in fact, have thought that. "I suppose not. But surely Art"—and here she cast her eyes heavenwards, to where she apparently believed Art resided—"is the greatest of callings, and should not be sullied by the sordid to-and-fro of commerce."

"You must have sordidly to-and-froed a bit to get Orfeo here in the first place," Peggy pointed out.

"We had some correspondence with the marquess. But I do not involve myself in *business*. I just . . ." Lady Farrow paused loftily. It had not occurred to Peggy before that a pause could be lofty, and she was friends with Arabella Tarleton. "I just create a space for Art to flourish."

Orfeo had slipped their hand into Peggy's. "Perhaps," they murmured, "we should leave?"

"We're not leaving," said Peggy firmly. She put her mouth close to their ear and whispered, "Flattery, caresses, and money, remember?" before turning her attention back to Lady Farrow. "So, this art-flourishing space you create? I'm going to assume its creation involves spending a certain amount of—oh, what do you call it? That stuff you give to tradespeople? Money, maybe?"

Lady Farrow fluffed up like an irate housecat. "One cannot put a price on the proper ambience."

"Well, actually, people do put a price on it, and you, at some point, pay that price."

"This"—Lady Farrow was still radiating displeasure—"is an aesthetically barren conversation, and I mislike it intensely."

Peggy felt Orfeo tense beside her. But Peggy didn't care whether her conversation was aesthetic or not. "And it'll be over," she said, "the moment you recognise that you should value Orfeo at least as much as you value candles and uncomfortable chairs."

"How dare you." This was evidently such an affront to Lady Farrow that she swept to her feet. "There is no-one in London, except possibly my husband, who holds artists in higher regard than I."

"And you know what's a really good way of showing regard? Paying people."

Lady Farrow opened her mouth, then closed it again, then frowned thoughtfully. And finally, in more moderate tones, she offered, "That's . . . that's very strange."

It wasn't how Peggy had envisioned guiding the conversation to the required conclusion, but she was willing to be flexible if it got her what she wanted. She shrugged. "Artists are strange people. You know how it is: the more artistic they are, the stranger they get."

A spark of understanding flashed in Lady Farrow's eyes. "Ah. The artistic temperament. Of course, of course."

"And one of Orfeo's"—Peggy dropped her voice to stage-whisper, despite the fact they were standing right beside her—"*particular quirks* is that they like to be paid for their work. Best just to indulge them."

Abruptly contrite, Lady Farrow swept towards Orfeo and took their hands. "Orfeo, I'm so sorry. I . . . I've been so inconsiderate."

"Not at all, cara, not at all." Orfeo kissed her gently on both cheeks. Then slanted a sly glance towards Peggy. "I understand I am very peculiar."

"Not peculiar," declared Lady Farrow. "A *genius*. The marquess didn't make any of this clear in his letters."

Orfeo's mouth twitched. "That I am a genius?"

"I meant about your . . . your requirements."

"The marquess," Peggy put in, "didn't suggest Orfeo should be paid?"

Lady Farrow waved an airy hand. "Oh, he did. Just not that it was important."

Somehow Peggy managed not to roll her eyes.

"Of course," Lady Farrow went on, "my husband usually deals with financial matters."

"You don't have money of your own?" asked Peggy.

"Yes, yes"—Lady Farrow was looking dangerously close to finding the conversation aesthetically barren again—"but I don't pay any attention to it. My mind is reserved for higher things."

It was at this juncture that Orfeo uttered a sigh of theatrical longing. "How sad," they murmured, "for my muse to be so terribly unnurtured."

Lady Farrow paled. "Dearest Orfeo, please do not despair. We shall go immediately and ask my husb—" She broke off, uttering a little cry of distress. "Alas. It is the afternoon of his poetry salon. One cannot interrupt poetry. One simply *cannot*."

"We shall return at a more convenient—" began Orfeo at the same time Peggy cut over them with, "We'll wait."

"Wait?" repeated Lady Farrow.

"Yes." Peggy nodded. "Until he's finished."

"Until poetry is finished?"

"Well, how long does poetry take to finish?"

Orfeo's smile was just for Peggy: a moment of shared mischief. "As long as it needs."

"I knew you would understand," said Lady Farrow.

"No, but . . ." Peggy was damned if she was letting this go. "A rough estimate?"

Lady Farrow pursed her lips thoughtfully. "There was one occasion that lasted for thirty-six hours. But then Lord Yardley had a funny turn, and a doctor had to be summoned."

"Was he all right?"

"Not really. He went to France."

Peggy stole a glance at Orfeo, so breathtakingly lovely in Valentine's clothes, and felt some almost imperceptible shift in the depths of her heart. She didn't want to put any sort of word to it: she just knew that she desired Orfeo, was interested by them, and—above all—that she liked them. Liked them in a way that made her believe herself genuinely capable of heroism. Not just her usual pragmatic supportiveness, the same pragmatic supportiveness that had seen one Tarleton happy and the other at least not actively responsible for murder, but something bolder and sweeter. Something truly valiant. Like a knight upon the jousting field, her lover's colours a bright promise upon the end of her lance.

"This thing," she said, "that your husband's doing. Is there food?"

Lady Farrow looked confused. "I . . . I believe so?"

"All right then." Peggy straightened her spine and pushed back her shoulders. She could do this. She could do this for Orfeo. "Take us to the poetry salon."

Chapter 21

Lord Farrow's poetry salon was far worse than Peggy had imagined. It was nothing but artistically inclined gentlemen draped over chaises or staring moodily out of the windows. Plus, the food was limited, consisting mainly of grapes, plain biscuits, and the boring kinds of cheese. The soft white ones that tasted of rind and halfheartedness.

Lord Farrow had welcomed them, and indeed his wife, warmly enough, but he had also made it very clear that he would talk no business until poetry—or *poesy*, as he insisted on referring to it—had received her due. Peggy had no idea how they were supposed to ensure the satisfaction of an abstract concept, so in the meantime, she satisfied herself by trying to fit increasingly large triangles of brie into her mouth.

A lily-pale gentleman in a lavender waistcoat drifted up from his chaise. "Ahem," he said. "I may have prepared a little something. If the company is willing to indulge me."

Unfortunately, the company was willing.

"Algernon," exclaimed Lord Farrow, with what appeared to be genuine enthusiasm. "How wonderful. How we all loved your last piece. What was it again? 'Ode to the Sundial That Plunged from Lord Willoughby's Garden'?"

The various guests offered a susurration of appreciation.

"Oh . . ." Algernon blushed prettily—or would have blushed prettily had it not clashed abominably with his waistcoat. "That was a mere trifle. I feel my voice has matured considerably in the interim."

"Unlike this cheese," said Peggy. Except her mouth was full, so what she said in practice was "Unffurfththcnnnfff."

Which everyone took as a comment on Algernon's previous verses that they wanted to agree with.

"Ahem," said Algernon again, once silence had fallen. "I call this 'Ode to the Hyacinth That Bloomed in Lord Willoughby's Pot.' But it's a working title. And only the first stanza is really fit to have eyes upon it, so"—he glanced down demurely—"please be gentle with me."

"I'm sure Lord Willoughby would be gentle with you," suggested Peggy, "if you asked him."

Algernon blinked. "He is very amiable and even-tempered. I suspect he's gentle as a matter of course. Anyway, I . . . I, um, present 'Ode to the Hyacinth That Bloomed in Lord Willoughby's Pot.'" He gave one final ahem and began to read, his hands trembling upon a piece of paper grown flimsy from wear.

"O! Lovely hyacinth, so purple crown'd
That proudly thrusts from out its earthy bed
Of all of nature's bounties most renowned
I kneel before your pot and bow my head
In gratitude I huff your heady scent
And with my fingers pinch your trembling stem
I gaze upon your petals moist with dew
And think how sweet it is, how innocent
So I compose this humble requiem
To all my fragrant memories of you."

There was what Peggy took to be an appalled silence. And then, almost as one, the company began to click their fingers.

"Oh . . . er . . ." Algernon bobbed his head like a sparrow upon a hedgerow. "Thank you all so much. I mean . . . it's . . . it's still very much . . . it's not yet fully formed."

Peggy cut herself a fresh wedge of cheese. "Unlike Lord Willoughby's hyacinth."

Lord Farrow was nodding. "How right you are, Margaret. That image was developed most fulsomely, Algernon."

"Marvellous," agreed another gentleman, running a hand through a profusion of dark curls that somehow looked windswept despite the fact they were indoors. "Such vivid writing. One almost felt transported, as if one knelt before Lord Willoughby's hyacinth oneself."

A third gentleman—brawny type, in tight-fitting breeches, who Peggy had a vague sense usually ran with the Corinthian set—offered a rumble of approval. "Yes, I was particularly struck by the intricacy of the details, like the dew and the scent. The way you engaged all the senses."

By this time, Peggy had eaten most of the available cheese. With a tug upon her sleeve, Orfeo drew her down beside them on a chaise. "Peggy," they whispered, "I think I do not need so very badly to be paid and that these gentlemen should get laid."

"We're not leaving," she whispered back. "We've come too far."

"That may be what is called a sunk cost."

"So"—an older gentleman with a rather melancholy aspect rose from an armchair in a corner of the room—"I continue to work upon the longer piece I've mentioned on sundry previous occasions."

For the first time, there came the stirrings of discontent from amongst the company. "Still, Haxby?" asked Lord Farrow. "How many stanzas is it now?"

"One hundred and seventy-three."

Lord Farrow made a convulsive movement, like a repressed shudder. "And you don't think you've done all you can with that particular poem?"

"It never feels quite . . . complete." Haxby was frowning. "I feel like I'm missing something. Something important."

"Sometimes," offered Algernon, "that just means you have to let go of one idea and move on to the next."

Haxby was still frowning. "But I don't want to let go? This is the poem I think . . . I need."

"Very well. Very well." Lord Farrow subsided onto a velvet pillow. "Please do share with us as you will."

Haxby pulled out a pocket-sized notebook, its pages covered in dense script. "I've made," he began, "some changes to the opening canto."

"Again?" exclaimed Lord Farrow in some dismay. It was the first time Peggy had felt any connection to him.

"Well"—Haxby riffled back and forth through his notebook—"I got to thinking that perhaps I would do better with the ending if I could perfect the beginning. Although"—he squinted at his own handwriting as if it had become alien to him—"I remain uncertain if I have yet."

"Please"—Lord Farrow spoke through gritted teeth—"just share what you have."

"Of course." Haxby stopped riffling with a visible effort. "So this is an excerpt from 'To a Friend,' which, as you all know, is a somewhat longer work." And then he read:

> "We were like brothers, long ago
> When we in youth's full bloom
> Walked arm in arm both to and fro
> And shared one tiny room
> And how we'd talk into the night
> Such pals, such bosom friends
> You were my one true shining light
> Alas! How soon it ends!
> Those nights I'd lie there in your arms
> We'd talk as good chums do
> Of politics and ladies' charms
> And . . . other topics too.

I ever think of those sweet days
Yes, evermore and oft
My mind drifts back through time's white haze
To our one-bedroom loft
The best of men, my heart's great song
The wonder of my life
I miss you deeply. How I long
For you to meet my wife."

Polite finger-clicking followed.

"Ah . . . sorry." The Corinthian was the first to speak. "But what did you change exactly?"

Having been about to reclaim his seat, Haxby paused, caught in a strange half crouch. "Oh, too many things to mention."

"Mention some of them?" pressed the Corinthian.

"Well, I moved one of the commas in the second verse. I think it changes the flow of the line quite substantially."

There was a silence.

"Don't you agree?" asked Haxby.

Everyone agreed.

Then Lord Farrow turned hastily to the Corinthian. "Do you have anything for us, George?"

"As a matter of fact," said George, "I do. Inspired by a recent trip to my hunting lodge."

"Delightful," declared the windswept gentleman. "I simply *adore* a hunting lodge."

Algernon pouted. "I don't think I've ever been to one."

"Do you know Sir Comewithers?" Peggy roused herself from a dolorous stupor where time had no meaning. "I'm sure he'll take you to his. It might take your mind off Sir Willoughby's hyacinth."

"I'm not much of a huntsman, though," Algernon demurred.

"Believe me, Sir Horley won't mind."

"Look"—George's chin was jutting out somewhat aggressively—"we're all great admirers of Sir Willoughby's hyacinth here, but can I read my own damn poem now?" He glared at Peggy. "It's a sonnet. Do you know how hard a sonnet is?"

Peggy had already been involved in one fight at the Farrows', so she did not say, "Is it as hard as Sir Willoughby's hyacinth?"

"There's quatrains," George went on, as if they'd been invented to personally vex him. "And a rhyming couplet."

"Please." Lord Farrow gestured encouragingly. "We'd dearly love to witness the emissions of your Muse."

George was clearly not one for paper, preferring to recite from memory. "'Craggy Dell,'" he said. Then shot a darkling look at Peggy. "A sonnet."

"Peggy . . ." One of Orfeo's hands came to rest upon Peggy's knee, fingers curling tightly. "I know you are doing this for me, but—much as the rumoured cures for the pox—I am coming to believe the remedy worse than the ailment. Also, you have eaten all the tedious cheese."

"I'm so sorry," Peggy whispered.

"You have to get us out of here, mio principe."

They were right. This had been a terrible idea. And the worst/best thing about it was that Peggy had come up with it all on her own, with nary a Tarleton in sight. "I'll . . . I'll try to think of something."

"*A sonnet*," bellowed George, unimpressed by Peggy and Orfeo's distraction. And then at only a mildly lessened volume,

> "There is a ploughman works in a craggy dell
> An honest man whose hands are horny-rough
> I watch him and he casts on me a spell
> And I bethink me, 'Is it not enough,
> To dig one's hoe in rich sweet-smelling loam . . .'"

Leaning close to Peggy again, Orfeo said softly, "If this continues, I am most sincerely going to kill myself with a grape."

"'And know the satisfaction of your toil
Instead of living in some grand old home
And struggling within the ton's great moil?'
I ask, 'Should I not reach that wholesome man—'"

In desperation, Peggy leapt off her feet and starting applauding. "Bravo! Wonderful! I love it."

"What the devil?" exclaimed George furiously. "I hadn't finished. There was another quatrain and that damn rhyming couplet."

"Really?" Peggy did her best to look innocent. "But I was *so moved.*"

George bristled. "Are you ridiculing me, Delancey? These are my feelings, in this sonnet. Do you know how difficult it is for a man like me to have feelings? I'm very athletic."

"You really are," sighed Algernon, longingly.

Peggy was about to protest but then recalled that she, too, was athletic, and that going for a ride or taking a brisk walk with one's dog was highly preferable to the majority of feelings. Maybe George should have tried writing a poem about that. It would certainly have spoken to Peggy, regardless of how many quatrains and couplets it had.

Then, "Margaret?" Lord Farrow was glaring across the room. "Do you have something to say about George's sonnet? Something so artistically vital that it merited this interruption?"

"Yes," said Peggy, with all the conviction she could muster. "I mean, I have something to say in general. About all your, er, lovely . . ." She gritted her teeth, conviction wavering. "Poesy."

The twelve or so assembled gentlemen turned curious eyes upon her.

"Of course, it's very . . . affecting," she tried, "and everything. And full of emotions and images and . . . things."

Lord Farrow's glare was, if anything, intensifying.

"It's just," she rushed on, "I wonder if any of you had maybe considered having sex together? You know, instead of all the . . . um. Poetry?"

"Instead of poetry?" repeated Lord Farrow, thunderously.

"Or *as well* as poetry."

There was a very long silence. To Peggy's relief, it seemed more bewildered than hostile.

"Why"—Algernon was the first to speak, his voice a little hesitant—"why would we have sex with each other?"

"Because I'm getting the sense you might like to?"

"That's an odd and very specific sense to have got," said the windswept gentleman.

"What can I say?" Peggy shrugged. "I respond to poetry on a very deep level."

Algernon was still wearing a contemplative expression. "And you think this would help our writing?"

"I don't think it could hurt."

"But we're all gentlemen?" Algernon pointed out. "Can gentlemen have sex with other gentlemen?"

"Darlings." Orfeo climbed languidly to their feet. "Anyone can have sex with anyone if they wish it, and the other person wishes it too. And"—they glanced to Lady Farrow, who had been in the corner, either half-asleep or lost in the poetry —"their partner does not object."

She started slightly. "Oh? What? They want to make love with each other? No. Why on earth would I object?"

"Is this true?" Algernon, his eyes agleam with newfound passion, rounded upon Lord Farrow. "Can gentlemen make love with gentlemen?"

Lord Farrow seemed, for the first time that afternoon, out of his depth. "I . . . I don't see why it can't be true?"

"My God." Algernon threw his hands up despairingly. "I wish somebody had told me that before I wasted all this time on bloody poetry."

"But you're a beautiful poet," wailed Lord Farrow. "So elegant, so refined, your words stir my senses like your fingertips are caressing my soul."

"Oh, shut up, Clement." Algernon launched himself across the room and into Lord Farrow's arms. "And fuck me like Milton did the Homeric epic."

"But Lord Willoughby's hyacinth . . ."

"There is no Lord Willoughby," cried Algernon. "It has always been your hyacinth."

"*My* hyacinth?"

"Yes, the one over there." Algernon pointed at the purple-crowned hyacinth that was, indeed, thrusting proudly from a pot upon Lord Farrow's desk. "Although, in retrospect, I was probably thinking about your penis."

Perhaps inspired by Algernon's example, four gentlemen had risen as one and then fallen together onto a chaise in a muddle of limbs and unwinding cravats. Another stood by the fireplace, clinging to the mantelpiece, as a fifth claimed his mouth with a kiss and a sixth kissed him . . . elsewhere.

Peggy turned to Orfeo. "This is better, right?"

"Inexpressibly. Do you wish to partake?"

She took a hasty step back as a pair of poets, in the midst of tearing each other's clothes off, nearly rolled over her toes. "Probably not? If you don't mind?"

"Not at all. Orgies can be very repetitive."

"Good to know."

At that moment, a desperate cry rent the air as a gentleman who had not hitherto spoken leapt to his feet. "Haxby."

Haxby, who was perched on a chair, looked up from his notebook. "Yes, John?"

"I . . . I have felt it too."

"You have?"

In a surge of synchronous motion, they rushed into each other's arms. "My dearest friend."

"Beloved companion."

"I would . . . I would love to meet your wife."

The room had become a mass of bodies, kissing, clutching, embracing, writhing. Hand in hand, Orfeo and Peggy tiptoed discreetly away.

In the entrance, they met George, who was pulling on a many-caped driving coat.

"You're not staying?" Peggy asked politely.

"Fuck no. I'm going back to my hunting lodge. See if I can find that ploughman."

And, with that, he strode away.

Peggy sighed. "I've not done a very good job of this."

"At least you got me out of the poetry salon."

"After getting you into it."

"Details." Orfeo pulled her to them and kissed her with an easy assurance that made Peggy unexpectedly fluttery in the stomach and weak at the knees. "I adore that you tried."

"Trying isn't—" she began.

Except then they kissed her again. "Peggy, shush. If I wanted to have my life managed, I would still be with the marquess, would I not?"

It was an idea Peggy misliked about as much as Lady Farrow misliked aesthetically barren conversation. "I bet he's never accidentally thrown you an orgy."

"Of course not." There was the slightest of pauses. Damn Orfeo and their impeccable sense of timing. "I am perfectly capable of throwing my own orgies, thank you so very much."

Chapter 22

It had made sense to Peggy, once she had committed to pursuing Orfeo in earnest, to move from Valentine's townhouse into her own. Or rather, her parents'—which they never used, far preferring each other, their projects, and the country. She was sure Valentine would have been only too glad to accommodate another guest, but it felt strange and uncomfortable to be welcoming Orfeo to someone else's home. Especially when the home also contained the former love of Peggy's life who had previously nursed a tendre for Orfeo.

And perhaps Peggy just wanted to be alone with them. To have some taste of what it might be like if it was not her house—well, her parents' house—but *their* house. Although, in practice, what it felt like was Orfeo kissing her cheek and vanishing almost immediately because they "had something to do."

Which left Peggy slightly at a loose end and trying not to feel— well. She wasn't resentful exactly. So just hadn't quite expected Orfeo to indulge their newfound sense of freedom . . . without her? But then, considering her attempt at an afternoon excursion had involved an argument, far too much poetry, and an orgy, she wasn't sure she could wholly blame them.

That left her to settle into the house—apologising to Radish, the butler, for the abrupt arrival, having her things moved from Valentine's, eating a solitary meal at a ridiculously large table, and experiencing not so much a sense of freedom as a sense of emptiness. Which wasn't about

Orfeo, or shouldn't have been. They weren't the next hook for Peggy to hang her life upon.

No. Peggy's life was her own business. And that, she reflected, was part of the problem of having spent so long being in love with Arabella Tarleton: it always gave you something to do. Even if, as she'd lately come to understand, you couldn't write your own story in the margins of someone else's. Still, she had no regrets. Say what you would about the Tarletons, they could spin quite a tale. And having to think about yourself was scary.

Because Peggy knew she could keep drifting if she wanted. She had money, supportive parents, friends, lovers when she wanted them. But it had somehow become not enough. Perhaps it hadn't been enough for longer than she'd realised.

"Who are you, Peggy Delancey?" she asked a glass of brandy later that evening.

The glass of brandy seemed quite confused by the question and had no answers.

"What do you want, Peggy Delancey?"

Once again, the glass of brandy was not forthcoming.

So, she started small. Town didn't really suit her. She missed her horses and her dog. She missed being able to go where she pleased and do what she pleased—the fact that leaving her house alone wasn't deemed a threat to her virtue or her purse. Growing up amidst her parents' ramshackle contentment had been mostly frictionless, at least until they'd packed her off to Surrey to learn how to be a lady from her mother's sister. Needless to say, it hadn't taken, but nobody really seemed to mind, and in the end she was spending about as much time at her aunt's as she was at home because, by then, she'd met the Tarletons, and been swept along by their stories, their dreams, the easy acceptance they scattered like starlight.

"I want to live in the country," Peggy informed the glass of brandy. "I want . . ."

The ordinary things she'd told Orfeo she'd wanted. The home of her own. A relationship to last a lifetime. Not that wanting those things stopped her wanting Orfeo now. Would likely stop her wanting Orfeo when they were gone. It was a relief, in some respects, to realise the only time she'd ever lied to them was when she'd made claims about what she *didn't* want.

Of course, she was still lying about that a little bit even now.

"I think," she started. The glass of brandy was, in its way, quite a good listener. "I think I probably want . . . I think I do want . . ." She finished her glass of brandy. Thought of her mam and dad, their companionable breakfasting, their endless delight in each other's habits, the stitched-together warmth of their parenting, wrapped round her life like a quilt. "A family," she told the empty room.

And immediately felt like a fraud.

Because wanting something like that—wanting *that*—was the only thing the world expected from women. And what did that say about Peggy? Nothing, she was sure, that some people didn't already think. But wouldn't she just prove them right? And herself wrong?

Except then Orfeo's words drifted back to her. Words, she realised, she had been holding tightly inside her ever since they'd spoken them. Could she really have what her parents had, or something like it at least, and still be herself? Still be with someone who whirled her heart around like fallen leaves in autumn with their wildness and beauty?

She glanced down at her hand. It was nothing like as elegant as Orfeo's, which were the sort of hands portrait painters would flatter their sitters with. No, Peggy had peasant hands, rough and broad-palmed, callused from fencing and riding. Nevertheless, she turned her palm up, then down again.

"Neither this," she murmured, "or—"

And then the door burst open and Orfeo swept into the room, their hair flying and their eyes bright. "Peggy, Peggy . . ." Catching sight of her slumped in her chair, clad only in pantaloons and a loose shirt, brandy at her elbow, they broke off. "You look very debauched, mio principe."

She made a vague attempt to pull herself together. "Do I?"

"Yes, like the sort of wicked storybook rake who everyone finds more appealing than the hero."

"I'm not very wicked," she pointed out. "And only a little bit rakish."

Orfeo dropped to the floor in front of her, folding their elbows on her knees, gazing up at her winsomely. "Perhaps I am come to beg you not to ruin my sister. Take me instead."

"Are you sure you wouldn't prefer to be with Belle?" She was, after all, another devotee of minor theatrics.

"Be with—oh, your odd little companion. No thank you." Orfeo's mouth curled up mischievously, the beauty marks upon their cheek shifting into fascinating new configurations with every flicker of their expression. "See, I have learned you do not appreciate it when I offer to fuck your friends."

"How considerate of you."

"Well, there are many things I may be accused of—vanity, pride, hedonism, impulsiveness, avarice . . . now I think of it, it must be that the deadly sins are my very favourites—but not that I am slow upon the uptake." Nestling their cheek against her thigh, they wound their free arm around her other leg. "Now are you quite sure you do wish to play rake and virgin with me? I perform both beautifully."

"Of course you do," said Peggy, laughing. "But I think I'd like us to try being Peggy and Orfeo first?"

Orfeo offered a sound of amusement, half-muffled against her. "The role of a lifetime. But first, may I tell you what I have been doing tonight?"

"I suppose."

They glanced at her in surprise, then rolled their eyes. "Oh, you are feeling funny, I see."

"I'm a funny person."

"Then perhaps I won't tell you."

Reaching down, Peggy gathered up a lock of their hair and stroked her fingers through it. "Tell me?"

"I went to the theatre."

"Aren't you back a little early?"

"Not to see a play." Their eyes had half closed in response to Peggy's caresses, but their voice had lost none of its edge. "To negotiate, or I suppose technically, re-negotiate my contract."

"To," repeated Peggy, somewhat startled. "Oh. I would have come with you. I could have helped."

They hid what was clearly the most impish of smiles against her knee. "I was not in need of an orgy, tesoro mio." She pulled their hair, not very hard, and they yelped far more dramatically than was warranted before loosing their rough laugh, for perhaps the first time unhindered. "I wanted to do it on my own behalf," they went on. "Do you understand?"

She nodded. "Yes. But I'll always be there, ready to start a fight or an orgy, if you need me."

For a moment, there was only the silence, and the crackle of the last of the fire's embers. Then, "I believe you."

Orfeo had spoken so softly that Peggy almost didn't hear them. But when she did, the words—simple as they were—dragged their fingers up her spine. Spun her heart like a top. "What did you re-negotiate?" she asked, trying to cover the intensity of her reaction.

"Well, being sent to prison made it difficult for me to meet my performance obligations."

"When I was trying to find you, the manager said you'd been replaced by an understudy."

"Darling"—Orfeo shuddered visibly—"an understudy is not Orfeo. Something I made very clear to that same manager when he claimed I had reneged on our agreements."

Peggy tried to imagine the scene. And then realised she could, easily and vividly. It made her smile. "How did you convince him otherwise?"

"Ah, it did not take much. It is my name that will fill his theatre for him, and it benefits him not at all for me to hold my own concerts or offer my services to his competitors. And look"—they reached into the interior pocket of Valentine's coat and drew out a crisp stack of notes—"Peggy, I have been *paid*."

She stared. "You have indeed been quite comprehensively paid."

"I insisted on a portion of it in advance. This is half of what I will earn for the whole season, minus a hundred pounds to cover my absence." Orfeo's eyes were wide. "Am I rich? I think perhaps I am rich."

"You are rich," Peggy agreed. "You could buy, oh, I don't know, at least two hundred and eighty hats with this."

Orfeo glanced again at the notes. "This is the strangest feeling."

"Theoretically you've always had this money."

"It is different, though, to hold what I have earned. To know it is mine."

Peggy felt a swell of pride for them. "You know what else is yours?"

"Mmm . . ." They considered the matter. "A severely overpriced hat I cannot recall purchasing?"

"No."

"A coat of black sable gifted to me by Alexander I of Russia?"

"No, but I'm going to have to see that."

"An unparalleled voice? Exquisite taste? Overwhelming beauty?" Orfeo paused, a hint of uncertainty in their manner at variance with their words. "Or perhaps you mean . . . you."

"I do mean me," said Peggy.

"How much do I owe you?"

"For me? I think you'll find I'm priceless."

Orfeo poked her. "For my debts."

Truthfully, Peggy hadn't kept a close accounting of them, and all the bribery hadn't helped. So she named an approximate figure that felt fair and hoped Orfeo wouldn't feel either patronised or exploited.

But they just nodded and counted out the banknotes with a flourish. "I have something else for you too. It was sent to the theatre."

Peggy had been intending to make an obvious and salacious joke. Instead, she frowned. "To the theatre? That seems a pretty damn inefficient way to contact me."

"Not if I am your point of connection. Here." From the floor beside them, Orfeo produced a parcel wrapped in brown paper and tied with string.

"If this is your way of giving me a present," Peggy said, "it's needlessly circuitous."

Orfeo's expression grew a little rueful. "Alas, I am too accustomed to being the one who receives the gifts—it did not occur to me. I will have to correct that in the future."

"I was joking."

"Nevertheless." Orfeo sat back on their heels. "You deserve to be showered in beautiful things."

In actual fact, Peggy had been told she was impossible to buy for. In material terms, she usually already had everything she wanted—which managed to say good things and bad things at the same time. "And if I mention you're the most beautiful thing I've ever seen?"

"Then I'd be more than happy to gift myself to you."

"You'd probably be more fun to unwrap than this." Peggy bit at the string and eventually managed to tear away the paper. "Oh," she said, in surprise. "My coat."

"You think because the duchess is a debtor, he is also a thief?"

Peggy squeaked. "What? No. Definitely not. I just . . . I forgot I'd given this to him."

"Why don't you try it on?"

Standing, she shook it out and slipped her arms through the sleeves. And it did fit better across the shoulders. It fit *much* better across the shoulders. And, while Peggy was far from an expert, having broken a window by throwing an embroidery frame through it at the age of eight, a new set of seams had subtly shifted the hang of the whole garment. She swished a little, unexpectedly moved by the sensation of not feeling a little bit wrong in her clothes.

"This is . . ." She cleared her throat. "God, I wish I had my own tailor. Or I knew a seamstress who could . . ." She stopped again. "Could we pay their debts? The duke and duchess? I don't know why I didn't think—"

"I doubt they would accept the charity."

"Even if it got them out of prison?"

"And what would they do afterwards? People who have not been abandoned by their friends and family do not linger long in Marshalsea. They have nowhere to go, nothing to—"

"What?" asked Peggy, when Orfeo showed no signs of continuing the thought.

They looked at the fan of notes in their hand. Then back at Peggy. "What kind of money would it take to . . . to . . . what is the word? Invest? In a tailor's shop."

"Oh God." Peggy blinked. "I have no idea. My dad might know."

"Your father?" Orfeo made a sound of amusement that didn't seem very amused. "What would you say to him? This is the Italian I have taken up with outside of wedlock; can you please offer them some financial advice?"

"No, I'd say, 'This is my friend,' or perhaps 'my lover' if you were comfortable with that; 'Could you offer them some financial advice?'"

"And he would not have me horsewhipped?"

"He'd be happy to meet you."

"No father is happy to meet the castrato who is involved with their child."

"Then," said Peggy a little sharply, "I guess I have a peculiar dad."

Orfeo waved a hand at her. "Come now, you wouldn't seriously propose to introduce me, would you?"

"I don't see why not."

"You cannot sew me neatly into your life, Peggy."

"I'm not trying—" she began. And then stopped because she didn't want to start or, perhaps, continue a fight. And certainly not to overshadow their happiness by tormenting Orfeo with everything they felt could not be theirs. "Look, I'm sure we can find someone to help you who isn't my dad."

"You are going to try again to persuade me to hire someone, aren't you?"

"Yes. Because that's what people with money do. But I'd rather"—Peggy drew them to their feet—"persuade you to come to bed with me."

"I could certainly be persuaded to do that," Orfeo conceded. "You will not change your mind again?"

"I didn't change my mind. I just wanted there to be no debts between us. And now there aren't."

"Merely," Orfeo pointed out, "a debt to pleasure."

Peggy nodded. "Then let's pay it the fuck off."

Chapter 23

They were stopped in the hallway by the butler, who had a message for Orfeo. They ripped it open on the way up the stairs, then handed the enclosed note to Peggy as some banknotes fell into their palm.

"I do not read well in English," they explained, with a touch of defiance.

"Because my Italian," Peggy retorted, "is brilliant. Anyway, this is from Lord Farrow."

"Oh. I am being paid again?"

"Yes. It says, 'Orfeo, you are such an inspiration.'"

Laughing, Orfeo swept ahead of her into the bedroom. "What am I to do with all this money, Peggy?"

"Spend it. Bank it. Whatever you like."

Orfeo flung up their hands, and the notes scattered like unseasonable snowflakes.

"Except," Peggy continued, "maybe don't throw it everywhere?"

"Why not? It is mine."

"Yes, but what if it—"

"I don't care."

With a flourish, because of course it would be with a flourish, Orfeo stripped Peggy's coat from her and threw it over the back of a chair. Then they were dragging her shirt over her head as they steered her across the room and pushed her onto the bed. Peggy went willingly enough, appreciating the way she could be hustled about and hastily disrobed without ending up with hair all over her face.

She reached for Orfeo, not sure if she wanted to kiss them, or pull their clothes off, too, and therefore attempted to do both. What followed was messy and breathless and only half-satisfactory on both counts, but it left them both laughing. And there were times, Peggy thought, that laughter brought its own gifts to carnality.

"Ah." Orfeo, who was straddling her thighs, tossed back their tresses. "I had not . . . planned for things to go like this."

Peggy sat up and stroked the smooth curve of their shoulder, where it emerged from their undone shirt. "I'm excited to know you planned how we were going to have sex."

"I always plan how I will have sex with people. What I will wear, how I will have them, what I wish them to tell their friends."

"I don't, as a general rule, tell my friends that kind of thing."

"Ah, but tonight you're sleeping with Orfeo."

"I'm sleeping with you."

"To tell you the truth, tesoro mio . . ." Sliding their arms about her, Orfeo pressed their face against the curve of Peggy's neck. "To tell you the truth, I am increasingly uncertain I know who Orfeo is."

"If it's any consolation," she told him, "I sometimes wonder the same thing about Peggy. But maybe we can work it out together?"

Their sigh warmed her skin. "Maybe."

"And if not, at least we'll be well fucked."

At that, they lifted their head, their eyes as lustrous as obsidian in the candlelight. "I shall ruin you with pleasure."

"Well." She grinned. "Good for me."

Orfeo helped her shed the rest of her garments, leaving her sprawled and tingly with anticipation upon already rucked-up covers. She waited for the shadow of self-consciousness that sometimes crept over her— what were breasts *about* exactly—but it did not come. Instead, she tucked an arm lazily behind her head and let Orfeo look at her.

"Bodies tell so many stories," they murmured. "Yours is so full of strength." They traced the hard muscles of Peggy's thighs. Spread the callused fingers of her free hand. "And beauty."

She gave a kind of lying-down shrug. "I do all right."

"What is this story?" Orfeo asked, as they leaned over her, the tips of their hair brushing her stomach as they followed the upraised edge of a scar that curved around Peggy's hip.

"Fight with a highwayman."

Their eyes widened. "I thought you claimed you were not in the habit of getting into fights."

"Yes, but what was I supposed to do? Let him take our money? Steal a kiss from my lady companion?"

Rolling atop her, they flicked a tongue over the ridge of her collarbone. "Is this even a little bit true?"

"Fine." Peggy cast her exasperated gaze towards the bed canopy. "It was a bush. I fell off my horse into a bush."

"And you were scarred for life?"

"It was a very prickly bush."

Orfeo laughed and nipped at her throat. "Tell me another story."

It took Peggy—languorous beneath Orfeo's attentions—a moment to think of any. She raised her left leg. "That ankle? The knobbly bit?"

"You were warding off a crocodile?"

"I broke it ice-skating."

"What happened?"

"Forgot how to stop."

Sitting back on their heels, Orfeo caught Peggy by the calf and tumbled kisses from her knee to her foot, knobbly bit and all.

Peggy pulled her arms back, stretching out her torso. "And if you feel here . . ." She demonstrated with her own palm. "There's this . . . kind of . . . indentation, I guess. From where Valentine hit me with a chair."

Orfeo's touch was impossibly warm, infinitely gentle. "He did what?"

"It was an accident. Belle had convinced some sapphic ladies to tie him to a chair."

"That seems outlandish even by my standards."

"It's . . ." Peggy paused. "It was a whole thing." She pushed her hands under their shirt and drew them all the way up the sinuous curve of their spine. "Your turn?"

"Me?" Orfeo repeated. "Oh, I was mutilated as a child. Otherwise, I am perfect."

"You *are* perfect," Peggy told them.

"Indeed," they agreed, too much in their voice to be easily untangled: pride and shame and hope and sorrow and anger turned brittle over time. "Now"—they slipped from her grasp like a fable—"let me demonstrate another reason I am celebrated across the length and breadth of Europe."

It took them less than three minutes to prove their point, not that Peggy personally felt they had anything to prove. Certainly not to her. In any case, her capacity for discussion had been severely compromised—as Orfeo had probably intended all along. She had thrown a leg over their shoulder, spread the other wide across the bed, and was doing her utmost not to buck against Orfeo's mouth like an unbroken steed. Because . . .

"Oh my God," she muttered. "Oh my *God.*"

Orfeo's eyes glittered at her from between her thighs. "This is all me, Peggy darling."

She heaved in a breath. And still felt breathless. "Stop talking. And do more . . . more that."

Their laughter swirled against intimate places, already sensitised by caresses, and Peggy wondered if she was going to die. Die in a good way. Die in a "Definitely worth it, she went happy" way. She'd always thought the notion that you could be good at sex was a myth. That everyone was sufficiently different that it was just a case of giving a damn. Learning what you could. And maybe that was what Orfeo was doing now. But she had never had anyone devote themself to her pleasure with such singular focus. As if she was a piece of music to be mastered. Or not mastered. Remade. Through them and with them.

"Orfeo . . ." She tugged restlessly upon their hair.

"You want more of me?" they asked.

Dazedly, Peggy tried to function. "Want everything," she concluded.

"That can be managed."

Resting on a knee, they wriggled their breeches partway down and settled once more between Peggy's legs. The heat of their arousal against her own was wonderfully gratifying, and Peggy—who had been trying to avoid anything that might feel too controlling to Orfeo—couldn't help pulling them close. Kissing the taste of herself from their mouth. To her surprise, they met her almost desperately, breath breaking against her lips, when she had thought them as certain upon her body as they were upon the stage.

She drew back a little. "Are you all right?"

They gave a sharp nod, their hair caught in damp clusters about their brow. "Why would I not be?"

"I don't know," Peggy said. And then, in the hope of making them laugh again, "I mean, you're about to be inside me, so you should be thrilled to bits."

"Oh . . ." They dipped their head, sounding amused, but still a little shaken. "I am. Believe me, I am."

Are you sure felt very much like the wrong question for both of them at that moment. But it was hard to know what would be the right question. Especially because Peggy couldn't quite tell if there needed to be a question at all. Orfeo's desire was clear in their body. In their harsh breath. In the hungry, seeking way they fit themself to Peggy. But there was something in their eyes she didn't quite recognise. Or rather, that she did, because she had seen it once before at Lady Farrow's soiree: that touch of distance.

Just as she was about to say something, Orfeo tilted their hips, and pressed forward—not rough, but certain, and Peggy just melted helplessly around them in eagerness and welcome. There were, she knew, abundant ways to enjoy yourself with someone else, but she was, as she had always said, at heart a simple person. And there was a blissful simplicity to holding someone, moving with them, feeling their warmth and their weight, floating free in the pleasure of physical connection in whatever form it came.

Peggy wished Orfeo was as naked as she was. But she didn't mind that they weren't. She tightened her legs around them and fucked up lazily, contently. Was pleased by Orfeo's deep shudder of response. Though then they rolled against her, using the knowledge they'd garnered with tongue and fingertips to send her careening into the sexual stratosphere. She wasn't one to claw people up—she didn't really have the capacity because, given what she enjoyed doing with her hands, blunt nails were best—but she clung to Orfeo hard enough she was sure she'd left crescent moons upon their shoulders.

If they minded, they gave little sign. Their eyes were half-closed, their mouth a tight line, something at once determined and yet still distant in their expression. It was like they were trying to overwhelm her somehow, and, to be fair, it was working. Frankly, Peggy couldn't imagine how anyone could be with Orfeo and not be a little overwhelmed. They certainly hadn't exaggerated their reputation. Their body, dedicated to the satisfaction of hers, moved with power and precision. Peggy might have thought them almost tireless if not for the slide of perspiration between them and the stampede of their heart pressed to Peggy's. It was a performance of consummate skill. Dazzling. But it *was* a performance. And that . . .

That made Peggy feel lonely.

"Orfeo?" She caught their face between her hands and stilled them. "Are you with me?"

They had never seemed less themself. Even on stage. "Where else would I be?"

"I've no idea. Look . . ." She broke off. Then tried again. "Are you . . . do you like this?"

At last, they seemed to see her. "Peggy." Her question had obviously horrified them. Not an ideal state of affairs when one of you was actively inside the other. "How can you . . ." Their tone gentled. "Of course I do. I have wanted to see you in ecstasy ever since my voice made you faint with it."

"That could have been a grape." Probably not the point at hand. "I mean," Peggy went on, "that's . . . that's great. But I'd quite like to see you in ecstasy too?"

Leaning over her, they pressed kisses to her brow. Her eyelids. Her mouth. "Let me give you this."

That didn't help her feel any less lonely. "I'm not sure I need to be given something, Orfeo."

"And neither do I," they said sharply.

Even Belle hadn't managed to fight with her mid-coitus. Peggy wasn't sure if she was exasperated, amused, or impressed. "Then can't we share something instead?" she asked.

Now they were actually scowling. "We are joined. I am pleasing you. Are we not sharing this?"

"I'd be a lot pleased-er," Peggy told them, "if you didn't look like you were trying to conjugate irregular Latin verbs."

"Excuse me?"

"Like you're doing something stressful and slightly unpleasant."

"I'm sorry." It was as if whatever fire had been animating Orfeo had been abruptly quenched. They folded over her, shaking slightly. "I'm so terribly sorry. It was not unpleasant. That is, it was wonderful. You are wonderful. I am aflame for you. But . . ."

"But what?"

"But . . ." Their voice had faded to almost nothing. "It hurts. A little," they added quickly. "It hurts a little."

Peggy squawked. "Why are we doing something that hurts?"

They pressed themself against her, their hair spreading across them both, heavy with sweat, and lustrous. "It doesn't. Not usually."

"Then what's different?"

"I don't know. I think . . . I am not used . . ." They uttered a sound of vexation that, to Peggy, seemed oddly fragile. "Normally, I enjoy to perform and show my prowess. To prove myself the best my lovers have ever had. And then, of course, take my own gratification. I am not a saint."

"You're the Catholic. I'll take your word for it. But I'm pretty sure being unselfish in bed isn't how people get . . . sanctified? Is that what they call it?"

Orfeo sighed. "Oh, stop it. You cannot laugh me out of this."

"Out of what?"

"*This*," they repeated. "It is wretched. Why can it not be with you as it is with everyone else?"

"At a wild guess? Because you like me."

Gently, Peggy extricated herself and Orfeo rolled onto their back, a hand flung across their brow in a pose of such theatrical despair that it came perilously close to comical. "Did you not promise that liking you would make it better, though?" they asked. "And, instead, I am impeded by my own reactions."

"Oddly enough," said Peggy, "I'm not discouraged by that. I'm the opposite of discouraged."

"*I'm* discouraged. All I wished was to . . . show you . . . ah." They broke off. "I do not know what I wished to show you. Something—someone—you will remember. And now you will remember me for all the wrong reasons."

It was the first time Orfeo had spoken of their parting, beyond their insistence that it would inevitably happen. "As if I could under any circumstances forget you," she said.

They offered only a disgruntled noise by way of answer.

Peggy tried again. "I'm not some curious aristocrat lingering by the stage door hoping for a couple of hours and a story. I don't want you to perform for me. I want you to be with me."

Beside her, Orfeo had gone very still. Peggy hoped it was a good still. An "I am listening to you and you are making sense" still.

"I want to be your lover," she finished. "Not your audience."

For a long moment Orfeo was silent as well as still. Then they shifted onto their side, propping their head in their hand. "The things you say, mio principe."

"I mean them."

"I know you do. That is what startles me."

"Startles you?"

"Dazzles me in turn, tesoro mio."

Peggy, too, moved onto her side, mirroring their pose, sliding a sly knee between their thighs. Her sense of anticipatory languor was returning, desire beating its wings softly but not yet frantically. She pressed her palm against them through their breeches, where she felt them hard and eager still. "You'll say if I . . . if it hurts?"

Laughing, Orfeo clasped her wrist and drew her to them more firmly. "This doesn't hurt me. It was the . . . the ache of unfulfilment. Normally that is not something that concerns me. With you, I found I was very concerned indeed."

"Well"—Peggy wriggled closer—"I'm pretty concerned about that too. For both of us. What's the best way to make it happen?"

"Internally, but do not think that means it does not please me also to fuck."

"By fuck, do you mean penetrate?" asked Peggy. "Because, to me, it's all fucking."

"Is that a complexity of language I have failed to grasp? Or a complexity of you?"

Peggy thought about it for a moment. "Could be either?"

"Then be aware it . . . it may take me a while. Or"—with a sharp gasp, Orfeo arched into her tightened grip—"or perhaps not. It is strange to talk of this."

"Surely it's stranger not to?"

"I begin to wonder how you've spent your time with your lovers."

"Put it this way," said Peggy, "you've had more orgies. And I've had more conversations. Now . . . internally you say?" She let them go, flipped onto her stomach, and peered under her bed, looking for her chest of goodies.

Orfeo's breath brushed her shoulder as they joined her. "You did tell me you were well endowed."

"Do you have a preference?" she asked.

"Pick your favourite. I'm sure"—Orfeo's tone grew teasing—"I can accommodate."

Simple, butter-soft leather—to match her harness—suited Peggy just fine. She was in the middle of equipping herself when she felt Orfeo's hands upon hers, helping with the straps and buckles.

"Ingenious," they murmured.

Peggy, who had been temporarily obliged to leave the bed, put her hands on her hips and struck a pose. "You like it?"

"I'd like you in anything, Peggy. But this is"—Orfeo cast her a glance through their lashes—"pure provocation." Crawling forward, their eyes still upon her, they parted their lips and drew the tip of their tongue lingeringly up Peggy's shaft.

"Fucking hell," she said, clutching at their hair to steady herself. "Who's being provocative now?"

"You have met me, darling. I am always provocative."

Grabbing her bottle of oil, Peggy dumped it liberally over her cock. "You are about to be so fucked."

Orfeo laughed as Peggy pushed them onto their back and pressed between their legs. "Do you mean penetrated? Because I have lately been told it is all fucking."

By way of answer, Peggy lined herself up and drove into them, not hard enough to hurt, but hard enough to satisfy. To give Orfeo that moment of resistance and then the long, sweet slide of being filled. Taken. Pleasured. Their head fell back against the sheets, exposing the column of their throat—a scattering of beauty marks there, dancing in the hollow of it—and their mouth opened on a rough moan that reminded Peggy of their laughing. Something beautiful and true, and just for her.

"Oh yes." She leaned over them, letting their bodies lock, hip to hip and chest to chest. "Sing for me."

They cradled her face between their hands. "As I sing for no-one else. Not even myself."

"Tell me . . ." Peggy was already breathless again, that combination of arousal and physical exertion she always found so wonderfully satisfying, as she began to rock inside Orfeo. "Tell me if I do . . . if I hurt . . . or I'm too . . ."

They made an exasperated noise. "One can have too much conversation, Peggy."

"You said you don't like feeling controlled. I don't want to—"

"Dio caro." Orfeo writhed wildly against her, their hair dark snakes upon the bedspread. "I have said too much in fear. I want you in ways I did not know it was possible to want. Fuck me, or be fucked by me, but—for the love of everything—let us fuck. Let us fuck the stars from the sky."

Peggy sat back on her heels. "You got it," she said.

They did not, in the end, fuck the stars from the sky. But—Peggy concluded—they did everything else. Gently, curled together like pieces of punctuation in a very naughty book, with Orfeo's head tipped back to rest upon Peggy's shoulder, their face naked in pleasure. Then more roughly, with Orfeo upon their knees, their spine bowed before her, sweat-gilded gold as Peggy braced herself upon their hips, her every thrust shattering their breath into cries. And when Peggy was, at last, herself undone, Orfeo rode her, eyes gleaming and hair flying, while Peggy stroked all their fascinating curves. Finally, though, they moved together, both kneeling, with Peggy behind and Orfeo cradled against her, hands free to caress as they would. Until with a sound that made Peggy weak with tenderness, they found their completion, their joy spilling bright, and almost clear, across Peggy's fingers and the sheets.

For a little while after, all they could do was gasp and cling, but then Orfeo helped her out of the harness, and pressed their fingers to her, exactly where she needed, and probably one or two stars *did* fall out of the sky. She certainly yelled a couple down and saw their afterimages in silver flashes as she landed in a sprawl upon Orfeo's still-heaving chest. Where, to her dismay, she couldn't think of a single thing to say. At least, nothing it felt the right time or place for.

"Well," she managed finally, "prowess proved, I guess?"

Orfeo flinched slightly beneath her. "You know it was more for me than that."

"Aren't you always reminding me things can be both?"

At that, they gave a soft laugh. "You need to stop making me want the impossible."

"I can't help what you want."

"Then you need to make me stop believing in them."

There was a pause, Peggy's thoughts too fast for her body, which only wanted to lie there in perfect peace and contentment. "Can't we—"

"Peggy, please." Orfeo drew their fingers lightly across her shoulders to soften their interruption. "I would rather not waste my time with you in lamenting what cannot be. I would rather embrace everything that can."

They were right. And it was nothing Peggy had not thought for herself. But she had never been good at governing her heart. It always over-spilled inside her like a too-ripe fig. Then again, she had always known it would. And she had chosen this—chosen Orfeo—anyway. Just as she had once chosen Belle. Because, no matter how hard she tried to be practical or cynical or whatever else she sometimes felt might be better, she believed love was worth it. Even if it took its own form. Came with its own compromises. Painted your future different colours to the ones you'd only half dared to dream of anyway. "You got it," she said impishly.

And was rewarded by Orfeo's rough throaty laugh.

She snagged one of the blankets with her foot and drew it partially over them before nestling herself back against Orfeo. "So what does this *everything* we're going to embrace entail?"

"Well"—Orfeo's voice grew dreamy—"I shall expect you to come to my every performance."

Peggy almost jolted off the bed. "Seriously?"

Orfeo was laughing again, this time gleefully. "No, darling. I am tormenting you."

"Thank God."

"But we should," they went on, their hand sliding beneath her breast, thumb gliding across her nipple, "do plenty of this."

"On the agenda."

"And I might, after all, appreciate having someone to assist me with my finances. For what is the point of wealth, even transient wealth, if you cannot use it?"

"What are you going to use it for, though?" asked Peggy, with a comfortable yawn.

"Well, I will assuredly want new hats."

"Assuredly."

"And I would like to help my . . . my . . ." Orfeo paused a moment, as if they were unsure of their words. "My friends in Marshalsea."

Peggy was about to say something about going into business with someone being a big step. But Orfeo wasn't a Tarleton and didn't need her to be the voice of reason. They'd had restriction enough in their life. "You're a good person."

"I am not, as we have discussed on several occasions. But they were kind to me. That is a rare thing."

Leaning up, Peggy kissed them. They tasted, still, a little bit like her. Which was the sort of thing that always made her feel possessive and soft at the same time. "So," she said, when they drew apart, "singing, sex, secretary, hats, friends . . ."

"All the rudiments of contentment." Orfeo smirked. "And a party."

"A party?"

"Why not?" they asked. "I have always been someone for whom parties were given. I wish to have one of my own."

"What kind of party?"

"Well . . ." They paused. "It must be splendid."

"Goes without saying."

"But it must be more than mere spectacle." Another pause. "It must also be real. Ah, I have it. A masquerade. People are at their truest when they think they're in disguise. It will be"—Orfeo's voice swooped up in triumph—"a *come as you are* masquerade."

Peggy wrinkled her nose. "You don't think we're in danger of sending out mixed messages there?"

"No?" Then Orfeo glanced down at her, a flicker of uncertainty in their eyes. "But can we contrive it, do you think?"

"A masquerade ball?"

They nodded.

Peggy pondered. "I don't see why not. I mean, some people will pretend we don't exist. But I think the people who matter will be there."

"What a notion."

"People pretending we don't exist?"

"No, darling, I am more than used to that." Orfeo's arms tightened around her. "People who matter."

"You know," Peggy told them, "you're always going to matter to me. Wherever you are in the world. Whatever you're doing or whoever you're with. You don't have to stay with me to have that."

Orfeo made a faintly wounded sound as they pressed Peggy onto her back and covered her. She was still slick and sensitive, so they slipped inside her effortlessly, locking them together. They were both tired and sated, but the closeness, and the shared heat, was welcome. Orfeo's patience seemed inexhaustible as they drew her slowly, oh so slowly, towards arousal. There was a touch of fear in it, Peggy could feel that: longing locked behind unspoken words. But she let Orfeo speak with their body instead, responding with her own. And when she came for a second, and then a third, time, the pleasure was soft and wrenching, and almost made her cry with the sweetness of it.

Chapter 24

"Peggy, this is impossible." Orfeo paced the room, the jewels set on silver chains woven through their hair chiming together. Their things had been, at least, partially retrieved from the marquess's house, which meant trunks and boxes were strewn across Peggy's bedroom and out into the hallway, and Orfeo had been able to put aside their borrowed austerity. They were in a full-skirted, floor-length coat of shot silk that shimmered blue and purple as the light caught it, worn over dark breeches and extravagantly clocked stockings. "I do not like any of these men."

To be fair, Peggy hadn't liked them either. "I think maybe the second one was not . . . not the worst?"

"How am I to put my trust in someone who views me as little more than an upstart foreigner?" demanded Orfeo. Their extravagant, silver-embroidered shoes were heeled, adding to their already striking height, and turning each step into punctuation. "I certainly do not wish to give them money."

Peggy sighed, rubbing the back of her neck to ease a crick from it. She'd asked Valentine about hiring a secretary, been directed back to Periwinkle, and from there to an agency who had been initially very helpful and then much less helpful when they'd discovered who the work would be for, and eventually consented to send whatever suitable candidates they could find. None of whom had turned out to be remotely suitable. Mainly because Orfeo was right, and they'd given very little impression of seeing the job as anything other than demeaning.

Frankly, it was disappointing. Especially because it had required both of them to get out of bed.

"You see," Orfeo was saying, "why I have not your ease with engaging people in my business."

"We might still find someone."

"I am not hopeful. Moreover, I am due at the theatre in a matter of hours."

Needless to say—after some intensive vocal work—Orfeo's return to the stage had been a triumph. And news of some highly scandalous party was beginning to spread, though the actual business of organising it had fallen to Peggy. Orfeo's idea of organisation involved sweeping into rooms and saying things like "Our colour story shall be cerulean and pearl" and "I want panthers and peacocks to run free amongst the guests," and "We shall serve only champagne so that we may all drink sunlight." Mostly Peggy had found ways to make it all happen, but she drew the line at panthers and peacocks: panthers because she thought it would not be good for the guests, and peacocks because she thought it would not be good for the peacocks.

Rising, she shook out her skirts and rang the bell for Radish. "Is there anyone left to see?" she asked.

The butler, who had been with the family for years and had developed—as was so often the case with long-standing retainers—an air of implacability, seemed very mildly placced. "There is one, yes."

"Great. Send him up."

Radish's nostrils flared expressively. "I am not sure the young . . . young personage is entirely respectable."

"Well . . ." Peggy shrugged. "Neither are we."

As it turned out, however, Radish was partially correct. The final applicant looked dishevelled to say the least, his clothes visibly too big, his cravat appallingly tied, and his hair knotted unconvincingly up inside the hat he seemed to realise, slightly too late, he couldn't remove.

Peggy and Orfeo exchanged glances.

"Hello," said the newcomer, in a deep voice that could not have been comfortable to maintain.

"Er," said Peggy. "Hello. I'm Margaret Delancey . . ." She offered her hand to be shook and nearly lost the whole arm. "And this is Orfeo."

Having seen Peggy's experience with hand shaking, Orfeo took a step back and gave a languid wave instead. "And you are?"

The brim of the young man's hat was falling over one of his eyes. "Bob."

"Bob?" repeated Peggy.

"Yes," said Bob. "Bob. Bob Everley."

"And"—Orfeo's mouth was twitching with mirth—"you wish to be my secretary."

Bob nodded, and his hat slipped down a little farther. "Yes. I'm a motivated self-starter who is also a team player."

"What does any of that mean?" asked Peggy. "And please do take a seat, if you like."

"It means I'm a good person to employ," Bob rushed to assure her. "Full of good employable qualities." He sat down, one ankle tucked behind the other, then gave a start and spread his legs extravagantly.

"And you wish"—Orfeo perched on the arm of the sofa, swinging a foot idly, shoe shimmering in the late-afternoon light—"to be employed by me?"

Bob chewed his lower lip. "Why wouldn't I?"

"Well . . ." Orfeo's voice was silky smooth. "Because I'm a degenerate Italian whore."

To Peggy's surprise, Bob blushed but otherwise remained calm. "I don't see that's any of my business."

"I don't suppose it is," Orfeo agreed. "But is there, perhaps, any of your business that might be relevant to me?"

"My business?" Bob squeaked.

"Such as, what experience do you have? What is your education? Your background?"

"Oh." Bob looked relieved. Then freshly shifty. "I'm not *formally* educated," he conceded. "But I'm quick and clever and good with numbers, and I've been responsible for my family's accounts and investments since I was twelve years old, and"—he rushed on passionately—"I warrant I could hold my own against any man."

"Pardon?" said Peggy.

"Against any *other* man," Bob finished firmly.

"And this . . ." Orfeo made a gesture, a certain gentleness creeping into their eyes and tone. "This is your preferred way of moving through the world?"

Bob shuffled in his chair. "What do you mean?"

"There is no wrong answer here."

"I . . ." Bob's chin was pointy and naturally stubborn. "I still don't know what you mean."

Another gesture from Orfeo, this time of dismissal. "I gave you my truth. Perhaps you will someday wish to share a little of your own. For now, though, Bob—"

"Except," Bob said abruptly, "you weren't truthful at all."

"Pardon me?"

"You said you were a . . . well. You said some things. But you're not: you're an opera singer. I've seen you. You were incredible."

"Ah." Orfeo smiled. "Now you are trying to flatter me into hiring you."

Bob's eyes, which were clear and grey, fringed by softly curling sandy lashes, looked up at them winsomely. "Is it working?"

Orfeo was silent for a moment. "You said you managed your family's investments?"

"Yes. Except my father kept gambling them away."

"That's unfortunate," said Peggy.

"It's all right." Bob shrugged. "He's dead now."

There was a pause.

"I mean," Bob went on, "it's not all right he's dead. It's just . . ." He swallowed. "It's easier. That he is. In some regards."

"I'm interested," Orfeo offered, to stop Bob squirming, "in perhaps going into business with a tailor?"

Bob perked up immediately. "Oh. Retail. Hmm . . ."

"Hmm?" Orfeo turned the sound into an enquiry.

"Somewhat risky, if I'm honest. But I suppose people will always need clothes."

"What would be less risky?"

"Guns. People definitely always need guns."

"I do not," said Orfeo, "wish to invest in guns."

"In which case probably national debt shares, or rents and mortgages? I have an inkling this railway thing might be big at some point."

Orfeo glanced again towards Peggy, who shrugged in what she hoped was a supportive way. "I am quite set on the shop."

"We can make it happen." Bob gave a decisive little nod, and his hat fell into his lap. He scrambled to put it back on. "I . . . I assume your income is inclined to fluctuate? Feast-or-famine-type situation?"

"I wouldn't know," Orfeo admitted, "but that seems probable, given I am either working or I am not. Peggy, is this making much sense to you?"

Peggy shrugged. "Not really. But then, my father's money is all in mines, and I intend to treat my own inheritance the proper English way: buy land and sit on it."

"Well"—Orfeo spread their hands—"since I do not as yet have the resources or, perhaps, the inclination for that, I will instead put my trust in . . ." Again, their mouth twitched. "Young Bob here."

Bob sucked in a breath. "You will? Really? What if I . . . what if I go astray with your fortune?"

"There is only so astray you can go, darling. Most of my fortune is tied up in hats."

"Tied up in hats?"

"Best not to ask," Peggy suggested.

"You mean . . ." Bob was still sucking in breaths. He put his hands firmly on his knees. "I have the job?"

Orfeo smiled. And, again, there was that unusual touch of gentleness in it. "You have the job."

"I have a job," Bob repeated. He had entirely forgotten to moderate the pitch of his voice. Then he gave a tormented kind of groan. "Oh no, I can't do this."

"The job?" enquired Orfeo. "Because you have given me every indication that you can."

"No, I can do the job. It's . . ." Breaking off, Bob made another tormented noise and gnawed his lower lip. "Look, I . . . I don't think I want to lie to you. Even for this. I'm probably going to shock you both rather, but . . . the truth is, I'm not actually a man."

Bob seemed to be expecting something, so Peggy left the acting to Orfeo. They gave a convincingly shocked gasp.

"I'm a woman," Bob explained. "I thought you wouldn't give me a chance unless you thought I . . . thought I wasn't."

"I am terribly amused you believed that," murmured Orfeo. "Almost flattered in fact."

"And this isn't how you like to dress?" Peggy asked. "You wouldn't rather we—"

"What?" Bob looked startled. "God no. Why would anyone like to dress like this? It's itchy and uncomfortable and I had to put a rolled-up sock in my drawers."

Peggy let out a relieved sigh. "So *that's* what that was. It's unravelled by your knee, by the way."

"Lord have mercy." Bob hastily slammed her thighs together.

"I was not sure whether you were to be congratulated or commiserated." Rising from the sofa, Orfeo crossed back to Peggy and dropped an idle kiss upon her brow. "But who are you, if not Bob?"

"I'm still Bob," said Bob. "Well. Roberta. But my family have always called me Bob."

"The family that includes the deceased, gambling father?"

"Yes, I didn't lie about anything else, I promise."

"Did you say your last name was Everley?" asked Peggy. The name was passingly familiar to her: respectable people, she thought, the excesses of the father aside. They were far below the touch of someone like Valentine—even, perhaps, the Tarletons, whose history carried no whiff of trade—but the Delanceys did not like to give themselves airs. "Is your mother supportive of your professional ambitions?"

Bob hung her head. "She doesn't know. But"—she looked up again—"I am nearly three and twenty. I am old enough to be making my own decisions. Besides, we must support ourselves somehow."

"Who is we?" asked Orfeo.

"My mother, my younger sister, and me. My mother, of course, wants us to solve our problems through marriage."

"It's a classic for a reason," said Peggy.

"Yes, but it never works, does it?" Bob huffed in frustration. "Alexandra—my sister—is very beautiful, and Mama is convinced that if we just bring her out properly, a duke will fall in love with her."

It was, Peggy suspected, the dream of most mamas with beautiful daughters. "It could happen?"

"It could," Bob agreed, with a sigh. "But my sister is far more likely to be swept off her feet by a handsome nobody with a soft heart, and I could well end up catching the eye of a duke myself, due to sheer narrative irony, and what a mess that would be."

"I can see you've thought this through."

"I have." Bob nodded. "So it really is best for everyone if I can be a secretary."

"What about when I am travelling again?" Orfeo spoke up abruptly.

"I would love to travel," declared Bob, with real yearning in her voice. "If nothing else, it will get me away from dukes."

They raised a teasing eyebrow. "You seem very concerned about dukes."

"I am," said Bob, greatly wearied. "There is something about me that feels as though it inexorably attracts them. I think it is my ordinary looks coupled with my striking eyes, alongside the fact I am mostly sensible yet given to impulsive attempts to control my own destiny."

Peggy thought about it. "I can see why dukes might go for that."

"And you are really willing to"—Orfeo was still hovering by Peggy's side, though their eyes were on Bob—"to help me? Manage my time and my finances and my—"

"Whatever you need," said Bob simply.

And Peggy—all too conscious of Orfeo's uncertainty and how much it cost them to admit it—could have hugged Bob in that moment. Even if she did have strange ideas about socks.

"You have no idea how grateful I am, Orfeo," Bob went on. "I've tried to get all sorts of jobs, and nobody would give me a chance. But now I'm glad they wouldn't, because"—she flashed the sort of face-transforming smile that would probably overwhelm the heart of any passing duke—"this way I can look after my family somewhat, my sister can have her season, and I will get to see the world in the company of a famous opera singer."

"That does seem like a very happy ending," said Peggy.

Bob bobbed eagerly. "Yes, and I can always marry a duke later if I change my mind."

Chapter 25

Peggy had rather imagined that being with Orfeo—in whatever way she *was* with Orfeo; she hadn't felt a need to ask about it—would have been like being with Belle. Not, she supposed, that she'd really *been* with Belle either. She'd just been *there*, which, it turned out, wasn't the same thing at all. Orfeo, of course, was busy, between the theatre, the hours of vocal practice they undertook daily, and their plans with Bob, but it was not the sort of busy that Peggy felt excluded from. She liked seeing them this way, more engaged with the world, rather than simply performing for it, and liked knowing she'd been a small part of that change. Truthfully, it inspired her in return. Not to do anything particularly exciting, she would have been the first to admit, but she'd started looking at houses. Places to lease, somewhere she could call her own for a while, not too far from London, or too far from Devonshire, with land for walking, riding, watching the sun rise and set over. It pleased her and saddened her at the same time. Finally, she was doing something for herself—something she should have had the courage to do a long time ago—but there was no escaping the fact she was planning for a life without Orfeo. And she did not *want* a life without Orfeo. But she knew she could not live a life *for* Orfeo either. Belle had taught her that.

It was strange, too, not to be living in the pockets of the Tarletons. She missed them, and hoped she was missed in return, but not enough that she didn't also recognise a little distance was good for all of them right now. Besides, she found there was an unexpected pleasure in being the someone that someone else came home to. And Orfeo always did come home to her, in the early hours of the morning, with the scent of the theatre—sweat and paint and exultation—caught in their hair like smoke. Later, Peggy might ask, "Who admired you best, who wanted you most?" and sometimes Orfeo would tell her, and sometimes they would laugh and say "Darling, everyone," and then they'd talk until dawn in that foolish, nothing way that lovers did, their words as golden to each other as the first sunlight of the day.

Occasionally, though, it was Peggy's turn to do the returning. She'd been visiting a property in Oxfordshire called Hadwell Hall—a name she personally found auspicious—with her parents, who had been, as should have been expected, embarrassing. Her mother had demanded a complete occult history of the place, and her father had bombarded the housekeeper with increasingly obscure domestic questions, like how long it took to carry a bucket of hot water from the kitchen to the master bathroom, or if they'd ever had any problems with rising damp or termites. Probably these were important things to ask when you were intending to rent somewhere, but Peggy was too busy falling a little bit in love.

It was one of those slightly higgledy-piggledy houses that had clearly been added to since its sixteenth-century founding without much rhyme or reason: it was a sandstone square, with mullioned windows, a triangular sloping roof, and a wing jutting out like a spaniel's wayward ear. The current owner was, according to his steward, a great traveller and, if the stuffed crocodile that took pride of place in the entrance hall was anything to go by, a great eccentric. In any case, Peggy liked the crocodile. For whatever reason, the taxidermist, perhaps not knowing very much about crocodiles, had positioned it on its hind legs, with its front claws extended before it and its long-snouted mouth open in an expression of mild exasperation. It was as if it was saying "Oh, what the fuck now," and it was exactly how Peggy wanted her visitors to be greeted. Other delights included an entire roomful of cuckoo clocks, a full suit of samurai armour that Peggy hoped had been obtained with the owner's permission, an enormous skull of who knew what on the upstairs landing, a collection of canoes in the stables, and—to Mrs. Delancey's satisfaction—stories of an angry ghost monk in one of the cellars.

The five-year lease would give Peggy ample time to get used to having a house of her own to manage and, perhaps, to look for one that would be hers to manage for the rest of her life. Her parents seemed approving enough, despite the presence of only a single spirit, and Mr. Delancey's ongoing fatherly concern about the bathrooms, so she dispatched them back to Devonshire and returned herself to London, eager to see Orfeo and tell them all about the crocodile.

They were in the library, with Bob and the Duchess of Marshalsea, who was re-introduced to Peggy as Cecil Fitch. The little gathering had something of the air of a council of war. Clearly tailoring was serious business.

"Where's the duke?" Peggy asked, leaning over Orfeo to kiss them lightly. They were in dark-green velvet today, the train of their dress swept elegantly behind them, their hair pulled back and held in place with long golden pins.

Cecil's eyes were soft and sorrowful as he glanced up from the maps, plans, and ledgers cast across the table, all annotated in Bob's meticulous hand. "He didn't want to come. He didn't think there was anything for him out here anymore, and . . . apparently I don't count."

Whatever Peggy had been expecting, it wasn't quite this, and she had no idea what to say. "I'm sorry?" she tried. Because while she was as familiar with stubborn pride as anyone, she couldn't imagine choosing to stay in Marshalsea a day longer than you had to. She'd only been there twice herself and had as good as vowed never to return.

"I'm sorry too." Cecil's attempt at indifference was far from convincing. Even less so when he dashed what was clearly a tear from his eye with his sleeve.

Bob, clearly dressed more to her comfort in a neat cotton print day dress, made a valiant effort to turn the conversation back to Peggy. "How was your trip?"

"Good," she said. "Really good. I saw this house called Hadwell Hall, which I'm thinking of taking—"

"So everyone in the neighbourhood," put in Bob, "can get excited that Hadwell Hall is let at last?"

"I don't think they'll be that excited when they discover it's been let by me. But," Peggy offered, "I'll do my best to insult a young lady at a country dance."

"What's the house like?"

Peggy was somewhat surprised at the giddy sound that emerged from her mouth. "Wonderful. I want to live there so badly. It's so . . ." She tried to think of the right word. "*Peculiar.* There's butterfly bushes in the kitchen gardens and a summerhouse in the shape of a pineapple and—"

"Peggy." To her surprise, it was Orfeo who cut over her, their attention fixed on the papers spread before them. "We are somewhat in the middle of something just at the moment. Do you mind if we discuss this later?"

"Um," said Peggy. "No. I mean, no." Because it was fine, wasn't it? Perfectly reasonable. Except Orfeo had never spoken to her like that before, even when they'd been angry with her. There was a coldness that was both unexpected and possibly half made up, since Peggy could well have been overreacting to absolutely nothing. "Of course not," she went on, overcompensating to her overreacting; "I'll get out of your way."

At last, Orfeo looked at her, something that was not quite apology in their eyes. "That was not intended to be a dismissal."

"Don't worry." Peggy rose, as if it was what she'd been intending all along, shaking out her coach-crumpled skirts. "I need to change anyway. Too much travel and too many petticoats."

She did not wait for anyone to stop her—or worse, to not be stopped—but went upstairs to wash and change. She really had no reason to be hurt. She *had* interrupted. And Orfeo had no reason to care where Peggy settled down, for they had made it very clear that settling down was not for them. Then again, the traitorous thought flitted across her mind: she'd found reasons to care about the things that Orfeo cared about—the opera, for example—just because Orfeo cared about them.

"My problem," Peggy told no-one in particular, for she lacked both dog and decanter, "is that I have a *type*." And her type was people who saw the world on their own grand terms, to whom Peggy's small world—even if it did contain pineapple-shaped summerhouses and disgruntled crocodiles—was always going to hold less significance.

Still, it wasn't as if she could choose who she wanted. And, even if she could, she doubted she would have gone looking for someone exactly like her. Not because she had anything against herself, but because she thought it would be downright strange to desire what you already had or were.

Opening her wardrobe, she found a pair of comfortable buckskins and the coat Cecil had re-worked for her. She was glad he was out of Marshalsea—frankly, she didn't like to think of anyone there, whatever had led them into debt—and glad for Orfeo too. The tailoring business might not have been reliable as, say, guns, but Peggy suspected Bob had been right in her assessment of Orfeo's fluctuating income, and it would be good for them to have something stable. Something of their own that would last, that they could return to. That wasn't, well, her. If it couldn't be her.

Her mind drifted unbidden back to Marshalsea, where the duke presumably still waited. She wondered how he was doing, how Cecil was, what had passed between them when they parted, knowing that the only way for them to be together was for one of them to compromise their future.

Peggy swore, knotting her cravat quite viciously. She knew it was wrong to project too much of yourself onto someone else and call it understanding. But she wasn't feeling especially useful right then, not to Orfeo, and certainly not herself. Perhaps she could, at the very least, be useful to someone else?

Pausing only to grab a bottle of brandy and some coins for Tampin, Peggy called for her carriage and told the coachman to take her to Marshalsea.

So much for never going back.

❦

The prison was not easily forgotten, and yet somehow it looked worse than Peggy remembered. It probably didn't help that only yesterday she'd been peacefully bathing in the soft golds and greens of Oxfordshire, and now she was drowned in London grey. And you couldn't get greyer than Marshalsea. From the flaking iron of its spike-topped walls to the late afternoon sun that washed the rectangle of the prison yard in shades of worn-out slate.

Tampin pretended not to recognise her, but it was only to extort a bigger bribe. And, soon enough, Peggy was climbing the rotting wooden staircase to the room Orfeo had temporarily occupied. Somehow, without two of its occupants, it seemed even smaller, even darker, and even dingier than it had before—as if their presence had conferred more life than their bodies had taken up space. The duke was sitting at the rickety table, in the same place he had before, though he was in his shirtsleeves, no sign of his lovingly handmade coat.

He stared at Peggy with dull eyes. "What are you doing here?"

She plonked the brandy down in front of him. "I thought you might want some company."

"I haven't touched a drop of liquor in seven years. It did me no damn good when I did, and it took me too damn long to learn that lesson."

Peggy stared at the bottle on the table. "Oh shit," she said. "Sorry." Grabbing it, she pulled open the door and yelled for Tampin. "It's your lucky night," she told him, shoving the brandy at him. "Enjoy." Then she turned back to the duke. "That turned out to be a really ill-judged gesture."

He waved a regal hand at her. "Oh, sit the fuck down."

Peggy sat the fuck down.

"What are you doing here?" he asked again.

"I really did think you might want some company."

"I've met you twice."

"I didn't realise there were selection criteria."

Folding his arms on the tabletop, the duke regarded her. There was something sharp and unexpected about his attention, at odd variance with the rest of his appearance, like being stabbed by a stiletto while you were ducking a blow from a club. "I'm none of your business, Peggy of the Up-Your-Arse Delanceys."

"So, what?" Peggy was half wishing she hadn't given the brandy away. The duke might not have had a use for it, but it would have steadied her. "You're just going to rot in Marshalsea?"

There was a long silence. Peggy wondered idly if she was going to get thrown out on her ear.

Then, with the air of someone who might have given up a tooth more easily, and probably had, the duke said, "There's nothing for me out there."

Peggy blinked. "Cecil?"

"He doesn't need me. His new friends will take care of him."

What Peggy was about to say, she knew, made her the most absurd of hypocrites. But she couldn't not say it. "I think you're more to the duchess than someone he needs."

The duke shook his head. "He has his life ahead of him."

"And what about your life?"

"Ended long before Marshalsea." He ran his blunt fingers with strange tenderness over the scarred wood of the table. "I'm someone here. At least he'll remember that."

He hadn't punched her yet. Not that she really thought he would—he was a man too familiar with violence to use it lightly. "I think you're making a mistake."

"I don't give a fuck what you think."

"Well, I think you're a coward too."

At this, the duke—apparently unmoved—gave a snort. "If I wouldn't change my mind for my duchess, do you think I'd do it for you?"

In those terms, it did seem like a vastly daft notion. Peggy made one more attempt. "No, but I'm guessing Cecil didn't get it. Whereas . . ." She steeled herself. "I do."

Another snort from the duke, even less encouraging than the last.

"Listen," Peggy said, "I'm a very fortunate person in all sorts of ways. I'd never pretend otherwise. But that doesn't mean I don't also know what it's like to live like you're building a house of cards."

"What are you talking about?"

"Treating everything you do and everything you are as if it's fragile. As if you could knock it over at any second and end up with nothing. So you just stop building. Tell yourself that it's fine, that it's enough, that it's better to keep what you have than risk trying to get what you want."

Abruptly, the duke rose to his feet. And Peggy swallowed a yip because he really was an absolute mountain. But he did nothing threatening at all, just stood there, looking vast and helpless, with his hands clenched into fists by his sides. "I've got nothing to give him," he growled. "He's beautiful and talented and . . . and special. And I'm a broken-down old prizefighter who thought he was too proud to take a fall and pissed away everything he ever earned."

Peggy knew the duke had quite a turn of phrase when he was in a mocking humour, but this was the longest speech he'd ever given on his own account. Long enough for all trace of the Duke of Marshalsea to fade from his voice and his bearing until all that was left was a man. Wounded by himself and the world, half-lost in his own sense of shame.

"What's your name?" Peggy asked.

He hung his head, breathing heavily as though he was back in the ring. "Henry. Henry Reed."

Peggy rose, with the oddest conviction that if she said the words she was about to say, she had to believe in them. "Sometimes," she told him, "loving someone is enough."

Orfeo, who was not performing that night, was already in bed when Peggy got home. Henry Reed's debts had been of such long standing that they had as good as been forgotten, and so it had taken very little to discharge them, and she was now well versed in the arts of bribery and corruption. Actually leaving had taken somewhat longer, though all Henry had taken with him was the patchwork coat. As Marshalsea's gate closed heavily behind him, he had stood upon the threshold, like some enchanted prince from a fable, his face turned, in half-fearful wonder, towards the sprinkling of stars that arced across the cloud-rough sky. If either of them had harboured any concerns over the choices they'd made, they were put to rest by Cecil's greeting. Without a single word, he had flung himself into Henry's arms, and they were still embracing as Peggy slipped away.

She stripped to her shirtsleeves in her bedroom, uncertain whether she wanted to disturb Orfeo or not. They had fallen asleep in the manner of someone for whom that had been their intention—still mostly clothed, surrounded by sheet music that it still astonished Peggy they could make head or tail of. It was clearly an evening for fairy tales because they had an air of magic about them to Peggy, with their unbound hair tangled over the pillow, and their face soft in slumber. Gathering up the papers—Orfeo cared little for the safety of banknotes, but they would not want their music crushed and crumpled—Peggy set them carefully upon the bedside table. Then leaned over Orfeo and kissed them gently awake.

They gave a pretty sigh and stretched languidly, their eyes fluttering open. Predictably theatrical of them, perhaps. But you did not fall in love with Tarletons and take up with opera singers because you objected to theatre in your life. Besides, Peggy herself always woke up like a startled hedgehog.

"Where did you go?" Orfeo murmured, sleep still clinging to their voice, roughening its edges. "I was rude to you, and I shouldn't have been."

Peggy kissed them again, banishing remorse. "Don't worry about it. You were busy. And it gave me time to get the duke out of Marshalsea."

"So that's what you've been doing?"

She nodded, trying not to be too pleased with herself.

"You must have been quite persuasive. He was adamant he would leave only on his own terms."

Settling down beside Orfeo, she began to card her fingers through their hair—something that always made them dreamy with pleasure beneath her caresses. "And he did."

"Ah, mio principe. You are such a wonder."

Peggy was about to protest that she very much wasn't, but then she recalled what Orfeo had told her about accepting compliments. "Yes," she said nervously. "Yes, I am."

"Though not very modest."

She spluttered. "Oh my God, you were the one who—"

Her protests were lost in Orfeo's laughing. "I am teasing you."

"You are taking advantage of the fact"—Peggy tried very hard to sound stern—"that I'm culturally sensitive about praise."

"Yes." Orfeo nudged into her hand, apparently unconcerned Peggy might pull their hair. "That is what amuses me."

"You're a monster," Peggy told them, with neither rancour nor conviction. Just affection.

"I pride myself on it."

They didn't. But Peggy let them have their bravado. "How's the planning going?"

"Well . . . that is. I think it is going well?" Orfeo paused, uncertainly. "I do not have enough experience to judge. But we are looking at potential properties, and Bob has drawn up an agreement between Cecil and I, laying out how my investment is to be returned from the profits of the business."

Having about as much insight into tailoring as she did the opera, Peggy made an encouraging noise. Frankly, she would have made an encouraging noise whatever they'd been talking of; she just liked to hear them speak. The precision of their language and the ripple of their accent, how private emotion textured their voice in ways that performance did not.

"Oh, Peggy," they went on softly, "I like it very much, having Bob to manage my affairs. Nicholas thought it was best for me to think of nothing but music and the indulgence of my appetites. But I prefer this, being in control of what I do and what I earn. And it would never have occurred to me . . . I would never have dared . . . without you, tesoro mio. You clearly have a talent for getting people out of prisons."

"Well"—Peggy rolled onto her back and drew Orfeo down onto her chest—"I'm pretty good at putting myself into them."

Orfeo settled against her with the ease of established familiarity, their hand curled at her neck, fingers fit to the base of her throat. "You may believe that. But I have never believed it."

So much for getting better at accepting compliments. Peggy knew she was blushing. But she thought ignoring them was probably a step up from denying them. "What else have you been up to?" she asked, gesturing in the direction of the sheet music.

"I am trying to decide what I shall sing at our party."

"What are the options?"

Orfeo turned their face up to Peggy's, their expression slightly distant. "Perhaps I shall keep it a surprise."

"You know it'll be a surprise to me even if you tell me exactly what you're doing."

"You insist upon this ignorance," said Orfeo, nipping at her throat, "and yet you respond so strongly to music."

"No, I responded to you."

"I will probably choose one of Porpora's arias."

"Ahhhh," said Peggy. "Porpora."

Orfeo laughed. "He was the teacher of both Caffarelli and Farinelli. But he has been rather eclipsed by Hasse, Handel, and Vinci."

"Ahhhh," said Peggy. "Hasse, Handel, and Vinci."

"Darling, the opera I am performing in right at this present time is by Vinci."

"Oh," said Peggy, chastened. "Um. Why was Porpoise eclipsed?"

"Nicholas always described his work as fostering a discomforting vocal sensuality. But he also writes in a very technically demanding way. I presume without his tutelage, singers sought easier material."

"Not you, though?"

"Not I," Orfeo told her, with the deliberate arrogance she found so entrancing. "I like things to be a little challenging, for me and for others."

Peggy wouldn't have thought to describe a piece of music as "fostering a vocal sensuality" if it stuck its tongue in her ear. For all Orfeo made much of her pleasure in their singing, she wondered if they missed having someone like the marquess in their life who actually understood what they were talking about. She nearly asked, but the words felt so cloyingly needy in her own throat she swallowed them again. "You can challenge me with your discomforting vocal sensuality any day," she said instead.

"Oh, can I now?" As they pushed themself to their knees, Peggy suspected Orfeo's aim had been to pounce on her. But they got tangled in the sweep of their dress and simply sprawled over her, laughing.

Catching her hands in theirs, Orfeo pinned her to the pillow and kissed her amidst a tangle of velvet, their body still warm from sleep. And Peggy was only too happy to kiss them back. For a while at least, until—amidst the happy haze—her brain remembered something.

"Oh, Orfeo," she said, half-muffled against their mouth. "This house—"

Orfeo's hand was between her legs, the heel of their palm pushing exactly where Peggy liked it.

"I'm trying"—Peggy's breath was already coming too quickly—"to tell you about a house."

Their glance was wicked. Their touch, if anything, wicked-er. "Can't you do both?"

Peggy's spine arched, and she kicked a heel restlessly against the bed. "Clearly not. And . . ."

Was it worth it? She couldn't tell if it was worth it. Because, while the house was amazing, so was Orfeo. Especially what Orfeo was doing right now. And about to do in the next two to three minutes.

"And," Peggy went on, stubbornly, "if I didn't know better, I'd say you were deliberately trying to ensure I couldn't."

Orfeo paused.

"Don't you care?" she asked. "Or does what I want not matter to you because it's not what you want?"

"I'm being selfish," Orfeo admitted. "Though not because I do not care."

It felt more than a little foolish to be accusing someone of selfishness or carelessness when their hand was positioned where Orfeo's hand was positioned. "Then what's going on?"

"I suppose . . ." They hesitated, then curled back into Peggy. "I suppose I did not think . . . I was not prepared . . . that it would be quite so painful to hear about the life you will lead without me."

In some ways it was almost comforting to learn that Orfeo felt as Peggy did about the prospect of their parting. But she hated the thought of hurting them, even more than the possibility of bearing hurt herself. Uncertain what to say, or do, she simply wrapped her arms around them and drew them in tight.

"I'm sorry," they whispered. "I want you to be so happy, Peggy."

"I'm happy with you."

"But I cannot give the kind of happiness that lasts. The happiness that belongs to home and family."

"Well . . ." Peggy gathered their hair together and draped it over one of their shoulders, finding the bare skin at the nape of their neck. She stroked, the tiny hairs dancing beneath her fingertips. "Maybe I can give that to you."

"You can't." Orfeo's voice was flat. "I am not made for it."

"What does that even mean?" Peggy asked. "What are any of us made for?"

With a rough noise of protest or exasperation, or protest and exasperation, Orfeo rolled away from her. "Don't pretend we are the same. You have choices that I do not."

Peggy—whose mind had been turning such things over ceaselessly as she looked over the houses of strangers—thought, like most things that mattered, that this was true in ways that were complicated, and not necessarily as true as Orfeo thought them, in ways that were even more so. She could have told them that the world at large believed her made for certain things and that admitting she wanted them for herself felt like betrayal, triumph, and surrender all at once. She could have told them she thought that sometimes the only way to have a choice was to make it anyway. But she knew it wouldn't help either of them to argue. Their time together was too precious. And besides, she wasn't sure she would get the words right.

So she gathered herself and did a little pouncing of her own, rucking Orfeo's skirts up between them as she pushed between their thighs. Orfeo's stockings were pristine white silk, against which their skin shone like polished wood.

Orfeo's lashes shimmered green to match their dress as they fluttered them at her. "Now who is distracting whom?"

"Do you mind?"

"Not at all."

It took very little from Peggy's fingers and mouth to rouse them to full hardness, at which point she dispensed with her drawers and breeches and sank down upon them. Their hands came to rest upon her hips, guiding her movements, and leaving her own hands free to wander. She caressed the gentle swell of Orfeo's chest beneath the bodice of their dress, and the long, lithe lines of their torso, missing the intimacy of skin, but enjoying the tease of being so intimately joined and yet kept apart at the same time.

"I like this look on you," said Orfeo, smiling up at her.

Peggy stripped off her cravat, leaving her shirt gaping at the neck and sliding down her shoulders. "Hot and half-naked?"

"Hot, half-naked, and bouncing."

She laughed and Orfeo gave a sharp gasp because, apparently, laughing when someone else was inside you was *quite* a thing. And suddenly she could barely catch her breath, partly because she was being energetic in various different ways, but also because her heart felt it was too busy splitting down the middle to keep oxygen moving usefully round her body. "You . . ." The words were spilling out of her like blood. "You . . . you could still choose me."

"Mio principe"—Orfeo's voice rang distantly in her ears—"to choose each other is to choose nothing else. I will not do that to you nor you to me."

"No, but," Peggy tried. "Can't we—"

Orfeo flipped her onto her back then, driving into her hard enough to steal speech. Their eyes were full of that familiar pride and sorrow, and Peggy clung to them, dizzy, sad, a little desperate, climbing tumultuously towards orgasm, letting them give her that instead.

Chapter 26

"And this is it?" asked Orfeo, staring at Peggy's offering.

"Look . . ." Peggy sighed. "It's very difficult, actually, to source a shark."

Orfeo gave what Peggy had come to think of as one of their prima uomo flourishes. "The oceans are full of them."

"Well, next time you want a shark, you can get your own damn shark. Also, do you really think a shark is going to have a good time at a masquerade ball?"

Orfeo prima uomo-ed again. "It isn't supposed to be having a good time. It is supposed to be looking magnificent. Same as everyone else."

"I know it's a non-traditional approach," said Peggy, "but I'd like our guests to, I don't know, enjoy themselves at our party?"

"Darling, the guests are mostly English. You are culturally incapable of enjoying yourselves at parties unless you are in someone else's country, in which case you embarrass yourselves beyond all reason. And"—Orfeo drew themself to their full impressive height—"none of this explains why I requested a shark for the ballroom and you have supplied me with . . . with . . ." Orfeo poked the tiny knitted shark that was balanced in the centre of Peggy's palm. *"This?"*

Peggy rolled her eyes. "It's because, *as I have already explained to you*, I made the decision *not* to make a shark's life miserable. So I tried to find, you know, a stuffed one or something, but nobody would sell me one. And then I heard of this . . . crafting person who said she could make me one out of wool. Which, to be fair, she has done. It's just she neglected to mention it would be three inches long. Although . . ." And here Peggy felt herself obliged to be fair again. "I suppose I could have worked out for myself that an elderly woman in a cottage in Kent probably couldn't knit a life-sized shark in less than half a week."

There was a long silence.

"Thank you," said Orfeo finally, picking the diminutive creature up, "for my shark. He may live with my blue rose."

"But . . . you made me take the blue rose away."

Orfeo glanced away, a dusky flush upon their cheeks. "I collected some of the fallen petals after you left and pressed them in my sheet music. I may not show it well, but I treasure all your impossible gifts, Peggy."

"I treasure you," Peggy told them.

And went to kiss them, as deeply as they deserved to be kissed, except they gave a wild cry and pushed her away. "What are you doing, you barbarian?"

"Um." Peggy blinked. "My lips? Your lips? I thought they might want to . . . renew their acquaintance."

"You will smudge me."

Obligingly, Peggy stepped away from the dressing table, where Orfeo had been busy for quite some time. "You realise you're going to be late?"

Orfeo scrutinised the perfect glister of their mouth in the mirror. "Of course I'm going to be late."

"Orfeo, it's your party. You can't be late to your own party."

"You should *always* be late to your own party."

"Right. So . . . I'll go and greet our guests on my own, should I?"

Orfeo rose, sweeping towards Peggy in a waft of satin and perfume. Then brushed the barest of kisses across first one cheek, then the other. "You are splendid, thank you." They tilted their head slightly as they regarded her. "Admittedly, splendid in a way I do not, at present, comprehend. But splendid nevertheless."

"It's my costume."

"Luxuriant." Orfeo stroked their fingers through the curling beard Peggy was hoping she could unglue again at the night's end. "Should I recognise you?"

"You very much should, yes."

"Beard. Spiky crown. Disconcertingly large . . . horn?"

Peggy re-settled her horn against her shoulder. "It's my horn of plenty. A small horn of plenty would be a horn of scarcity. Orfeo, I'm *Hades*."

"Is not Hades the god of the underworld? What would he be doing with a horn of plenty?"

"Well . . . I think it's because he's sort of god over all, as well. Because everything dies. And maybe something something abducted wife something something agriculture? But my theory . . ." Maybe Orfeo was right and Peggy's horn was a bit *too* big because it was turning out to be hard to maintain a grip on. "My theory is that it's so he doesn't get confused with Zeus on vases. Given they're both beardy spike-crown wearers with a shared interest in assaulting women."

"And this is whom you have chosen to personate?"

Peggy was starting to wonder if she'd thought any of this through. She flail-gestured between them. "Orfeo . . . Hades . . . Hades . . . Orfeo."

"Darling, I do not think we had a good relationship. You imprisoned my wife."

"She died. I was just doing my job."

"And then refused to release her."

"Again, just doing my job. People don't get released from the afterlife. The fact I was willing to make an exception for you, and only you, probably says something."

"Yes, it says I am a masterful maker of music."

"You see," Peggy exclaimed, vindicated. "You moved me. I wanted you."

"And I just wanted my wife back."

Peggy scowled. "You say that, but I'm increasingly convinced this has nothing to do with her. Maybe she just wanted to get on with being dead. Probably she was sick of having to be her husband's muse all the time."

"I'm sure," said Orfeo, with dwindling conviction, "we could have had that conversation on our escape from Tartarus."

"Except you didn't escape, did you? You glanced behind you."

"To ensure my wife was still following me, as you had promised."

"Or," Peggy finished, "you were looking back *at me*."

Orfeo looked like they wanted to argue but had no idea how to begin, and Peggy felt more than a little smug at having backed them into a mythological corner. No matter how spurious.

"And the fact I never wed again?" asked Orfeo, tentatively.

"You were too busy doing pederasty."

"Oh dear."

"Until"—Peggy caught their hand—"you came back to me. To make love and music in the underworld for all time."

Orfeo's expression flickered between amusement, longing, and exasperation. But all they said was, "I see."

And Peggy thought it best to leave things there. A little bit for emotional reasons, but mostly for practical ones, like the guests who would be imminently arriving.

Assuming, of course, they did arrive. Because a masquerade ball thrown by an opera singer and their lover was either going to be the event of the season or cast them both beyond the pale forever.

Something Peggy should probably have cared about more. But in a strange sort of way it felt like a win-win.

❧

So Peggy wasn't ruined. She had, in fact, joint-hosted the event of the season. Probably the event of several seasons because it had just the right air of scandal. Of secrets flaunted but still kept. And the absence of an unhappy shark diminished the atmosphere not one jot. People arrived with their lovers, with several of their lovers sometimes, and dressed very much as they pleased. Bonny had come as a small, round Achilles—who should, in no way, have been trusted with a sword, and Peggy had, in fact, divested him of it—while Valentine made an elegant, indulgent, oddly convincing Patroclus.

"And I," Belle had announced, "made this myself."

Peggy surveyed her in some bewilderment. "Why have you come as a seven-headed ostrich?"

"I have not come as a seven-headed ostrich." Belle's eyes flashed indignity. "I am *riding* a seven-headed ostrich. And it is not an ostrich."

"Flamingo?" suggested Peggy. "Dodo?"

Belle stamped her foot, which Peggy realised was actually the foot of the ostrich/flamingo/dodo, and what she had taken to be Belle's legs were fake legs draped over the creature's body to produce the illusion that Belle was riding. "It's not any kind of bird," she said. "It's a beast. With ten horns. And I was going to write the names of blasphemy all over it, but I couldn't think of any, so I just wrote the names of people I didn't like."

"There's . . . there's a lot of people you don't like."

"And whose fault is that?"

"Could the blame," suggested Peggy, "maybe lie somewhere in the middle?"

"No," said Belle. "It is all them and not at all me, and they are terrible anyway."

"Er . . ." Peggy was still scrutinising the flanks of the scarlet beast. "Just to check. I'm not on there, am I?"

"Peggy." Belle's indignation fell away. "Of course not. Why would you think that?"

"Well, I sort of . . . ran off with Orfeo and didn't really . . . I don't know." Peggy found she was scuffing her foot against the ballroom floor. "I wasn't avoiding you."

Belle was gazing at her with wide, pristine blue eyes. "Why would anyone avoid me? I'm *such* a delight."

"I feel like I've been a bad friend."

Tucking the golden cup that Peggy was relieved to see was not filled with abominable things under her arm, Belle reached out a hand to Peggy. "You have always been the best of friends to me, Peggy. I simply thought, perhaps, it was my turn to be a good friend in return and make space for you to see what you needed. Instead of hoarding you and inadvertently making myself an obstacle to your happiness."

"Belle, I . . ." Peggy blinked against a sudden prickle at the back of her eyes.

Belle made a dismissive gesture. "Please don't expect me to be this selfless very often. Because I missed you. I missed you a lot."

"Oh God." Peggy flung her arms around Belle, ostrich and all. "I missed you too."

"You're squashing the signs of the apocalypse," protested Belle. But she still let herself be hugged. Peggy eventually drew back, gave her a fierce, searching look, and asked, "You are happy, though, aren't you?"

"I mean," said Peggy. "I used to wish I had the knack of falling in love with uncomplicated people. But now I just think . . . *fuck that.*"

Belle considered this for a moment. "I have always felt *fuck that* is an underrated form of happiness. In fact, it might be my very favourite."

"And," Peggy added, "I'm leasing a house with a crocodile and a pineapple."

"What kind of crocodile? What kind of pineapple?"

"You can visit and see for yourself."

"I will. Though"—Belle struck a pose as best she could while managing a seven-headed ostrich costume—"if I find either the crocodile or the pineapple substandard, I will leave again immediately."

"As you should."

A smaller pause. "And what about Orfeo?"

"Orfeo . . ." Peggy sighed. "Orfeo and I are going to make the biggest mess of each other's hearts. But what's the alternative?"

"I suppose"—Belle was clearly out of her romantic depth already but determined to be supportive—"you could not do that?"

"I'd rather be someone who gets their heart broken than someone who never dares their heart at all." Looking back over the past few months, it was impossible for Peggy to imagine how they might have gone if not for Orfeo. She felt like she'd . . . she wasn't sure *changed* was the right word exactly. Become more of herself. And not because of them but with them.

Now it was Belle's turn to sigh. "That's the sort of thing Sir Horley would say. For all the use it's done him."

"Is he coming tonight?"

Belle shook her head. "We've barely seen him. He's been in the country."

"At his hunting lodge?" asked Peggy, hopefully. Going to his hunting lodge always cheered Sir Horley up.

"With his aunt."

"Is there anything we can do?"

"Don't worry"—Belle leaned in conspiratorially—"Bonny and I will take care of it."

That was very much the opposite of reassuring. "What? How? You're not going to murder his aunt or something, are you?"

"Peggy." Belle gave a squeak of outrage. "No. We have learned our lesson about plots and adventures better suited to fiction. We intend to resolve this maturely."

"I really don't think," began Peggy. But before she could articulate precisely what she didn't think—mostly that the Tarleton definition of maturely might not map to the rest of the world's—she had to excuse herself in order to greet the next set of arrivals. Lord and Lady Farrow, simply attired but wearing what Peggy guessed to be the masks of their favourite muses, were arm in arm with Algernon the former poet, who was wearing a green-sleeved gown of purple silk embroidered in gilt stars, a myrtle wreath upon his brow. Peggy had no idea who he was supposed to be—he did seem to independently like purple—but he did look absurdly pretty.

"I really must thank you," said Lady Farrow as soon as her husband and his lover had vanished into what had become a genuine crowd and, if Peggy wasn't careful, would become a crush.

She caught Radish's eyes and indicated for him to open the terrace doors in the hope it would encourage her guests to disperse a little. "Er. Must you?"

"You and Orfeo both. For what you did at the poetry salon."

"The, um." Peggy wasn't sure how to phrase it. "Orgy?"

"Well, perhaps not that exactly. It was rather hard upon our soft furnishings, especially the Axminster."

"Sorry," said Peggy.

Lady Farrow waved her apology away. "I more meant, what you told us about men being able to have sex with each other."

"No problem. Glad to be of help."

Pressing in close, Lady Farrow took Peggy's non-horn-grasping hand in hers. "It has been so wonderfully freeing. Do you know how much more time one has to spend on one's passions and pursuits when one is not obliged to sleep with one's husband?"

"No?"

"So much more," declared Lady Farrow, squeezing Peggy's hand. "And everyone is so much happier." Gazing across the ballroom to where Algernon and Lord Farrow were dancing, she uttered a sound of deep contentment. "Look at them. They're inseparable. And they've hardly written any poetry."

"I'm very happy for you both," said Peggy. "Very happy for all three of you."

"Oh, it extends beyond the three of us." Lady Farrow gestured to the quartet about to vanish onto the terrace together. "That's Haxby and John, and their wives. We shall probably have them over to dinner soon."

"How intimate," came another voice, audibly sneering. "How artistic."

Peggy turned, to discover George at her elbow. He seemed to have eschewed either costume or disguise, having come in ordinary evening dress, without a mask, and was already well past inebriated.

"George"—Lady Farrow sneered back—"I see you have made every effort tonight."

"I have made an effort," protested George.

"Then who are you supposed to be? You look exactly as you always do."

"I . . ." George tried to look haughty but mostly succeeded in looking drunk, due to the fact he was drunk. "I am Mr. Darcy."

"So," clarified Peggy, "you've chosen to come to a masquerade ball as a fictional man who lives in the present day, is about your age, dresses like you'd dress, and has no particular distinguishing features?" She paused. "I like it."

Lady Farrow sniffed. "If Mr. Darcy attended his social engagements foxed, this was not something the author chose to share with us."

"I bet he did, though," said Peggy. "I mean, if your aunt was Lady Catherine de Bourgh, wouldn't you?"

Abruptly, George lost interest in the conversation. "Oh, fuck pride and fuck prejudice."

"Pay him no mind." Lady Farrow snapped open her fan. "He's been in a mood for weeks."

"I'm not in a mood," retorted George. "I'm having feelings. It's just they're bad feelings. And everybody else is having good feelings. So I also feel lonely. And even if I wrote another sonnet, there'd be . . ." He hiccoughed. "There'd be nobody to share it with."

Lady Farrow moved her fan in front of her face, as if to form an actual barrier between her and George. "Excuse me. You are marring my capacity to appreciate beauty."

George gazed after her sullenly. "Well . . . good."

And since he showed no sign of moving on, Peggy felt obliged to ask, "What's wrong?"

By way of answer, George offered only a disconsolate noise.

"How was your . . ." Peggy had tried to block the poetry salon from her memory, and she slightly resented having to think about it again. "Plough person?"

For a moment, George said nothing. Just breathed heavily and looked tormented. Then the words burst out of him. "He was so beautiful, Peggy. Like a landscape given form. With these deep-brown eyes like . . . like wet earth in the morning. And his hands. So big and horny—"

"I remember about his hands," interrupted Peggy hastily. "What happened?"

"There's a shepherd he likes." George toed angrily at the ballroom floor. "What does a shepherd have that I don't have?"

"Sheep?"

"I have sheep," bellowed George. "Well. My estate has sheep. You know what this is? It's . . . it's discrimination based on my class and economic status. I was willing to look past such things. To conjoin our worlds. And he was not. What does that say about him?"

"What's his name?"

At the very least, George stopped bellowing. "What?"

"What was the ploughman's name?"

"I don't know?"

"Maybe," Peggy suggested, "that's why he prefers the shepherd."

"He didn't want my sonnet either." George slumped to the ground, causing two young ladies dressed unimaginatively as nymphs to fall over him. "I should have stuck to pugilism. Pugilism has never rejected me. All you have to do in pugilism is hit people."

"I know the feeling," said Peggy.

"It's not supposed to be like this. I mean"—George gestured at himself somewhat wildly—"look at me. I'm handsome, strong, and rich. That should be the end of it. I shouldn't have to have all these feelings or suffer all these setbacks. What am I going to do?"

George didn't seem to be actually speaking to her so much as addressing his complaints to absent and indifferent gods. But Peggy answered anyway. "You could start by drinking some water. As in . . . a lot of water."

"I think I'll just lie here. The floor is nice. The floor is my friend. I like the floor."

This bit of floor was definitely not George's friend. It was putting him in imminent danger of being trampled. "What if you lay on, say, a bed?"

Like a whale abandoned by the tides, George rolled a little to his left, then a little to his right, and finally gave up. "My bed is cold and empty like my heart. Also, too far away."

"Come on"—bending down, Peggy tried to haul him upright again—"let's get you somewhere, um, else."

Peggy was beginning to remember why she didn't like hosting parties. Why, for that matter, she didn't like parties in general.

In the end it took three footmen to help Peggy bundle George upstairs and into one of the guest bedrooms. She tucked him in, left instructions for the staff to check on him regularly, and hurried back to the ballroom. Thankfully, her absence had barely been noted. People were too busy masquerading—which was to say, flirting, intriguing, and dancing—and Peggy took a moment to breathe. To bask in a quiet sense of accomplishment. She might not have chosen, for herself alone, to hold a ball. But in doing it for someone else, it had become hers too. More hers than sorting out someone else's scrapes or following them around supportively while they cast themself into unnecessary adventures.

And then Orfeo arrived. And Peggy had no thoughts left for anyone else.

Chapter 27

Orfeo's gown was tier after tier of white feathers that floated around them as they walked; its bodice was encrusted with glistening, bloodred stones and cut in V so deep it dipped to their waist. Peggy wasn't sure if it looked like a heart or a wound, but that was probably the point, to be beautiful and discomforting at once. Upon their powder-whitened hair, they wore a headdress of swan feathers, silverwork, and rubies. Their lips, too, were painted a stark red, and there was a sweep of the same colour across each eyelid. Heads turned as they passed. Conversations faltered. And Peggy shivered with a kind of shocked longing for this glittering, impossible masterpiece who was also the lover who laughed with her, whispered with her, lay nightly in her arms.

By the musicians, whose hiring Orfeo and Bob had overseen together, there had been erected a small dais. As Orfeo stepped onto it, the room fell silent in earnest.

For a moment they were silent, too, simply looking back across the sea of faces turned up to theirs, whereas Peggy would have dissolved in horror beneath the scrutiny. Then they offered a scarlet smile. "Grazie, friends, for joining us tonight. In return: a song."

Their eyes found Peggy in the crowd, and it felt like they never looked away, though, of course, they must have. She had thought that having seen Orfeo on stage several times now might have prepared her better for their voice. But, if anything, it was the opposite. At the theatre, they were a character: a young soldier, a thwarted suitor, a man torn between love and duty. Tonight, they were simply Orfeo. And whatever they were singing—something achingly slow and piercingly sweet, pure stripped-bare sorrow—was probably going to make Peggy cry.

Which, at least, wasn't fainting but wouldn't have been, in her estimation, much better. She tried to hold on to everything she'd said to Belle, because she believed it still, except just then it was impossible to do anything except feel overwhelmingly, unbearably *sad*. And she was almost angry that something so sad could also be so beautiful. Because it wasn't beautiful. When Orfeo left, it would be ugly for both of them, and all the loveliness in the world couldn't change it.

Some truths, Peggy thought, were just too fucking real.

Like the slowing wings of a dying sparrow, Orfeo's rippling coloratura was falling into silence, swept away by the strings. Thankfully, Peggy had seen enough opera now not to be fooled by this. And, sure enough, just as the music itself seemed on the brink of fading, Orfeo's voice shattered them all afresh—as if whatever drove their song was simply too powerful to abandon. They surged through a dizzying series of rapid trills and flourishes, half-desperate, half-furious, the melody almost stumbling to keep up with them. Peggy couldn't tell if they were imploring or defying. But this particular broken spiderweb of emotions was familiar enough.

Far too familiar, in fact. And Peggy wasn't sure what was worse: resenting a piece of art for not speaking to you or having to face up to the fact it was.

Oh fuck, the song was getting sad on her again. Though this time there was a weariness—a creeping resignation—that infused Orfeo's effortlessly powerful voice with fragility. It didn't sound even remotely similar to weeping, really, but if someone had asked Peggy to describe how music might weep, she would have said *Like this*.

Surreptitiously, she wiped her eyes with her beard.

And then something happened, something that Peggy sensed more than she fully understood, the same way you sensed how an opponent might strike or a horse might shy. The same instinct that made you want to fling yourself in front of the people you loved no matter what burst over the horizon. Except she couldn't fling herself in front of Orfeo. They were on the other side of the room. And she had no idea what she was trying to protect them from or why she was suddenly so sure they needed it.

Instead, she twisted round, frantically scanning the guests. Not that frantic scanning was required. The stranger in the doorway would have been recognisable simply by his dusty clothes amidst the extravagant costumes.

Peggy had never heard Orfeo miss a note, not even in practice, but they did then, their voice stumbling as a person might, helpless and ungainly. They could probably have recovered themself—surely that was the sort of thing you trained for—but they didn't. They just let themself fall, into the silence of a thousand broken things.

At last: "N-nicholas?" said Orfeo.

The man in the doorway simply turned and walked away.

"Nicholas." Orfeo's voice lifted into a cry. "Nicholas."

Descending from their dais, they hurried after him, their skirts a flurry of shedding feathers that, scattered haphazard upon the ballroom floor, had no magic to them at all.

☙❧

Peggy shoved her horn of plenty into the arms of a startled woman and ran after Orfeo and the marquess. Though, as it turned out, they hadn't got farther than the entrance hall.

"Ah." The marquess's eyes flicked to her. "This must be your new friend."

"What are you doing here?" asked Orfeo, their tone so full of conflict and uncertainty that Peggy had no idea what to do.

To that, the marquess offered the faintest arch of a brow. "I was given to understand you were in some kind of trouble. Having rushed back to England on your behalf, I am relieved to discover you are not. Indeed, you seem to have no need of me whatsoever."

"You left me in debtor's prison."

"Giovanni." The marquess looked, and sounded, sincerely shocked. "When have I ever not come for you?"

Orfeo's whole body wilted like a storm-battered flower.

"When have I ever not stood by you?"

For this Orfeo, too, seemed to have no answer.

The marquess smiled, and there was nothing of the villain in it at all. Nothing of the villain in him either. He was younger than Peggy had thought he would be from what Orfeo had said of him, handsome enough, and softly spoken, with an air of natural elegance.

"I enjoyed your performance, by the way," he remarked. "A little indulgent, in places, and—as you shouldn't need me to tell you—somewhat under-practised. You know it is not enough simply to feel a piece. You must master it too."

When Peggy had last started a fight, it had been to a mixed reception from Orfeo. Probably it was not the sort of thing she ought to make a habit of. But did twice constitute a habit? Maybe she could punch the marquess now, and they could figure the rest out later.

"Yes," said Orfeo. "I know."

Again, the marquess smiled. His manner was so assured, his demeanour so calm and conciliatory, that some part of Peggy was beginning to wonder if she was being irrational—maybe even just jealous—in disliking him. It didn't help that his face was a little drawn, and there were dark circles beneath his eyes; he really had been travelling hard.

"Shall I see you later?" he asked.

Orfeo flinched very slightly. "Later?"

"When I've had time to rest and"—the marquess made a self-deprecating gesture—"bathe. I've missed you. I should like to hear how you've been and what you've been doing."

"I . . ." The voice that could fill a theatre was little more than a whisper. "I wish to stay with Peggy."

"And you're very welcome to," said Peggy, far too loudly in turn.

The marquess glanced between them. "You may do as you please, of course. But it is likely a mercy to both of you to end this now."

"What do you mean?" asked Peggy, when it was clear Orfeo wasn't going to.

"Forgive my bluntness"—the marquess paused delicately—"but you surely do not expect Orfeo to give up their career for you?"

Given how fraught the topic had the potential to become, the future had been something they had mostly avoided discussing. But now Peggy very much wished they *had* discussed it because their cowardice had made them vulnerable. Uncertain of each other in ways they should not have been. And the marquess's words slipped as neatly between her ribs as a dagger.

"Oh my God," she said, caught unawares and left reeling. "No."

Orfeo made an awkward, tentative movement. "Peggy, I . . ."

"And by the same token," the marquess went on, "you must be aware that there is no respectable life you can have with Orfeo."

Peggy could already tell that she was fighting alone. But she fought anyway, even though she didn't quite know what, or who, she was fighting for. "Maybe I don't give a damn about a respectable life."

"What about a life without family?" If the marquess had intended cruelty, it might have been easier to bear. But he spoke with insurmountable gentleness. "You will be outcasts. You cannot marry. You will have no children."

"We'll have . . . ," began Peggy.

"Each other?" enquired the marquess. "I'm sure that seems like a romantic idea today. How romantic, though, will it be in a year, in a decade, in fifty years, when passion has faded, when youth is gone, and all you have left is the memory of sacrifice?"

Peggy's hands had curled into fists at her sides. "Orfeo is not and could never be a sacrifice to me."

The marquess gazed at her, frowning slightly. Then seemed to dismiss her, his attention returning to Orfeo. "Giovanni"—his tone grew coaxing—"I understand what it is to want what the world denies you, but—"

"You do *not* understand," interrupted Orfeo, roused at last. "You think you do, but you do not. You cannot."

For the most fleeting of seconds, the marquess's frown returned. Then his face smoothed over again. "As you say. Nevertheless, you have a great gift, an extraordinary gift. One I sometimes think has come too easily to you."

Orfeo's eyes widened. "Too easily?"

"Imagine what you could be if you only worked." The marquess reached out a hand to caress Orfeo's cheek. It was only the fact that Orfeo did not pull away that stopped Peggy jumping across the room and biting him. "You were made for music, body and soul. You do not need the consolations of lesser men."

Silence fell across them, as smothering as velvet. There was a kind of shivering tension in Orfeo, like a harp string about to snap. But then they bowed their head in surrender, turning in to the marquess's touch, the movement shaking a tear free from their lashes. It slid softly down their cheek, leaving a streak of makeup behind, a comet with a crimson tail.

"Most are loved by one," the marquess went on. "You will be loved by thousands upon thousands. Most have no choice but to forge their legacy in blood. You will write yours across history itself."

Orfeo sighed. "It is true, I am fit for little else."

"You, my dear"—the way the marquess was looking at Orfeo, equal parts adoration and avarice, made Peggy's skin crawl—"are worth so much more than an ordinary life."

"You don't have to choose." Peggy's voice rang distantly in her own ears. She felt strangely separated from the scene, like she had blundered into the middle of a story that was being told about someone else, a play in which she had no part. Or had long since missed her cue. "You said yourself: not everything has to be *this* or *that*."

Finally, Orfeo looked at her. Their eyes were dark, blank stones. "There has never been anything for me to choose, tesoro mio."

"Come." The marquess put an arm around them and drew them close. "You have played at smallness long enough. Your art has suffered for it, and you have hurt her."

Orfeo made a choked sound. "I'm sorry."

"You have nothing to be sorry for." Peggy had meant the words as reassurance, but they came out like a slap—one she wished she could have directed at the marquess. "My only regret is that I took too long to kiss you the way I wanted to. I should have done it straightaway."

"Peggy . . ."

"Don't leave me, Orfeo." She knew she was begging. And begging in front of the marquess. But she would have done anything, just then, to show Orfeo that she didn't see them as he did. That they could be whoever they wanted. "Even if you have to leave, don't leave *now*."

"Oh, Giovanni." The marquess sounded so earnestly sympathetic it made Peggy's teeth itch. "Look what you've done."

"I'm sorry," said Orfeo again. "I'm sorry." And then they pressed their face against the marquess's neck, as they had sometimes done with Peggy. As if, this time, they were sheltering *from* Peggy.

And in a strange, fucked-up way, it helped. Because, while it made her profoundly, horrifyingly sad, it also made it easy to pretend she was angry. "Is that it?" she demanded. "Everything you ever said to me, everything you helped me believe, was wrong all along?"

Orfeo refused to lift their head. "It is not wrong for you."

"And what about Bob?" Apparently Peggy was far from pacified. "What about Cecil and the shop? Are you done with them too? Does none of it matter anymore? Just because"—she glared at the marquess, who regarded her mildly in return—"you've spent your whole life being told the only thing you can be is someone's . . . someone's opera pet?"

That was enough to slightly crack the marquess's placidity. "I made Orfeo a star. Before me they were—"

"I know." Peggy sliced a hand dismissively through the air. "Singing in church choirs. Same cage, different scenery."

From the frosty glitter of the marquess's eyes, she half thought he might be about to lose his temper with her. But he just smiled his empty smile and nudged lightly at Orfeo. "Giovanni, you have made a poor accounting of me."

"No," said Peggy quickly. "This is *my* accounting."

"Love is a charming deceiver, Miss Delancey." The marquess, damn him, offered a condescending chuckle. "You think you know Orfeo, and that has made you think you know me. But it has been a mere matter of months, whereas I have been with them for years. You are not their first passion; you will not be their last. But the art will always transcend you."

"I . . ." Orfeo's whisper was such a wisp of a thing that Peggy barely heard it. "I love Peggy."

"I'm sure you do," said the marquess, serenity restored. "But without music, you are nothing. A broken man. A wingless angel. A curiosity and a cautionary tale. Can you live like that?"

And, after a long moment, Orfeo shook their head.

"How can *you* live?" Peggy asked, rounding on the marquess.

The marquess's expression reflected only the faintest bemusement. "Easily and with pride. I believe in the beauty of this world, and I work tirelessly to preserve it. I have nothing to reproach myself for."

"But Orfeo's a person." Peggy flailed her arms in helpless despair. "They need more than . . . art and beauty and abstract shit."

"Perhaps," conceded the marquess, but there was something about the curve of his mouth that made Peggy wary. Something knowing and assured. A little cruel. "But if Orfeo truly believed they had any sort of future with you, why would they choose to sing you 'Parto, ti lascio, o cara'?"

"I . . . I have no idea."

He laughed then. "Oh dear. You really know nothing about opera, do you?"

"No." The marquess had meant to shame her, and yet the word rang out defiantly. "I don't. But I know Orfeo."

"Nicholas," said Orfeo suddenly, "I wish to leave. Take me away."

"Whatever you desire." The marquess paused. "But what was that about a shop? And a . . . Bob?"

Orfeo gave a listless shrug. "My secretary. And a business venture."

"My dear"—the marquess was watching Peggy as he spoke, a sharp triumph on his face—"why did you not tell me you wanted a secretary?"

"I don't know."

"Or to undertake, what was it, a business venture?"

"I don't know," repeated Orfeo, a little louder, as if the words were themselves a punishment.

"Well." The marquess was positively purring now. "I look forward to hearing all about it."

It was only then that he deigned to shepherd Orfeo away as they had requested. And Peggy was left staring after them.

The entrance of her parents' townhouse had never seemed at once so vast and so infinitesimally small.

Her mind was a useless waterwheel of churned-up thoughts. *I have to stop this. I have to go after them. But how? And if I do, what does that make me? Would I be no better than the marquess? Orfeo doesn't belong to me any more than they belong to him. To the crowds. To the church. Except I can't let them leave. Not like this. Not believing so little of themself. Not because of him.*

And yet she could not move. Because she did not know what to do.

They were almost at the door. The marquess was casting his coat across Orfeo's bare, silver-dusted shoulders.

If they look back, Peggy decided. *If Orfeo looks back, that will be enough.* It would tell her they wanted her still, that they needed her, that she could help them. That they could help each other.

But no matter how hard Peggy willed it, no matter how desperately she cried out to them in her mind, from her breaking heart, Orfeo did not turn.

They did not turn.

Chapter 28

Because Peggy was Peggy to a fault, she could not allow herself to lie with her face on the floor and wail until the moon cracked like an egg and the sky fell in. She was, after all, hosting a ball.

Time had as good as stopped beneath the artificial gold of the candles. It was, Peggy thought, the longest, most miserable evening of her life—including the time she had eaten a bad oyster and spent twelve hours curled around a chamber pot. At least when you were curled around a chamber pot, people didn't expect you to smile and make polite conversation. But smile and make polite conversation she did. And only Belle, in the end, saw through her. The problem was, though, Peggy knew if she tried to explain, she would fall apart completely, so she lied. Of course, Belle knew she was lying, but she pretended she didn't because, sometimes, that was what friends did for each other.

It was not until the early hours of the morning that Peggy's guests finally began to depart. Whatever else had happened that night, even if she had drifted through it like a shadow puppet of herself, hollow and insubstantial, she had thrown a marvellous party. One where, if Orfeo's exit and subsequent absence had been cause for gossip, there was enough other gossip—who people had come with, and who they had left with—that it didn't matter.

In the empty ballroom, where the candles had burned themselves to puddles of wax and the flowers had wilted to parchment, Peggy huddled into a corner. And there, upon the dance-scuffed floor, into the echoing silence, she finally let herself cry. She cried so hard, and so long, that the dawn pressed red and raw against her eyelids.

Some part of her, ever foolish, had perhaps been hoping Orfeo might come back. But it was now inescapable that they hadn't. And that they weren't going to. She tried to remember that she had chosen this, that she had known all along that what she had with Orfeo could not last. Orfeo had been honest with her from the beginning, and if she hadn't been honest with herself, that was her own fault. But she had prepared for a parting. Not for an ending. And certainly not an ending like this. With Orfeo giving her up—giving up everything—at someone else's behest.

Eventually she dragged herself upstairs, waving a farewell to a sheepish George, who was just leaving, and crawled into bed. Where she stayed, with the pillow intermittently over her head, for the next couple of days. It was not, however, wall-to-wall romantic devastation. Sometimes she allowed herself the brief respite of feeling utterly fucking pathetic instead. And, now and again, she contemplated going to the marquess's house. Trying to see Orfeo. Reason with them. Anything. But she did not imagine they'd speak to her. Rather, she imagined the marquess having her thrown into the street while she howled like an abandoned dog.

No, what Peggy really wanted—really needed—was to go home. So, she wrote to her parents and began the business of closing up the house. She had never particularly wanted to be staying in London, and yet her departure nevertheless weighed upon her as a failure. And to think, after Belle, she had believed herself so wise to the ways of love gone awry. Not inured, certainly, but resilient. Except now she understood she had only ever played at heartbreak. Perhaps because she had always known, on some level, that Belle would never love her. Orfeo, though. They did love her. They'd said so. And it hadn't been enough. Hadn't changed a damn thing.

Peggy was flinging boots into a travelling trunk and—unable to face humans of any kind—scribbling a goodbye letter to the Tarletons when there came a tapping on her bedroom door. It was an oddly familiar-sounding knock, but it could not have been Orfeo. They never knocked. They just swept in.

"What is it?" she called. Assuming it was probably a servant. Or Belle, perhaps. Then again, she was a sweeper-not-a-knocker too.

The door opened and Peggy turned, impatient with the effort of having to pretend that she wasn't falling apart. And there on the threshold, even though she hadn't asked for them, or thought to ask for them—even though it hadn't quite occurred to her that there was no-one she would rather have seen just then—were her parents.

She dropped the boot on her toe and barely noticed. "What are you doing here?"

"We thought we'd pick you up," said Mrs. Delancey, unconvincingly.

Peggy stared at her. The deepest, most dizzying sense of relief was fighting its way through the layers of her hurt. Her parents were here. She was going home. "You thought you'd drive down from Devonshire to take me back to Devonshire?"

Mr. Delancey nodded. "Your letter read a bit peculiar, pet. We thought mebbe you were not quite all right."

"It didn't seem especially peculiar to me." Mrs. Delancey pushed her spectacles farther up her nose, as they had a tendency to slide off. "But I trust your father's judgement."

"You get an instinct sometimes," explained Mr. Delancey. "When it's your child."

Peggy's shoulders slumped. "Well, instinct confirmed, I guess. Because I'm not even a little bit all right."

And then she burst into tears. And her parents sat her down on the bed, one on each side, and took turns to squeeze her hand or pat her knee or make reassuring noises when she tried—more wetly than coherently—to tell them what had happened with Orfeo. And, while Peggy thought she'd cried altogether too much over the last few days, it was different not to be doing it alone. Even if she'd been with friends, she would have felt obliged to pull herself together, in case they concluded—

Actually, she wasn't sure what she was worried they would conclude. That she wasn't the unshakeable, invincible, endlessly reliable paragon she had always found it safer to pretend to be. But that, she knew, wasn't fair either. Nobody had asked that of her. She'd just fallen into it and not known how to stop.

Until she'd met Orfeo.

But here, right now, with her parents, she only had to be herself. Even if that meant being wrecked, and small, and in need of comfort. Someone who, whatever else life offered her and took from her, needed the reminder that she was uncomplicatedly, uncompromisingly loved.

♧

They stayed in town for another day—mainly so her parents wouldn't have to get straight back in a coach—and then prepared to depart over an early breakfast. Because Mrs. Delancey did not thrive without breakfast. Peggy had not been particularly hungry for days, but she took some toast so as not to further worry anyone, and it did help a little. As did making mild gestures towards normality.

Orfeo was gone. Peggy's life lay before her. Someday, that would feel bearable again.

Of course, there was also such a thing as *too much* reality. Which was how Peggy felt about Valentine turning up, looking distraught and so dishevelled that he must have dressed without the services of his valet.

"Peggy," he cried, bursting into the dining room. "I need your help."

He clearly needed some kind of help. Valentine did not believe in getting out of bed before noon. "Um." She glanced at her parents, who were eating bacon and watching events unfold with the bemused expressions of people who found themselves the unexpected recipients of after-dinner theatre at breakfast. "I'm really not . . . I mean, I was kind of about to . . ."

"Please." Valentine cut over her attempted demurrals. Then seemed to notice her parents. He smoothed a hand through his tangled hair and gave a tense little bow. "I do apologise for interrupting your meal." Then he turned back to Peggy, frantic again. "It's Bonny and Belle."

And for some reason, this entirely unrevelatory revelation made Peggy feel the slightest bit more herself. "Surely not. They'd never do anything controversial or ill thought through."

Valentine made an astounded noise. Then an irate growl. "Could you perhaps not be dry? Just at the moment? It's not helping."

"Sorry," said Peggy. "What have they done?"

The words *this time* hung unspoken between them.

"Well . . ." Despite the urgency of his entrance, Valentine abruptly seemed to lose steam. He took an abstracted turn about the room. "I could be wrong. Or . . . or jumping to conclusions. Bonny's letters are not renowned for their coherence, even when he is not writing in haste."

"Valentine"—if Peggy had not interrupted, she thought he might have continued for some considerable time—"is there a point on the horizon?"

"I'm so sorry," he said, somewhat tormentedly. "And I'm so sorry to come to you like this. But I am inclined to—I have reason to suspect—that is to say."

"What?"

"I think the Tarletons have kidnapped Sir Horley."

Mrs. Delancey looked up from her coffee. "What interesting friends you have, Peggy darling."

"They've *what*?" asked Peggy, who had hubristically believed herself incapable of having her ghast in any way flabbered by either Bonny or Belle. And yet here she was, flabbered of ghast, and smacked of gob.

"And possibly his fiancée," added Valentine.

"Why?"

"God." He gripped his hair hysterically. "Why do those two do anything. Presumably they thought it was a good idea."

"How can kidnapping two people possibly be a good idea?"

"Are we allowed to play?" asked Mrs. Delancey. "Perhaps they want to bring them together in order to settle a matter of philosophical or scientific conflict?"

Mr. Delancey snorted affectionately. "Only you, love, would want to abduct someone for the sake of a scholarly exchange." He turned to Peggy. "I reckon it's far more like to be a romantic matter."

"How is kidnapping romantic?" asked Mrs. Delancey. "If someone kidnapped me, I would not feel romantically disposed towards them. I'd feel quite annoyed."

"I more meant two people who'll only admit their feelings under extraordinary circumstances."

Peggy gave her father a horrified look. "Dad, stick to mines."

"It was in that play." He appealed to his wife. "Remember? That play we saw. The one with the—the one with that man in it. And the bit with the—the thing."

"Ohhhhh." Mrs. Delancey nodded. *"Much Ado about Nothing."*

"How did you—" began Peggy. And then gave up. "I don't think it can be that. Sir Horley doesn't favour women, and no amount of kidnapping is likely to change it."

Valentine, who had been watching this exchange with the agonised expression of a man whose politeness was at war with his politeness, gave an impatiently polite cough. "This may be the Tarletons' way of forcing a conversation."

"Oh." Peggy let the potential consequences of a Tarleton-driven intervention sink in. "Oh shit."

Valentine's expression was ominous. "Exactly." He made a hopeless gesture. "Please help, Peggy. I don't even know where they've gone."

"I know where they've gone," said Peggy, both surprised and not surprised at how instinctive the knowledge was. "They'll have taken them to the last place they . . . um. Did a small amount of kidnapping."

"You mean, the home of Miss Fairfax and Miss Evans?" Valentine was apparently too distraught or too tactful to note that he had, on that occasion, been the kidnappee. "Surely they can't think that's what it's *for*."

Peggy shrugged. "I think it would have made sense to them. Thematic resonance or what have you."

"We have to do something, Peggy."

"Well, it has been five minutes since I was in a frantic cross-country chase, but . . ." She indicated her parents. "I was about to go home. I honestly need a . . . a bit of a break."

Valentine wrestled visibly with his conscience. "I understand. It's just I sincerely doubt my capacity to resolve this alone."

"My mam and dad came specially." At this point, Peggy couldn't tell if she was making excuses because she secretly wanted to fly off in pursuit of the Tarletons. Or because she didn't.

"Darling," said Mrs. Delancey, munching peacefully, "it's no trouble to us. It was a lovely journey. I read twenty-three books, and your father was only travel sick twice."

Mr. Delancey poured himself a cup of tea. "We'll always be here when you need us, pet. And we'll happily bugger off again when you don't."

Peggy glanced between her parents and Valentine, torn. "I . . . I don't know."

"You should never feel bad," Mr. Delancey told her, "for taking care of yourself. But if you want to go stop your friends kidnapping each other, then you don't have to worry about us."

Mrs. Delancey smiled at her husband. "We haven't been to town for such a long time. I would love to disguise myself as a man and take in a dissection."

While her parents debated the tourist attractions of the capital, Peggy took a moment to turn her heart upside down like she was looking for the last biscuit in the tin. Orfeo had been gone less than a week, and she was about one imploring look from running around after the Tarletons as though nothing had changed at all.

Except she'd changed, hadn't she? In ways that had nothing to do with whether she was with Orfeo or not, however much it hurt that she wasn't. She no longer felt like the only life she knew how to have was one she lived in the shadow of someone else's. That the things she wanted, small and quiet and ordinary though they were, need not exist in opposition to who she knew she was. And, in any case, no matter who she was, or what she wanted, she wasn't ever going to be someone who abandoned her friends. Even if her friends were very much the agents of their own disasters.

"All right," she said. "Let's go."

Chapter 29

They took Valentine's curricle, but Peggy drove. Partly because she was the better whip but mainly because neither she nor Valentine trusted he wouldn't fall asleep over the reins. As it happened, he fell asleep on Peggy's shoulder not long after they left London, and she thought it best to let him rest. He did not handle adventures very well.

Besides, it was less woe-inducing than she had feared to be alone with her thoughts. Not with the streets, and then the countryside, flying by, the wind in her hair, and the rattle of the horses' hooves upon the road. The world stretched before her like a cat shaking off slumber, and she stretched with it, feeling herself uncrumpling somehow beneath the cloud-swirled archways of the sky.

And if she ached more than a little for Orfeo still, distraction and distance helped, spreading little cracks through the pain, through which glimmered the memories of all the ways Orfeo had made her happy. Of their capacity for sweetness and bitterness both, their swift temper, and unassailable pride. Their rough laugh. Their shameless hedonism. The way they looked at her, sometimes, as if she was as fascinating and remarkable as they were. It wouldn't be today—it probably wouldn't even be next week—but Peggy could make out the edges of a time in the future when looking back would bring her far more pleasure than pain. There was comfort in that. Just like there was comfort in knowing her parents were there for her. As were her friends, in their own inimitable fashion—although she wished the one with her right now had a less pointy chin, because it was digging right into her.

Eventually Valentine stirred of his own volition. He gave a snuffle and a start, and sat up so violently that Peggy grabbed his arm to make sure he didn't go tumbling from the curricle.

"Oh God," he said, rubbing his eyes. "I had this nightmare that I was back—" He broke off, glancing round him wildly. "Wait. Where am I?"

"So," Peggy told him, "I have bad news about the nightmare situation."

Valentine slumped against her with a groan. "Why does this keep happening to me?"

"Because you're with Bonny?"

"All I want"—it was Valentine's most tragic voice—"is to be a very rich, powerful, and well-dressed man who gets to sleep until a sensible hour of one or two in the afternoon, and bathe uninterrupted at length." He flung his arms to the heavens. "Is that too much to ask?"

As in answer, the sky darkened, and a few drops of rain plopped heavily down upon them.

"No," said Valentine. He subjected the weather to a ducal glare. "Stop it. Stop it *at once.*"

Peggy patted him reassuringly on the arm. "We're nearly there."

They were not nearly there. But she didn't want to admit that to Valentine in case he burst into tears or threw himself from the vehicle. Thankfully, the rain didn't get too much worse, although—as was the nature of rain—it remained cold and wet and, therefore, made the people it landed on cold and wet as well.

The cottage was much as Peggy remembered it from her last visit, although, at the time, she'd mostly been focused on helping Belle run away from Valentine, for reasons that—retrospectively—seemed particularly Belle-like.

Hoping that it would be a relatively swift visit—one that would mostly involve dragging two Tarletons away by their hair—they left the curricle in the stable yard. Barely had Valentine rapped on the door when it was opened by a harried Emily Fairfax.

"Thank goodness you're here," she said, evidently unsurprised to see them. "Belle brought a strange woman here at gunpoint, and now we don't know what to do with her. The strange woman, that is. Well, we don't know what to do with Belle, either, but that's a given."

Valentine, being Valentine, was incapable of not honouring social niceties, no matter how irrelevant the situation rendered them. "Good afternoon, Miss Fairfax. May we come in?"

She blinked at him. "No, I intend you to resolve this matter for me on the doorstep in the rain."

"Thanks," said Peggy. "And sorry about this." She knocked the mud off her boots as best she could and marched inside.

Emily, stepping aside to admit them, gave a sigh. "I think Bonny and Belle have forgotten that just because I write sensational books doesn't mean I want to live one."

Peggy offered a sympathetic noise and made her way down the narrow hallway towards the living room. Given the success of Emily's novels—all published under the name Ambrosia Blaine—the fact that she and her partner, Miss Angharad Evans, were still staying in a cottage suggested they did so by choice, rather than necessity. Frankly, Peggy saw the appeal. Had always seen the appeal. To say nothing of the appeal of Emily herself, whose no-fuss hairstyle and demure gown did nothing to detract from the luminous intelligence of her eyes and the secretive sensuality of her mouth.

Enough of that, Margaret Delancey. She's a taken woman, you're on a rescue mission, and your heart is very, very broken.

The living room was just on the right side of cosy when it contained Emily and Angharad, and all of their various projects—Emily's books and pages, Angharad's painting materials—but it was very much not set up to accommodate the two ladies, Peggy, Valentine, Belle dressed as a highwayman (because of course she was), and the disdainful-looking stranger perched on a chair.

"Hello," said Peggy. "I'm Peggy."

The stranger, who for all her disdain was also extremely striking, with piercing green eyes and chestnut hair, regarded her with unexpected equanimity, given the circumstances. "Forgive my discourtesy, but in what way is that relevant to me?"

That rather threw Peggy. "Well, it's not. But I thought it might be, I don't know, friendlier?"

"I have been brought here against my will for reasons that remain elusive." The woman's gaze did not falter. "That leaves limited opportunity for friendliness."

Belle pulled down the scarf that was covering the lower half of her face. "This is Verity Carswile. Sir Horley's fiancée."

Peggy tried not to groan too loudly. "That's what I was afraid of."

Miss Carswile started. "What does Sir Horley have to do with this?"

"Yes, Belle"—Peggy shot her a look—"what *does* Sir Horley have to do with this?"

It was at this juncture that there came another knock at the door.

"Our home is not a coaching inn," cried Emily, her usually immaculate hair frizzing around her face.

Angharad gave her arm a reassuring squeeze. "I'll go."

She vanished into the hall, while the rest of them remained, frozen in a tableau of awkwardness.

"Inclement weather," Valentine remarked, "for the time of year."

Everyone stared at him.

"It will probably," he went on, "make the roads quite wet."

Everyone was still staring at him.

"And difficult to traverse," he finished.

"I hope you don't think"—Sir Horley's voice mercifully drifted towards them, along with the sounds of feet being stamped and coats removed—"that I haven't recognised you, Bonaventure Tarleton. You are the least convincing highwayman I've ever encountered, and I have encountered zero highwaymen."

Bonny made an unconvincing growling noise.

"Darling, why would a highwayman bring me to the house of my friends? I do hope this is some kind of peculiar sex game you and Valentine have dreamed up." Sir Horley paused for a moment, both verbally and, apparently, physically. "On second thoughts, I sincerely hope it is not. Because I cannot imagine either Miss Fairfax or Miss Evans would appreciate that."

"I might," offered Miss Evans. "But Emily assuredly would not. And I'm not sure we have the space to accommodate anything so logistically complicated."

The door opened, and Sir Horley bounced in with an air of indulgent exasperation. "If this is a surprise birthday party," he began, seeing them all assembled, "you're exceptionally out of season for—" His gaze alighted upon his fiancée, and the geniality slipped from his face like a mask crumbling. "Miss Carswile."

"I think," she said, rising, "for both our sakes I shall pretend I heard none of that."

Sir Horley had gone very pale. "What are you doing here?"

"I was brought here," returned Miss Carswile. "And if these . . . these people are indeed your friends, it's little wonder your aunt is concerned about your choices."

Nobody quite knew what to say to that. At least until Sir Horley turned upon the Tarletons with a snarl of "What have you done?"

Bonny and Belle exchanged nervous glances.

"We were trying to help you," Bonny said finally.

"Then God save me," Sir Horley retorted, "the day you decide to take against me."

His fiancée gave a shudder of mild distaste. "There is no need to take the Lord's name in vain."

"Certainly there isn't," muttered Emily. "For he doesn't exist."

This, Miss Carswile simply ignored, turning instead to the twins. "I find myself at a loss twice over: first that you seem to have formed the conviction Sir Horley is in need of assistance, and secondly that your attempt to provide this assistance took this particular form."

Of all unfortunate scenes that had taken place in this cottage—including the evening Valentine had spent tied to a chair—this was topping Peggy's list of the worst. On that occasion, Belle had been legitimately scared of Valentine, and Valentine had been legitimately angry with Belle, but it hadn't felt like this. Tense beyond anyone's power to remedy.

"Well," said Bonny at last, as though he was just beginning to recognise this wasn't going the way he had hoped. Whatever that was. "We thought perhaps it might offer you an opportunity to talk to each other?"

Miss Carswile tilted her head enquiringly. "And you are under the impression we need such an opportunity?"

"An opportunity," Bonny tried again, "to talk candidly."

"That's enough." Sir Horley's voice cracked across them suddenly, and without mercy. Peggy had never heard him speak that way before. "I will not subject Miss Carswile to any more of your nonsense. Come"—he took her arm—"we're leaving."

"It's not nonsense." Belle darted forward, trying to put herself between Sir Horley, Miss Carswile, and the door—quite a challenge, considering she was as short as Bonny and had none of his heft. "We just want you to be happy, and we don't think you'll be happy with Miss Carswile." She suddenly seemed to remember she was speaking directly to the lady in question. "No offence."

"None taken," said Miss Carswile, from—Peggy thought—a position of indifference rather than forgiveness.

Sir Horley, meanwhile, had the grim look of a man forced to defend something he didn't want. "Miss Carswile's mother is a long-standing friend of my aunt's. She's an heiress of good family and sterling reputation. It is I who should be grateful she's willing to marry me."

"It's quite all right." His fiancée's grip tightened on his arm. "I know you are."

"In which case," Belle went on relentlessly, "don't you think you ought to consider her happiness?"

Miss Carswile's spare hand drifted unconsciously to the simple golden cross she wore around her neck. "My store of happiness does not reside in earthly things."

"You might think differently," Bonny told her, "if you knew what earthly things you were going to miss out on."

"I will do my duty," snapped Sir Horley.

"But"—Belle made a pleading gesture—"what of Miss Carswile? Does she not deserve to be more than a duty? Does she, at least, not deserve your honesty?"

Sir Horley was trembling slightly. "I don't think *my honesty*, as you put it, will help anyone."

"I am inclined to agree," said Miss Carswile. Her austere, sculpted beauty made Belle look small and frivolous by comparison. "Sir Horley's aunt informed me of his unsavoury habits long before I consented to the engagement."

"His what?" cried Bonny. "There's nothing unsavoury about—"

Stepping up to him, Valentine drew him close, smothering Bonny's outrage against his shoulder. "Not now, my heart."

"What did she tell you?" Sir Horley cringed slightly away from Miss Carswile. "You shouldn't have to know about my—"

She waved him into silence. "There's no need to worry about that," she said soothingly. "In order to do the Lord's work, one must know the Devil's ways."

Still in Valentine's arms, Bonny flailed and made squeaky noises.

"Is that why you're marrying Sir Horley?" demanded Belle, glaring up at Miss Carswile with her hands on her hips. "Because you think you're . . . helping him?"

Miss Carswile glowed with fervour. "Of course I'm helping him. I am saving him from perdition. What greater good can one human being do for another?"

The conversation was not helping to settle the dread sloshing in Peggy's stomach. She tugged at Sir Horley's sleeve. "You don't believe that, do you?"

He shook his head. "I do not. But I do believe my aunt is correct that I have obligations to fulfil: to my name, to society, and to my family."

"What about us?" Belle pressed her hands to her heart. "Aren't we your family?"

At last, Sir Horley seemed to see them—Valentine and Bonny, Bonny still being aggressively hugged by Valentine, Belle standing before him like a tiny King Canute, Peggy uncertain what to do for the best but there nevertheless, and Emily and Angharad patiently enduring the invasion of their property. His manner had shed all traces of his usual impishness and insouciance, and Peggy thought, with a touch of shame at her own self-absorption, that it might be the first time she'd ever truly seen him.

"No more charades, Arabella," he said. "It has been entertaining, but let us not pretend it's more than that."

Belle's mouth tightened, and Peggy realised, with a pang, that she was struggling not to cry. "How can you say that? Of course it's more. *You* are more."

"No." The word was its own wall. The worst of it was that Sir Horley sounded neither angry nor sad. Just certain. "I played the merry fool for you. But it is time to ring the curtain down."

"That's not true," Belle protested, piteously. "You . . . you're my friend, aren't you?"

"And mine." That was Valentine, a stricken look on his face. "I hope?"

Sir Horley sketched them a bow, his eyes bleak. "Miss Carswile and I are leaving."

"Gladly," she said.

"No." Belle gave a wild cry. "No, you can't. You can't do this. It'll be like a prison to you. And it won't . . . it won't change anything. It won't make your aunt love you."

"What do you know of love?" He sneered down at her. And then at the rest of them. "What do any of you know of love? You're all so *fucking* self-righteous."

Sir Horley's sudden fury filled up the little room. Splashed itself against the walls in bright and ugly shades. It was hard, though, to be angry at him in return because he wasn't really angry at them. Nor, Peggy thought, was he really angry. His rage was a rotted log. Turn it over with a boot, and you'd find nothing but despair wriggling beneath.

"You think," he went on, "love is this grand entitlement. And why would you not; it comes to you with such *ease*. I mean, take you, my dear duke." He gestured to Valentine. "You spent your whole life blissfully oblivious of your own nature, and the second you had to confront it, this prince of sunshine and sparkles tumbles into your lap to kiss everything better again."

Valentine swallowed. "It . . . it wasn't quite like that."

"Oh yes." Sir Horley rolled his eyes. "You suffered terribly, having to wear an ill-fitting coat and go without a bath for three whole days."

"I can see," said Valentine, somewhat stiffly, "you have been harbouring some resentment towards me. For anything I have done to inspire it, I apologise."

Sir Horley's shoulders slumped, and his toned softened. "Keep your apology, Valentine, and keep your fairy tale. I'm happy for you, truly. But try to understand that most of us don't live in your world." He closed his eyes for a moment, and when he opened them again, all trace of warmth had gone. "We live in a world of compromises and sacrifices. A world where happiness is the exception, not the expectation."

"You *should* expect happiness," Belle told him, fiercely. "And you should expect love."

Sir Horley gave a soft laugh. "Not everyone is worthy of them, my dear."

And with that, he led his fiancée away.

Chapter 30

If Peggy hoped for respite from the journey home—they had left Valentine's curricle with Emily and Angharad, and piled into the carriage Bonny had employed for the purposes of unconvincing highway robbery—she was doomed to disappointment. Outside, the rain persisted, the drops tippy-tapping on the roof of the carriage like skeletal fingers. Inside, the mood was little better. Peggy had no idea what to say. *Well, we fucked that up* seemed unhelpful, if accurate. She felt a fresh pang of longing for Orfeo, not because she wanted or expected them to do anything exactly. But crawling quietly into their arms, surrounding herself with the scent of their hair, the smooth heat of their body, and pretending the rest of the world didn't exist seemed a far better way to end her day than continuing to feel terrible about everything.

Eventually Valentine broke the gloomy silence with "You have to stop doing this."

Predictably, Bonny bristled. "Trying to help the people we care about?"

"You know," said Valentine wearily, "that's not what I meant." He sighed and put his fingers to the bridge of his nose, like he was getting a headache. "I'm talking about these . . . I don't know what to call them . . . escapades? Theatricals?"

Bonny had that pouty mulish look he sometimes got when challenged. But then he crumpled. "We weren't *trying* to have an escapade. We were *trying* to make two people have a conversation. That's *mature*."

"From a certain perspective," conceded Valentine, "perhaps. But you still staged a kidnapping—"

"Only a little one."

"—and would it not have been better to converse with Sir Horley first?"

"Well, he wouldn't converse with us. What else were we supposed to do?"

"I don't know." Valentine made an ill-advisedly wild gesture and banged his hand against the roof on the carriage. "Not this?" He cradled his wrist. "Ow. When are you going to learn?"

Bonny's attempt to draw himself up haughtily was again restricted by the carriage. "I don't need you to scold me, Valentine."

"I'm not trying to scold you," said Valentine, in the face of all available evidence to the contrary.

"Then what are you trying to do? Because"—Bonny fluffed huffily—"it looks a lot like scolding from where I'm sitting. Which, by the way, is right next to you."

Belle, meanwhile, had said nothing at all. She was looking fixedly out the window, or at least at the pattern of waterdrops streaking the glass, her whole body turned tightly away from Peggy.

"Do you not understand," Valentine was asking Bonny, "that I, too, wish the world could work the way it does in books? Fiction makes sense; reality frequently doesn't. But life cannot always be bent to the shape we would prefer it to take."

Bonny's eyes glimmered blue-black through the gloom. "You're a duke. You bend whatever you want."

"I should not, though. You taught me that."

"Then, I want to unteach it," declared Bonny, pouting, "if it means letting Sir Horley marry someone who thinks . . . who thinks who he is is *bad*. All because his smelly aunt told him to."

"And how are we to stop him? Kidnap him again?"

"Can we?"

"No," said Peggy and Valentine together.

"So . . ." Bonny's voice trembled. "Then what are we to do? How are we supposed to help him?"

"I don't know. I—" Valentine broke off and then tried again. "I am beginning to think Sir Horley has been a better friend to us than we have been to him. And . . . and what happened in that cottage has probably damaged whatever trust he had in us beyond repair."

Belle, Peggy realised, was crying—very softly and undramatically.

"Darling," she murmured and tried to put an arm around her.

But Belle would not allow herself to be comforted. "Don't."

"It's not . . ." Peggy didn't want to say *It's not your fault* because that would have been a blatant lie. Although she also thought, in the grand scheme of things, there were limits to culpability here. "Sir Horley has to make his own decisions. Even if they're . . . you know. Absolutely fucking terrible."

"He . . ." Belle sniffed in a very damp, unladylike way. "He doesn't believe we care for him."

Peggy winced. "I'm not sure he believes anyone could care for him."

"That doesn't make it better," Belle wailed. "Now he is going to do an absolutely fucking terrible thing *all alone.*"

There was a long silence, Peggy racking her brain for something even a little bit reassuring to say.

At last Belle—having rejected Valentine's offer of an exquisitely monogramed handkerchief, which shone through the uncertain light like a white flag—scrubbed her face with her sleeve. "I," she announced, "am done with books. They have never steered me right."

"I'm not sure they're trying to steer you at all?" suggested Peggy.

"Aren't they, though?" Belle's tearstained face was set. "Romantic love was supposed to bring me happiness. Loving my friend was supposed to save my friend. Books either teach us that who we are is wrong, or they promise us things that cannot be. And, right now, I do not know which is worse."

Valentine gave a small, helpless hand flap. "Belle . . ."

"No," she said, sharply. "I am done. I am going to become a nun. That's what heroines always do in stories when—oh." She growled. "Goddamn it."

"How about . . ." Except Peggy didn't have a *how about*. She was an experienced how-about-er, especially where the Tarletons were concerned, and she had nothing. She was sad for Sir Horley, sad for Belle, sad for Orfeo, and sad for herself. And that felt like far too much sadness to cope with, the weight of it pressing down on her like an enormous thumb until all that would be left of her was a Peggy-shaped smear.

Truthfully, she couldn't have imagined today playing out otherwise. Except, in some ways, that was its own little tragedy. She had always tried to be the naysayer, the sensible one, the voice of reason when dragged into the latest round of Tarleton hijinks, but she had never once said nay. Because, at the end of the day, a world full of adventures, romantic reversals, grand gestures, and happy endings was simply *better* than a world without. It wasn't, after all, as if she hadn't been dreaming of winning Orfeo back, defeating Nicholas like some dragon from a fable, choosing love above everything, crying and laughing and kissing them in the rain.

"Let's just go home," she said finally.

And the rain that slicked the carriage windows grey remained ordinary rain. The kind of rain that made you cold and wet and uncomfortable. Not the kind of rain you embraced someone in.

It was probably for the best, Peggy told herself, that Bonny and Belle were growing up a little.

Even if it also cost the world a little magic.

༒

She was still telling herself this—and not believing it in the slightest— when they arrived back at Valentine's. Desperate to either stretch her legs or get away from the concentrated misery that was the interior of the carriage, Peggy jumped down without waiting for the stairs. This meant that she was first to spot the figure huddled on Valentine's doorstep. A figure her heart recognised before her eyes.

"Orfeo?"

They came unsteadily to their feet. And it was, indeed, Orfeo, dressed in simple black, with their unbound hair flattened to inky sheets by the rain.

Peggy made a sort of gasping noise as the world reeled around her. "What are you doing here?"

"Your mother said you were at the Duke of Malvern's, and his servants said you had gone out together, and I . . . I was not sure they would let me wait inside, so I waited here and . . ." Orfeo seemed to lose their grasp on what they were trying to say. And then, when they began to speak again, it was with such desperate rapidity that their words were almost indistinguishable from each other, half drowned in the pitter-patter of the rain.

"Peggy, Peggy, tesoro mio, ho sbagliato, ho torto, I am sorry, I was wrong."

There was water on their face that might have been from weeping, and they were trembling violently from the cold. Tearing off her coat, Peggy rushed forward with it, only for Orfeo to rush towards her in turn, dropping to their knees before her.

"I do not care about any of it," they said, wrapping their arms around her and pressing their face against her body. "Not the music. Not the fame. Not my future. None of it. Only you. Perdonami, per favore."

"Orfeo—"

"Ti prego."

"Please don't—"

They gazed up at her, starlight dancing in the darkness of their eyes. "It is too late? You no longer want me? Or it is too much to ask? To spend your life with someone who—"

"Let me finish," Peggy yelled. "I was only trying to say, *Please don't kneel down in the street. It'll hurt your knees.*"

"I'm not really so very concerned about my knees just at the moment, Peggy."

"Well, I'm concerned about your knees. Please stand up."

Orfeo stood up.

And Peggy was fully intending to say something sensible like *You're drenched* or *Here's my coat* or *You could have waited inside like a reasonable person*. But instead, the day and the week that had preceded it, thinking she had lost Orfeo forever, and now discovering she had not, descended on Peggy in a deluge so overwhelming she could hardly tell grief from joy. Bursting into tears, she flung herself into Orfeo's arms, and they held her as the rain came down and the cloud-defying moon washed the whole world silver.

⚜

Much later, they gathered in Valentine's library. Orfeo sat close to the fire, in a borrowed dressing gown, letting Peggy comb the tangles from their drying hair.

"Wait." Bonny was curled up on Valentine's lap as usual. "You left Peggy? You left Peggy, and we didn't know about it?"

"I didn't tell you," said Peggy. "I was going to. But the whole kidnapping thing got in the way."

"And"—Orfeo pressed a little closer to her—"I will never leave you again."

Peggy spluttered slightly. "Steady on. I think that would get on my nerves. I mean," she clarified hastily, "no further breakups, please. But I'm not the marquess. I don't want to own you."

"I do not think I would mind if it was you."

"Yes," said Peggy. "Yes, you would. And so would I."

It was strange to see Belle seated alone on the sofa she usually shared with Sir Horley, and clearly she felt that strangeness, too, for she was pressed right against the cushions. "You left Peggy for a marquess?" she asked, some of her customary energy returning in defence of Peggy.

289

Orfeo made a faint, pained sound. "Not *for* him. If I was leaving for anyone, I believed it was for Peggy."

"Um . . ." The damp weight of Orfeo's hair was silken and familiar in Peggy's hands. It smelled a little still of the rain. "You can't do something *for* someone unless they want the thing in the first place."

"Ah, Peggy, Peggy." There was a note of gentle remonstrance in their voice. "I am a selfish creature and have always been so. When the world has taken from you, you feel justified in taking back. But I did not wish my love for you to be selfish."

"How is loving me selfish?"

"Because it is as Nicholas said, as I have long known it myself: you will have to give up so much for me."

Peggy waved her hand at her assembled friends. "I don't seem to be a social outcast yet. Though if we're talking about sacrifices, you just offered to abandon your whole career."

"But you *want* a family. You have told me so. Music has always been a choice someone else made for me."

"Orfeo . . ." Gathering up their hair, Peggy draped it across one of their shoulders and then turned their face to hers. Their expression was wary, pain lingering like a promise in their eyes. "That might be how it started. But you love what you do."

"Not as much as I love you."

"It's not a competition."

Orfeo flinched slightly against her fingers but did not pull away. "If I love it so much, then why do I not work at it, as Nicholas says I should?"

"Because"—Belle spoke up suddenly—"your art belongs to you, not to him. What matters is what you create, not that a rich man approves of how you create it."

That won a smirk from Orfeo. "Few patrons of the arts would agree with you."

Belle shrugged. "Do you care?"

"It does not matter now."

"Listen"—Peggy drew their attention back to her—"I've been thinking about this . . . I've been thinking about this for a while, actually. And I don't see why anyone has to give up anything."

Orfeo laughed, in that harsh, bitter way they sometimes had. "You will be satisfied with a lover who spends at least half their time elsewhere?"

There was a pause, simply because Peggy did not want to deliver them an impulsive answer. Truthfully she was beginning to wonder if, in her way, she was as given to extremities as the Tarletons, for she had swung from telling herself she could not have a relationship that looked like everyone else's to believing she *must*. When she had known all along, yet somehow forgotten, that her parents' marriage worked because they had shaped it for themselves, for each other, and for her. "If it was you, and as long as you came back to me, yes."

"You say that, but—"

"I say that," said Peggy firmly, "because I mean it."

The corner of Orfeo's lips twitched with wry amusement, their beauty marks twinkling. "Do you have some pomegranate seeds for me to eat also?"

"Now you're just mixing all the myths together."

They sighed. "This will not work, Peggy."

"Why not? Unless"—she grinned at them—"this is your way of telling me you can't bear to be parted from me for more than a second."

"It will be a lot more than a second. My schedule is demanding. The marquess . . ." They trailed away. "Well, I suppose the marquess will have no say in what I do any longer."

"So you can set your own schedule. If anything, being less available will probably make you more in demand."

Hope flickered across Orfeo's face. "And you will not mind to wait for me?"

"Sometimes," Peggy told them, "I intend to come with you. But, sometimes, yes. I'll wait."

"That sounds *awful*," cried Bonny, before Valentine could hush him.

Peggy rolled her eyes. "Yes, well, I'm not you. Thank God."

"But you are you . . ." Orfeo drew her back to them. "And while I can take you at your word when you tell me such an arrangement would make you happy, there are still things you can never have with me."

"You mean," asked Peggy bluntly, remembering a conversation in a carriage that already felt lifetimes ago, "a child?"

Orfeo gave a little nod.

"I've thought about that too. We can still have a child, Orfeo. We can raise one—or even more than one—together."

"That"—Orfeo looked startled—"is not something I have ever considered before. Where would you get this child? From the fairies?"

"From my body. As long as you would accept them as yours."

Orfeo put a hand to their brow. "This is a lot, mio principe. I have never allowed myself to think of . . . of being a parent; it felt too painful an impossibility to contemplate—I am excited, I think, but also terrified."

"From everything I've heard," Peggy said, "that's a very normal reaction to parenthood."

"We must not run away with ourselves, though. The world would not be kind to someone born outside of wedlock."

"They wouldn't be."

There was a soft, sharp intake of breath from Orfeo. "If you are wed, what role am I to play in your life? In your husband's life? In the life of this child you say we are to raise?"

"Well"—Peggy felt herself blushing slightly—"I hadn't intended to say this in front of an audience, but I was kind of hoping to marry you, Orfeo."

Chapter 31

There was a moment of silence that quivered in the air. Then Orfeo put a hand to their mouth to cover a shocked rush of laughter. "Peggy, you cannot. The pope will not allow it."

She made a "Look around you" gesture. "Protestant country."

"It is still not possible."

"I think it's very possible. The world insists I'm a woman. And if we have a child, it will be hard-pressed to prove you aren't a man."

"But, but . . ." She had never seen Orfeo so flustered. "You are not a woman. And I am not a man."

"I know that and you know that, but we didn't make the rules."

There was another, intense silence. Then Belle gave an actual shriek. "Margaret Delancey, you are chaos incarnate. I *love* it."

Peggy flicked an imaginary speck of dust from her sleeve. "Thank you. Um." She realised Orfeo was yet to speak. Or for that matter move. "Are you . . . are you all right?"

"Oh, Peggy," they breathed, leaning their head against her shoulder. "Perhaps it is my turn to swoon."

"I don't recommend it."

"And . . ." Their voice trembled. "You truly want to do this with me? Music, family, all of it?"

"Hell yes, I do." Sometimes, late at night, with Orfeo asleep in her arms, Peggy had half wondered at a future for them both. But she had never imagined it could actually happen. That she and Orfeo would make it happen. "We can have everything we want," she went on. "Together. And nothing can stop us."

"Well"—Orfeo's eyes turned up to hers—"there is the small matter of this child we—"

"Me." Bonny bounded off Valentine's lap. "Pick me. I'll do it."

Peggy stared at him. Everyone stared at him. "You?"

He flung his arms in the air. "Why not? *Imagine*. A tiny me. A bijou Bonette. They will grow up with the finest arse in London. Don't you want that for your offspring?"

"Yes," said Peggy, "that is my dream. I want my child to have love, joy, freedom, education, security, the confidence to be who they are, and a really great arse."

"A really great arse will smooth their passage through the world," declared Bonny, with great conviction.

At last, Peggy managed, "You can't be serious?"

"Of course I'm serious. Look at my arse." Bonny wriggled it demonstratively. "It has brought me nothing but good fortune."

"No. I mean . . ." How did Peggy say this? While the desire to have a child was very real to her—had probably always been very real, once she'd admitted it to herself—the prospect of having that child with Bonny seemed beyond absurd. Not wanting to offend him, she waved her hands about.

"Oh, Peggy"—Bonny blazed with sincerity—"it would be the *best thing ever*. A gift from Belle and I, to you, our best friend. And my arse gifted to posterity." He stopped abruptly and whirled back to Valentine. "If Valentine doesn't mind, that is. Flower, would you mind?"

Valentine's face looked the way Peggy felt. "I have no notion."

"While I'm sure," Peggy said slowly and not sure at all, "this is a lovely idea, there are. Well. Practical considerations?"

Bonny's eyes went wide with outrage. "I don't have the pox or anything. My cock is pristine and beautiful; you could eat your dinner off it."

It was not an image Peggy needed right now. "I think I'll pass on that. But . . . you. You like men. Could you even—"

"I do like men," Bonny conceded. "Or one man very specifically at the moment and probably forever." He dropped his voice to a stagy whisper and eyed Valentine. "That's you, by the way."

Valentine seemed to be hiding a smile. "I am relieved to hear it."

"In any case," Bonny went on cheerfully, "I'm sure I could. Because it's not as if—I mean, you're not a—you're a . . . you're a *you*. And I've always adored you. It's just you liked Belle better."

"She did," Belle put in, with an undeniable air of smugness. "It's because you're quite annoying, Bonbon."

"I am not. I'm"—Bonny struck a pose—"*fabulous*."

Trying to keep the Tarletons even a little bit on topic was a labour that would have defied the power of Hercules. Still, Peggy tried. "But how are you even sure you'd be comfortable with. Well. My body type."

At this Bonny re-adjusted his pose, hands landing firmly on hips. "Because I'm already familiar with it. Well, not yours exactly. But that very delicious soldier I pined over for the longest time? Two whole weeks or something? He gave me *lots* of experience."

"Good to know," said Peggy.

"You seem to be raising a lot of objections," observed Bonny, getting pouty. "Is this your way of telling me that you don't find me attractive?"

"On the contrary"—Peggy was neither so foolhardy nor so insensitive as to insult someone who was trying to help her—"you're very attractive."

"Or you don't think I'm a suitable person to contribute to making a child."

Peggy relented. Truthfully, she could imagine far worse candidates. "It's not that. I just wasn't prepared for you to offer."

"That was very silly of you," retorted Bonny. "I'm incredibly vain."

"I'm not sure having a child out of vanity is the best idea?"

"And you'd be right," Bonny agreed, "if I had to be responsible for them in any way. But I won't because you will. You and Orfeo will."

In that moment, Peggy's vague hopes for the future felt very real indeed, and her heart seized with the reality of them.

"Yes." Orfeo's voice cut neatly through the quiet. "We will."

Peggy slipped her hand into theirs and gave it a squeeze. "If nothing else"—she took refuge in levity—"I'll have the singular distinction of having been with both Tarletons."

Peggy and Bonny exchanged glances.

"That's not even a little bit singular," Belle told her finally.

"Not," Bonny added, "at the same time, obviously. But you know what Surrey is like."

Belle nodded. "We were very stifled."

"And does this mean"—Bonny gave a gleeful little yelp—"you're saying yes?"

A friend, Peggy had to admit, was an infinitely more reassuring prospect than a stranger. And far less morally unpleasant than befriending someone specifically to ask them if they wanted to have procreative sex with her. Besides, a child could do worse than to have some Tarleton in their blood.

She turned to Orfeo, carding her fingers through their hair to spread the strands before the flames. "What do you think?"

They smiled at her, somewhat tentatively. "I do not know what I think."

That was fair. She wasn't sure what she thought either. Just that, for all she did not consider herself an impulsive person, she was giddy with possibility. "There's no need for us to rush into anything," she said. "Or to make each other promises of—"

"Tesoro mio . . ." Orfeo was laughing. "I would promise you the moon and the tides, if you wanted them. I would cast aside my music with no backward glance and follow you into the underworld with nothing but joy in my heart."

Peggy was not used to being spoken to quite like that. It made her blushy and fluttery and embarrassed to be so. "I . . . don't need any of those things."

"I know you do not," they told her. "Because you are the only part of my life that has not expected sacrifice. Before I met you, I could not have imagined you. I could not have imagined who I could be with you. I would marry you tomorrow, if I could."

"Same," Peggy croaked inadequately.

"I shall get you a special licence." It was not until Valentine spoke that Peggy remembered that she and Orfeo were not alone in the room. Or, for that matter, in the world.

"And when can we make a new Bonny?" asked Bonny, bouncing from foot to foot.

"Well"—Peggy frowned, slightly discomforted by some of the realities they were dealing with—"probably that would need to come before the wedding. In case of doubt."

"You," Belle told her, adoringly, "are going to cause *so* much scandal."

Bonny bounced even more bouncily. "Now, then? How about now? Can we do it now?"

"Er," said Peggy. Because now seemed very . . . very now?

"I think"—Belle rose from the sofa—"this would be a good time for me to go to bed." Crossing to where Peggy was seated before the fire, she bent down and kissed her lightly. "I am so happy for you, Peggy, and I will dance at your wedding." She subjected her brother to a severe look. "Be good, Bonbon."

He flicked back his golden curls. "I am better than good, Belladonna."

"I'd give you a child myself, if I could," Belle told her. "But my twin is the next best thing."

"I'm in the *room*," Bonny reminded them.

"Good night, everyone." Sweeping a neat little curtsy, Belle quietly let herself out.

It really wasn't like her to do anything quietly—she had, Peggy thought, been quiet in general—but there was a degree to which Belle wasn't Peggy's concern anymore. They were friends. They loved each other. That would always bind them. But Peggy's life was her own. It was taking her where she needed to go. To home, to family, to Orfeo. The most exhilarating adventure of all.

"You don't think," she asked Bonny, "you've had enough excitement for one day? You did kidnap someone earlier."

Bonny hung his head. "That was . . . that was a disaster. And I know I can't fix a bad thing by trying to do a good one, but—"

"But," Peggy finished for him, "you want to try anyway?"

"A little bit," Bonny admitted. "Mainly, though, I think I want to be part of something beautiful."

Orfeo rose gracefully from the hearthrug, shaking back their hair. "And that is laudable of you, Signor Tarleton. Yet you do not have to be part of something beautiful *immediately*, do you?"

"I . . ." Bonny looked confused. "Well. The thing is, *immediately* is my favourite time to do anything."

"And"—Orfeo drew Peggy to her feet with them—"is it your favourite time, mio principe?"

It was very much not. In a considered fashion, having maybe had one too many anxious conversations about it, was Peggy's favourite time to do things. "No," she admitted.

Bonny's face fell, though Peggy saw the relief that flashed across Valentine's. And that reminded her that Belle hadn't been the only quiet one in the room. Other than offering to intercede with the Archbishop of Canterbury for them, Valentine had been little more than a shadow in the corner. Given how possessive he was of his valet, she had no idea how he was feeling about sharing his lover—even if only temporarily.

"Under normal circumstances," Orfeo was saying, "I would have no qualms in bringing bodies carelessly together. But I have not, on those occasions, cared much for the bodies in question. This need not be a grand matter, but nor, I think, should it be a light one."

Leaning against Orfeo's shoulder, Peggy allowed herself a moment to bask in the pleasure of being truly understood. For her natural instinct towards caution to be treated as something to be honoured rather than something she had to be coaxed, cajoled, and chided through.

A smile glimmered upon Orfeo's lips. "And, forgive me a little self-ishness, but I have waited all day in the rain, changed the course of my life, and received—if I have not dreamed it—a proposal of marriage from someone who would change the course of her life for me. I am a little tired."

"I'm tired too," added Valentine, with soft and undukely plaintiveness.

"Oh my God." Bonny threw his arms wide in despair. "You people have no emotional stamina. You'd never survive in a novel."

"Frankly," said Peggy, "I'm at peace with that." She took Orfeo's hand in hers. "Come on, let's . . . actually I have no idea what we should *let's*. But let's do it together."

One of Orfeo's fingers stroked lightly at the dark shadows Peggy knew lay beneath her eyes. "We shall hold each other, talk of little, and sleep. Everything else may wait upon our pleasure."

"That sounds . . ." An enormous yawn caught Peggy by surprise. "Perfect," she finished.

Peggy swayed a little, feeling so wrung out it was almost peaceful, her thoughts fuzzy and impossible to pin down. Orfeo's arms came around her, as they had in the rain. There was a strength in them, for all their willowy languidness. The sort of strength that made Peggy occasionally able to relax her grip on her own. Except, when she did, it didn't make her feel any weaker. It just made her feel safe. Like her world could bear the weight of her. Like she would never truly leave home again.

Chapter 32

"I really thought we were done, you know." Peggy's fingers drifted over Orfeo's chest, where a delicate sheen of sweat made it shine like bronze.

They'd kept what she thought of as Valentine hours. Which was to say, they'd awoken at twelve, breakfasted in bed, and then made love upon crumpled sheets in the generous gold of the afternoon sun. They had been tentative at first, touching each other as if neither could quite believe the other was there, then urgent, spiralling together into ragged bliss, where hungry kisses tangled into words of love and need, and finally indulgent, testing the limits of satiation and pleasure. Which, as it turned out, had not been particularly limiting.

Orfeo curled a little closer. "I hate that I left. I hate that I hurt you even more."

"Well," Peggy reminded them, "you'd been talking about leaving from the moment I met you. I shouldn't have been surprised."

"And yet all the time, all I could think of was staying."

"You don't have to stay. You just have to come back." She tucked a kiss into the crease of their shoulder. "Which you did."

"Ah, Peggy." Their gaze grew abstracted. "In that moment, everything Nicholas was saying felt so real, and everything else so impossible. Like some dream I'd try to cling to past morning."

The marquess was not Peggy's business. But a spark of annoyance ran through her anyway. "He's wrong about you, Orfeo. And wrong about what your life can be."

"So I hope. But I also do not believe he intended to do me ill." Orfeo turned onto their side, nudging Peggy into a matching position that they might lie face to face. Close enough that Peggy could see the spaces between Orfeo's eyelashes and the runnels of gold that were only sometimes visible in their irises. "If he had, it would have been easier to leave him. In his way, he cared for me. And, until you, I had so little experience of being cared for that I would have accepted it in whatever form it came."

"If this is supposed to make me think better of him," Peggy muttered, "it's not working."

"He had"—Orfeo paused, thoughtfully—"particular expectations of me. Expectations I never gave him cause to question, because I did not know to question them myself. But he was trying. He let me keep Bob and Cecil, for example."

"Still not working."

Orfeo laughed, and hearing that—the unexpected rasp of it—went quite some way to soothing Peggy's irritation. "All I mean to say is, do not think too much upon Nicholas, for my life does not need a villain. It has a hero."

"Oh my God." Peggy hid her reddening face in the pillow. "I'm not. I'm just—kind of a person, really?"

"Then you are my favourite person."

Whatever incoherent thing Peggy offered in response to that was smothered by the pillow.

"It is not so great a compliment," Orfeo told her. "You may recall I do not generally think well of people. You have very little competition."

Peggy emerged, now tousle-haired as well as blushing, not that it mattered because she still had the smug, dissolute air of the comprehensively fucked. "It still counts. I've never been someone's favourite person before. I'm always an honourable third or in the running for second."

"Well"—Orfeo's usually sharp-edged smile was all softness—"you can be mine exclusively, unless we have a child, and then you will have to share."

"I accept those terms."

They shook on it with absurd formality, given they were both naked and in bed, and Peggy's mouth was still tender from Orfeo's kisses, her thighs slick with their pleasure. There was, she thought, a lightness to Orfeo that, for all their ready playfulness, had not been there before. It was not hers to lay claim to, or take responsibility for, but it made her feel light in return. As if happiness was a lightning bolt that could ricochet endlessly between them.

Pushing themself onto an elbow, Orfeo swooped a fingertip down the line of her nose, perhaps intending the frivolity of the action to distract her from the sudden intensity of their gaze. "And you really intend to marry me?"

"No," she said. "I propose to people frivolously for my personal amusement."

"Peggy . . ."

She grinned but stopped teasing. "Only if you want to. I don't need to put a ring on your finger to believe you're with me."

"Your friend is right—it will be a scandal either way."

"Ehhh." Peggy offered the verbal equivalent of a shrug. "I'm quite rich. I think it'll blow over into eccentricity, and then everyone will forget."

"I have made rather a practice of not being forgettable."

"Then, maybe we'll cancel each other out." Draping a hand over Orfeo's hip, Peggy stroked the velvet curve of their flank. "We don't have to be Bonnys about this. It doesn't have to be now."

"If we do get married," said Orfeo dreamily, "I shall wear gold."

"And I'm going to wear"—Peggy gave it some thought—"clothes."

"And this is truly what you want?"

"To wear clothes at my wedding? Definitely."

Laughing, Orfeo swiped at her, and she fended them off halfheart-edly until they were both breathless and entangled.

Peggy settled back against Orfeo's shoulder. "It's what I want." She pressed a fingertip to the hollow at the base of their throat, feeling the beat of their blood. There was something so strangely reassuring about bodies, the intricacies of breath and heat and skin, the powerful drive of them to continue, to live, to thrive. "Mostly for the sake of children, but also because . . . because we can? While so many can't. And so many others must."

"It is so very gratifying," Orfeo murmured, "to do a thing because one can. Though I think I am still learning how. It is not always simple, finding ways to make yourself free."

"It's not. I mean . . ." Peggy hesitated. She had grown used to holding her anxieties close to her in case they ended up looking small and silly when shown to others. "The truth is, I've always been scared that the only way I could get married was to be a wife. Or that having a child would make me a mother."

Orfeo tightened their embrace protectively. "Some people may well still draw those conclusions from our choices."

It was a consideration Peggy had wrestled with before. But she'd come to a new conclusion. "I don't care. What we do is about us. What it means is for us to decide, not for other people to tell us. And, besides, we'll know something they won't."

"Oh?"

"Mm-hmm." Peggy grinned, suddenly reckless. "We'll know we're fucking with them."

And then Orfeo was atop her, pressing her to the bed as they kissed her through their laughing. "We are going to have the most spectacular life."

꧁❦꧂

It was quite a bit later by the time Peggy made it out of bed. Orfeo she had left there, sated and slumbering, which was the most pleasing way to leave a lover, especially when you intended to return to them soon. They had not spoken overmuch of their time apart, but—slight though it had been—it had taken a toll on Orfeo too. At least Peggy had her parents and her friends, had she sought them out, but Orfeo had been alone. And still they had found the courage to cast off everything they'd known since leaving Italy. All for a chance at a future they'd chosen for themself. One they could share with Peggy.

The house was quiet, bar the discreet to-ing and fro-ing of Valentine's many servants. Peggy, who thought best when she was in motion, stepped out into the gardens to enjoy the breeze and what remained of the afternoon. To say nothing of Bonny's taste in horticulture—which appeared to have expressed itself in a gigantic fountain with a unicorn centrepiece, surrounded by extremely pink flowers.

She didn't actually have much she needed to think about. Mostly, she just wanted to give herself the option. There was something slightly disconcerting about discovering that you were perilously close to getting everything you'd ever wanted, especially when you'd spent a long time telling yourself you couldn't or shouldn't have it. Not that she'd ever lain awake at night daydreaming about falling in love with a beautiful opera singer. But if she'd known to, she absolutely would have.

Beyond the fountain lay a rose bower because, yes, of course Bonny would want a rose bower and, through that, a little wilderness area. Here everything was artfully overgrown and sufficiently dense that the light fell softly green through a canopy of leaves. At the centre stood an oak tree, its spreading branches furled in gold, with a swing hung from the sturdiest of them. It was so unmistakably reminiscent of one of Bonny's favourite paintings that all it needed was a beauty in a pink dress—skirts flying suggestively—to complete the scene. Instead, however, the swing was incongruously occupied by a moody-looking duke.

"Want a push?" Peggy asked.

Valentine, who had been nudging himself back and forth without much conviction, shook his head. "Thank you, but no."

"Want to talk?" She found a little stone bench and sat down on it. "Yesterday was quite . . . quite something."

"I feel like it ended better than it began."

Peggy pulled a face. "That wouldn't be difficult."

"Perhaps I shall try writing to Sir Horley," Valentine suggested. "I doubt he would welcome the sight of any of us just now."

Peggy pulled a slightly different kind of face. "Good idea."

"I thought pretending I merely tolerated him was part of our . . . our . . ."

"Dynamic?"

"And instead"—Valentine kicked at the grass with his perfectly shined boot—"I have made him believe I only tolerate him."

"I'm sure he doesn't think that deep down." Peggy paused. "Very deep down."

At last Valentine looked at her. His eyes were red-rimmed. "I have been a poor friend to him."

Probably they all had. But saying that to Valentine would have been the opposite of comforting.

Thankfully, though, she didn't have to say anything, but he went on, "I have no wish to be a poor friend to you as well."

Ah. "Is this about Bonny?" Peggy asked.

After a moment, Valentine gave a tense little nod. "I wish only for your happiness and for his."

"Our happiness isn't worth anything if it comes at cost to you."

"But"—Valentine swung fretfully—"this is about you and Orfeo and Bonny. Why would that be at cost to me?"

"Does it *feel* like it is, though?"

"I . . . I don't know," Valentine admitted. "I think I'm"—he swallowed—"a little concerned."

He wasn't concerned; he was afraid. And more than a little. "I don't need Bonny for this." Peggy offered a sly smile. "What he is bringing is not in short supply. At least fifty percent of the population can provide it."

Valentine came to a juddering halt. "But he wants to."

"Valentine"—Peggy tried to put this gently—"you've been with Bonny long enough that you should know by now that he wants all kinds of things. Many of which he shouldn't have. You can say no to him. In fact, you probably should. And often."

"I don't like saying no to him."

"He would want you to," said Peggy sternly. "Especially about something like this."

For a long time, Valentine was silent, the swing buffeted occasionally into motion as he shifted upon it. Peggy wondered if she was ever going to be able to think of *L'escarpolette* as an image of non-melancholic sauciness again. When he spoke, it was softly, almost to himself. "I know this is not intended to hurt me. That it *should* not hurt me."

"We're not always rational about the things that hurt us. Especially when there's love involved. Or sex involved. Or love *and* sex involved."

But Valentine batted her reassurance away like a bee. "I know it is . . . at the very least *unlikely* that Bonny will have sex with you and consequently fall out of love with me."

Peggy blew air through her teeth. "Oh, I don't know. It's pretty damn magical down there."

Valentine gazed at her in very real horror.

"Oh my God, I'm teasing. Of course he wouldn't. That's not how, well, *anything* works."

"How would I know?" Valentine asked. "I have never loved anyone but Bonny. Never desired anyone but Bonny."

"And Bonny," Peggy pointed out, "has desired almost anything in breeches for his entire life and only loves you."

Valentine uttered something between a wail and a groan. "But what if . . . if that changes?"

Leaning back on her hands, Peggy searched for words. "We can't stop things changing, Valentine. People least of all."

"So you're saying it doesn't matter what I do?"

Peggy blinked at him. "No, I'm saying that if you and Bonny no longer want to be together, that'll be about you and Bonny, and nothing else. But," she added quickly, "that's still not a reason to do something that makes you uncomfortable."

"I . . ." Valentine gave an anguished little swing. "I love him so much, Peggy. So much that I sometimes ache with it in a way that feels both beautiful and terrible at the same time. Please don't tell anyone."

"Your secret is safe with me," she said gravely. "Although I think Bonny might have noticed."

At this, Valentine finally smiled. "I may have indiscreetly given him that impression, yes."

"You're not going to lose him. Whether he does this with me or not."

"In abstract, I know you are correct."

"And you aren't going to lose me as a friend either."

"Thank you." Valentine dug another smile out of the depths of his apprehension. "But I think I knew that too."

"Why don't you come inside?" Peggy suggested. "You've been separated for longer than twenty seconds. Bonny's probably missing you."

Standing, she crossed the clearing and offered her hand to help Valentine down off the swing. He descended with surprising grace for such a tall man and stood, for a moment, looking down at her. The setting suited him, bringing out the verdant green of his eyes. Their unexpected capacity for warmth.

"I will not stand in your way, Peggy," he said.

She met his gaze, trying to assess whether this was the sort of thing you were supposed to say yes to or no to. "Are you sure?"

He nodded. "I would think less of myself if I allowed myself to be so governed by fears I know to be foolish."

"Nobody would think less of you."

"I know you find it a little absurd"—his smile was diffident—"that Bonny and I cleave so closely to each other. But this feels like something I genuinely cannot share."

"You don't want to be my child's very rich, influential godfather?"

His eyes widened. "I would love that."

"But it's not enough?"

"It is more than enough," he assured her. "I'm afraid I was thinking more simplistically, in that there will be an occasion when Bonny is with you and not with me."

"Oh. Well." Peggy squirmed a little. "Not an invitation I ever thought I'd be issuing, but you're. Um. Welcome to join us."

Valentine squirmed back. "I appreciate your . . . your generosity. But I do not think I'd be a useful participant."

"Listen," said Peggy firmly, trying to corral her brain away from places she did not want it to go. "I under no circumstances want you to be *useful*. I am very much *not ready* for that."

To her surprise, for Valentine was a very private man, he seemed to be genuinely thinking about it. "Would it not be strange for you, if I were present?"

"Only if you, I don't know, *stare* at me in a disconcerting fashion or comment on what's happening like you're at the opera."

Valentine looked almost comically appalled. "I wouldn't do any of those things."

"Then come? Orfeo will be there for me. Why shouldn't you be there for Bonny?"

"And nobody would expect me to . . ."

Clearly, Valentine had no notion what he could theoretically be expected to do in a sexual encounter involving two pairs of lovers, so Peggy took pity on him. "No. Friendship can mean a lot of different things. But our friendship is definitely the zero-fucking kind of friendship."

"Thank God," said Valentine, with unflattering fervour.

"And," Peggy added, "if seeing me with Bonny makes you the smallest bit unhappy, then you have to tell us so we can stop."

"I understand."

Tugging lightly on his hand, she began to lead him back to the house. "Promise?"

"I promise."

Peggy cast him a searching glance. He seemed a little nervous but was otherwise calm, and much less unhappy than he had been earlier. On balance Peggy thought she could trust him. "Just be aware," she said, "that this probably won't be a onetime thing."

"I beg your pardon?"

"I mean, it's not going to be our new hobby. But I'm probably not going to fall instantly pregnant in the presence of Bonny's . . . um. Little Bonny."

"He'd insist it was a very sizeable Bonny indeed."

"Very much not the point I was making."

"This all seems unnecessarily complicated," Valentine concluded, at his most ducal.

"I know," returned Peggy dryly. "It's only making a human life. Why would *that* require some finessing?"

As they came to the terrace with the fountain, there was a small human explosion from the direction of the main house, and Bonny came bounding out.

"Oh my God," he cried. "Val-EN-tine. I've been looking all over for you. It's been *hours*."

Releasing Peggy's hand, Valentine broke into a run and met Bonny halfway across the garden. They crashed into each other's arms, like lovers united after some monumental parting, while the setting sun got in on the action by illuminating them extravagantly in shades of pink and gold.

Peggy shook her head and left them to it.

Chapter 33

In a strange way, talking to Valentine had reassured Peggy too. Made her more comfortable with what she was intending, and with it being something she shared with Bonny and Valentine. The alternative would have been a relative stranger, albeit one she would have chosen carefully. But as she had told Valentine, friendship could encompass a lot. And her friendship with the Tarletons, she realised, could encompass this quite comfortably. She liked the idea of raising a child who would connect them all. A child who might, perhaps, have a child of their own who lived in a world where who you loved was not cause for speculation and who you were required no explanation. Peggy sometimes wished she had the power to create that world in one fell swoop, but she hoped she was helping to create it a little bit, by the not always simple act of being herself.

In any case, it had felt almost ordinary to retire one evening with Bonny and Valentine, as if the idea of having a child together had quietly made itself at home in all of their hearts. They took their time, two sets of lovers kissing like melodies in counterpoint, and Peggy let herself drift upon Orfeo's touch. Their mouth beneath hers, the fall of their hair through her fingers, soothingly reminiscent of other occasions—bright mornings and deep midnights—when they had lain together simply for pleasure. She could hear Bonny's soft moans and Valentine's deeper ones, and there was something comforting in that, too, the way their love was familiar to each other, as hers and Orfeo's was to them.

The shedding of clothes came equally slowly. The room was warm enough, and Orfeo's caresses sufficiently consuming, that Peggy hardly felt her own nakedness. She was, she thought, in a bit of a daze, robed in bliss, Orfeo's lips and hands brushing her body over and over until she could barely feel the seam where her skin met theirs. Except then she turned her head and caught Bonny glancing her way at exactly the same time, and that gave them both a fit of the giggles.

Valentine—who was wearing a full-skirted, quilted banyan embroidered with outrageously sensuous flowers—exchanged a rather bemused look with Orfeo. They were in one of their tantalising silken nothings that made Peggy positively feral with the desire to rip it off them.

"Why are you laughing?" asked Valentine, when it was clear that neither Bonny nor Peggy was stopping anytime soon.

Bonny made a valiant attempt to catch his breath. "We . . . we don't know."

"You have to admit," said Peggy, "it's a slightly unusual situation."

Again, Bonny stole a look at her. "I don't think I've ever seen you naked before."

"Well, I've seen you naked about eighty million times."

"Can you blame me, though?" asked Bonny. "When I have all *this*." He indicated himself with a sweep.

He was beautiful and, Peggy was relieved to note, in ways distinct from Belle, for all you could catch the echo of the other in their features. Stretched out beside her, one arm tucked behind his hand, the other loosely gripping his cock, Bonny was an extravagant full-blooming rose of a man, his skin flecked with golden hair and flushed with desire. He made her think of strawberries and cream on a Sunday afternoon: a treat to satisfying an indulgent mood.

Never one to countenance a silence, Bonny poked her in the arm. "What are you thinking? Is it flattering? It better be flattering."

"It's very flattering," Peggy told him. "I'm thinking you're delicious enough to eat with a spoon."

Bonny smirked. "Valentine doesn't use a spoon."

"Can I touch you?" Peggy asked.

Bonny's attention flicked to Valentine before he nodded. "Yes. Don't kiss me, though? I mean, not on the mouth. We talked about it and—"

The words vanished into an excited squeak as Peggy straddled him. "No need to worry," she said. "I've other uses for you."

"Umm." Bonny blinked up at her. "You want to paint me like one of your Fragonards?"

Peggy laughed. "Maybe later." Lifting herself up slightly, she slipped a hand between her legs and curled her fingers around Bonny's cock.

He gasped and gave a pretty little quiver, though he was still watching her, something half-curious, half-desirous in his dreamy blue eyes.

"Is this all right?" In that moment, Peggy wasn't quite sure who she was asking.

Orfeo pressed a kiss to the nape of her neck—it was a delicate thing, close-lipped, but the context, being touched by Orfeo while she teased someone else, made Peggy burn like they'd put their mouth between her legs.

"For me," they murmured, "yes."

"Definitely for me," added Bonny, nudging needily against her.

"And I." Valentine's voice shook a little. And Peggy froze, mistaking it for distress. But as he stepped closer, she realised it was ardour. "It is entrancing to watch you, Bonny." Like a prince caught in an enchantment, he settled himself close by. "Normally when I . . . when I am *involved*, I am too distracted to fully . . . to see everything." With what looked like a visible effort, he dragged his gaze from Bonny's face. "Touch him again, Peggy."

His tone was so unexpectedly commanding that Peggy almost laughed. "In my bedroom," she said, "we say *please* when we want things."

Valentine lifted a ducal eyebrow. "Well, we are in my bedroom. And you are atop my husband."

Their eyes met and held. And Valentine, it turned out, was much better at this than he was at sword fighting.

"Oh, Valentine," said Peggy, amused, "you do contain multitudes."

Beneath her, Bonny gave an attention-seeking thrash. "Hello. I would like to get touched, *please*."

"Touch him," said Valentine again.

Peggy glanced down in false deference. "Yes, Your Grace."

The position made her clumsy, but it didn't seem to matter. Bonny was an enthusiastic recipient, arching against her hand but equally eager to press himself against her thighs and up between her legs.

"I love it," he declared, "when I can feel how wet you are with my cock."

Orfeo was still kneeling behind Peggy, not close enough to crowd her, but close enough that the heat of them licked softly up against her, as constant as a shadow. "Maybe"—their voice swept past her ear on a ripple of warm breath—"we could make her wetter."

Bonny's eyes grew round. "Oh my God, yes. Yes yes yes."

"Yes?" The question was for Peggy.

She leaned back, letting her head rest upon Orfeo's shoulder. "Yes."

One of Orfeo's hands joined hers between her legs, their long fingers tangling with hers in a space that quickly became all heat and slickness. Peggy was not quite prepared for the intimacy of it, Bonny's cock between them, and her own body spread greedily in response to the uncertain friction. It was the sort of pleasure to drive you to delirium—endlessly tantalising, never fully satisfying—and it would have been too much to take alone. But Orfeo was there to steady her, and Bonny's urgent whimpers were like Ariadne's thread leading her safely through the labyrinth of sensation.

"I could watch you like this forever." Valentine was stretched out on his side next to Bonny, gazing at him in avid wonder. "You are exquisite in the throes of bliss."

Bonny somehow managed to make a helpless gasp carry a suggestion of outrage. "I'm . . . *always* . . . exquisite."

"Especially exquisite. The way your eyelashes flutter like threads of gold and how sweat shines upon your skin like diamonds. The tender ripple of your throat. And, oh, Bonny, *your mouth*, stretched open in a torment of rapture, so pink and glistening and *eager* as if it wants to be fucked."

Peggy's fingers had stilled with Orfeo's. Somehow the word *fucked* uttered with such determined relish in Valentine's lofty, aristocratic tones was one of the most delightfully obscene things she'd ever heard.

"You can fuck it if you like," Bonny offered, with the air of a man for whom receiving lewd paeans was an everyday occurrence.

"Oh . . ." Valentine looked at once tempted and abashed. "Perhaps not—not on this occasion."

"You do you, Valentine." It was not an ideal position—physically as well as mentally—to be reassuring from, but Peggy tried her best. And then, wanting to help him through his sudden self-consciousness, she asked, "Is there anything else you want to order me to do to your lover in your bed?"

"Tell her to fuck me," Bonny said immediately, and somewhat predictably. "If I don't get fucked soon, I'm going to *die*."

"Well?" Peggy flexed her hips, pressing down hard against Bonny's cock and Orfeo's fingers, sending a shock of sensation all the way up her spine. "Shall I fuck him for you?"

There was still a bright flush upon Valentine's cheeks. But something rather wicked flickered across his face. "I understood that a *please* would be required."

Bonny flailed. "You're both monsters."

Leaning over him, Peggy licked a long stripe up his chest. "You heard what he said. Ask him nicely."

"Monsters," repeated Bonny. In his head he probably sounded put-upon. How he actually sounded was thrilled. Peggy's teeth grazed one of his nipples, earning an exuberant squeal. "Please please I'm saying please." Delaying his own gratification had never been one of Bonny's talents. "I'm saying all the pleases."

Sitting up again, Peggy braced herself on her knees, poised above Bonny. He was so ready for her she could almost feel the beat of the blood in his cock.

Bonny twisted, trying to see both her and Valentine at the same time. His face was a picture of desperation. *"Peggy."* She had never heard her name used as an imperative before. *"Val-EN-tine."* He stretched one of his hands across the bed, clasping Valentine's tightly. "I love you."

"And I you," Valentine told him.

He nodded to Peggy, she felt Orfeo's hands settle on her hips to guide her, and she slid effortlessly down Bonny's length—a perfect burst of relief and pleasure that made her head fall back and her eyes close.

"You . . ." His voice was unusually hushed for a Tarleton. "You look . . . beautiful . . . handsome . . . Which do you prefer?"

"All of them," she said, the words coming treacle slow, as her body took over, her hips rolling as she worked Bonny's cock inside her.

"Then you look all of them like that."

"She is magnificent, is she not?" Orfeo glided their palms up her body, cupping her breasts gently, for they knew she wasn't always in the mood to be touched there.

Today, though, Peggy wanted to be. She wanted to be touched *everywhere*. And even pressed against her as they were, Orfeo felt too far away to her. Turning awkwardly, she caught their lips in a rough kiss. They met her, parted for her, let her fill her mouth with the taste of them. But it was still not enough.

"Orfeo," she whispered. "Orfeo."

Their answering kiss was gentle. It moved over her like sunlight. "I am here, tesoro mio."

Peggy slowed her pace, rocking against Bonny, amused—in some distant way—by the efforts he made to match her. And there it was. The most Tarleton of truths: selfish in all contexts but one. She curled a hand behind her to draw Orfeo closer, craving the familiarity of their skin against hers, something to ground her amidst so many new sensations. It was not that doing this with Bonny seemed so very strange anymore—he was one of her oldest friends, and if someone had asked her to imagine what he'd be like in bed, she would have answered *this*—but it was Orfeo she loved. And the shape of that love felt ever more distinct, its colours ever more vivid, when sharing space with the love she felt for Bonny and the love she felt for Valentine.

"Orfeo," she said again. "I . . . I need you."

They kissed her neck, her shoulder, the edge of her jaw. "You have me."

"N-no . . ." The way she longed for them had become a clawing thing. A thorn at the heart of bliss. "Inside me."

"You are sure?" Orfeo asked.

Peggy made a sound, half laugh, half sob. "I'm fucking sure." She took a steadying breath. "You know how I like it."

"I do." She felt the whisper of Orfeo's hair across her naked back as they turned to Valentine. "Is there oil?"

"Of all kinds," Valentine told him.

"Any will suffice."

"Sooo"—Bonny's voice had swooped higher than Peggy had ever heard it—"remember how I said I was going to die? Well, I'm just letting you know that I have died. And I'm currently ascending to the afterlife."

Peggy dropped to her elbows and kissed his chest—directly over his heart, whose wild thundering she felt against her lips. "You're being wonderful."

"I know I'm being wonderful," snapped Bonny, "but I hope you don't expect me to last much longer."

There was the clink of a glass vial, and the scent of roses filled the air. Roses and something slightly citrusy—bergamot? Because of course Valentine and Bonny would have scented oil. Or, indeed, a range of scented oils.

"Especially," Bonny was saying, "if Orfeo—if Orfeo . . . *ooooooooooh.*" His eyes fluttered closed. "Is that . . . Orfeo?"

"Just my fingers, darling. Should I be offended?"

"What? No—I . . . *oooh—oh—ooooooooh.*"

"That is me," Orfeo murmured, more than a little smugly.

"Oh my God." Bonny clutched at the sheets and at Valentine. "I can feel you. I can feel you . . . through . . . inside."

"I can feel you too," said Peggy. "Go slow."

One of Orfeo's hands she could feel against her body, where they guided themself inside her. The other was at her hip again, cradling her and steadying her. "Whatever you wish of me."

Peggy's breath was burning in her throat. Her pulse beat like a phoenix. "This. I wish this."

Orfeo entered her with unshakeable care. The stretch and the pressure built, reached the brink of overwhelming, but never went beyond it. Peggy closed her eyes and let her body open itself completely—to Orfeo, and to the child that she realistically knew they probably weren't creating right now but would at some point. She felt her own strength, her ability to give and take, to find joy and to be free. And then she felt Orfeo, pressed tight against her, as deep as she could take them.

For seconds . . . minutes . . . Peggy had no idea, none of them moved, lost to themselves and each other. And when Orfeo, at last, began to move smoothly inside her, Peggy—filled, pleasured, cherished—spun away like a sunbeam. Her orgasm was a ripple of heat that gathered itself in all the hidden places of her body and moved through her in endless waves, making even the tips of her toes tingle with the power of it.

And Bonny—still alive, despite his insistence to the contrary—was little more than driftwood, pulled along with her.

"V-Valentine," he gasped. "Kiss me."

Which left Peggy to experience his climax in the shudders that racked him. The rest he gave to Valentine, clinging to him, as he pressed everything he felt to Valentine's lips. Exactly as it should be. Just as Peggy, when her shaky limbs permitted her any sort of movement, folded herself into Orfeo's arms. Exactly where she should be.

Epilogue

Tesoro mio,

Or "dear Peggy," as I believe you English have it. As you can see, I have with the help of Bob been working on my English reading and writing. Frankly, if I wait for your Italian, we may both be dead.

You will be relieved, or more likely indifferent, to learn I have yet to be excommunicated. Nor am I aware of any attempts to dissolve our marriage. I did meet Nicholas in Paris some weeks ago, who insisted we would be ruined, but you were quite correct that, now we have our stellina, he has little grounds upon which to move against me. In truth, I do not believe he would, even if he could. He only offered me words of anger after he had offered me words of love. Love indeed. I told him he did not love me, he simply wished to have me. How welcome it is to know the difference.

I have been, as I am sure needs no explication, a great success. I am increasingly rich, Peggy, famous and desired. My own desires, however, remain entirely yours. I hope this, too, requires no explication. But I nonetheless wish to explicate because I wish you to know my love always, even when, especially when, I am far away. I used to dream of music, of bright lights and endless applause. Now I dream of you and of home. Of grey English skies and green English fields. Your silly dog, that pineapple house you revere so unreasonably, and, of course, our stellina. For all that the last time I beheld her, she looked like a disgruntled hedgehog. Does she still look like a disgruntled hedgehog? I do not care. I love her with the same unstinting fervour some of us are inspired to by pineapple houses.

Strange, I think I used to dream of stars, too, their distance and their pure light. I felt I belonged among them, like some cold, unreachable thing towards whom others would turn their covetous eyes. How fine it is, instead, to have a star of one's own. Even a star who looks like a hedgehog. And a prince to cherish her with.

All my love, always,

Orfeo

ACKNOWLEDGMENTS

Huge thanks to my editor, Lauren Plude—and to the Montlake team as a whole—for being incredibly supportive through this whole process. Special mention to the mysterious Bill S. for being one of the best copyeditors I've ever had and the equally mysterious Elyse L. for her musical-nerd eye and a fantastic proofread. And, as ever, none of this nonsense would be possible without my amazing agent, Courtney Miller-Callihan, and my assistant, the incomparable Mary.

Please find below the full text of George's poem, "Craggy Dell." I felt bad for him that he got interrupted because, y'know, sonnets are hard.

CRAGGY DELL

There is a ploughman works in a craggy dell
An honest man whose hands are horny-rough
I watch him and he casts on me a spell
And I bethink me, "Is it not enough,
To dig one's hoe in rich, sweet-smelling loam
And know the satisfaction of your toil
Instead of living in some grand old home
And struggling within the ton's great moil?"
I ask, "Should I not reach that wholesome man
And take his great strong horny hand in mine?"
And he could teach me what a ploughman can
And I could show him all that's great and fine.
Alas! 'Tis all the burden of my heart
That this man's world and mine are set apart.

ABOUT THE AUTHOR

Alexis Hall is determined to marry into money, as his grandfather drank half the family fortune and gambled the rest. He lives in a tumbledown mansion in a fictional county, and his valet doesn't even have a humorous name.